PRIDE AND
Twelve Short Sto.
Pride and P.

Alice McVeigh has been published in contemporary fiction by Orion/Hachette, in speculative fiction by UK's Unbound (using her middle names), and in historical fiction by Warleigh Hall Press. Her novels have won innumerable awards, including being shortlisted in the final seven novels for the 2024 UK Selfies Book Award, joint runner-up for Foreword Indies' Book of the Year 2022, and BookLife Quarterfinalist 2021.

Alice spent her childhood in Asia (South Korea, Thailand, Singapore, Myanmar), her teenage years in McLean, Virginia, and her adulthood in London. She arrived in London to study cello with Jacqueline du Pré, married and spent fifteen years travelling the world with London orchestras, including the BBC Symphony and the Royal Philharmonic, before taking fiction seriously.

Alice has long been married to Simon McVeigh, Professor Emeritus at the University of London. They share a daughter, Rachel – currently a PhD student in Chinese literature at Harvard – two long-haired mini-dachshunds, and a second home in Crete. Alice also wastes many hours watching professional and playing (very) amateur tennis.

Also by Alice McVeigh

Austenesque

Susan: A Jane Austen Prequel
Harriet: A Jane Austen Variation
Darcy: A Pride and Prejudice Variation

Contemporary

While the Music Lasts
Ghost Music
Last Star Standing (by Spaulding Taylor)

PRIDE AND PERJURY

Twelve Short Stories inspired by
Pride and Prejudice

Alice McVeigh

Warleigh Hall Press

This edition first published in 2024

Warleigh Hall Press
International House
36-38 Cornhill
London, EC3V 3NG
www.warleighhallpress.com
All rights reserved

© Alice McVeigh, 2024

This book is a work of fiction and, except in the case of historical fact,
any resemblance to actual persons, living or dead, is purely
coincidental. The author certifies that absolutely no AI was used in
the writing or plotting of this novel.

ISBN (eBook): 978-1-7385461-0-7
ISBN (Paperback): 978-1-7385461-1-4

Cover design by designforwriters.com

Cover portrait (Sir Thomas Lawrence, *Lady Maria Conyngham*) courtesy
of the Metropolitan Museum of Art, New York

For Rachel

Contents

Acknowledgements

Nine of these short stories have *Pride and Prejudice* as their inspiration – the final three were inspired by *Emma*. I have also recklessly borrowed characters from Austen's *Mansfield Park* and *Northanger Abbey*, especially in 'Pride and Perjury' (a finalist in Chanticleer's International Book Awards). I also created quite a few!

I remain intensely grateful to my amazing husband Simon, who brilliantly line-edited this volume while finishing his own *Music in Edwardian London* (published by Boydell and Brewer, released May 2024). I'm also forever indebted to Phil McKerracher, dear friend and unflappable tech/website/newsletter guru. Grateful thanks too go to designforwriters.com and to the Metropolitan Museum of Art for the cover. My ARC team was also wonderful, spotting typos, scribbling early reviews and even assisting with the chapter order. Erica Saltzman, Peter Sheeran, Rebecca Fuller, Neil Andrews, Laura Farnsworth Nielsen, Harri Whilding, Amanda Kai, Karen Quigley, Carol Briggs, Teresa del Giudice, Cindie Snyder and Sarah Pope were all outstanding.

Finally, I have dedicated *Pride and Perjury* to our amazing daughter, Rachel. Every IVF was worth it!

A.M.

The Housekeeper's Tale

'I will go to Meryton,' said she, 'as soon as I am dressed, and tell the good, good news to my sister Philips. And as I come back, I can call on Lady Lucas and Mrs. Long. Kitty, run down and order the carriage. An airing would do me a great deal of good, I am sure. Girls, can I do anything for you in Meryton? Oh! here comes Hill. My dear Hill, have you heard the good news? Miss Lydia is going to be married; and you shall all have a bowl of punch to make merry at her wedding.'

(from *Pride and Prejudice*, Chapter 49)

It might be said that I started it, for it was I who first said to Mrs Bennet, 'I understand, ma'am, that Netherfield has been taken at last.'

'Why, whomever by?' she asked, for she detested the recent additions to its design. I told her by a young fellow by the name of Bingley.

'Married?' she supposed, but I understood that he was not.

'Engaged?'

'Apparently not, ma'am. But he is said to be very pleasing – handsome, rich, well-spoken – and with no side to him, neither.'

'Unmarried!' she cried. 'Well!'

Then she was banging on the door to the library, her nerves all a-flutter. I was pretending to be examining the dust in the stairwell, just to hear what clever thing Mr Bennet might say, for the master *will* have his little joke.

'Mr Bennet, oh Mr Bennet,' she cried, entering. And he, lifting his eyes from his great book, wished to know whether it was a flood or an earthquake, or the return of the Messiah with a choir of angels.

'My dear! Hill has learned that Netherfield is taken at last – a young man, single, charming – and why, you must call upon him!'

'Is he some sprig of the nobility? Or a Parliamentarian, perhaps?'

'No, he is a Mr Bingley!'

'And I suppose,' said Mr Bennet thoughtfully, 'that a man named Bingley might be as great an encumbrance at Westminster as a fellow by any other name.'

'Yet you will call on him, will you not?'

'But for what reason?'

'Why, for the sake of our *girls*, Mr Bennet! For he must have four or five thousand a year, and fine manners besides!'

'So, I am to leave my books and ride to Netherfield to smirk and fawn upon some young fool in hopes that he might wed one or more of my daughters?... I think not! However, should Mr Bingley yearn for my acquaintance, he is most welcome to call – for, to be sure, we cannot be above a few miles from Netherfield.'

She half-slammed the door as she departed but he only cried, 'Take care, my dear, lest you alarm the angels.'

Upon observing me in the stairwell, she said, 'Oh, Hill, what a fine thing for my girls! A rich young fellow with a property *must* wish for a wife – for what else could he have to wish for?'

A quiet life was my guess, never having had one, but – truth to tell – most fine young men do wish to settle and to father a son, though – more's the pity! – the master never did. Then the mistress said, tapping her nose with great signification, 'I would be glad, Hill, if you could mend Miss Jane's lace collar.'

2

She was thinking that Miss Jane might be the next mistress of Netherfield, and – truly – why should she not? – for Miss Jane has no equal for sweetness or fine looks. (I *should* call her Miss Bennet, now that she is grown, but – having wiped her tiny nose and cleaned her little face since she was four – oh! she will always be Miss Jane to me!)

I trotted upstairs to fetch the collar. Then I bustled down to the kitchen, where Bessy was attacking the silver, and told her, 'And here is one for you, my girl, for I lack your deftness with the needle!'

'The French collar? What is amiss with it?

'It wants repairing, the mistress says.'

'Mercy! And why was I never told as Miss Jane was to be presented at court?'

'Nay, for she is not – but the mistress fears that, should the new master at Netherfield observe imperfect lace on Miss Jane's collar, he will return to town in a dudgeon, and not wed her after all.'

'The mistress,' said Bessy, rubbing the spoon rather harder, 'would do a good deal better to leave such things to nature. But I would do more than that for Miss Jane, for she always says, "Thank you kindly, Bessy," unlike *some* as I could mention!'

To which I said amen, for the Bennet sisters could be a trial, and no mistake. I cannot help but like Miss Lizzy, though she is quick enough to cut herself. But Miss Mary *does* put on such airs, while Miss Kitty could whine for England! And as for Miss Lydia, she *will* go her own sweet way, for she is her mama's pet, even though she had – stubborn-like – refused to be the boy that they had wanted.

For the next few days all we heard from Mrs Bennet was, 'When do you intend to go to Netherfield, Mr Bennet?' and 'A little ride, just around the road, would soon clear the phlegm in your chest, my dear!' And all the while he protested that he would not, not for a kingdom, till I felt rather sorry for her. But what did he do yesterday but go, and all without mentioning it to a single soul?

Then the mistress blesses herself, crying, 'How good it is of you, Mr Bennet! You girls will never understand quite how good, but for *you* he would do anything!'

Which might be true, at least as far as Miss Lizzy is concerned. Wicked, they are – the pair of them – for the mistress would not recognise a tease were it to bite her in the leg, while the master cannot be serious for two minutes together.

And ever since he confessed to having called at Netherfield, she is never far from the window, in hopes of seeing Mr Bingley cantering up on his snow-white horse to carry Miss Jane and her French lace collar away!

❦

Well, the new master of Netherfield has called at last and is very fine-looking indeed. A face as open as a puppy's – a fine, fluffy, cream-coloured puppy with wide eyes and a shock of fair curls. And the moment he lifted his head after bowing to Miss Bennet, I thought, 'Hey-day!' – because he looked that startled and coloured so.

Then Mrs Bennet introduces the others, and then Miss Lydia, bold as brass, pipes up to hint about how Netherfield was once famous throughout the county for its balls and its dancing. And then Mr Bingley allows as how he wishes Netherfield to be famous for its balls again. And then Miss Lydia practically screams for joy… and then I was obliged to come away and heard no more.

Bessy was in the kitchen, perturbed. 'Where has young James gone?'

4

'He was told to go to Lucas Lodge, by the master.'

Bessy frowned, and I guessed that she was thinking, not about the Lucases, but about their maid, Marietta.

Now Bessy and James, a footman, have always liked each other, though *she* is twenty-nine and lost her husband three years ago and better, while *he* is not yet twenty-one and a great deal too lively to settle down.

Indeed, so unruly was James, when first he came, that Mrs Bennet wished that the master would dismiss him. But the master would not, for James and he both relish their little jokes, and – in my opinion – Longbourn is none the worse for them.

As for the Lucas's maid Marietta, I have never heard a word against her though, of a Sunday, her gown is in such a style, and her cap set so very jauntily, that one might mistake her for one of the Miss Lucases, herself!... But if Lady Lucas's housekeeper does not choose to rebuke her, 'tis not *my* place to do so.

❖

Then there was indeed a ball, though only a public ball at Meryton, and not the private ball that the girls are so wild for – though, to be sure, *I* can see very little difference. For are they not all dancing the same dances to the same fiddlers, and with the same young men, besides?

But such a business! – with every servant at Longbourn driven frantic with the girls needing something adjusting to their gowns or their petticoats or their hair or their shoes or their stockings. While I was driven half-distracted with the missus, who had mislaid the amethyst pendent that she had quite set her heart upon Miss Jane's wearing.

In the end, I found where it had fallen, and very lovely Miss Jane looked as I fastened it about her throat.

And as I finally heard the wheels of the second carriage disappearing down the drive I said, 'Bessy, I beg you put the kettle on for I am quite worn out,' and Bessy not only did but made the tea as well. Though 'twas unusually silent at the second table, for James was driving Mrs Bennet and the younger girls to Meryton in the second chaise – on its last legs, at least in James's opinion – so that all the young ladies might not have their gowns crushed inside the first.

I hoped that young Bingley would ask Miss Jane to dance, but Bessy doubted it, for the Netherfield party – *if* they made an appearance, for even that was uncertain – included 'ten or twelve young ladies,' each of whom Mr Bingley would be obliged to dance with before even being introduced to Miss Jane.

Into the silence, the new butler said, 'If I may say so, I still believe that Miss Bennet looked uncommonly well as they set off, and such as any young man might request an introduction to. 'Twould be the salvation of the family should she marry high, for then it might not signify whether the master had one son or fifty!'

I suspected that fifty sons would be a worse affliction than the five young ladies the master was already plagued with, but I did not say so. Bessy said, 'The way *I* see it, Mr Spencer, is that this Mr Bingley would be a fool *not* to choose Miss Jane!'

And Cook said just the same.

Mr Spencer is still so new that we are all a little wary of him, but he has this advantage over the previous butler, of not drinking the cooking sherry. His only weakness appears to be his pipe, for he likes to sit before the fire of an evening, a pipe in his hand and a great book on his lap. I suppose the master will like him, for the book is by Shakespeare, and he so fond of it that he quotes from it all day long.

For example, he said to young James, with a twinkle, 'Farewell, and let haste commend your duty.' And to Robin, the boots, 'What fates impose, that men must needs abide; it boots not to resist both wind and tide.'

Upon which Robin confided to James, 'I think 'e is touched in the head!' But James shook his head saying, 'Better'n the last one, my lad! Better'n the last!'

If Mr Spencer is 'touched', he is respectful with it, and he has asked my advice about the master's jokes and the missus's nerves and thanked me.

Late that night, for Bessy and I waited up to receive them, I learned there are *not* in fact any number of young ladies staying at Netherfield. Instead, there are but two, both sisters to Mr Bingley. And so he *did* indeed ask Miss Jane to dance – twice – and was overheard describing her as 'the loveliest creature he had ever beheld'.

Well! You can imagine the mistress's state of mind. It was but one step, to her way of thinking, from *that* to lawyers' settlements and to St Georges Hanover Square, for she – though so often prey to despair – is just as prone to the wildest hopefulness.

But though Miss Jane seemed modestly contented, Miss Lizzy was *not*, for some other rich young fellow had described her as 'not handsome enough' to dance with, and though she mocked him for it – she is a girl of spirit – I thought her secretly not best-pleased. For she is quite pretty enough, though neater and darker and not as blooming as her sister.

Miss Lizzy was not alone in being a little discontented, for Miss Lydia had been told off for laughing, Miss Kitty had had her shoe rosette trodden on and Miss Mary had lacked for partners… though *that* was the case for them all, beyond Miss Jane.

I daresay it is something in the water – but it does seem to be the case that, for every young gentleman hereabouts, there were three young ladies born, while the regiment to be quartered in Meryton village is yet to come. But when it does… Lord! we shall probably wish it away again!

❧

It was Mr Spencer who, probably unaware of Bessy's interest in the business, mentioned that James was 'walking out' with the Lucas's maid, Marietta. I was sorry for it and must have said something aloud, for he asked, 'Sorry? Why might that be, Mrs Hill?'

He said it not unkindly, for he seems a decent fellow. But as he is so recent an addition, I could never betray poor Bessy. So I said rather hurriedly, 'Oh, 'tis only that James is so young, Mr Spencer!'

'Young, do you call him? He is a year older than I was, when I was wed.'

I blushed and forbore to ask what had befallen his wife. And then regretted not asking, for – to be sure – he had not been obliged to mention her. 'Tis a nervy business having a new butler in command, after so many years with Mr Broadbent, before!

As for James, he is so struck by his new love that we are all losing patience with the pair of them. It is 'Marietta does not care for cheese… Marietta says that Sir William Lucas would sleep all afternoon, if he was able… Marietta thinks very thick boots never look well… Marietta believes that, were it not for Miss Lucas, everything at Lucas Lodge would fall to rack and ruin within a fortnight.'

Bessy teases him. ('What, has Marietta no opinion of the rector, then?' or 'But of course even the *bishop* must agree with Marietta!') On Sundays, he attends her at Lucas Lodge after the second service, while his whistling – I have reason to believe – is trying the patience even of the equable Mr Spencer for, as he told young James, 'If music be the food of love, play on. Or better still – forbear!'

Though in truth we are not as well-off as we were before, whistling or no, without James's good temper and quick wit of a Sunday. And Bessy bangs the saucepans rather more often in consequence.

❧

The militia have finally arrived and – in the case of *one* young officer – are already causing rare havoc in the breast of every woman in Meryton. Every young lady in the world, it seems, is quite smitten by the gallant manners and fine looks of Lieutenant Wickham, who is coming to dine on Friday. Apparently, his demeanour is so delightful and his manners so handsome, as to make even Miss Lizzy's clever little head spin. (As for Miss Kitty and Miss Lydia, *their* passion is not to be credited.) Even the mistress told me wistfully, 'Ah Hill, how Lieutenant Wickham puts me in mind of Colonel Benedict, when I was a girl! How we all yearned after Colonel Benedict! And yet, la! – is it not strange? – I declare, I cannot recollect what became of him, whether he perished in the war, advanced to general, or became a missionary in foreign parts!'

And I chanced to overhear Miss Lizzy tell Miss Jane that Mr Wickham had been willed some fine position only to have been robbed of it by Mr Darcy – the same grand gentleman who was so uncivil about Miss Lizzy's looks at the ball. What a pity it is that people cannot be kinder to one another, as the rector so often says, if so laboriously!

On Tuesday, Bingley's sister invited Miss Jane to Netherfield, to ride together or to read novels together, or to assist her with whatever it is that very fashionable young ladies like to do. Which the mistress was most anxious that she should, wearing her French collar all the while. But just as she set off for Netherfield, there was – most unluckily – a shower of rain, and poor Miss Jane got wet right through.

So now she is confined at Netherfield with a chill, and Miss Lizzy insists upon attending her. And today, after Miss Lizzy departed through the mud and the dirt, the master proposes that, once she catches Jane's cold and commences to sneeze, Miss Mary might go to Netherfield to attend *her* – and then Miss Kitty might then go thither to attend Miss *Mary* and then – why – Longbourn might be as peaceful as it had been before there were any girls at all, to the relief of man and beast… He has a wicked sense of humour, the master.

But Miss Mary was not at all diverted, for she went upstairs and began to thump on her pianoforte till Bessy said that it was more than any Christian should be obliged to bear.

✦

Mrs B. has taken the youngest two to visit at Netherfield, whether they catch Miss Jane's germ or no. And the master says to me at tea-time, 'Marvellous quiet, Hill, is it not?' And I agree but Mr Spencer says nothing, so the master jokes, 'And do you not enjoy Longbourn in so peaceful a state, Mr Spencer?'

But Spencer says, discreet-like, ''Tis not my place to say, sir.'

'Tell me, Spencer, were you never married yourself?'

'I was, sir,' says he, 'but we were never blessed with children.'

And the master: 'Ah. Be careful what you wish for!'

I was relieved to learn from the missus – her nerves still a-flutter – that Miss Jane is better. ('And Netherfield so lovely in the sunshine, Hill! And Jane shall go down to supper tonight. And Mr Bingley was as charming as ever, though his sister rather fancies herself, and Mr Darcy is so odiously self-satisfied... But how I blessed myself to see dear Jane sitting up so prettily, her lovely eyes shining!')

As I told Bessy, she is as clear as clear that the Netherfield ball will see Miss Jane settled there, till kingdom come.

'Perhaps she may, but many's the slip 'twixt cup and lip!' said Bessy.

And Spencer said – or likelier, Shakespeare – 'There is a divinity that shapes our ends, rough-hew them as we will.'

⁂

This afternoon the mistress was in a mood of rare excitement for the master had kept all knowledge of his cousin's being expected, probably in case she burst a blood vessel with joy, till the very day itself. Bessy and the rest were no more impressed than I however, for a little notice would have been most welcome. Though Mr Spencer *did* say, in resignation, 'As the Bard put it, "What's done is done".' (Not one of the Bard's best lines if you ask my opinion, though no one did.)

'Oh Hill!' cried the mistress. 'We *must* get some fish in, for we have a visitor – and the Blue Room must be readied, and I must speak to Spencer, as soon as may be. 'Tis Mr Bennet's own cousin, a Mr Collins, from Kent!'

I doubted that fish would be possible – and felt astonished at her excitement, for the master's cousin was next in the entail – the heir to Longbourn, no less – and she had always begrudged his very

11

existence, before. Then I thought harder. 'And his wife, ma'am?'

'He has no wife,' said she, 'yet!' And absolutely winked. As I live and breathe, she winked at me!... And I guessed that Lizzy was to be the one, for Jane was, in the mistress's mind, as good as engaged already. And, after a hectic time seeing that all was done, we lined up, from Spencer and myself down to Robin – all scrubbed up and tidy, for a wonder – to do the heir of Longbourn honour.

I cannot think him an ill-looking fellow. He is perhaps five and twenty, a little heavy, though tall enough to carry it off. But he certainly lacks Mr Wickham's advantages of manner and the master had started in with teasing him even before tea, though the fellow was too dim to see it. During tea – according to Bessy – on and on he talked. About his beloved patroness, the daughter of some Earl or other down in Kent – about his humble abode and its many improvements – about his ambitions for the new school, and about the number of Her Ladyship's windows, till Bessy protested that she was as grateful not to be a Miss Bennet as she had ever been in all her life, for 'one of them is for it, sure as eggs are eggs.'

And when I went upstairs to assure myself that he was contented with the Blue Room he said, 'And so you are Mrs Hill! In that case, it is my ardent duty, as well as my pleasure, to thank you for your thoughtful, kind and generous efforts on behalf of my poor self!'

'I trust that the room is to your satisfaction, sir?'

'Immaculate, my good Hill, immaculate! Quite charming! The paper, the linens, the view from the windows complete!'

Now I had naught to do with the view from the windows, nor with the paperings, either, but I *was* glad about the linens, for Bessy had taken a deal trouble with them and all with only a few hours' warning. After that he favoured me with a minute description of his rectory in Kent – its aspect, its orchard, and the number of rooms it had upstairs.

The door being ajar, Miss Lydia poked her curly-topped head in and said, with the straightest face you ever saw, 'I think Hill might be curious to know about the dimensions of your housekeeper's room, cousin!'

Upon which, to my astonishment, he proceeded to describe it. And Miss Lydie had only been teasing! But Mr Collins is tone-deaf to humour – the master would not leave off teasing him downstairs – so much so that, according to James, the mistress ought to have put a stop to it. But there! – she has her own reasons for wishing Mr Collins's rectory to be shown in the best possible light, for she is only in doubts whether it should be Elizabeth or Mary who should be the mistress of it.

But it was not two days later when he offered – to Miss Lizzy – and was rejected. What a day *that* was! – for the first we knew of it was when Mrs Bennet summoned me and the phial of sal volatile for emergencies, which I rushed to fetch. Then I was stumping up the stairs, leaving James and Bessy laughing till they wept on each other's bosoms in the kitchen. And upstairs, 'They will be the death of me, Hill, altogether! I cannot bear another moment of being alive! What have I done – I ask you – to deserve such base ingratitude, but to sacrifice and sacrifice again for the selfish little chit only to laugh at me with her lazy and thoughtless father? Of all the daughters in all the world, Lizzy is the most heartless! And who will look after *her*, I beg, after her father is gone? Not I, I vow! She can go into the streets and sell flowers, for all I care!'

I tried to calm her, though I could not blame Miss Lizzy for all that and neither, I believe, could any of her sisters.

It is beyond my poor skill to describe how irritating Mr Collins could be, for he is neither stupid, nor ugly, nor rude. As Spencer said by the fire that night, he 'lacked the gift of seeing himself as others saw him'. His self-satisfaction in his patroness's wealth, in his humble abode, in his person altogether – is beyond bearing. And it should be remembered, too, that Miss Lizzy has been very little seen in society and, even if the highest in the land thought her not quite pretty enough to be dancing with, surely she need not sacrifice her young life to oblige her family! After all, the days of forcing young ladies into wedlock are – I am glad to say – long since passed.

Perhaps, as Bessy slyly suggested, 'Miss *Mary* might be prevailed upon to like him?'

And the last I saw of Mrs Bennet that day she was knocking on Miss Mary's bedroom door.

❦

While some of us – and I include the mistress here – were thinking of Miss Mary, we had reckoned quite without Miss Charlotte Lucas. Who, as neatly as possible, laid her trap. 'Twas Bessy saw it first, for she was waiting at table and later reported, 'I caught Miss Lucas giving that Mr Collins the eye – you mark my words, she shall be pricing new curtains for that humble abode of his, before long!'

But I could not believe it, for Bessy *can* talk rather wild, and Miss Lucas is a very sensible young lady, and a particular friend of Miss Lizzy's. So I was taken aback when, late that evening, Mr Spencer said much the same. We have got into a custom of sitting by the fire, putting the world to rights, me with my knitting, and he with the Bard – for his father, so he told me, had been a schoolmaster.

And what he said was, 'Miss Lucas does not normally visit every day, as she has done of late, and her attentions towards the young man are unusual. She may well be attempting to assist Miss Elizabeth of course, for he has certainly been rather cold to *her*,

14

ever since that eventful morning!'

'Why *that* was my own guess, Mr Spencer! For they are thick as thieves, Miss Lizzy and Miss Lucas, and always have been.'

'Just so, Mrs Hill. But were she to come again tomorrow, and *again* attempt to engage Mr Collins in conversation, then I believe it possible that Miss Lucas is going beyond obliging her friend and is considering her own advantage, instead... I could be wrong, of course.'

⁜

But she did come again. And 'twas only the day after that, very early indeed – just as the sun was cresting the horizon, as I was standing on the front steps enjoying the birds, when he passed by. He was supposedly going for 'a refreshing walk' but – truly – all the best walks are in t'other directions, and *he* heading straight towards Lucas Lodge. Then I remembered what Mr Spencer had said – and wondered.

I had not been left to wonder long before news of the engagement, though not precisely announced, seeped through the neighbourhood. Miss Lucas – never pretty but certainly clever enough – had agreed to wed Mr Collins, and thereby to make him 'the happiest of men'.

The mistress was furious. 'I never trusted her, the two-faced creature! Oiling about, pretending to be helpful... What chance had poor Mary, fluttering those sparse little eyelashes of hers?'

'Yes, ma'am,' said I.

'And *he* in just fit state to be flattered, thanks to Miss Lizzy's disdaining him as rudely as she did!... I cannot *believe*, Hill, that any person, in the history of mankind, ever had more burdens to bear than I! An eldest daughter – so lovely, so gentle – still unmarried! A second daughter as cross and contrary as Lizzy is! A third with no talent to console her cousin, a sulky fourth, and a fifth who finds losing her home a source of humour!'

'I daresay that – ' I began.

'And when salvation appears, in the form of a perfectly well-spoken and most acceptable young fellow, who could have imagined me so thwarted? *Why* could Lizzy not have accepted him? They would have made an ideal pair – for he is solid and reasonable and could have directed her wild fancies into more sensible directions! How charming she would have looked, delivering soup to the poor of Hunsford! With what grace would he have introduced her to Lady Catherine and to all the other great people of Kent! And when Mr Bennet goes to his reward, *we* might have remained! Oh, was ever a mother in the world more tormented than I?'

Well, I could not immediately recollect, though I expect Shakespeare could have thought of several, but it had always seemed to me that the mistress was not so badly off. Most English people do not have manors, but work for a living, instead. Had she contrived to give the master a son she would have been rich indeed! – but there! the rich never see themselves as we do – they *will* compare themselves to the Bingleys and the Darcys, instead of to everyone else in England!

❧

The mistress's nerves next flared after the Netherfield ball, another triumph – by all accounts – for Miss Jane. I swear, the mistress fully expected Mr Bingley to arrive, with his proposals, the very next day. Then – that day having gone by – she pinned her every hope on the dinner that Bingley and his sisters were engaged for on the Wednesday although, as she reminded me, 'We must not include Mr Wickham, for *that* Mr Darcy does not like him.'

Because he had been unkind to Mr Wickham, was my own thought. People are rarely very fond of those they have injured – 'tis not in human nature. But I said not a word, for I ought never to have overheard what Miss Lizzy told Miss Jane.

But Mr Bingley never did come to dinner.

At first the story was put about that Mr Bingley had been 'called to town on business' – though nobody could conceive what business that might be, for while his grandfather and even his dead father had been in trade, Mr Bingley himself had nothing to do with it.

The mistress was convinced that he was seeing his lawyer before rushing back to offer to Miss Jane. But then one day passed, then several others. And then his sisters and the husband of one – and Mr Darcy – all followed him back to London, leaving Netherfield as empty as it had ever been.

And then the mistress decided that there was a love child, and that Mr Bingley was arranging to leave the child all his money, and that Netherfield would never see him more. And then it was, 'But Hill, oh Hill, how unfair is it, that I wait all this time for a pleasing young man to come, and when he does he falls in love with Jane, only to go away again!'

Now I cannot believe in the love child, for Mr Bingley does not have the look of such a man (Mr Wickham?... perhaps!) But a thousand things could keep a man in London beyond a love child, for gentlemen quite often keep houses there and who can say what else they might find in town to attend to, or on which to waste their idle hours? For, though I have never been to town myself, nor am ever likely to be, Mr Spencer says that London is a wonder.

Then the mistress takes to her bed, to make as much trouble as she could, for it was all, 'She will never get him now, Hill!' and I said all that I could to give her a little hope, for Miss Jane is so beautiful that Mr Bingley could never be her only admirer and, if Miss Jane should only go up to London once more, why, there must be a thousand fine young men for her to choose from!

But Mr Spencer did not quite agree with me. He said, 'She is very attractive indeed, Mrs Hill – most attractive. However, many London men prefer to wed their relations, to keep their property in the family – or else to marry ladies whose families are in trade, for the sake of their fine fortunes. They might secretly prefer to marry Miss Bennet, but the money sways them. For "In love the heavens themselves do guide the state/Money buys lands, and wives are sold by fate."'

'Oh, do not say so!' I cried, 'for the entail –'

'The *entail* is half of the problem,' said Bessy, who had been listening while doing her polishing. 'But not the whole of it, for men are half the problem, themselves!'

She had been in a disparaging mood ever since James had been 'Marietta-ing'. ('Marietta says that Miss Lucas shall have three fine new gowns… Marietta says that *she* would never have wed Mr Collins, upon any consideration… Marietta says that lettuce is a stupid vegetable, for it tastes of nothing at all.')

I shared a glance with Mr Spencer, and he changed the subject. But once he had gone up to his room, I dared to say to Bessy, 'Supposing this Marietta is as two-faced as you say, and James as deluded as you believe, he is never likely to prefer you when you are so unkind about men in general!'

After that she tried to treat him better, though they never seemed to joke as they had used. But then, not even the master's wit was as polished as usual, as the days that Netherfield stayed empty stretched into weeks.

✦

'There is no pleasing her,' James said discontentedly.

'Then ignore her,' said I. 'Marietta will come round soon enough. And, if she does not why, she is not worth fretting over.'

Despite James' discomfiture, there was a new spirit of hopefulness in the house, for the Gardiners had come for Christmas and had invited Miss Jane to return to town with them, thereafter. I had been obliged to endure all the mistress's imaginings upon the subject, for she was certain that Mr Bingley would no sooner hear that Miss Bennet was in London before he would be pounding down the Gardiners' door to offer to her. Though how he was even to learn she was there neither I nor Mr Spencer could conjecture.

But London always seems a place of possibilities, and 'tis likeliest that Mr Bingley is still there. He has kept the lease of Netherfield, though no one, not even his own housekeeper, is sure how long it has still to run.

And how lovely Miss Jane had looked, as she stepped into the carriage with the Gardiners' sweet-voiced children! – In that moment, I could not imagine that she would not have *some* adventure in town, one way or another! But James was still fretting that Marietta was merely 'toying' with him.

'She is almost never serious – at least, with myself – yet I cannot resist her,' said he. 'And how she knows it, the impudent chit! She is so quick! The way she teases Mr Phipps, the butler!'

'And does he not object?'

'No, for he is not slow and steady like Spencer is but quizzes her in return. When she is in a mood to charm, no one could be more charming than Marietta! Yet she can sulk every bit as well as Miss Kitty herself. As I told her – how she laughed – she can be as lovely as Miss Bennet, as witty as Miss Lizzy, and as daring as Miss Lydia. But she is never like Miss Mary, ha!'

'No one,' said Spencer, who chanced to be passing, 'could be like Miss Mary, beyond Miss Mary indeed!' Though I still feel sorry for Miss Mary, pounding away on her instrument when no one wishes to hear her, and fixing her hopes on that Mr Collins to no avail.

❖

Such a time as it has been since I have written – and with a bad pen as well – but that much has happened! For to say the truth, the family has been at sixes and sevens ever since Miss Lydia eloped with that deplorable Wickham, who turned out to be as wicked as wicked can be.

Aye, you read that aright. Miss Lydia eloped, the giddy young creature, while she was staying with Colonel Forster and his wife down at Brighton. Not only *that* but Miss Lizzy had actually dared to warn the master that she might – and he had only laughed at her! As Mr Spencer said, and rightly, 'An easy temper is a blessing in a master but a disaster in a father.'

'Well, I cannot understand that Wickham,' was Bessy's view. 'What fool would have wed Miss Lydia when half Meryton would have had him? Why, even Miss Lizzy –'

'Wed her?' said Mr Spencer, quite sharpish. 'Who says that he will wed her? 'Tis a longish way to Scotland. And, if he *fails* to wed her, why, the whole family comes to grief!'

Bessy said, 'Aye, I should certainly think twice, if I were he, for Miss Lydie is so troublesome! In fact, were I Mr Wickham, I should leave the silly girl and her trunk by the side of the London Road and drive on to Scotland without her!'

And James holding his sides with laughing – even though the mistress is dying. Or so she says.

'I shall die of this, Hill,' she cries, 'for there never was a better girl, nor a kinder and sweeter one, than my dearest Lydia! But men are deceivers ever!'

'Quite, ma'am,' says I, thinking that it was Miss Lydia, and not myself, she should have been lecturing to about men, for then her lecture might have been of rather more use.

'The best girl in the world! And me lying here, dying!'

'But with respect, ma'am, it could have been still worse, for a great many families have survived an elopement – and in the nobility as well, as Mr Spencer himself says.'

'Dying! Dying!'

I longed to ask if some camomile tea might set her to rights, but it did not seem respectful, what with her dying – though, to be sure, she was not. And so I went to the kitchen and left Miss Jane to comfort her instead. For the master is still with Mr Gardiner in town and Miss Lizzy not yet returned from the north – but Miss Jane is home, which is a blessing.

At the second table that night I said, 'The mistress told me, "Men are deceivers ever."' And Bessy impertinently wished to know whether Marietta thought *James* a deceiver, and James pretended to hit her with the plum preserve.

But two hours later Mr Spencer took out his pipe and filled it up, saying sombrely, 'My dear Mrs Hill, the young ladies will never marry up, after this.'

'No more they will, Mr Spencer. But surely they *will* still marry?'

'If 'tis an elopement, they might,' said he, as grave as the grave the missus thinks she is toppling into.

'But it *is* an elopement!'

'So we have been assured, Mrs Hill, but –'

'But what?'

Spencer avoided my eyes – the first time I had known him to do such a thing. Then he said with lowered voice, 'I have heard scandalous things about this Wickham – things which I could never repeat to you or to any lady and – in addition – scandalous things about money.'

I felt a little confused, because I am no lady, for a lady must have her own house. I only repeated, 'Money?'

'Debts. Debts of honour, so 'tis said.'

'Surely you do not mean *gambling*, Mr Spencer?'

'I do mean gambling, Mrs Hill,' said he heavily. 'I am very sorry to shock you, but he is said to owe a great deal. Ten to one, he cannot *afford* to wed Miss Lydia, even should he wish to! In which case, she will become a fallen woman.'

'Oh heavens! Do not say so!'

'And all because of the master's fatal flaw – the flaw of his character, as in Shakespeare.'

I knew nothing of Shakespeare's flaws – but, of course, Mr Spencer's father had taught him a good deal. 'What flaw do you mean, Mr Spencer?' I asked at last, for he was still staring into the fire, and his pipe quite gone out.

He said, 'It is the quality that brings down the principal player, in every tragedy. In *Macbeth* 'tis ambition. In *Othello* – of course – 'tis jealousy. But in Mr Bennet's case, it is indolence. Miss Lydia wanted discipline – wanted it badly – but her own father only bestirred himself enough to laugh at her.'

I could not defend him, for had not Bessy always said the same? But I could not help asking, 'But surely – it is the *mother*'s duty to correct her daughter?'

He sat looking into the fire for a terrible long time, while I feared he could not disapprove me more, or else that he was falling asleep over his pipe, as had happened once before. But finally he said, 'You are a very wise woman, Mrs Hill.'

✦

At last, the master returned from London, dusty, weary, and defeated, for he and Mr Gardiner had never found them. He would hardly touch his food, though Cook had roasted lamb in the manner he loved best. Meanwhile, the mistress moves – by the hour, it sometimes seems – from their 'ruination' to her dying – and from her dying to her expecting, every moment, a joyful express from Gretna Green – and from expectation to arguing with Lady Lucas on account of that lady's daring to ascend the stairs to what Bessy secretly calls the 'room of ruination'.

Thus in the morning it might be, 'My nerves, Hill, are not in fit state to endure such anguish!' And ''Tis all that Mrs Forster's fault, Bessy, for she never looked after her. That one false friend will be the ruination of us all!' But after luncheon she can listen to Miss Jane's reading some novel by Miss Burney and complain, 'Well, *I* can see nothing so very clever about it,' and at four o'clock she can brag to Lady Lucas, 'Why, any moment now, I warrant you, we shall learn that little Lydie is as wedded as you and I, ourselves!' But in the evening she might be banging on about the ruination again – till I heard the master tell Miss Lizzy that it was an education to him to learn that ruination could feature in quite so many guises.

I cannot help thinking that – in some ways – we servants are better-off than the young ladies, for *we* have something else to do and to think about, while the poor girls have only to hear about the ruination and to listen to Miss Mary on the pianoforte.

But I must have been tempting fate, for no sooner had I thought this when Mr Spencer and I, coming down the stairs, discovered James in tears in the butler's pantry, and Bessy patting his shoulder hard enough to injure it.

'Why James!' I cried. 'What has happened? Are you poorly?'

'Nay, 'tis Marietta,' said Bessy, with satisfaction.

'Marietta!'

'Aye. She is walking out *now* with the Lucases' butler – with Mr Phipps, himself!'

'Great heavens,' said Mr Spencer, but all I could think was that James looked younger than ever, his face awash in tears and his heart quite broke.

'Oh, my poor boy,' I cried, and he clung to me as if I was his last hope on earth.

'I loved her so!' cried he, burying his head in my shoulder. At which Bessy began to bang her pots and pans about, rather like Miss Mary and the pianoforte.

Mr Spencer said kindly, 'I am very sorry, James,' and, just under his breath, 'Frailty, thy name is woman!' – which might have been the Bard or might not have been, for *I* could never swear to it.

But once James was cool enough to listen, I said, 'My poor James, I am truly sorry but – if she is two-faced – surely 'tis better to know sooner rather than later? Also, is not Mr Phipps a great deal older than she?'

'Yes, for *he* is 32,' cried Bessy, 'and *she* is but twenty!' Which surprised me, for I had always thought Mr Phipps far nearer to forty than thirty – nor could I think twelve years so shocking a difference, for there had been ten betwixt my own parents. 'She is a chit and a hussy and no better than she ought to be!' added Bessy.

'But was she actually engaged to James?' I asked.

'*That* she was not, for whenever he asked, she would say neither yea nor nay.'

24

Then I went to beg Cook to heat up a bit of brisket for poor James, though 'twas meant for the young ladies. But when I finally made my way, with heavy heart, upstairs to Mrs Bennet, I learned that the miracle had happened. For though there were still no angels in the garden, the mistress hailed me with almost as much joy as if there *had* been. 'Hill! Hill! There has been an express from Mr Gardiner' – and I knew, by how her ribbons bobbled, that the news was good – 'They are found! – and they are to be wedded on Friday! And you shall all have a bowl of punch to drink Miss Lydia's health!'

I instantly wished Miss Lydia joy – while silently thanking God for the end of the ruination.

The master too seemed mightily relieved – according to Bessy, who waited on the top table in James's place. For James had gone to bed, on purpose to cry himself to sleep.

But I cannot help marvelling, for all that.

Miss Lydie, the first to be wedded! 'Tis a turn-up for the books, and she will rub it in quite unmercifully but the worst – I do believe – must surely be over. Miss Lydia will become Mrs Wickham and – as Mr Spencer reminded me, we must forget that we ever heard a single word about the gambling. Which is a common enough fault for a young man of breeding, though my late husband had never any patience with it. But that evening Mr Spencer stoked his pipe, which comfortable smell always puts me in mind of my father, and said, 'Mark my words, Mrs Hill, there is more to *this* than meets the eye.'

'I daresay, although – to be fair to Miss Marietta – she and James were never quite engaged. And who is to say that 'twill end in a match with Mr Phipps? For she seems so unsteady!'

'I was referring to the match at Longbourn, Mrs Hill.'

'But – but surely Mr Wickham could never weasel out of it, with the articles signed and the date all fixed!'

'Could he not? And even should he go through with it, what are they to live on?– for according to the innkeeper at the Bull and Bush, he owes a very great deal – and not only to various shops but, they *do* say, to some young lady besides.'

'Not to anyone we know, I hope?' I asked, quite in jest, but Mr Spencer did not return my smile.

'They do say, to the Lucases' Marietta, Mrs Hill.'

'No!'

'So it is said.'

'Good gracious! Does – does James *know*?'

'I believe not.'

'But she could surely never have been with Mr Wickham while she was stepping out with James!'

'It seems so.'

'I cannot believe it! – though Bessy *did* say that Mr Wickham had an eye. And that he pinched her on the bottom, as well.'

'He appears to have gone a good deal farther with the Lucas's Marietta. Though *she* – luckily or unluckily – has no connections to bribe him into wedlock, as Miss Lydia has.'

'Bribe!'

'Bribe, Mrs Hill. I cannot but think that Mr Wickham has been bribed, by Mr Gardiner or perhaps by the master, into wedding Miss Lydia. There will have been something of the sort, you mark my words!'

I must have seemed witless, I was that shocked. I said, 'You mean, to save the chances of her sisters –'

'– and the family honour, indeed.'

'But 'twas *never* the master!'

''Tis likeliest to have been Mr Gardiner, then. We must hope so, at least. Because, had the *master* borrowed to save Lydia's honour… well! James, and perhaps others on the staff, might have to be let go.'

'Oh, do not say so! If poor James was dismissed – and his heart quite broke –'

'I agree,' said Mr Spencer, just pressing my hand. 'Though I trust that the broken heart might be mendable. I have sometimes wondered whether Miss Bessy – but never mind!'

How warm his hand was, upon my wrist!

'I do hope as it might be mendable, Mr Spencer,' I said, and then I left him and went up to bed, my feelings all in disorder.

❦

The news about Marietta and Mr Wickham was not long a secret, and James flung straight from misery to fury. That Marietta had been flirting with both Wickham and the butler Phipps 'beneath his very nose!' – 'How could I not have seen?' and 'How could she ever have done it?' absorbed him to the point where he could attend to nothing properly… Then at long last Lady Lucas heard, and instantly dismissed Mr Phipps and Marietta both.

The master as usual *would* have his little joke, saying gravely to Mr Spencer, 'And so, my good Spencer, when are you to run off with Bessy? For my wife will never be content until her household is as much gossiped about as the Lucases' is'!'

And Spencer, with that little smile, 'I would oblige you, sir, in everything within my power – but I am very sure that Bessy would never have me.'

'Well, well, you shall never know until you try,' said the master tolerantly. His mood had altered, and overnight, too. At first he had sworn never to see the Wickhams more, neither in this world or the next, whether they be wed or no. Then we had endured more of

27

ruination from the mistress. And finally, his two eldest daughters had persuaded the master to endure it.

And so on the evening of their wedding day, and in the Gardiners' own carriage, Mr and Mrs Wickham returned to Longbourn. And *she* as charmed with herself as possible in a pretty new gown and *he*, as Mr Spencer quipped, 'as handsome as handsome does not always do'. And Miss Lydia immediately starts in at upstaging her sisters, taking precedence at dinner even over Miss Jane, till every servant in the house lost patience with her.

I did not serve at dinner of course but, when Lydia came downstairs to show off her fine clothes, she cried, 'Oh Hill, do you not simply adore my new gown and pretty shoes?' and nary a word about my chilblains. Though, as I had expected no better, at least I was not disappointed.

But soon enough the Wickhams were gone, for his new regiment is to be quartered in Newcastle, and the latest excitement is all about Mr Bingley – just as it was all those months ago – for his housekeeper says he is returning to Netherfield. Though Bessy, in imitation of the master, says, 'I shall not be mending Miss Jane's collar, for I was assured before, if I mended it, that Mr Bingley would wed Miss Bennet and yet he did not!' – which made James fall about laughing.

The mistress seems almost as fidgety as during the ruination, for not even Mrs Emmerson at Netherfield is certain when Mr Bingley is to arrive – and perhaps nor is Bingley himself, for he was always rather a sudden young gentleman.

'Twas on Wednesday when I heard the mistress cry, 'Mr Bingley is come to visit, he is indeed, and that Mr Darcy with him!' and Miss Jane's face as pink as if dipped in hot water and Miss Lizzy's as white as if she might faint… And both Mr Bingley and his friend looking as uncomfortable as possible. (Although I must just say that, though Mr Bingley is the friendlier, that Mr Darcy *does* draw the eye.)

I could see no symptom of particular regard between Mr Bingley and Miss Jane – but that evening, when I mentioned it to Mr Spencer by the fire, Mr Spencer said, 'Sometimes, Mrs Hill, a man can feel too much to be comfortable. At any rate, that was my own impression. For "When heaven doth weep, does not the earth o'erflow?"'

I tried to take consolation from this, for the words were so poetical, but it seemed to me that a man who felt too much to be comfortable might – and for that very reason – soon be off. And how I hoped and prayed that he would not!

But what a topsy-turvy time we are having!

For 'twas only the next day when Bessy came to me and said, 'My dear Agnes, I have something to tell you.' And I was dreading that she would leave, for Bessy – for all that she is so headstrong – is such a friend. But she said, 'It is this. James and I are – are walking out together. And I know that I am too old – it is only what everyone will say – but I have loved him for so long, as you must know – and he is so very dear to me!'

I knew not what to do except to kiss her, and to hope that it was for the best. Then she asked me to let Mr Spencer know.

It was very much easier to tell him than I had thought, for I had only to say, 'Something Bessy has begged me to tell you, Mr Spencer…' before he interrupted, 'So James has asked her to walk out with him, has he? Excellent!' Then he put down his pipe and said, 'A consummation devoutly to be wished!'

I was not certain what a consummation might be, but it was clear that he was very well-pleased, while James seemed every bit as delighted walking out with Bessy as he had ever been with the Lucas's Marietta. And Bessy teased and bullied him as much as ever – or rather more – and I cannot help hoping that this 'walking out' might end in the banns being read, for she sings as she sorts the dishes, and then he tickles her to make her stop.

As for Mr Bingley, he never tickles Miss Jane, for young gentlemen cannot – but the way he looks at her gives me such hopes! And then last Friday I met Miss Lizzy on the stairs, with swimming eyes. 'Are you well, Miss Elizabeth?' I asked.

'Oh, Hill! Forgive me,' recollecting herself and wiping her eyes with the back of her hand, 'I am more than well. For Jane has accepted Mr Bingley!' And this with a light in her eyes that made her suddenly every bit as lovely as her sister – for there was never anything between the two of them, to my mind, as to which was the prettiest.

I could not find words, but she understood and shook my hand, saying, 'I know you feel for us, Hill – and I thank you for it, most gratefully!'

Which was very handsome of her, as well.

＊

After this, of course, Mr Bingley has been underfoot to such an extent that Mr Bennet wonders aloud that he does not surrender his lease at Netherfield and move into the bedroom shared by Miss Jane and Miss Lizzy, instead. Which is quite wicked of him. And then the mistress complains that he – Mr Bennet – is never properly grateful for anything.

And accompanying Mr Bingley, as often as not, is Mr Darcy. But because Mrs Bennet wishes for Mr Bingley to be allowed time with Miss Jane, she schemes for them to be alone together in the shrubbery or in the woods. Which Miss Kitty detests, as she and Lizzy are then obliged to remain with Mr Darcy who, for all his fine looks, never seems to have two words to say to anybody.

And so, this morning, we had Miss Kitty threatening to stay behind with Mary but Mrs Bennet would not have it, for 'unless Lizzy and Mr Darcy are engaged – ha! –which no one has yet told me of – or indeed, unless Kitty is herself engaged to Mr Darcy, then you must *both* attend him. Unless someone can persuade Mary, who is more obstinate than the rest of you all put together. For I shall never have it said that I allowed a daughter of mine to walk alone in the woods with a young man to whom she is not engaged.'

And Kitty submitted. Though as she put on her bonnet she told me, and very seriously, 'Hill, I may be home just a little behind the others, for I must see Maria Lucas – I must indeed!' (For she and Maria *will* have their little disputes, just as their mamas do.)

I kept an eye out for their return, in hopes that Miss Kitty might look a little happier but, instead, there was Miss Lizzy walking at quite a distance from Mr Darcy, not that there was any ill nature in it, for she turned on the path and gave him one of her loveliest smiles – which was more than I expected, for had not he begun their acquaintance by pronouncing her not handsome enough to dance with?… Though I was even better-pleased, not five minutes later, to see Kitty walking arm-in-arm with Maria Lucas – setting an example that, in my own opinion, their mamas would do well to follow.

But the joys of the day were not yet over, for Bessy stopped me as I was going up to bed, and said, 'Mrs Hill – Agnes – you should know that James has asked me to marry him. And I dearly hope that you might approve.'

'Why, Bessy!' I cried. 'Do you want to make me weep, after all that we have been through, with the mistress's nerves and the master's jokes, and the eloping and the expresses and all the ruination that we have endured together? Oh my dear, I wish you both every joy in the world, for you deserve it all!'

Then she embraced me and I went up to bed, marvelling. And how I longed to mention it to Mr Spencer the next day – though, one way or another, I could not. But as we were all celebrating Miss Jane's engagement, he said in his toast how he hoped that the air of Netherfield might be as conducive to marital happiness as the air of Messina had been for Beatrice and Benedict. Then he looked at James, and almost winked. That was how I knew that he had guessed.

And that was not all, for what the master had always thought the greatest joke, of Mr Darcy's offering to Miss Lizzy, turns out to have actually happened! While even if that Lady Catherine might be ill-tempered enough to cut Mr Darcy it cannot signify, for Mr Darcy has all the money anyone could wish for – and Miss Lizzy will be even richer than Miss Jane!

Everyone exclaimed on the brilliance of the match, and a great many jests were made about Miss Lizzy's lack of handsomeness on the one hand and her great slyness, on the other, for not a single soul in the house had ever suspected. Not even Miss Jane, for it had all taken place down in Kent and Derbyshire. And who knows but, had Lydia never run away, that Miss Elizabeth might not be already wedded to Mr Darcy?

The master was so relieved as to make most of the jests himself and, as for the mistress, instead of that 'strange and difficult man whom she could never understand Mr Bingley's liking', Mr Darcy seems almost her favourite of the two, for Cook complains that no meat nor fish not any other food is good enough to set before 'that Darcy'. Though he hardly eats at all but only looks at Miss Lizzy in such a way – oh! I believe I should faint, should anyone look in such a way at me!

But Mr Bennet told Cook that Mr Darcy and Lizzy would soon

be gone to the Archbishop to be wedded, and that she could then return to her usual dishes, which he greatly preferred.

'Twas only a joke about the Archbishop but Cook was very well-pleased all the same.

✦

The night before the young ladies' double wedding, Mr Spencer and I were sitting comfortably by the fire – for Bessy was out with young James and Cook and the rest had gone up to bed. He had his great tome before him and I had my needles, for I was embroidering Bessy a cap for a wedding present.

'And so,' said he, "All's well that ends well."'

'It does indeed Mr Spencer, and no young ladies could deserve it better than Miss Jane and Miss Lizzy. And who is to say but that Miss Kitty and even Miss Mary might now fall in the way of gentlemen almost as fine? 'Tis no wonder the master seems so contented! Imagine, if they were all settled – and no need for cutting off any entail!'

'And imagine the state of Mrs Bennet's poor nerves, Mrs Hill, should you be right!'

'She will have to fall to arguing with Lady Lucas, just to keep her pores open. For unless she has something to fret about, she will work herself up into a fever and all for nothing!'

'An exhausting manner of living,' was his opinion.

''Twould not suit me, I am sure.'

'Nor me. But we seem to agree about most things, Mrs Hill, do we not?'

'Aye, true enough.'

And the fire crackled a little louder while Mr Spencer refilled his pipe. Then he said, 'Mrs Hill, I am glad that we are alone tonight, for I have something rather particular to ask you.'

'If 'tis about the locking up, James will see to it – and Bessy will see that he does.'

'It is not about the locking up. Mrs Hill, I lost my wife on this day eighteen years ago, and the new-born baby with her.'

'Mercy!' I cried, moved and astonished enough to put down the cap. 'I am grieved to hear it, indeed. I lost my husband nigh on eight years since, myself.'

'She was a wonderful woman, Mrs Hill – good-hearted, warm, generous, affectionate. I have never believed myself,' said he, looking into the fire very steadily, 'to have seen her equal.'

'I should think not,' said I – though he must have seen a great many women, of course, over eighteen years.

'Until recently,' said he. Then he turned his eyes towards me, and – and the look there was not far from the look in Mr Darcy himself, glancing down at Miss Elizabeth. I blushed all the way to my cap, wondering if I was dreaming it.

'I have been hoping for some time, Mrs Hill, that you might be feeling something of the same, but did not dare to ask, for fear that I might be mistaken. But I put it to you now, my dear, my very dear Mrs Hill. Could you think on it perhaps, and let me know if the fondest wish of my heart might not someday be answered? That, as the Bard of Avon so fervently believed, to the marriage of true minds, there might be no impediment?'

And I could say nothing, absolutely nothing.

Because it seemed to me as if, all along, through all the year's trials and tribulations, he had always been there, supporting me.

But I could *say* absolutely nothing. I could only just look.

Then he embraced me.

⬥

The next Saturday, we visited the master in his study. He seemed alarmed, for we had never called on him together before. Nor was it Mr Spencer's usual time for collecting the hired staff payments.

'Great heavens! A deputation! There has been no accident, I hope?'

'No, sir.'

'And I trust that neither of you is thinking of giving notice, due to missing Miss Lydia so grievously. Has the work been too much for the pair of you, with regard to the double wedding?'

'Nay, sir,' said Mr Spencer very steadily. 'Instead, we had a second double wedding in mind. James's to Bessy – and mine to Mrs Hill, here.'

'Good heavens! Well, well! Mrs Hill, I wish you joy. I congratulate you, Spencer. Truly, I could not be better-pleased! And young James and Bessy as well? Under the circumstances, I believe that Cook must wed young Boots and make a thorough job of it!'

Then he shook Mr Spencer's hand – and my own as well. He did, indeed.

One Good Sonnet

From the diaries of Mr Paul Perkins

Mrs Bennet said, 'I do not like to boast of my own child, but to be sure, Jane – one does not often see anybody better looking. It is what everybody says. I do not trust my own partiality. When she was only fifteen, there was a man at my brother Gardiner's in town so much in love with her that my sister-in-law was sure he would make her an offer before we came away. But, however, he did not. Perhaps he thought her too young. However, he wrote some verses on her, and very pretty they were.'

'And so ended his affection,' said Elizabeth impatiently. 'There has been many a one, I fancy, overcome in the same way. I wonder who first discovered the efficacy of poetry in driving away love!'

'I have been used to consider poetry the FOOD of love,' said Darcy.

'Of a fine, stout, healthy love it may. Everything nourishes what is strong already. But if it be only a slight, thin sort of inclination, I am convinced that one good sonnet will starve it entirely away.'

(from *Pride and Prejudice*, Chapter 9)

It has come to me at last. I have met the only woman in the world for me – the one true love of my life! But I have very little chance, for she remains in town for only three weeks, after which she will disappear into the country!

This is how it happened. I was at the Little Theatre with Toby when he said, 'My word!' and leaned forward, rapt.

'What is it?' I asked, for I should not have been surprised had it been something as silly as a quiz of a hat, or that some fellow we had been to school with had surfaced in naval dress, or something of the sort.

'It is a divinity,' said he. I had a pretty crisp retort prepared yet, as I followed the line of his pointing finger, I gasped, instead.

'Who on earth…?'

'Perhaps not "of earth," at all,' said Toby, shaking his head. But then he started on about the prospects for his brother's racehorse as if nothing out of the ordinary had occurred. While I was so struck that I could think of nothing beyond – somehow – meeting her. And there I was blessed by a stroke of great good luck, for she was seated in a box with Mr Gardiner, a member of my club and – though I could not recall ever sharing more than two words with him – at least we had been introduced. After the first act was finally finished, it took me an age to work my way around to their box, where I was admitted.

Gardiner said very pleasantly, 'Mr Perkins, is it not? May I introduce my wife? – and our niece, Miss Jane Bennet, who is visiting from the country.'

I bowed as neatly as I could for, close to, the niece was more divine than ever. I was also conscious that people were glancing at us – at her, I should say – from all round the theatre. Either for this or for some other reason she blushed, and the access of creamy peach made her look prettier than ever.

'I trust you are enjoying your visit?' I asked tenderly.

'Oh, very much,' said she, and her voice… I cannot describe its lightness, its delicacy, the way in which she fingered her little fan. 'The Gardiner children are so delightful!'

I imagined her in a portrait, that lovely arm around some fair and tiny bairn – wisps of golden hair, a velvet gown.

I said, 'Ah. And what ages are they, ma'am?' and Mrs Gardiner said that, though the eldest was not yet ten, they were all exceedingly well-behaved – except when they fought over the attentions of their cousin Jane. Here I saw my chance. 'But who,' I inquired, 'would not fight for the lightest word from their cousin Jane?'

At this Miss Bennet blushed still more as I rapturously reflected that, whilst Jane was never a favourite name of mine, it was one of marvellous usefulness in terms of poetry, for even a very mediocre wordsmith could find rhymes for 'Jane'… I politely inquired as to Mrs Gardiner's opinion of the play. (An attractive lady with a lively eye, but nothing in comparison!)

'It is silly,' said Mrs Gardiner, 'but silliness can be remarkably diverting, as my husband was saying just before you arrived.'

'The acting,' said her niece, 'is quite marvellous. Mrs Siddons is remarkable!'

I concurred, though Toby and I had found her insufferably affected not fifteen minutes earlier. Such is the effect of so luminous a beauty upon man's reason! Then Mr Gardiner returned with John Thorpe.

Now I have no difficulty with Thorpe, in a general way. We had endured the same school, and the same house within it – but I have never forgotten his terming me 'Pretty Perkins' and other odious and mocking names, as he was – which he remains, of course – some years my senior. We younger lads had found him quite the bully. I have not presented a very persuasive case for our friendship – for he loved himself and I detested him. Still, his introduction to Miss Bennet was made in due form, and John bowed above that lovely hand.

'So how long do you intend to grace London?' he asked, amongst other fatuities.

In the end we left together, Thorpe shaking his head. 'I wished, like you I suppose, to get a closer look. She is well enough, not bad at all. Eyes a little too close together, perhaps.'

'Her eyes,' I told him fervently, 'resemble the limitless glory of a sun-drenched June afternoon. As for her grace, she cannot shift her fan from one hand to the other without stopping my heart. And her voice! It falls upon the ear like dew from some cupped bluebell!'

Thorpe peered at me. (Come to think of it, were not *his* piggy eyes a little too close together?) He said, 'You do know, my good fellow, that she has scarcely a penny?'

Now Plato himself remarked, 'The madness of love is the greatest blessing of heaven'. Thus, though the heart sank a little, 'twas only a little as Thorpe continued, 'Her family estate is entailed upon some cousin and – so 'tis said – mortgaged to the hilt, besides. And five daughters – How they must have blessed themselves! Daughter after daughter, and no means left of curtailing the property's entail!'

I said, 'It *is* unlucky. But such an eldest one!'

'True, and I suppose the family must hope that if *she* could but entrance some fellow of substance, the younger daughters might stand some chance. They might ride upon her coattails. But looks, you know – looks never last. A few seasons from now – 'twould lay my house on it – she will be no more than another plump matron watching the sensation of the season dance past!'

'Never!' I cried, thinking, 'the poetic glory of her whole soul is in those orbs of heaven's blue!' And, before I could forget so felicitous a phrase, I scribbled 'orbs – h'ns blue' onto the back of my theatre ticket.

'Well, well,' said Thorpe tolerantly. 'At least you cannot say that I failed to warn you! Oh, hallo, Darcy, I had not heard that you were in town.'

'I am generally in town at this time of year,' said Mr Darcy, acknowledging me politely – though, after a few comments of no particular meaning, I found myself too in awe of him to remain. Darcy had overawed me since our schooldays, for he had been the richest lad there, and with an air to match...

I wrote ecstatically in my diary late that night, 'It has come to me at last – love!'

And dreamed of bright orbs, suspended in an agate sky.

The next few days were frustrating indeed! On Tuesday I called at the Gardiners, but 'no one was at home'.

I left my card – with Mr Paul Perkins, Esq., embossed in its centre. I tried again on Wednesday, but the ladies were again not at home – nor were they were anywhere to be seen at the concert that evening.

When finally admitted, on Thursday, I found that I was not the first young fellow to be lured by the newcomer's charms. The room seemed packed, and Miss Bennet most perplexedly besieged... On her right, Lady Millington was, most passionately, recommending her dressmaker – on her left, Sir Humphrey was attempting to interest her in a speech he intended to deliver at the House of Lords.

Her aunt appeared to have forgotten me, then her expression cleared. 'My husband's friend, Mr Perkins, of course!'

I murmured something about the play and added, 'I publish a soupcon myself.'

'About soup, do you mean?'

'A literary compendium, one of interest to all artistic and thoughtful people.'

'How delightful! Essays, I suppose.'

'Mostly poetry, ma'am. And reviews.'

'I expect you were reviewing the play the other evening?'

I could not pretend that I had been but explained that, while well enough, the play concerned was lacking in significant form. For some reason however, I sensed that Mrs Gardiner was a little *distrait*. I spent the next twenty minutes attempting to get close enough to Miss Bennet to speak to her. Her modesty was not my friend, in that the attention she received – and she just fifteen! – seemed almost too much for her. Feeling rather indignant, I almost repented of coming. But then a lucky chance of sitting beside her arose.

'Good day, Miss Bennet. All this attention distresses you a little, does it not?'

'It does, Mr Perkins,' said she, with a sigh that quite wrung my heart. 'But it has nothing to do with *me*. It is my aunt's nature that is so attractive. It can be no surprise that she is popular! And then, I slept rather badly. I find it difficult to sleep, when parted from my own bed.'

'I believe your home is in Hertfordshire?'

'Near Meryton. But even Meryton is only a village.'

'I imagine it quite in the country, where only the screech owl might be heard in the night?'

'Indeed, while here there is always some early fellow pushing his cart across the cobblestones, or some rider in a violent hurry – And then, once I am awake I start to think, and then there is no hope of rest again! However, my aunt's physician has promised me a sleeping draught.'

ONE GOOD SONNET

And just when I was gathering enough courage to suggest that the clarity of her gaze did not suggest any dearth of slumber, her aunt declared that her niece was weary and should go upstairs. After which the visitors, who had mostly come to assess the extent of her divinity, soon dispersed.

✦

Oh Jane, fair maiden, like a wayward star
Thy beauty's light didst pierce my feeble heart,
In yonder theatre, radiant near and far,
I saw thee first, but now we drift apart.

Thine eyes, like gems, did sparkle once that night,
Thy smile, a scent of sunshine in the gloom,
My heart with longing took an upward flight,
But now – alas! – I fear my love's entombed.

Shakespeare or Coleridge might, I daresay, have made something of such a theme, but I found myself assailed by doubts – for example, with regards to the sun's possessing a scent. It is always the same, with my writing, I am so excessively sensitive! It might be fine – it might even be genius – but I find myself forever fretting that it might, perchance, be rather poor instead.

In the end, I determined to call upon the Gardiners again.

✦

I was earlier on Friday. Mr Gardiner said, 'What a pleasure to see you again quite so soon,' and Mrs Gardiner remembered me at once. I found my muse reading to a small girl. What a delightful picture they made! – her lovely head bent close to the girl's, the illustrated book between them.

'Oh, Mr Perkins,' said she. 'This is my eldest niece, Beatrice.'

'Beatrice, how delightful! Ah, how I wish I was an artist!'

'Why, I thought you were?'

'An artist with a brush, Miss Bennet. I doubt that my poor words' – for they had been particularly poor that morning – 'could do as much!'

'I very much wish, Jane,' pouted the child, 'that you would finish the story!'

'Perhaps I might oblige?' I suggested.

The little girl looked dubious. 'Would he do, Jane? For he has *such* long hair!'

'I believe,' said Jane, with a laughing look that made me instantly resolve to have my hair cut that very day, 'that Mr Perkins would do a great deal better than I! For he is a writer himself, Beatrice.' With the result that I found myself reading about Little Red Riding Hood, with the lovely Miss Bennet not five feet away.

With so fair a chance, I instantly determined to give of my all. How I threw myself into the role, particularly when given the chance to act the grandmother or the wolf! Mrs Siddons could not have done more. In truth, it is possible I did rather *too* well, for Beatrice gave a little squeak and hid her face in her cousin's skirt, crying, 'Oh, Jane! The wolf is quite *quite* horrid!'

'Oh my dear! Mr Perkins is only pretending!'

But little Beatrice was eventually borne off by her mama, most urgently wishing to be assured that there were 'no wolves in London'.

Jane shook her head at me and said, with that delightful laugh, 'You never confessed, Mr Perkins, to being quite so gifted at acting! We shall have wolves, I suppose, till Sunday, or until something else comes along to captivate Bea's imagination.'

Chastened, I said, 'I had always supposed children rather partial to drama.'

Miss Bennet smiled for some reason and asked what I had been working on.

'Oh, a mere something or nothing, Miss Bennet. A sonnet.'

'How lovely! Upon what subject?'

'Um… upon beauty.'

'Nature, I suppose, provides a poet's greatest inspiration.'

'I am sometimes inspired by flowers and verdure,' I admitted, being unwilling to admit that my view of her, across a crowded theatre, had been my sole inspiration. 'If you are fond of the art, you should attend at the de la Tours. Only the best are invited to read, so the standard of poetry is unexceptionable!'

'I doubt,' said she, colouring, 'that my uncle knows them.'

I rather doubted this as well, for the de la Tours are the most crashing snobs in all the world, and her uncle Gardiner – though urbane and intelligent – was in trade. I also recalled Thorpe's dismissal of the Bennets as possessing 'not a penny'. But what mattered *that*, with so lovely a face and figure? I asked, 'Have you ever been painted, Miss Bennet?'

'Painted? Oh, never! Who should wish to paint me?'

'I think,' I said boldly, 'that any number of my artist friends could wish for nothing better! But you live in so quiet a way that they will likely never encounter you.'

'And surely *that* is for those ladies with husbands rich enough to long for their portrait?'

It was true, portionless as she was, that most men in a position to commission a likeness would disdain the idea of wedding her. Thus I said, 'I hope you slept a little better last night?'

'Oh, perfectly! The herbal tincture was quite as horrid as Little

Robin Hood's wolf, but nothing could awaken me this morning. Its taste was quite different from the one Mama uses but has as strong an effect!'

'Your mama is a delicate sleeper?'

'She sleeps well enough, but her nerves are not strong, so there is some draught she takes, when afflicted. And then, having to teach five daughters… the strain is sometimes almost too much for her. But whenever Papa urges her to procure us a governess she never will, for she is convinced that we have not money enough, and that she can teach as well as any other!'

Soon afterwards Mrs Gardiner returned, and I left to call on a friend. I did not get far before I stopped, for the day was fine, and I afire with ideas. The result of which are below.

> *For fate it seems hast still most harsh decreed*
> *That we shall, so rarely, cross paths so frail,*
> *For Jane, my love, so gentle and so sweet,*
> *In sorrow's chains, I must forever wail…*

⧫

Today – catastrophe! I was just passing by St Martin-in-the-Fields, and vaguely considering rhyming 'Jane' with 'pain' (perhaps a trifle obvious?). Then John Thorpe accosted me. 'Ah, Perkins! Fancy a flutter at billiards, for the usual stakes?'

I was too wise to accept, for Thorpe is as adept at billiards as he is lacking in the finer sensitivities. After I had declined he said, as if struck by a thought, 'Oh I say, I heard something at the club the other day, about your divinity!'

I wish now that I had possessed sufficient alertness to politely inquire to whom he might allude. As it was, I merely said, 'Miss Bennet?'

'The same. Apparently, the family is not as unexceptionable as is pretended.'

'Nay, I never heard a word spoke against Gardiner, either at Brooks's or elsewhere!'

'Nor I, and her *father* is well enough – but, great heavens, her mama!'

'She has nervous trouble, I understand.'

'Nervous trouble? That is a new way of describing an opium eater, however!'

'And what is *that*, I pray?'

'Surely even you must have heard of the rage for opium, here and even in the country. Why, ladies who frown in judgement at our mildest liquor are downing the paregoric by the vat!'

'And what on earth is a paregoric?'

'Why, a tincture comprising honey, liquorice, camphor, oil of aniseed, a little wine – and opium of course.'

'Opium!'

''Tis *that* to which the ladies become addicted, Lady Addison, for one. How do you think she contrives that wild glitter in her gaze?' Here Thorpe tapped the side of his nose in an annoying fashion. 'While Lady Diana takes it of an evening, for she can sleep in no other fashion. Though she is careful not to indulge during the day. At least, I have never seen *her* giddy, nor her gaze affected.'

'Do you truly mean to suggest that *Mrs Bennet* –'

'Quite. The lady is a martyr to her nerves and is said to have no other method of dealing with them. And to have a quite splendidly brilliant gaze, besides!'

'Poor Miss Bennet!' I cried, much moved. 'To have a mother so afflicted! Think of all that must devolve on her and her sisters – and perhaps upon their housekeeper, as well.'

It occurred to me that the poor lady's nerves could not be

assisted by her situation for, should *Mr Bennet* perish, she and her every daughter might have nowhere to live. Such a worry would be enough to make any lady turn to laudanum!

Now, I knew of men who took opium, while every literary soul had heard of the sad fate of Topham Beauclerk, who had perished of it. But the notion that society *ladies* might become dependent on such drugs for nervous disorders still appalled me.

Thorpe said, 'I learned it all from Sir William Lucas, as great a bore as ever donned a pair of trousers. He was up from the country yesterday, when he overheard a couple of members praising Miss Bennet's sweet looks. I cannot think that *she* has the slightest notion about it, however. Probably she – young and innocent as she is – merely feels sorrow for her mama's nervous affliction!'

At this I mourned in spirit for my love. How unlucky, to have not only a lazy and careless father, mired in debt, but a desperate and dissolute mother as well! Yet, far from besmirching Miss Bennet's allure in my eyes, this information only served to cast her as a distressed and noble heroine, as in a play. Oh, if only I was no poet – though I do sometimes doubt that I *am* one – but the richest of gentleman instead, so that I could offer her a comfortable home and relief from all her worries! If only I was a Lord Aldringham or a Fitzwilliam Darcy, the kind of fellow who might marry whomever they fancied, let the world say what it may!

◈

To my delight, I observed Miss Bennet again at the concert that evening. I heard her aunt say, 'Surely not that man again?' and looked around to see of whom she might be speaking. Likely Sir Hubert Culbertson, who was eyeing Miss Bennet, with undoubted satisfaction, the hound!

'Miss Bennet!' said I. 'This is a pleasure I did not anticipate.'

'Jane is excessively fond of music,' said her aunt.

'If only I had my sister Lizzy's talent for it!' cried she.

'I thought that last duet quite charming,' said I.

'Oh, enchanting! Though my Italian is so poor I did not comprehend it all.'

''Tis an overrated language,' I informed her. 'I am forever having to explain to Italians why their poems in English will not translate, or why I do not dare risk losing half of my subscribers by publishing poetry in their own language... But the duet was not badly done.'

'And the quartet – I had never heard an oboe before!'

How wonderfully bright her eyes were, like new-minted cornflowers! I said, I hoped soulfully, 'Ah, the oboe, or *hautbois*! Its mournful mellifluence resembles the foreboding shadow of autumn on some August afternoon!'

At this point Mrs Gardiner chanced, for some reason, to cough into her handkerchief. I seized on the opportunity to ask Miss Bennet whether she ever promenaded in Hyde Park, a practice to which London society in general is greatly addicted.

'Oh, yes – we were there on Wednesday, with the children. They so enjoyed pushing little paper boats across the ice!'

'And has little Beatrice recovered from the wolf?'

'Oh, *that* is all forgot! And truly, if there were nothing to fear in a fairy story, we should not tell them... Is not the moon glorious through that window?'

I quoted, '"The moon is behind, and at the full/ And yet she looks both small and dull/ The night is chill, the cloud is grey/'Tis a month before the month of May." Not my own,' I added hastily. 'Coleridge's.'

'Never mind,' said Mrs Gardiner with a little laugh. 'After all, not even Coleridge could contrive to write splendidly all of the time!'

I reflected that the gift of comprehending poetry is given to few, though Jane's eyes were liquid with feeling. Thus, I could not imagine that I had quoted Coleridge *entirely* in vain...

❦

I could not call on Miss Bennet for the next few days, to my deep frustration, for my mother had chosen this moment to arrange a visit to town.

Now if Mama has a fault – and I could name you any number – it is that she is frustrated by my unwedded state, and most fervently wishes the situation amended. Thus far, there is no dispute between us, for I wish my state amended still more fervently than she. However, whilst my whole soul is wedded already – to Miss Bennet – Mama is forever urging me to court a neighbour of her own, a Miss Jennings, who couples a goodly amount of money with the kind of laugh which goes in one ear and refuses to come out the other. Thus, when Mama wrote me a note begging me to call at the Jennings's, where she was staying, I could instantly understand the purpose behind it.

The morning after their arrival I called as promised at eleven and – to my relief – learned that the wealthy widow was out, that her daughter Miss Jennings had gone for a fitting, and that Mama was alone.

'I do not know,' said she querulously, 'why you *must* live in town. The air is quite appalling.'

I could see nothing amiss with the air, and said so.

'Oh!' cried she, 'It is nothing like the air of the country. The gardens – even Mrs Jennings's own – are a mere burlesque of any proper-sized garden, while there is nothing but noise and rush and disruption all about! I cannot see how any *proper* poet could contrive to work –'

'How is good Mrs Jennings?' I asked, in hopes of calming her.

'Oh extremely hearty, shockingly hearty. I sometimes wish her rather less so, in that I might have more time to read. But so good-natured!'

'I trust Miss Jennings is well?'

'Perfectly so and in remarkably good looks, as I hope you will agree, when you take us to Hyde Park this afternoon.'

'This afternoon!' I cried, dismayed, for I had hoped to visit Miss Bennet then. Here was a week gone already – and my goddess had but three!

'Surely you have made no plans for this afternoon?' asked Mama, with a rather steely look.

Thus, I had no choice.

My mother had married a man a great deal her senior who, always poorly, died before I could possibly recollect him. So, although Mama still possesses his property, that property is – very probably – all that I shall ever inherit.

Perhaps for this reason, Mama's ambitions for me have always been limitless – she is forever yearning for me to distinguish myself, in some fashion or other. Once I left university, she urged me to enter politics, which I despised. To quieten her, I studied law, but never completed the course, since when I have rather drifted with my poetry and my magazine – neither spending nor amassing much, while fighting off Mama's immediate ambitions with regards to Miss Jennings. (To be clear, the *second* Miss Jennings. The eldest is married already, to a fellow called Middleton.)

Now I have no objection to Miss Jennings – beyond, that is,

marrying her. She is cried up everywhere, and justly, for being both pretty and lively. However, she combines these advantages with a most irritating laugh – very nearly a whinny – and with a startling lack of regard for the arts. She sings badly, paints appallingly and has never, in the entire course of her existence, picked up any book of fancy, without secret hopes of injuring it.

Still, as there was no means of avoiding it, I duly perambulated with Mama, Mrs Jennings and her daughter in Hyde Park that afternoon. Conceive my dismay, as I saw my muse in the distance, walking between her aunt and uncle. I could not imagine that Mrs Jennings would be acquainted with the Gardiners – and was in an instant quandary as to how to behave. Would it be ungentlemanly of me not to introduce them? And whatever would Miss Bennet think, to see me promenading with *another* young lady? (Unless she was too modest to be aware of the strength of my regard?)

As the Gardiners drew closer to us I grew more and more agitated. Gardiner kindly acknowledged me, while his niece met my kindling glance – and blushed.

'Why, whatever ails you?' asked Mrs Jennings after we were safely past, in her usual boisterous fashion, 'You look as if you had seen some species of ghost!'

'Not at all,' said I, buoyed up by my love's delicious blush.

'The young lady is all perfection,' said Miss Jennings, with that horsey laugh of hers. 'Pray, who is she?'

'She is a Miss Bennet,' said I reverently.

'There is one every season,' said Mrs Jennings, shaking her head. ''Tis a regular thing. Some poor young lady with but one good gown, who quite jolts society with their fine looks, only to slip back into the country, and never to be heard of more. Poor dears! – 'tis not their fault, bless them, that God gave them pleasing looks with scarcely a penny!'

'But perhaps such is *not* the case with Miss Bennet?' her daughter inquired, laughing.

Miss Jennings's laugh always started very high and descended, and whenever I endured it, I longed to procure some blunt instrument, with which to do unspeakable things.

Instead, I gloomily conceded that Miss Bennet was very nearly portionless, leaving both ladies exceedingly well-satisfied. (In parenthesis, what could be more comfortable or more gloating than such pity, particularly in the breasts of society females?)

Still, the sunlight that day had the angled clarity of the Italian coast, while the contour of the grass resembled a field of emeralds.

'What are you doing?' inquired Miss Jennings, observing me flourishing my pencil.

'Ah, nothing!' I told her, 'Just nothing at all!'

And then she laughed...

※

Before Mama could command me to wait upon the Jennings the next day, I took care to call upon the Gardiners. Mrs Gardiner said, 'Oh, Mr Perkins! We are just departing, to call on some very dear friends of mine. Perhaps you might care to accompany us – that is, if you have nothing better to do?'

I fell into step beside Miss Bennet, who was sporting the prettiest silver-pink boots I had ever seen. ('My aunt's,' she confided, 'for they are grown too small for her feet, ever since her last confinement. Have I not great good luck, Mr Perkins?')

'They are reminiscent of a rosy-fingered dawn!'

'How poetic you are!'

'Not my own,' I was obliged to admit. 'I studied Homer's *Odyssey* at school.'

'My father owns it,' said she, rather wistfully, 'but not even Lizzy has read it. And Lizzy is much the cleverest of us.'

'No one could be cleverer than you!'

'Nay,' said she, very seriously, 'two of my sisters are very much cleverer. As for the youngest pair, they are children still – Lydia is only nine.'

'Five daughters is a very great number.'

'And a very great misfortune, in my family's case,' said she, with a grave lightness, 'but it is what it is!'

I was as smitten by her calm judgement as by that perfect chin. In her place, I could not help thinking, Miss Jennings would have laughed like some species of hyena. Just at that moment, Miss Bennet stumbled. Instinctively, I caught her arm and set her right.

'Thank you, Mr Perkins – I am grateful. That tree root caught me all unaware! I slept so poorly last night that I am walking in a daze.'

'I do hope,' said Mrs Gardiner anxiously, 'that you have not twisted your ankle, Jane?' – though she denied it.

Later, I had recourse to a coffee shop. After I had allowed my sensations to resonate throughout my consciousness, I wrote the following:

> *Oh Jane, fair maid, by yon soft theatre's grace*
> *Thy beauty held my senses quite in thrall*
> *'Twas there that first unveiled thy glorious face*
> *Thy laughter like a soft wood pigeon's call...*

✦

'Well, *I* think that she would have you.'

'I think not,' said I, courteously omitting any reference to that deplorable laugh.

'Charlotte is a lovely girl!'

'Miss Jennings is very attractive indeed,' said I, concealing my private doubts that a young lady of 23 might usefully be termed a 'girl'. (Miss Bennet, at nearly sixteen, *might* be – Miss Jennings, I thought *not*.)

'She is said to be admired by Mr Palmer,' said Mama.

'An excellent fellow!' said I – though I had met him only twice and thought him very satirical indeed.

'He has a very good property, down at Cleveland.'

'Which is why, my dear Mama, if she is already courted by Palmer, she would never accept of *me*.'

'I did not say *courted*,' said she, rather sharply, 'but he attends at the Jennings's with great regularity. I daresay it will come to that, in the end.'

'You mean, unless I try harder, Charlotte Jennings will likely fall prey to Mr Palmer,' I said, with a smile.

'Prey!' cried she, affronted.

'Well, is not that what it comes down to, in the end? 'Tis an auction, when all is said and done, with well-born ladies judged upon their pedigree, their fortunes, their looks and their accomplishments, for gentlemen to bid for, one against the other.'

'What an extraordinary idea!'

'Nay, I assure you, 'tis how young men calculate and – I would wager my life on it– how young ladies calculate, as well. Palmer will be debating, "Is she is rich enough, pretty enough and sweet-natured enough for me to bid upon?" Whilst *she* will be calculating, no less judiciously, "Palmer – not an ill-looking fellow – a pleasing property, no family to speak of, and apparently making rather a name for himself for wit, in the House of Commons."'

'Well, and if she likes him, there can be no harm in such advantages –'

'– though whether she *likes* him seems a relatively minor consideration –'

'– while Charlotte has always had a great regard for you. Why, you played together as children!'

'And played very prettily, I daresay. But *now* we are more like easy friends. If Miss Jennings thinks of me at all, which I doubt, it would be along the lines of, "I do not dislike Mr Perkins, but his property is less extensive than Mr Palmer's, his family less distinguished – and he is, when all is said and done, a mere publisher of poetry and essays." At the same time, her every friend will be urging Palmer's suit, especially as she is twenty-three.'

'Which is no sort of age at all!'

'Nay, twenty-three is exactly the age when a young lady quite longs to give over practising the pianoforte in favour of consultations with her housekeeper, and to cease attempting vague sketches of roses, in favour of embroidering baby caps.'

And with *that*, I flattered myself at having silenced her.

I left the house early the next morning, at an hour when the Gardiners were normally at home. Mr Gardiner said, 'Ah, Perkins! We were surprised to miss you at the theatre.'

'I would have gone, however my mama is in town.'

'I am glad to hear it. The ladies are within.'

And, just as I entered, I heard Miss Bennet say worriedly, 'But Aunt, what must I do?'

'I daresay,' said Mrs Gardiner, 'that all will still be well. You mother is not so unsteady as to –' Then she saw me, and added swiftly, 'But here is Mr Perkins come.'

How I longed to know what had happened to poor Mrs Bennet!

But I dared not inquire. Instead, I held Miss Bennet's hand a fraction longer than usual and murmured, 'Miss Bennet.'

She wiped a few tiny drops from her 'orbs of heaven's blue' – which looked still more dazzling than usual – and said, 'You *are* kind to call – but I must shortly depart for Hertfordshire.' While Mrs Gardiner rang for some refreshments, she added, 'My poor mama!'

And – rather than to allow her to distress herself – I said tenderly, 'I know.'

She lifted her eyes. 'What!'

'I greatly fear, Miss Bennet, that your poor mother's – situation – though far from common knowledge, is known to a select few.'

'But so distressing!'

How I longed to fold her to me! Instead, I urged, 'You must be strong, Miss Bennet, not least for your younger sisters' sakes.'

'Oh, I shall – at least, I hope to be!'

'I am very sure you will be,' said I, much moved, and kissed her lovely hand. 'But... you *will* return to London, will you not?'

'I am certain of it,' said Mrs Gardiner, 'at some time or other.'

I left – feeling an urgent need for the refreshment which the distraught Gardiners had never offered me.

Thorpe was at the club and – for a wonder – not infesting the billiard table. Upon observing my countenance, he said, 'Ah! I suppose that you have heard. I am very sorry, but 'tis just as I had always suspected. Like mother, like daughter!'

'Might I ask,' I demanded haughtily, 'what, in the name of heaven, you might be referring to?'

'Why, to the little Bennet girl. Her mama, as is well-known, is deep in opium.'

'I know, I know! So, *she* must return home, to support her sisters.'

'That may well be the story put about… but I cannot see how *she* could assist!'

'What on earth are you implying?'

'Why merely that Miss Bennet has the same condition as her poor mama! Those eyes, which so many find so brilliant, are laden with tinctures of opium! So says Toby Smith, at least. And so Sir William Lucas himself confessed, not two nights since, to Lord Haversham.'

I wavered as if to fall but could say… not a word.

My goddess… an opium eater?

Thorpe continued with remorseless satisfaction. 'So the little maid will trudge back to the country, there – doubtless – to eventually consent to wed some fat squire, one prosperous enough, at least, to keep her in laudanum. A sad fate for so fair a creature! – But 'tis as well, you know, to learn the truth before you might become rather too attached. Truly, she looks as fresh as a dewdrop. One would never have thought it, indeed!'

I fled from him as from the devil, to walk about the park, and there to attempt to make sense of it all, dazed with shock and even horror. That my sweet love should be as fragile as her own mama! At first, I could not begin to believe it.

Yet looking back… Her acknowledgement of not sleeping, for *that*, no doubt, had probably been the origin of the business… Her 'dazed' trip, where I had caught her on the walk in Hyde Park… that hectic alteration of complexion…the glassy-eyed brightness of her gaze at that concert… And even her artless words! ('For, once I am awake, I start to think, and then there is no hope for it, whether in town or at Longbourn!' – 'But my dear aunt's physician has promised me a tonic that will help'… 'The tincture with herbs' taste is quite different from the one Mama uses, but has as strong an effect.')

Oh, heavens – a tonic, indeed!

Oh woe, woe! – that one not yet sixteen might be as afflicted as her aged mother!

'Are you quite well, Perkins?' asked my friend Toby, spotting me letting myself into my lodgings. 'I did hear, from Thorpe, that –'

'Nay,' cried I, 'I shall never be well again!'

＊

Oh Jane, frail relict of the restless night!
How destiny did part us, wreck of ancient tombs
Thy soul and mine torn from each other's sight
Midst thunder'ous heralds of impending doom...

＊

(from *The Times*)

The marriage has been arranged and will shortly take place between Mr Thomas Palmer, of Cleveland, Somerset, and Miss Charlotte Jennings, younger daughter of the late Mr Herbert Jennings and Mrs Jennings, of Marlborough Street, W1.

(Mrs Perkins to Mrs Jennings)

I daresay my Paul could have wooed and won her, my dearest friend, had he only been content to listen to advice from older and wiser heads! But poets, you know, are a law unto themselves, and poor Paul is no exception...

(John Thorpe to Paul Perkins)

My dear Perkins, I must admit that – ha! – apparently I quite mistook Sir William Lucas's comment with regard to little Miss Bennet. <u>Not</u>, I must just mention, about her mama, who has only recently suffered some kind of hysterical fit, something not uncommon in those who indulge in opium. But apparently Miss Bennet herself is perfectly well, and only in need of the occasional sleeping draught, as is so common these days. Grieved to have misled you, but – as I told Sir William Lucas – the fault was truly his, in the first place! I expect I shall see you about, perhaps for billiards? Yours etc., John Thorpe, Esq.

It has come to me at last, the one true love of my life! The others were mere shadows of this molten passion, and as nought, in comparison – Oh Olivia, Olivia, sweet love of my life, and the poetry pouring out forth in foaming torrents! Those red-gold locks – that hazel gaze – that tiny hand!

Olivia! Was there ever a name more sweet?

I just met a girl called... Olivia!

Valentine's Day at the Bennets'

'I am fifteen,' said Lydia, 'and I have been fifteen this long age – I am very nearly sixteen – and yet no one has ever troubled themselves to send me even a single valentine.'

'No one,' Kitty reminded her, 'has ever sent any of us a valentine. Not even Jane.'

They sat in gloom for a moment, contemplating the sorry state of their existence. Then Lydia said, 'But that fellow in London wrote some verses on Jane, at least. At least she had *that!'*

'Perhaps, were we to go to London, some gentleman might write verses on us?'

'But *that* could never happen, for Papa detests London.'

'Yes, and Mama seems to have given over visiting our Aunt Gardiner,' said Kitty.

'I do not suppose I shall ever go to town, till I am dead.'

And they remained seated on the bench, meditating upon their parents' unreasonableness.

Then Kitty said, 'There is still the curate, Mr Thompson.'

'Yes, yes, we all know what the curate said to Mama! – But there is a very great difference between praise of her "five fine girls" and sending even one of those girls a valentine… and it would be so delicious! There were such sweet ones in the magazine our aunt sent to Mama. The one with the little white lace fringe!'

Kitty clasped her hands together. 'And the one with the

61

embroidered hearts… I should *die* of rapture should someone send me a valentine with embroidered hearts!'

'People do not die of rapture, Kitty, not even in novels… But the embossed hearts *were* exceedingly pretty and then, the verse!' And Lydia dreamily recited,

> *Thou art my love and I am thine*
> *I drew thee to my Valentine.*
> *The lot was cast and then I drew,*
> *And Fortune said it should be you.*

'It should be you,' repeated Kitty. 'Oh! I should die of rapture should Mr Thompson the curate –'

'– or one of the officers –' added Lydia, temporarily suspending her objection to death by rapture.

'– or one of the officers – send me a valentine!'

'And if that officer was Wickham!'

'I should not be as particular as you for all the world,' said Kitty. 'For, though Mr Wickham *is* unusually well-looking, I should not mind any other officer, instead.'

'But not Mr Lindsay, or Mr Bucknall.'

'Oh, never! For *they* are wed already.'

And they sat for a moment, while Lydia thought of Wickham and Kitty thought of the curate Thompson, though his nose *was* rather long. Suddenly Lydia jumped up. 'I have had an idea, Kitty, which might perhaps work!'

'What kind of an idea?'

'A scheme, a most excellent scheme! What say you to our employing our dear, good Aunt Philips in the cause? *She* is always up for a spot of mischief. If she might, perhaps, be willing to drop a little hint about valentines while the officers were about –'

Kitty's eyes widened. 'Why, I think she might!'

'And the officers are so very often about. They seem to prefer *hers* to any other house in Meryton. And if she *did* perhaps drop a hint, then our sad dearth of valentines might be ended!'

※

February 11th

Their Aunt Philips being agreeable – she was almost always agreeable, a noisy, rotund, jovial woman – Lydia turned her attention to teasing her two eldest sisters.

''Tis nearly Valentine's Day,' said she. 'Might not Mr Bingley send you a valentine from London, Jane?'

'Heavens, no,' said Jane, with a blush.

'Even should he wish to,' said Elizabeth, 'I cannot imagine him doing it. 'Tis not the fashion of the fashionable world.'

'But the London magazines –'

'Magazines are obliged to busy themselves with some foolishness or other,' said their father, 'lest they lose subscribers. And the more foolish their matter, the better pleased their subscribers.'

'I cannot consider *myself* a foolish subscriber!' cried his wife.

Mr Bennet hastened to reassure her. 'No, my dear, you must be well up the ranks in terms of magazine subscribers, if not quite the *crème de la crème*.'

And, while Mrs Bennet was attempting to determine whether or not she had been insulted, Mary pronounced. 'Valentines,' said she, 'are of no very recent origin. They are associated with the saint of that name, who assisted persecuted Christians during Roman times. He was also said to have accomplished miracles such as restoring sight to the blind, while his name-day is even mentioned in *Hamlet:*

> *Tomorrow is Saint Valentine's day,*
> *All in the morning betime,*
> *And I a maid at your window,*
> *To be your Valentine.*

'Oh! Delightful!' cried Kitty, while Lizzy objected, 'But *that* was only in a speech by Ophelia, when she is already quite mad, and busying herself with bestrewing the Danish court with herbs and flowers!'

After luncheon, the two youngest sisters announced their intention to walk to Meryton, just to see how their Aunt Philips did.

Mr Bennet said drily, 'As she enjoys perfect health, as well as an excellent digestion and a famously good temper, it puzzles me as to why she need be so constantly inquired after... Surely her stream of visiting militia has nothing to do with it?'

'Nothing at all, Papa,' said Lydia, without a blush.

'And so, my dear Aunt,' asked Lydia, not five minutes after entering her house, 'did you dare to ask the officers?'

'Dare to ask – Lord! I should think I might have sufficient courage for *that* – and whilst they were stuffing themselves with my muffins! Between ourselves, there was not a single muffin left afterwards and Cook not best-pleased!'

'And was Mr Wickham among the company?'

'Nay, he was not –' but, upon seeing Lydia bite her lip, her aunt cried, 'Your *face,* my love! Of course he was, and Denny and Pratt besides!'

'What a tease you are!' cried Kitty admiringly. But Lydia persisted, 'And did he say anything about valentines?'

'Oh, la! They said all sorts, between muffins... Wickham said something, and Denny said something else, and then Pratt made us all laugh. And 'twas *then* when I said, "Why, my own five nieces – the sweetest girls in all the world, I vow – have never received a single valentine between them!"'

And with these tidings, the girls were forced to be content. For though they later wandered to the farthest end of the High Street in hopes of encountering an officer – or, at very least, a curate – they were obliged to retrace their steps without a single sighting, even of a red coat disappearing down some side-street or into the Assembly.

'I do not think there is a single young man alive in this pokey little town,' said Kitty despondently, after they had turned round.

'There is no harm in trying… though it *is* provoking!'

'Miss Lydia and Miss Kitty, I believe?' He had emerged, almost soundlessly, from some house they did not know.

'Why, Mr Wickham! We were just speaking of you, not a moment ago. Your ears must have been burning!'

'Charmed to hear it. Though my ears' – he murmured low enough that only Lydia could hear – 'do not burn quite so easily. So, what do you in Meryton, besides improving the look of the place with your flowerlike youth and beauty?'

'We were inquiring after our aunt.'

'A delightful woman – so warm, so hospitable!'

'You may well say so,' said Lydia archly, 'for we have already heard how you scrounged her every muffin!'

'We are sad fellows in the militia, Miss Lydia. I should not entrust us with any muffin – and certainly not with a muffin I cared a very great deal for. I would not give – *this* – for the chances of any muffin's survival, in our immediate vicinity.'

'And *before* we heard about the muffins,' said Lydia, with a sly little glance, 'we were speaking of St Valentine.'

'Ah! I know nothing of St Valentine. He was omitted from all my years of schooling.'

'Well, he was very good I believe, and all that,' said Lydia, attempting, without success, to recall Mary's information, 'and it was he who first had the very good notion of handing out valentines to ladies that he liked – I do not know how many.'

'What! The good saint sent valentines to more than one lady at a time?'

'Yes – no. Truly, I am not quite sure!'

'I think,' said Kitty, 'to *one* lady – or to two, at most.'

With such livelinesses they persevered along the way he had to go and, just as they were bidding Wickham farewell, they had the good luck to fall in with the curate.

Mr Thompson was a young, earnest and bespectacled young man, who came from a very good family afflicted – like the Bennets – with sadly little money. Until the militia was quartered in Meryton he had seemed extraordinarily fascinating, but he had long since been supplanted. In Lydia's secret opinion, by this point, only his taking up a commission could have saved him.

'Good day, Mr Thompson! Are you going to the rectory?' asked Kitty.

Though he did not seem entirely certain, Lydia captured his proffered arm. He was nothing in comparison to an officer but he was still a man – and it was Lydia's simple creed that any man was better than no man at all.

'Well, you must know where you have *been*, at least!' she teased.

Mr Thompson had been at The Hollies, where several family members were unwell, adding, 'The Lisneys are such excellent people!'

'I expect they were coughing a good deal,' said Lydia sympathetically. 'Kitty here is forever coughing but, while our

Papa believes she only does it to annoy, *I* am convinced 'tis for the purpose of garnering attention, instead.'

'It is only that my lungs are weak, just as the Lisneys' are.'

'Your lungs – impossible! I assure you, Mr Thompson, that – except for our *second* sister, who could outrun a deer – Kitty is much the quickest. After Lizzy, she is the quickest I ever saw!' Mr Thompson did not doubt it and Lydia added, 'How excessively good you are to bother with people who are always poorly – *I* should never have the patience!'

'I am very sure you would,' said Mr Thompson. He then asked Kitty if she was not chilled, as she kept rubbing her hands together.

'Not at all,' she lied, for they had been on the prowl for so long a time – from one end of the High Street to the other – that she had several times wished for her gloves. 'So, are you very busy looking after sick people?'

'To a degree.'

'And do you never attend the Meryton balls?'

Mr Thompson coloured deeply. 'I doubt that the rector would consider it suitable, but *I* should have no objection.'

'If you do ever venture,' said Lydia generously, 'I shall persuade the master on the night to find you some famous partners! We do not always attend, however... Tell me, what do you know about Saint Valentine?'

'He is not a saint that I have studied to any great extent.'

'Well! They say that he lived in ancient Rome, where he healed the poor and gave money to the sick – or the other way about – so you and he would have had no end of things in common! And he was the first to send pressed bits of coloured paper to ladies whom he liked – you know, valentines.'

'In that case,' said Mr Thompson, shaking his head, 'he and I might have had very much less in common than you suppose, Miss Lydia. I cannot imagine being bold enough to send any young lady a valentine!'

'What a pity,' said Lydia briskly, 'but I would still recommend you try. After all, no one can be assisting the poor every moment – 'twould be unreasonable – the poor themselves would find it annoying! At any rate, the fourteenth of February is the proper day – and, of course, you need not sign it.'

'You were far too bold,' complained Kitty, after he had bidden them a hasty farewell. 'You might as well have said, "We wish to receive a valentine before our elder sisters, might not you contrive it?" '

'No, no, he understood me, I believe. And – oh, Kitty – did you observe, just now, Wickham's eyelashes? They are longer than Jane's, I vow!'

'I did not – but I *did* observe the hour, and Papa will quiz us unmercifully.'

'He may quiz me as much as he chooses,' cried Lydia. 'Imagine how much in need of amusement he must be, holed up with thick, dull books all day!'

❖

February 12th

Mr Bennet, in fact, had other things than books on his mind. It was not his life situation – on which he preferred not to brood – but something rather more mundane.

He had pledged assistance for the church window fund, and he had no notion where to put his hands on the amount required, even going so far as to entreat his wife to discover which of their daughters had exceeded her allowance. He rather suspected Lydia, for she was not only his wife's prime favourite, but much the most adept at wheedling – while he himself could never tell one gown or cap from any other.

But there it was. The rector had sent him an obsequious yet still urgent reminder – and from his sickbed besides – but where was he to find the requisite amount, when every shilling he possessed simply slipped away? And there were the servants' wages as well, though those would not be required till Saturday...

＊

February 13th

Denny teased, 'And so, my bonny laddie, have you made a valentine for the lovely Lydia? With a crown of encircled hearts and roses enough to sink a ship of the line?'

'I would not,' said Wickham, shaking his head, 'wish to get the lady's hopes up, and all for nothing!'

'If she has mentioned it once this past week, she has mentioned it fourteen times. Perhaps we might persuade Pratt to make her a valentine?'

'I fear – all modesty aside – that 'tis I she has her eye upon. While I have not the slightest intention of giving a valentine to any lady. Probably ever.'

'Only imagine the devastation of every young lady in Meryton, were they to hear you!'

'If there was *any* young lady I would think of,' said Wickham, 'it would be Lydia's elder sister.'

'She is well enough – but rather too soft for me.'

'Not Miss Bennet – but Miss Elizabeth, instead. She has Lydia's vitality, Miss Bennet's beauty and a brilliant wit, besides. What a pity she has likewise hardly a penny!'

'But little Lydia in such a case would never forgive you – and she is excellent fun, Miss Lydia, in her way.'

'Never fear – have I not sworn never to do it? – Do you fancy a touch at billiards, for the usual stakes? You managed to thrash me last time, if you recall, so I must claim my revenge!'

❖

February 14th

The rector's gout having worsened, he told his curate, Mr Thompson, 'I fear that you must go – for I am sure I am unequal to it – and ask Bennet for the remainder that he promised. He is the last, and the window finished, and the workmen due their pay… Having five daughters and an entail must be his excuse, in all conscience, but he promised me fifty, and fifty I must have!'

'But how might I persuade him?'

'Why, you must say that you are grieved to intrude, but that the sum is needed, and *that* as soon as may be.'

'And if he will not descend from his study?' asked the curate.

'If he will not descend, my good Thompson, then you must ascend, instead! 'Tis up the main staircase, the first room on the left – the best room in the house for my money, were it not covered from floor to ceiling with dust-covered books!... From memory, an ornate door.'

'First on the left, with an ornate door,' repeated the curate. 'Very well sir, I shall try.'

'You must not try, Mr Thompson, you must succeed – I thank you! And I wonder if you could, as you will be passing, put *that* in

70

the Clemmings' door? You – ah – you need not wait for a reply.'

The curate set off at once. He was repeating to himself, 'I *am* grieved to intrude… I am *grieved* to intrude… I am *most* grieved to…' – while attempting to determine which sounded the most courteous – as he passed the Clemmings', entirely forgetting the envelope in his pocket. As he trod along the drive at Longbourn he believed himself to discern a masculine figure at an upstairs window… He very nearly told the butler that he was grieved to intrude before inquiring, 'Is Mr Bennet within?'

'He is in the library, sir.'

'Very well,' said the curate nervously, 'then in that case, I shall –'

'Mr Thompson! What a pleasure!' cried Mrs Bennet, observing a single man and triumphantly seizing her chance. 'You must join us in a little tea, I beg!'

Trapped, he was shepherded into the drawing room, where he found Kitty disputing with Mary over whether Kitty was quite frighteningly ignorant for not knowing that Henry VIII greatly preferred Jane Seymour to Anne Boleyn. Lydia was just retorting that *she* much preferred Anne Boleyn, for she had never merely faded away in childbirth, but had had her head cut off, instead.

They graciously suspended their argument upon spotting the curate. Miss Bennet helped Mr Thompson to coffee – Elizabeth handed him a scone – and Lydia impudently inquired whether he had brought a valentine. The curate laughed unconvincingly at this, and put the envelope for Mrs Clemmings securely upon the coffee table where, to be sure, he could not forget it…

⁂

71

'But what is this?' asked Jane. 'Mr Thompson has left an envelope behind – and one without a direction!'

'It will be a receipt for Papa,' said Elizabeth at once, 'concerning the repair to the church windows.'

'We shall see,' said Mrs Bennet, and proceeded to open it.

The girls were just resurrecting their disagreement about Anne Boleyn when her eyes grew wide. She sat down – quite hard – and cried, 'I shall faint, I do believe – and not addressed to anyone in particular!'

'That, Mama,' sighed Lizzy, 'is because he *meant* to take it to Papa when he left us. I shall take it upstairs myself.'

'You shall not! For why should the curate make a valentine for your *papa*?'

The girls all gathered round. 'A valentine!'… ''Tis small, but absolutely charming!'… 'A valentine, indeed! But for which of us is it intended?' Then Lydia cried, 'Oh, Kitty! I shall die of laughing! All he needed was the slightest hint, indeed!'

'Whatever are you talking about, child?'

'Only *this,* that when Kitty and I were inquiring after our aunt yesterday, we fell in with the curate. And as we had just been thinking of it, I happened to mention St Valentine's Day –'

'– and how much we both longed for a valentine –' added Kitty.

'– and though he only blushed, and said he knew nothing of the saint –'

'– yet still, he must have gone away and thought –'

'– and *this* is the result of all!' finished Lydia.

'Great heavens!' cried their mother. 'But for which of you is it intended?'

'Is there no clue within?' asked Elizabeth.

'None at all!'

Mary said, 'It is my assumption – in such a case – that the curate prefers either Kitty or Lydia. And that his gesture was likeliest prompted, to some degree, by your conversation in the High Street. For inside it only says, "For your special day" with two hearts, and several flowers. But how very odd, not to specify!'

'Unless he meant it in jest?' asked Lizzy.

'If he did,' cried Lydia, 'then 'tis a lovely jest! My dear Kitty, we must hang about the vestibule till he comes down, to see which of us he looks at – and if he colours!'

'Oh, I do not dare!' cried Kitty, clutching the valentine to her.

'You *are* tedious,' said Lydia, 'for now I shall be obliged to haunt the vestibule quite on my own! For, though 'tis not Wickham, 'tis still our very first valentine!'

A few moments later, Mr Thompson descended, greatly relieved, with the money for the rector in his pocket. He vaguely wondered if there ought not to have been something else in the same pocket, but he could not quite recall what… Lydia glanced mischievously up at him. What a piquant face she had!

'I think it was a lovely surprise,' she said, fluttering her lashes rather oddly.

He supposed she meant his visit.

'Why thank you,' said he. 'And how kind of you to see me out, Miss Lydia!'

⁂

The curate did not recollect the envelope for Mrs Clemmings till he had walked to the Rectory, handed Mr Bennet's contribution to its housekeeper, and trudged home to remove his boots, with a great sigh, before the fire… And when he *did* recollect leaving the envelope at the Bennets', it did not concern him, for he had forgotten that the widow's name had been omitted. The note could be nothing beyond a note of thanks regarding the church windows – Mrs Clemmings was famously generous. He assumed that one of the Longbourn footmen would deliver it to the lady, instead.

Meanwhile Mrs Clemmings, a plump and pretty widow, looked out of her window and sighed.

Perhaps it was only a foolish fancy, but she *had* wondered whether Theodore – the rector – might not have recollected her birthday – and on Valentine's Day to boot. He had been so excessively attentive of late!

But she supposed that it was not to be.

The rector was full of gout, but simultaneously full of hope. It had been a push – a valentine, indeed! – but, he rather fancied, a push at an open door.

The truth was, he could not believe the widow Clemmings inconsolable.

Perhaps, at this very moment, she might be opening his valentine…

Captivating Mr Darcy

From the diaries of Caroline Bingley

Her figure was elegant, and she walked well; but Darcy, at whom it was all aimed, was still inflexibly studious. In the desperation of her feelings, she resolved on one effort more; and, turning to Elizabeth, said, 'Miss Eliza Bennet, let me persuade you to follow my example, and take a turn about the room. I assure you it is very refreshing after sitting so long in one attitude.'

Elizabeth was surprised, but agreed to it immediately. Miss Bingley succeeded no less in the real object of her civility: Mr. Darcy looked up.

(from *Pride and Prejudice*, Chapter 11)

October 9th

It struck me sometime between three and four in the morning, by the Netherfield clock.

Surely anyone who has read this far must have already guessed what I mean to divulge? It can arouse no real astonishment, surely? And yet, if you are truly innocent and unaware – if, in short, I am obliged to spell out *every single tiny thing* – then here it is... I am in love with Mr Darcy!

(Note: Is not Fitzwilliam the most *entrancing* name?)

Naturally, I have long esteemed him – he is by far the most delightful of Charles's many friends – but admiration is not the same as love. One does not awaken in the night with the revelation that one admires someone.

So, when was the moment? Was it, perhaps, when he was teasing my dear Louisa about the unripe tomatoes – that little sideways smile in my direction? Or was it instead on our first ride, here in Hertfordshire, when I observed that slant of sun alighting upon his dark hair?

In either case, is it not curious to think that beneath this very roof – and not a hundred yards down the hall – Mr Darcy lies, that same dark hair tousled on his pillow, entirely unaware of my fond regard!

Of course, I must acknowledge that I have very little hope, for he is as far above me as is any creature in existence. He has brilliance, genius, fire – indeed, he seems to recollect every word that he has ever read!... And not only are his *manners* all perfection – those who find him too reserved can have no taste worth mentioning – but he has all the best parts of breeding and looks and wealth besides! (I have already written here of Pemberley – the noble fall of ground, the great façade, the gilded rooms filled with astonishing portraits... Surely, in all England, there can be no more glorious place!)

He is not – it must be admitted – an earl, nor even a baronet, yet there is more nobility in Mr Darcy's expression than in all the portly dukes, upstart baronets and snuff-ridden marquises that it has been my ill-luck to encounter. My comfort here must be that surely *no one* could truly be worthy of such a one. Not even Lady Diana, the queen at our school, for – between ourselves – *she* struggled even to recall the dates of Henry VIII. Despite her beauty, connections and the grovelling admiration of our every teacher, *she* would bore poor Darcy within a half-hour!

But then... do I not rather bore him myself? When – to be

brutal – has he ever evidenced any partiality for me? (But then, when has he ever evidenced any partiality for *any* lady in particular?) Perhaps part of his charm is that he appears so entirely self-sufficient? My brother Charles is forever falling in love – with Lady Diana for an entire season, and for any number of others for a fortnight or so. But I do not believe that Mr Darcy has ever been in love.

Oh, I shall not think of him. I shall never think of him again, I vow! I shall never… And then, for the same reason, he is never gossiped about, for he pays precisely the same attentions to us all, doing everything correctly and nothing to excess! Oh! If only he had some imperfection, such as Charles's fickleness or Mr Hurst's sloth – but I can think of nothing, unless to be unusually serious and good-looking might be reckoned an imperfection.

Fitzwilliam!

I wonder if anyone has ever *dared* call him William? Or even Fitz. (Fitzy! What a delightful thought!)

But my problem remains. How might I possibly get – Fitzy! – to notice me?

⬥

October 10th

At breakfast – where I could hardly bear to meet his gaze – Mr Darcy agreed to ride to Meryton with Charles. I felt relieved once they were gone for – after warning Louisa that I had something quite shocking to tell her – I shared my revelation of the previous night. Although, to Louisa, it seemed no revelation at all! Instead, she sighed and drummed her fingers upon the chair, saying, 'You silly creature, of course you are in love with him. I should think for the past six weeks, if not for the whole of the past half-year!'

'But how might you know, better than myself?'

'Oh, heavens! Because of the way you dog his footsteps, the way you hang upon his lightest utterance, the way you endorse his every opinion... The question is, instead, how *can* you have been so self-deceived, and about your own feelings besides?'

How I stared! I must admit that Louisa has always been quick – she had been the quickest at maths in all the school – but this was beyond anything! I swallowed my pride therefore and said, 'But my dear Louisa, do advise me, I beg. Whatever shall I *do?'*

She laughed. But upon catching my expression, she finally said, 'Well, if you are truly serious, and truly willing to be guided by me, you must behave quite differently from how you normally behave.'

And *that* was the beginning of the plan.

♦

October 11th

Here is what my dear sister shared with me. It might not be exact – Louisa talks so quick! – but I am very sure that this is the sense of it.

1) *Men do not wish to be hounded.* By this she seemed to mean, that men need time to be left on their own. (Perhaps this is the reason why her own husband, Mr Hurst, is so often asleep on the settee?)

It is best therefore not to be continually plaguing them, but to be gracious when they seek our company, instead.

2) *While agreeing with men might be pleasing, it can be carried to excess.* For this reason, Louisa advised that I limit myself to only *three* agreements with Mr D. each day.

(nb. She later amended this to *two*.)

Oh, dear!

3) Such attentions as are offered – to any man – ought never be accompanied by what Louisa derides as 'puppy-dog' looks, suggestive of adoration.

(nb. How fascinating it all is! And I cannot help marvelling where she learnt it, for we were never taught anything half so useful while at school.)

4) *I should make a point of appearing to love books a great deal*, as Darcy is excessively fond of reading. 'Tis the only part of him that I should like to alter, really, for there is nothing duller than a book. Still, there it is!

5) A lady in love should seek to 'mirror' the behaviour of their loved one.

When I inquired what this 'mirroring' consisted of, Louisa considered and finally pronounced, 'If *he* appears thoughtful and bookish and wrapped up in some text, *you* must pretend to be in similar state… If *he* seems restless and longing to ride out, *you* should seem equally so… If his movements are quick, your music should be lively – but if he appears pensive, then try to express his hidden depths in your song… I mean, should he *have* any depths, for most men – I vow – are born without.'

I wished to ask whether Mr Hurst possessed hidden 'depths' – but did not dare.

❖

For all of these reasons, when Mr Darcy that afternoon inquired as to whether I might care to walk down to the ponds, I said, 'I would love to, as a rule, but I simply *must* finish this chapter!'

At this he absolutely started, as if astonished! My own joy was incomplete however, because he took his favourite pointer to the ponds instead – and how I wished that I had been the pointer!

Once he and the dog were safely from the house, Louisa said, just under her breath, 'I did not think that you could have resisted, and so stoutly, too. Well done! Well done, indeed!'

'But –' I began.

'Nay,' said Louisa, 'but me no "buts". Only wait – and see for yourself if it does not answer.'

Well, it did not answer, or not swiftly enough to suit my hasty temper. But after dinner, while I was reaching, most unhappily, for that interminable tome by Goethe – which I had only selected upon *his* recommendation – Mr Darcy said, 'Let us go into the garden, Miss Bingley, as the evening is so fine' – and offered me his arm.

As we walked – I was quite dizzied by the closeness of those dark, dark eyes – he chose to speak first of the book – *The Sorrows of Young Werther*, it is called, and very dull besides... But the sensation of leaning on his arm was worth it all! I kept thinking, almost in ecstasy, 'Fitzwilliam!... William!... *Fitzy*!'

For this reason, I was less than prepared when he inquired my own opinion of Goethe's style. I believe I said that I thought his style 'rather comic'.

'And what of the sorrows of Werther?'

'Oh! Most affecting!'

He coughed a little, for some reason, and turned the subject. Yet I had this much encouragement, he *did* beg that I accompany him. Perhaps Louisa's plan is working, after all!

◈

October 15th

Well, it is over at last – I refer, of course, to the appalling Meryton ball. This was our real introduction to Hertfordshire society, and how lamentable it proved! There was nothing beyond underbred men and flouncing women, musicians who ought never to have been employed, an uneven dancing floor, and a room heated at one end but quite extraordinarily chilly at the other... I was in rather good looks, but Louisa had warned me not to look at Mr Darcy, and upon no account to simper.

Though still a little confused as to what constitutes a 'simper', I took very good care not to perpetuate one. But it was so difficult not to cast looks in his direction – for he looked delightful in his black-and-gold waistcoat – and how I longed to know when we would dance! I knew that we *would* dance, for it would have been most incorrect of him to neglect to ask, as he is visiting at Netherfield – and I have never known Mr Darcy to be incorrect.

It is wicked of me but I sometimes think that I should rather like him to be incorrect, as it might give me a little encouragement...

Annoyingly, 'twas Louisa who benefited from my attempts *not* to look at him, for he petitioned her first, while I was engaged by a gentleman so clumsy that I was twice obliged to rescue my gown. At the end of those dances, when Mr Darcy approached me, I *hope* that I failed to simper, but dare not depend upon it.

Now I had just *peeped* into the second volume of *The Sorrows of Young Werther* (I quite long for the worst to happen to Young Werther, between ourselves). So, when I mentioned the significance of the two linden trees he looked rather startled, and rather impressed. However, when he asked me what I supposed them to represent, I could not recollect, and turned the subject to the musicians, instead.

I have writ earlier in these diaries of Mr Darcy's dancing, which is all perfection. Despite this, I believe, no one paid us the slightest mind, for Charles was dancing with the eldest Miss Bennet. And here, it must be admitted that, at least in *one* case, the Bennet sisters' reputation for looks is not ill-founded. Jane Bennet is perhaps the loveliest creature I have ever seen, excepting Lady Diana – and of modest and gentle address – advantages Lady Diana could never possess, even if handsomely paid. The second-eldest Bennet sister is herself not unattractive in a rather satirical style – but the youngest three nothing out of the common way.

At any rate, Miss Bennet quite captivated poor Charles – he danced with her twice, hung about her between the dancing, and even attended her at supper. While Mr Darcy, after parting from me, doubtless disappointed the hopes of many by adjourning directly to the cardroom. (Perhaps he could find no other so intriguing, after my hard-won insights on *Young Werther*?) I live in hopes!

※

November 12th

Today went quite wonderfully well. First, Mr Darcy admired my embroidery. Now, here I should admit that it was not *entirely* my own effort, for Louisa had started it and, upon my getting in quite a muddle, I asked my maid Sarah to extricate me from it. I later discovered that she had taken it a good deal farther. (Really, she is invaluable!)

Which is a good thing because, after the men left to spend the day with Sir William Lucas, I found myself in rather a muddle again... And so, I proposed to Louisa that we invite the eldest Miss Bennet to Netherfield. Louisa was agreeable. However – *most* unfortunately – the threat of a storm put Charles off his scheme and – still worse – when Miss Bennet arrived, she was almost immediately taken ill with a violent fever.

Her sneezing made her look rather less enchanting – and I must confess that I liked her the better for it. But Charles's alarm was profound, and after Louisa had bustled her upstairs, even Mr Darcy said, 'The lady does look most unwell. Were I in your place, Miss Bingley, I should send for local assistance.'

'You mean, the apothecary?' I asked.

'I did not mean the blacksmith,' he said drily. Hoping that he was teasing – for nothing advances intimacy quicker – I instantly dispatched one of the footmen, but the apothecary was unluckily at some deathbed or other.

And yet, his confiding tone! Be still, my beating heart!

$$\maltese$$

November 13th

Matters worsen. Today – *so* encroaching – the second-eldest Bennet daughter appeared at Netherfield, unasked, unwished-for and uninvited. Either the family has but a single horse or else a second horse was not to be procured, for Miss Eliza had walked – actually *walked* – over liquid hills and muddy dales, ankle-deep in dirt – to visit a sister who is not, after all, perishing.

There was mud absolutely *strewn* about the vestibule.

Despite her instantly removing upstairs to see her sister, I am convinced that her actual intent is to entrance Mr Darcy. (Recollect that after the ball, Mr Darcy conceded, in my hearing, that she had 'fine eyes'. Though I can see nothing so very fine about them. They are as dark as his own, but small and rather shrewish, in my opinion.)

Regardless, Miss Eliza's campaign of captivation is doomed to fail. Due to lacking the advantage of Louisa's sisterly advice, she is going about the business in quite the silliest way. Instead of ignoring Mr Darcy, she defies him. Instead of showing him no attention, she mocks him. Instead of being discreet and self-effacing, she positively *baits* him! I only hope he can see through it!

At one point this evening, for example, Mr Darcy was describing his notion of a truly accomplished woman. (Did I imagine it or did the woman he describe – excellence in languages apart – rather resemble myself? I like to think so, at any rate.) But Miss Elizabeth ridiculed his list of accomplishments, claiming that she had never met a woman in which so many advantages were united.

Was not that intolerably rude? – for, and *in that very room*, was not only myself but my dear Louisa, who can embroider, net screens and has some Italian, besides. While I play and sing and have been known to cover a screen! I even attempt to write poetry – though I never mention the poetry in company, as Louisa says I ought not… At any rate, once Miss Eliza had finally returned upstairs to Jane Bennet – who is sadly still poorly – Charles persisted in considering her 'pretty' and Mr Darcy refused to condemn her for coming (the mud has since, thankfully, been removed from the entrance).

Worse, the apothecary finally appeared, and pronounced Miss Bennet quite poorly. They could both be here for *days and days.*

I composed a little poem, just now.

> *I do not like Miss Bennet, E.*
> *I do not think that she likes me.*
> *I wish that she would go away*
> *And take her sister Jane today.*

There! How accomplished is *that?*

✦

November 15th

No, I cannot like Miss Bennet, E. – yet last night Louisa most strenuously advised that it would be advisable to *pretend* to, lest I appear 'churlish' or even 'envious' to Mr Darcy. Apparently, this is now part of 'the plan'. Oh, dear!

And so, for that reason, I asked Miss Eliza how she had slept, I consulted her preferences with regards to dinner – and this evening, I even begged her to accompany me in perambulating about the drawing-room, observing 'how refreshing it is to walk, after sitting for so long in one attitude'. (Truly, it was only *Werther* I wished to escape but, with Mr Darcy so immersed in its second volume, of course I could not say so.)

Miss Eliza agreed, whereupon Mr Darcy instantly closed his

book. However, he still declined to join us, observing that there could be only two reasons why we wished to walk together and that his presence 'would interfere with either.'

'Two reasons!' I cried. 'Why, whatever can you mean? I cannot imagine. Can you, Miss Bennet?'

'Not at all,' was her response, 'but depend upon it, he intends to be severe on us, and our surest way of disappointing him will be not to inquire.'

'But so mysterious! How I long to know what he means by it!'

'I have not the smallest objection to explaining,' said he. 'You either choose this method of passing the evening because you are in each other's confidence and have secret affairs to discuss, or because you are conscious that your figures appear to the greatest advantage in walking. If the first, I should be completely in your way – and if the second, I can admire you much better as I sit here by the fire.'

(Admire by the fire! Why, Mr Darcy is a poet, as well!)

'How shall we repay him for so infamous a speech?' I protested – though secretly delighted, for he had never admitted to 'admiring' my figure before or approached half so close to an agreeable little flirtation, either.

'Nothing easier,' said Miss Elizabeth. 'We can all plague and tease one another. Intimate as you are, you must know how it is to be done.'

'What, laugh at calmness of manner and coolness of mind? Nay, Mr Darcy may hug himself – he is not to be laughed at.'

'Mr Darcy is not to be laughed at!' she repeated. 'That is an uncommon advantage, and uncommon I hope it remains, for I dearly love to laugh.'

Mr Darcy then acknowledged that he had made it his study 'to avoid such faults of character as might expose a strong understanding to ridicule'.

'Such as vanity, or pride?' she inquired archly.

'*Vanity* is a weakness indeed. But *pride* – where there is real superiority of mind, *pride* will always be under good regulation.'

I asked, 'Your examination of Mr Darcy is over, I conclude?' And she returned, 'I am convinced that Mr Darcy has no defect. He owns it himself, without disguise.'

'No, there is a tendency in every character to some evil,' said Fitzy. (And how divine he looked as he said it!) 'My temper is too little yielding. My feelings are not puffed about with every attempt to move them. My temper would perhaps be called resentful – and my good opinion, once lost, is lost forever.'

'Implacable resentment *is* a shade in a character!' cried Eliza Bennet. 'But you have chosen your fault well, for I certainly cannot laugh at it.' Soon afterwards she went upstairs to join her – far more agreeable – elder sister.

I do trust that Darcy can see through her for – as Louisa later observed – he does appear to pay her some attention. But as Jane Bennet's recovery continues apace, with any luck they shall both be gone tomorrow – and I am giving away no secrets when I say that they will not soon be re-invited, for Darcy is altogether too intrigued by them. Though, as I reminded my sister, he *did* speak of admiring my figure as he sat by the fire. ('Was not that promising? I scarcely knew where to look!')

'Quite,' said Louisa thoughtfully. 'However, you were not the only young lady whose figure he was admiring.'

Which was, of course, true. However, once alone in my own chamber, I could not help indulging in a little daydream of myself, in a new silk gown, leaning on Charles's arm, walking down the long aisle at St George's Hanover Square towards Mr Darcy's powerful shoulders and handsome chin, those dark eyes bent on mine… All this, and Pemberley as well!

I should be the envy of every woman in London!

❖

November 16th

I ignored Mr Darcy most perseveringly for the whole of the morning and throughout most of the afternoon, when he was anyway in Meryton, so I had no other option. However, after tea – the sun having burnt off every drop of rain – he proposed that we walk. I accepted at once, and my cleverness in studying that awful Goethe finally paid off, as I was able to say 'quite' and 'indeed' in all the correct places.

He said a good deal about German romanticism. (Note to self: ask Louisa what it means.) I finally dared to turn the subject to something rather less confusing, in short to Miss Jane Bennet, who was to join us in the evening before her departure, but Mr Darcy merely acknowledged her beauty.

'Of course,' I suggested – recollecting his notion of 'fine eyes' – 'she cannot compare in looks with her sister, Eliza.'

'I disagree,' said he. 'Miss Jane Bennet possesses the superiority, at least in *that* regard.'

I was so delighted to hear this that I made some exceedingly witty jests with regard to Miss Eliza being his choice as bride – her 'elegant aunt and uncle in Cheapside', her mother's 'swift intelligence', the 'quiet reserve' of her younger sisters etc. I finished, 'Of course, you must not dream of having your wife's portrait painted, for what painter could hope to reproduce *such* fine eyes?'

But *then*, just as I was beginning to enjoy myself, who should turn directly into our path but Louisa – with Elizabeth Bennet! I knew not which way to look – for they might well have overheard me, though Louisa later admitted that she had *not*... She was a little brusque with me however, not only for not waiting for her, but for agreeing to accompany Mr Darcy at all.

I suspect that this qualified as 'hounding', in Louisa's opinion.

Jane Bennet did indeed join us at supper, looking most becomingly fragile, and Charles could attend to no one else. It was 'Are you warm enough?' and 'Should not you move a little closer to the fire?' – though she seemed perfectly well to me. Louisa later complained of his not paying the rest of the party the slightest attention. (''Tis more than my life is worth, trying to keep such a family in order!')

But *there*, of course, she must have been referring to the Bennets.

◆

November 26th

And so, today was the day of our own ball, here at Netherfield!

When this was first proposed – by Charles, of course, as one might have expected – I pretended great indifference, cleverly 'mirroring' the precise amount of enthusiasm displayed by 'Fitzy'. But Charles was in no mood to be gainsaid, and it has been delightful to be swept up in all the preparations – for, by all accounts, it has been *years* since Netherfield last saw a ball. And imagine my joy when Mr Darcy secured me for the first two dances, at breakfast.

I said, 'Of course! How delightful!' and did not mention my pleasure above twice thereafter.

And now, my hair perfected and my new green gown enchanting I feel quite charmed at the prospect… Now, where is that Goethe quote that I so laboriously inscribed?

❖

Well, the ball is over, and my feet absolutely aching from so much dancing… First, about the ball – then, what Louisa said – then I truly *must* sleep!

When Mr Darcy and I were dancing he admitted that he had never thought of Werther as comic before and commended my interpretation as 'unique'. (Did not I do well? Dare I not think, *very* well?) Also, I recollected that Goethe quote, about love. ('What torment it is to see so much loveliness passing before us, yet not dare to lay hold of it!')

Which neatly summed up my feelings soon afterwards, upon seeing Mr Darcy dance past while I was partnering one of the officers… Perhaps a man ought not to be described as having 'loveliness', though? Disappointingly, he was dancing with Elizabeth Bennet. (She does not dance too badly.)

But afterwards he came up to me and asked if I could, perhaps, do him a favour, and for this reason: 'Miss Elizabeth Bennet has heard the tired old rumour that I ill-treated Mr Wickham. I wonder if you might be kind enough to disabuse her of this notion?'

I wondered that he should care what any member of the Bennet family thought of him, but of course I agreed to make a point of it and to find a moment. But he said, 'She is by that pillar, just behind you,' and so I promised to do my best.

Crossing to her, I said, 'I understand that you are quite delighted with George Wickham! But you have imbibed *quite* the wrong notion about Mr Darcy for, as to Mr Wickham, he has always been particularly kind to him, which is far more than he deserved, for he has behaved quite infamously to Mr Darcy in return. Also – I cannot imagine Wickham mentioning it, but he is, in fact, merely the son of the former steward at Pemberley!'

Though she then claimed that he had. Mentioned it, I mean. So then I said, very politely, 'Excuse my interference, it was kindly meant!' And went to report to Mr Darcy that I had done all that he had asked, but that the lady had not appeared entirely convinced.

Yet even had she been, that evening – taken altogether – must have ruined any conceivable chance of Darcy that she might ever have possessed, for it could *not* have been more mortifying for the entire Bennet family.

First there was some cousin of theirs, an unctuous, podgy creature patronised – as who is not? – by Mr Darcy's aunt, Lady Catherine de Bourgh. (And *that* was exceedingly witty too – truly, I am in rare form tonight!)

At any rate, this Collins fellow had the effrontery to positively *prance* up to Mr Darcy and dare to introduce himself, without Mr Darcy's having taken the slightest notice of him beforehand, and without even the *pretence* of having been properly introduced!... As I whispered to Louisa, 'Has the family no shame?'

Apparently, none at all, because at dinner Louisa overheard Mrs Bennet crowing that her beloved Jane was destined to be 'mistress of Netherfield'! Whilst the youngest Bennet girl was meanwhile simply *shrieking* at the sallies of some of the officers, and Miss Mary – the third daughter and much the plainest – was *not* to be shifted from the pianoforte. Having rendered Clementi's C major in the most affected manner possible, she then proceeded to favour us with tedious Italian songs until her own *father* implored her to desist! At that, even dear Louisa's lips twitched.

But once all the guests were gone she said, and very seriously, 'My sweet Caroline, *something* will have to be done about that Bennet girl.'

I am not quite sure what she meant by this, but she will doubtless explain it in the morning.

❖

November 27th

Today we had a council of war – so exciting! The moment Charles was again closeted with the estate manager, Louisa commandeered Mr Darcy and myself. We followed her onto the south lawn, where not even a servant could conceivably overhear us. Then Louisa said, 'He is exceedingly far gone. He is very far gone, indeed!' And Mr Darcy affirmed, 'I have never seen him so in love. Not even when so bewitched by Lady Diana. He could scarcely take his eyes from her!'

'I suppose you must mean Miss Bennet,' said I. 'Do you think him in actual danger, then?' and Louisa did.

'And so do I,' said Darcy. How marvellously stern his countenance was! I felt rather a thrill, in that moment. So strangely *intimate* a moment!

'We must keep him away from her,' said Louisa, 'and I do not despair of it, for he goes to London tomorrow. You and I must follow him there, Caroline, and – somehow – persuade him to remain.'

'But if he loves her –' I said, unable to repress a little glance at Darcy, who was frowning. His hair was a little disordered – in *much* my favourite way.

'Love? – what nonsense!' cried Louisa. ''Tis merely a little fever of admiration, for which I cannot blame him. It is not *Miss Bennet* who is impossible. I should have no objection to Miss Bennet, beyond the misfortune of her birth, were it not for her appalling mother –'

'– and her unspeakable cousin,' said Mr Darcy.

'– not to mention her dreadful sister on the pianoforte. I thought she would never have done!'

Mr Darcy added, 'And – I must say it – even her father. Perhaps you failed to observe, Miss Bingley, but Mr Bennet made not the slightest effort to control his wife and daughters. He seemed almost diverted instead. I entirely agree with Mrs Hurst. Miss Bennet is delightful, but the family is not to be borne!'

I so longed to agree, but I could not quite recall how many times I had agreed with him since breakfast. And so, I merely *looked* my agreement, instead.

Louisa said, 'And so, we are as one.' (As one with Mr Darcy! Fancy!) 'We must follow Charles to town, and there we must somehow persuade him to remain. But how? – for he is almost as well-pleased with Netherfield as he is with Miss Bennet!'

'I believe I know a way,' said Mr Darcy suddenly. 'Were Charles to imagine the lady entirely indifferent, he would never wish to see her more. If I was to suggest that Miss Bennet was merely flattered by his attentions –'

'– for she accepts admiration from every creature with precisely the same complacency –' said Louisa.

'– our difficulties might be at an end.'

I could only admire how the divine cleft in his chin deepened as Louisa said, 'Indeed, Charles has ever had a low opinion of himself. Modest as he is, such a scheme might well answer. And you would truly be willing to do it?'

'I would do much more,' said Mr Darcy – so nobly – 'rather than to see a friend of mine allied to such a family!'

In the end, I wrote Miss Bennet a little note. The others read it and Mr Darcy said that it was quite perfect except in one or two little particulars and that, after I rewrote it, it was perfection itself. And such a smile as he gave me! And so, now we are co-conspirators. How closely it seems to draw us together: Louisa, Fitzy, and myself!

❦

January 6th

As soon as he arrived back in town, Mr Darcy did as he had promised. Poor Charles appeared deeply depressed afterwards, but dear Louisa was relieved, observing that she 'doubted we shall ever see Netherfield more'. But as Shakespeare put it, though why he used the Scottish dialect I cannot recall, 'The best-laid schemes of mice and men gang aft agley' and it was no time at all before Mr Darcy confided, 'I have heard ill tidings abroad.'

'You mean, in America?' I asked.

'Well, in America also. But what I meant was that the eldest Miss Bennet has arrived in London.'

'Dear me!' I cried. 'But are you quite sure?'

'I saw her at the Little Theatre, attending – I presumed – her uncle and aunt. There was no possibility of mistake.'

'I had quite forgot her relatives at Cheapside,' said Louisa, frowning. 'Why, she might be in town for weeks!'

'And weeks,' I added helpfully.

At this – how my heart sped! – Mr Darcy said, 'And not only that, Miss Bingley, but she will likely call upon you. There was a sufficient level of intimacy in Hertfordshire as to make that not inappropriate.'

'But how might I prevent her?' I asked, and the other two exchanged glances.

'We cannot prevent her from calling,' said Louisa, 'for *that* must be impossible, but we can at least prepare for it. Should she call, Caroline, you must be exceedingly formal. I suggest that you confine your comments entirely to the weather. There is always perfect safety in the weather.'

'Or to the last concert you attended,' said Mr Darcy. At this my heart rather sank, for the moment I have left a concert I can never recollect the first thing about it.

But Louisa said, 'The weather will suffice. Perhaps her health. And very brief sentences. We might practise this evening, in my dressing-room.'

Thus when it happened – when Miss Bennet *did* call – she found me perfectly prepared.

'How delightful to see you,' I said, rather coldly. 'I hope your family is well?'

'Oh! Perfectly.'

'We have been having charming weather, have we not?'

She hesitated a little, and said, 'Just so. Except for the rain.'

'Of course, with that exception,' I said, quite masterfully. (If only Mr Darcy had been there!) 'And I trust that tomorrow might prove equally clement.'

She agreed – well, she could scarcely *fail* to agree. And at the end of a discussion in which the pavements, the dirt and the crowds all played their part, she said, 'I do hope, Miss Bingley, that we might meet again!'

'Oh,' said I, 'I daresay that we shall.'

And that was masterful too, as I neither encouraged nor

discouraged this pretty hope. (Only think how fortunate it was that Charles was not by! – though Charles is insufferably sociable, and rarely at home for two hours altogether.)

When I related my triumph to Louisa, she said, 'Yet we are only half-safe, for her call must be returned… I know! The coachman shall take you to her uncle's, and wait for you, and you shall not remain above five minutes. *That* should perfectly convey your message.'

'What message?' I asked.

'Why, that this little – episode – must conclude the friendship! That, sweet and gentle as Miss Bennet is, you have not the slightest intention of continuing the connection.'

I asked if I was to discuss the weather again – I believed that I had done rather well with the weather – but Louisa thought not. Instead, she worked out a series of short observations for me to memorise, without mentioning the weather at all. And when I returned – from darkest Cheapside – and made my report, she believed that I had performed to admiration.

It was not *quite* the end of our frights, for I saw Miss Bennet in town on two later occasions – and both times Charles was attending me. And the last thing we wished was for him to learn that Miss Bennet was in London!

The first fright occurred at the theatre, where Charles was luckily too engaged with the play to notice. On the *second* occasion, however, we were in Oxford Street when I saw her approaching, presumably leaning on the arm of her uncle. And there, as I later told Louisa, I towed Charles into a jeweller's, despite his reluctance, pretending that 'the most divine earrings were within!' And I stayed there, inspecting earrings, till the lady and her uncle had quite passed by.

I preened myself on my clear thinking for some little time thereafter.

✦

July 30th

Unbelievably, those provoking Bennets are encroaching, yet again! Truly, some women have no shame! My brother comes to London and Miss Bennet arrives in London! Darcy travels to Derbyshire and Eliza Bennet dares to appear – and at the very gates of Pemberley itself! It is, quite simply, pursuit!

I heard about it first from Darcy's younger sister, Georgiana, who said as innocently as possible, 'So, have you ever met this Miss Elizabeth Bennet, whom my brother so longs for me to know?'

'Miss *Elizabeth* Bennet?' I repeated, shocked.

'I believe that was the name… She and her relatives were being shown around Pemberley when Fitzwilliam returned yesterday, and he seems most insistent that we call upon them. Is she' – this nervously – 'so very clever and remarkable?'

I considered for a moment before responding. Then I said, 'Her *sister* is remarkably pretty – even beautiful – but Miss *Elizabeth* Bennet is ordinary indeed.'

'But remarkably accomplished?' asked Georgiana hesitantly. (But then, she is often a little nervous.)

'Why, she has no accomplishments to speak of, in comparison with you! She plays a little, and sings a little, whereas your voice alone –'

'Ah, but you know how difficult I find performing before other people!'

'Yet Miss Eliza Bennet can scarcely be said to play and sing at

97

all. As for the *third* Miss Bennet – though it has been months since the ball at Netherfield, I have yet to excise her tinny little voice from my head!'

We met Miss Elizabeth the next day. She looked as bronzed as a nut and very much coarser than in Hertfordshire, but when I remarked upon it, Mr Darcy said that he could not conceive of there being the slightest difference, beyond her being 'rather tanned, a not unnatural result of travelling in the summer'. As I wrote to my sister, perhaps I had made a tiny mistake, by mentioning it?

How I wish she was here, to counsel and advise!

Louisa wrote back by return of post, urging me to be as friendly as possible, to the Gardiners in general and to Miss Eliza Bennet in particular, and to evince not the slightest awareness of their encroaching ways. I did this to admiration, though possibly *slightly* blundering by saying, 'I recall – ha! – your little quip, Mr Darcy, down at Hertfordshire, when you said of Miss Eliza, *"She* a beauty! – I should as soon call her mother a wit!"* Yet I believe you thought her rather good-looking at one time.'

For some reason Mr Darcy looked rather nettled – a touch of dyspepsia, perhaps? – as he said, 'It has been many months since I have regarded Miss Elizabeth Bennet as one of the handsomest women of my acquaintance.'

So annoying! – but I decided not to mention it to Louisa, all the same.

❖

The little luncheon at Pemberley is over – but I fear that is not the only thing to be over, for my hopes (of 'Fitzy') have dimmed a great deal. Despite her indifferent teeth, despite her brownness, and despite the rather shrewish look in her dark eyes, Mr Darcy seemed – though she was far less teasing than usual – absolutely struck by Eliza Bennet's lightest utterance. He paid more attention to her than to Georgiana, herself!

'Is all lost?' I wrote to Louisa, and she wrote back, 'I expect so. But you must do your best because – recollecting the mother, the cousin, the younger sisters – there *may* still be some measure of hope.'

And thus I most perseveringly admired his fruit, and his trees, and Georgiana's new pianoforte – but all to very little effect, because the gaze with which Mr Darcy watched Miss Eliza was like nothing so much as a cat regarding, most earnestly, a fresh bowl of cream.

She and her relatives left the area very suddenly – breaking several engagements – almost rudely, in fact. However, I gloomily determined, as Charles and I made our own adieux, that it would not be long before the worst would come to pass, and Pemberley, instead of being my own, would belong to – that Bennet girl.

As for studying Goethe, which I have done till my head ached – *that* was of no use at all.

❧

September 16th

'Tis all over.

Charles has declared his intention to go down to Netherfield – and Darcy has promised to attend him. Even Louisa has given over amusing herself with jokes about the Bennet family. And when I mentioned our wonderful conspiracy to save Charles from their machinations, she only shook her head. 'I greatly fear,' said she, 'that Charles now believes himself to have mistaken Miss Bennet's feelings entirely. I shall be *vastly* surprised if, by the end of next week, she is not engaged to him.'

I was sorry to hear it, but still sorrier to think that our close confederacy with Mr Darcy was ended. So cozy a confederacy! I said, 'And Miss Eliza Bennet?'

'There, too, I rather suspect the worst,' said Louisa. 'But there is nothing in the world that we can do about it.'

✦

October 20th

Louisa has been proven, yet again, most astute.

Charles and the eldest Miss Bennet plighted their troth only a week before the announcement of Mr Darcy's engagement to her sister – at which his aunt, Lady Catherine de Bourgh, vowed that she would never set eyes on him again.

And so, I shall never be the envy of London, walking down the aisle of St George's Hanover Square towards... Fitzy!

I shall never be mistress of Pemberley, either.

There *shall* be a new Mrs Darcy – but it shall *not* be me.

Really, it is all exceedingly annoying.

Then I recalled *The Sorrows of Young Werther* and consoled myself. I thought, 'Well, at least I shall never have to finish it.'

✦

October 22nd

I practised a good deal, under Louisa's tuition, till I could accomplish it with perfect conviction.

'No, no, not the least affected! Truly, Mr Darcy was never my sort. He is well enough, to be sure, but too – intense, too serious, too bookish for my taste. We should have been miserable together. *Such* a good thing he never offered to me!... And, of course, I was always particularly close to Miss Eliza Bennet, as was. One of my dearest friends, in fact. So quick, so witty – and with *such* fine eyes!'

All Hallows' Eve at the Bennets'

Not a syllable was uttered by either; and Elizabeth was on the point of going away again, when Bingley, who as well as the other had sat down, suddenly rose, and, whispering a few words to her sister, ran out of the room.

(from *Pride and Prejudice*, Chapter 55)

'Well, I am quite determined to try,' said Lydia.

'Try what?' inquired Kitty.

Lydia glanced swiftly around and lowered her voice. 'Why, the mirror, of course!'

'But only think! What if, instead of – instead of *that,* you should see a skull?' And Kitty shuddered.

'I shall not see the skull, I am quite convinced. Instead I shall see, reflected with my own in the mirror, the face of the man whom I shall marry!'

''Tis nothing but a silly old wives' tale,' observed Mary, who had been listening, 'but then most of the country customs to do with All Hallows' Eve are silly. The ancient Celts, for example –'

'Well, *I* should be far too afraid,' said Kitty.

'Too afraid even to watch me, as I try it?'

'Indeed – for fear of the skull.'

Lydia clasped her hands dramatically. 'But what if, upon seeing Wickham's handsome visage, I should faint dead away?'

'In such a case,' sighed Mary, 'you would recover the instant you failed to receive the slightest attention – though truly, anyone silly enough to believe old wives' tales, must be capable of anything.'

Lydia put out her tongue at her and turned back to Kitty. 'Mrs Forster said that it is best to wait till midnight, or even later.'

'Then Mrs Forster is wise beyond her years,' said Mary. 'For by midnight you shall both be most soundly asleep and will never stir till morning.'

Lydia nudged her confederate. 'Do you suppose, Kitty, if *Jane* were to do it, that she might see – ha – Mr Bingley's face in her mirror?'

'Perhaps she might – but 'tis useless to speak of it, for she would never do it, nor Lizzy either.' And they shook their heads at the dullness and stupidity of their elder sisters.

The Bennet family marked All Hallows' Eve, the eve of All Souls, in no particular fashion. With dinner finished, Mr Bennet was reading and Mrs Bennet sewing, while continually harping on her displeasure with her friend Lady Lucas, who had twice forgotten to send her a promised recipe. ('For – and this is the truth of it – had *I* forgotten, and had *I* omitted to send a note, she would have cut me for a fortnight, and I should never have heard the end of it till I was dead and buried! But simply because her husband happened to have been mayor at the luckiest time, she is allowed to lord it over me forever and ever…')

Mr Bennet did not even pretend to listen while Lizzy, writing a letter, seemed similarly unmoved. Only the gentle Jane commiserated. 'I am sure,' said she, 'that she will recollect, repent, and ask her daughters to bring it tomorrow.'

'Well, *I* cannot think so! – Her memory, always weak, is

become entirely unreliable. And she is grown so self-centred that she thinks of nothing beyond herself and her children!'

'Yet with so many to supervise, and the youngest to instruct, surely that can occasion no surprise?'

'Nay, not at all – not in the least – for *that* is their governess's province. *She* can have nothing to do, beyond forgetting her friends, abusing her housekeeper, and copying her sister's new bonnets – for her sister has a London milliner.'

'If you are correct in your information,' said Lizzy drily, 'then her diligence does her no service, for she must dress to less advantage than any lady in Meryton.'

Her mother ignored this civil reflection, adding, '*We* of course never had a governess. No, all the work, all the difficulties, all fell upon me. Not that I complain – I have not the nature for it. Oh heavens, there are the chimes. Time for you to go to bed, my dear Lydia, and Kitty as well.'

Normally, such a pronouncement would have occasioned a combination of outrage and grief on the part of her two youngest, amidst pleas from her third that *she* should be classed with Jane and Eliza rather than with Kitty and Lydia. However, that particular All Hallows' Eve, with Mary having already retired, the two youngest fled without a murmur, leaving Mr Bennet to trust, with heavy irony, that they were not sickening for something.

'They are well enough,' was Lizzy's opinion, 'but they have been hatching some silly scheme the whole evening.'

'I am delighted to hear it,' said her father. 'For without such diversions they might become responsible, even civilised, and so great a change as *that* your mother's nerves could never bear.'

'What was that about my nerves?' inquired his lady tersely.

'Nothing, my dear. I merely alluded to my respect for their fragility.'

'Well and as to *that*, can anyone wonder? With the weather so capricious, without the slightest security for my declining years, and with friends as thoughtless as Lady Lucas, 'tis a wonder my nerves are not in pieces!'

At this her husband and daughter exchanged glances but said not a word, for once Mrs Bennet had begun upon her nerves, the less said the better. Meanwhile the youngest girls were readying themselves for bed, and annoying Mary in the next room with their urgent giggles and sudden bursts of energy.

They waited until they had heard Jane and Lizzy retire, and their parents likewise, before Lydia dared light her candle. It shed a ghostly glow around the bedroom. Lydia whispered, 'That pile of clothes upon the floor. Does not it resemble… a dead body?'

'It far more closely resembles a pile of clothes,' giggled Kitty.

'Shh! Do you not see how ominously the draught from the window makes the candle flutter? What if it is our grandmama's ghost returning to earth? For did she not perish in this very room? And is it not the witching hour, when the barriers 'twixt the world of the dead and ours are lowered, that occurs but once a year?'

'Oh! Stop it, do,' said Kitty, nervously. 'You know it is not really so!'

'Shh, how you hamper me! How can I possibly summon Wickham to my mirror if you persist in interrupting? For' – a touch of drama – 'the hour is advanced, and midnight approaches!'

Kitty considered reminding her sister about the possibility of her espying a skull but decided against it. She even fretted lest her own constant fears about the skull – how terrible it would be for Lydia to die before she married! – might somehow make this catastrophe likelier. She watched in silence as Lydia combed her hair, the better to lure Wickham's spirit, and lifted her mirror. Then, to Kitty's puzzlement, she waved her left hand about as if to conjure up a mist, or smoke.

'Take the candle farther away,' whispered Lydia. 'Only a "darkened" mirror will attract vibrations from the other sphere!'

'*What* other sphere?'

'Never mind! Just move back a bit, do!'

Obediently, Kitty retreated but – unluckily – the untidy Lydia had left her workbooks on the floor, where they ought never to have been. Thus it happened that poor Kitty tripped, fell backwards with a stifled cry, and crashed noisily into the dressing table.

'You clumsy creature – you have quite broke the spell!' cried Lydia crossly, still keeping her eyes firmly upon her mirror. 'But never fear, because I can already just see –'

But what Lydia imagined she saw will never be known, because at that point their door burst open and the face joining Lydia's in the mirror – rather than a tender Wickham's – proved to be the furious Mary's, instead.

'And how, might I ask, am I supposed to get any rest at all when you silly children decide to break up your furniture in the middle of the night? How am I to work, to practice, and to excel? Oh, you are utterly impossible!'

'My *elbow!*' moaned Kitty, from the floor.

But Lydia was almost howling with laughter. 'The visage in the mirror… the barrier betwixt… the other sphere… Oh, Lord! I shall go quite distracted!'

A still-indignant Mary made the most of her tale of woe at the breakfast table, to Mr Bennet's intense amusement. Unfortunately for Mary, it was not the kind of joke likely to be thrown away, either on Lizzy or her father, while even her mother laughed at her, though also at her sisters.

Mary's annoyance was to endure. Upon their return from church, she went straight to her room, where she began to pound scales upon her square pianoforte – up and down and down and up, until Mr Bennet hastily retired to his library and his elder daughters decided to walk. There was a pleasant path from the edge of the Longbourn property, which wended its way along a wood, ending in a pond large enough to be called a lake. There they sat together on the little bench, watching ducks disputing over some water rushes.

'Rather like our sisters,' said Jane, with a sigh.

'Very like,' said Elizabeth, 'but truly, Mary was in the right. It hardly reflects well on Lydia's principles, to be summoning spirits to her bedroom on All Hallows Eve!'

'It does not.'

'And it is just the kind of behaviour that our relatives ought to address. Else Lydia's high spirits might one day become ungovernable.'

'I fear,' said Jane, 'our Papa and Mama are not serious – at least, not in that way. Why, Mama positively encourages Lydia to dwell upon the officers, because she herself so loved the company of officers at Lydia's age!'

'And Papa will only laugh at them.'

'To be fair, Lizzy, 'twas *you* who said that the crash Mary heard was the prospective husband's realising the horridness of his fate and attempting to run away!'

They both laughed and Lizzy cried, 'True, very true, I am guilty! – yet I still fear that something rather more serious is required.'

'I expect Papa *will* notice Lydia, at some point or other.'

'Oh, he may – he will – but he will be too indolent to do anything about it… But Jane, there is something else. Did you hear Kitty mentioning Wickham? Actually Wickham! You do not imagine any risk to Lydia *there*, do you?'

'Why, none at all! Wickham loves to flirt with every young woman, though with no serious intent. As for Lydia, she was – and only recently – so charmed with the newest officer Henderson that she could not say enough in his praise!… Are not these hazelnuts ripe? Why do we not collect a few, and roast them over the fire?'

Lizzy looked at her archly. 'And, if we should, I assume you know the old tale about hazelnuts?'

'I have not the slightest idea. I *have* heard the tale about apple peel, however.'

'It is only a country custom. To explain, were I to take this hazelnut and *this*, and to name the first, perhaps, Jane Bennet and the second – let us say – Charles Bingley, and to put them side by side above the fire –'

'No, no. This is every bit as silly as Lydia's mirror!'

'Just hear me out. Were I to do all this, why then, after the fire had popped and roasted every nut that it could, if *those* two nuts were still curled up side-by-side, then J.B. and C.B. might be supposed likely to – to go through life side-by-side, in the same way.'

Her sister rose, rather hurriedly. 'What an absurd game! I believe I ought to scatter our every nut, that you might not be tempted to try it!' Despite this, and with Lizzy still laughing, they pocketed their nuts and took the winding path back to Longbourn.

But for whatever reason, Elizabeth did not forget her idle fancy. Instead, she – all unobserved – slyly put one mark on one hazelnut and two marks on another, before nestling them together near the flames, for – after all – Jane need never know.

And Jane did *not* know – not for a year – what Lizzy observed that evening. It was only after the wedding that she told her sister that the two marked hazelnuts… were not to be parted.

The Bennet Girls' Easter Bonnet

Lydia was too much fatigued to utter more than the occasional exclamation of "Lord, how tired I am!" accompanied by a violent yawn.

(from *Pride and Prejudice*, Chapter 18)

Longbourn, Hertfordshire

'I hate Lent,' said Lydia, 'and I cannot see the point of it.'

'We are supposed to give something up, I believe,' said Kitty. 'The rector said a good deal about it last Sunday.'

'I expect he did, but I was only counting the number of times he cleared his throat.'

'How many?' asked Kitty, interested.

'Sixteen. And he has such small and piggy eyes.'

'Piggy!'

'*Very* piggy. Truly, not even regimentals could save him.'

'Yet once Good Friday comes and Lent is over,' said Kitty, 'then we shall have hot cross buns.'

'Yes! It is shockingly dull not being allowed a single sweet – except for one on Sundays – simply because we are in Lent. I have not had a morsel of sugar since pancake Tuesday! Were I in Parliament, I should abolish Lent altogether.'

'I do not think,' said Kitty, 'that a single representative could do so much, not even if he were Prime Minister.'

'It would be very poor fun being in Parliament, and Prime Minister besides, if one was never to get one's own way,' said Lydia.

✦

Rosings, Kent

'And wherever did you meet Mr Darcy?' inquired Lady Catherine, almost in disbelief.

Elizabeth lowered her eyes and said, 'He was visiting in Hertfordshire with his friend, a Mr Bingley.'

'A very agreeable young man,' said Charlotte Collins.

'An exceedingly agreeable man,' said Lady Catherine majestically. 'I know of no more agreeable man, in my entire acquaintance, than my nephew Darcy.'

This silenced the two friends, as Charlotte had been referring to Mr Bingley instead – and as Lizzy had never met a man whom she considered *less* agreeable than Darcy.

'And so, he arrives on Thursday?' asked Charlotte.

'Indeed,' said Lady Catherine, 'with Colonel Fitzwilliam.'

'Who is also *most* agreeable,' added Mr Collins hastily.

Lady Catherine pursed her lips, as if considering which of her two exemplary relatives she considered the most agreeable, but finally assented.

Later, Lizzy relieved her feelings in a letter to Jane: *Rosings itself is well enough – far grander than anything I have ever seen in Hertfordshire – but unimaginably dull, for Lady Catherine has cowed her poor daughter Anne into insipidity, whilst she pronounces indisputable judgement on everything from the weather*

112

to the window tax, only to be most fervently seconded by our cousin Collins. And, as if that was not sufficiently annoying, Mr Darcy and his cousin arrive on Thursday.

Once they were alone, Eliza said playfully to Charlotte, 'Am I nowhere in England safe from Mr Darcy?'

'What!' teased her friend. 'How dare you complain, when he is so excessively agreeable?'

'Lady Catherine would say *that* of any creature in the world, to whom she chanced to be related.'

'It is still a great shame that you have taken so cordial a dislike to Mr Darcy, for we shall probably see a great deal of him. Cannot you attempt to overcome it?'

Elizabeth shook her head. 'Does he infest Rosings very often, then?'

'Not he, for this is his first visit since I was married.'

'And is there no other great family hereabouts, who could shoulder some part of the burden?'

'Well,' said Charlotte, 'I told you of the Johnsons, who live in a very great way down at Warleigh Hall. But her Ladyship does not approve them, as they were in trade, and as Mr Johnson is rather vulgar. The nearest family with whom *she* cares to associate live past Westerham – which is doubtless why we are summoned to Rosings so often.'

Elizabeth sighed. 'I suppose that, if we are summoned, why, we must go! And Mr Darcy will presumably return to town soon after Easter, as there can be nothing here to detain him.'

✦

THE BENNET GIRLS' EASTER BONNET

Longbourn, Hertfordshire

'We could dye Easter eggs,' suggested Kitty.

'I should rather walk down to Meryton,' said Lydia. 'Far rather.'

'But – if you recollect – there is very little point, for the militia are engaged in their exercises.'

'True, I had forgotten. They seem forever at their exercises!'

'Well, it *is* their purpose, I suppose,' said Kitty.

'But surely there is some fellow fit to flirt with?'

'We could call on the Jones's, in case their son has come home.'

'I suppose we could,' said Lydia, gloomily. 'I daresay that flirting with Frederick Jones is better than having no flirting at all.'

❦

Hunsford, Kent

'Well, I think that he admires you,' said Charlotte, rather slyly.

Elizabeth coloured. 'No, it is only that his manners are unusually pleasing, as you mentioned the other day. And – as who would not? – he relishes a little respite from Her Ladyship.'

'I was not referring to Colonel Fitzwilliam, Lizzy.'

Lizzy laughed. 'What, Mr Darcy? – impossible! For he – as is known throughout all greater Hertfordshire – regards me as only *tolerable*!'

'And yet, opinions have been known to alter – minds have been known to change.'

'Not his. How could it, indeed? – for he, in common with his aunt, is always in the right!'

Charlotte persisted, 'Yet he regards you a great deal.'

'He regards his aunt a great deal too and, I daresay, with much the same level of interest. As for why he remains, I cannot conceive.

114

He seems to put off their departure, so provokingly, from day to day! – though the Colonel's pleasing manners *do* compensate for his cousin's.'

Charlotte said no more, but as she fed her hens she thought, 'Why, indeed! Cannot she see that Darcy puts off his departure on her account, and on her account alone? Truly, I cannot think that I imagine it... The way he listens when she speaks, the way he attends when she sings – I am as sure as I have ever been of anything that he greatly admires her. But how might such admiration end?'

After another evening spent at Rosings, during which she closely observed both men, Charlotte slipped into her husband's study. 'Forgive me, my dear,' said she, 'I do not wish to disturb you.'

'Then leave me, I beg – for I am shockingly behindhand with my Easter sermon. For that reason, I trust that this might be a matter of some moment, and not merely that the cat has been ill again.'

'Indeed, I believe it might be – a matter of some moment, I mean.'

'But so, dear wife of my bosom, is my Easter sermon. For Mr Johnson said only the other week that he looks forward to my sermons with the same impatience as he does the *Racing News*, while Her Ladyship herself –'

'What I have to say does concern Her Ladyship.'

He leapt to his feet. 'Great heavens! Why did you not say so at once? Is she poorly? Is she distressed? Whatever can have occurred?'

'Why nothing – but I believe that something *might* occur. In short, I suspect that Mr Darcy might rather admire Eliza.'

Mr Collins cried in consternation, 'No, for *that* must be impossible!'

'I believe it to be true.'

'Then, my dear Charlotte, something has gone amiss with your usual good sense, and for the following reasons. First, it could never have been lost upon *me,* should it be so. Secondly, even *I* was stooping low in offering to her while, as for Mr Darcy – well! And finally, as you know, he is engaged already – to Miss de Bourgh.'

'So Her Ladyship is forever reminding us. But it has never been announced all the same, and I cannot think he wishes it. In truth, I have yet to see the slightest symptom of regard on *either* side, though Miss de Bourgh is so tepid that I might perhaps have missed it. As for his wealth and importance, no one acquainted in the slightest with Lady Catherine could be ignorant of either, for she is nearly as proud of Pemberley as of Rosings, itself.'

'And justly so! And justly so! Why, Darcy must be one of the twelve richest men in all the country, who are neither of the nobility or else some upstart general or other! Could such a man as that admire my cousin? Impossible!'

'Unlikely, perhaps – but *not* impossible.'

Mr Collins got up, strode about and said, 'Forgive me, my dear wife, but it is, indeed, impossible. I have not sufficient time, just at present, to instruct you in the not inconsiderable difference – nay, the enormous gulf – betwixt Elizabeth Bennet and –'

'And yet unequal matches take place every day – or else one should not read about them! I believe I have an – instinct, in such matters. And I fear that Lady Catherine would never forgive us, were her daughter slighted in favour of my friend!'

'In such a case, Her Ladyship would have every right to hold us blameable – but I believe instead that your imagination or – still likelier – your partiality for your friend, has led your judgement astray. But now – truly – I *must* get on, for I promised to attend the whist club tonight, and to call upon the curate on the way.'

As Charlotte returned to the kitchen, she reviewed this conversation. She was not disappointed, for she still trusted that the seed she had planted might bear fruit. But did she *wish* it to? – For she had little doubt that even Lizzy's detestation would disappear, were she to fancy Darcy at her feet – and *then*, what might not the great Mr Darcy be able to do for her husband? Lady Catherine's ire would be nothing, in comparison! And Charlotte believed herself to have, the previous evening, observed a gaze so intense, so concentrated, from Darcy towards Eliza that nothing but the strongest passion could account for it.

She thought, 'How fortunate Lizzy is to have such natural wit and untutored charm as can bewitch even the man whom – of every man in the world – she most detests!'

As for her own husband, she had done her duty – and no wife could do more.

♨

Longbourn, Hertfordshire

'I am bored,' said Lydia. 'I am the boredest I have ever been, in the whole of my life. I do not believe anyone in all the world could be more bored than I!'

'I do not think,' said Kitty, 'that "boredest" is a proper word.'

'It is, now that I have used it,' said her sister.

'We could make an Easter bonnet,' suggested Kitty.

'We could, had we a bonnet worth the trimming, but we have none.'

'There is Mama's old biscuit-coloured bonnet. She said we could have *that* if we liked, because it makes her feel tired just to look at it.'

Lydia clapped her sister on the back so hard that she coughed. 'Why, so she did!'

'But could we mend it in time, for Easter is not far off? And what have we here to trim it with?'

'La! I cannot think! Perhaps... the border to my discarded tippet?'

'No, for that is sad indeed,' said Kitty. ''Twould not improve a bonnet, but make it uglier, instead.'

They sat disconsolate for a moment. Then Lydia cried, 'Mama has not worn her pink ribbons this long age! We could use those to frame the bonnet and – I vow – *Mama* will never miss them!'

'You mean the broad, pale pink ones, with the lace edge?'

'Yes! Were we to press them and sew them onto the bonnet, and to choose a few snowdrops – or feathers, perhaps – it might look delightful! Then I could wear it to the first Easter service and you to the second.'

'Or the other way about?' suggested Kitty – for not everyone attended the second service on Sundays.

'Or, I suppose, the other way about,' said Lydia.

❖

Hunsford, Kent

'Eliza is unwell,' said Charlotte, 'and cannot accompany us to Rosings.'

'She must, lest Her Ladyship take offence!' cried Mr Collins.

'But surely, no one could take offence at someone's being unwell?' asked Charlotte.

'Lord!' cried her young sister, Maria. 'I feel for Lizzy, most sincerely! To be ill on the last evening that we shall be in company with Mr Darcy and Colonel Fitzwilliam! For do they not depart for town tomorrow? And Her Ladyship promised a made dish that will likely astonish us all!'

'Eliza is not in the least hungry,' said Charlotte. 'And it might well offend her Ladyship, were she to push away each dish, untasted!'

Mr Collins frowned. 'I cannot think that many young ladies would turn down such an honour as an invitation to supper at Rosings!'

His wife reflected, rather drolly, that supper at Rosings was an honour that Eliza had enjoyed for several weeks, so it would not be strange if some of its novelty had worn away. But to Eliza, resting upon the settee, she only said, 'Can I fetch anything that might assist you?'

'Silence and tranquillity,' said Eliza, 'would be of more use than anything else.'

'Would you prefer me to stay?'

'No, no – for you must make my apologies to Lady Catherine, of course.'

Charlotte found her husband lurking in the hall. He said, 'I still worry, my dearest, that her refusal has some air of disrespect about it.'

'We must trust in Her Ladyship's usual generosity, in that case. And – perhaps – you might suggest that we wished to spare her delicate daughter, lest Lizzy's disorder prove infectious?'

'Now *that,*' said Mr Collins with enthusiasm, 'is a happy thought, a happy thought indeed! Perhaps something along these lines, that her lovely daughter is a jewel too rare to be put at risk, eh?'

'Ah, yes,' said Charlotte. 'Quite.'

✦

THE BENNET GIRLS' EASTER BONNET

Longbourn, Hertfordshire

'I think,' said Kitty dubiously, 'that the *design* of the bonnet is well enough, but that the colour is tame.'

'We might dye it,' said Lydia thoughtfully, 'with Cook's Easter dye.'

'The one she uses for the eggs, do you mean? For *that* is so very dark a red!'

'True. I do not know that my colouring is best-suited to dark red – nor yours, either.'

'No,' said Kitty loftily. 'My colouring is softer and more elegant, like Jane's.'

'You mean, pallid and washed-out!'

Lydia was just quick enough to escape and to run, laughing, into the garden.

❖

Hunsford, Kent

'What! Mr *Darcy* came here?' asked Charlotte, quite sharply, of her flustered maid.

'Aye, ma'am, and he *would* see Miss Bennet, whether she wished it or no.'

'And you admitted him?'

'Mr Collins's orders, ma'am, were always to admit him, should he call, and Colonel Fitzwilliam just the same.'

'And were they alone together for very long?'

At this the maid dissolved into tears. 'I know I should have stayed by, ma'am, but I was *that* distracted with the cat that I forgot – I did indeed! I never even heard when he departed!'

Charlotte said, 'Never mind, Mary. It may be for the best.'

While thinking, 'To leave his aunt and all the rest of us, and to insist upon seeing her… Oh, it could be only one thing! Though I should not be surprised if she refused him!' But to Mary she only said, 'Did Miss Bennet go upstairs early?'

'Yes ma'am, she did, with some valerian tea. I took it up to her myself.'

'And how did she look?'

'Oh, quite poorly, ma'am.'

'Well, we shall see if she is better in the morning,' said Charlotte.

But if he had offered and she had refused him, and Her Ladyship was to learn of it… Oh, it did not bear thinking of!

❦

Longbourn, Hertfordshire

The bonnet was ready for Easter, dark crimson thanks to Cook's dye, and prettily trimmed with snowdrops and the purloined pink ribbands. Lydia wore it at the earlier Easter service, where the curate complimented her on it, and Kitty at the – less well-attended – later one. She felt a trifle peeved that it suited Lydia's colouring rather better than her own.

❦

Hunsford, Kent

Elizabeth pushed Darcy's letter into her pocket, promising herself never to think of it ever again.

Had there ever been a more insulting proposal – or a more outrageous letter of excuse?

121

But only a moment later, she was retrieving it, re-reading it and repenting, as deeply as she had ever repented anything, her taunts the previous evening about Darcy's cruelty to Wickham.

'You take an eager interest in that gentleman's concerns,' he had said, with a heightened colour... Why, he had very nearly accused her of caring for Wickham! And it had been entirely her own fault, for it truly *did* appear that she had misjudged both men – and badly, besides! Mr Darcy's offering so great a sum might very reasonably have compensated Wickham for the sought-after living... and really, how dared Wickham confide so personal a matter to a comparative stranger in the first place?

The truth was that she had made a fool of herself over Wickham, with that beguiling manner of his, his superb figure, that little dimple in his chin – but never again would she permit herself to be so imposed upon. She would be a great deal more guarded in the future against men of his stamp, a man wicked enough to attempt to elope with Darcy's young sister!

As for Mr Darcy, *he* would do well to mend his manners, if so spoilt a fellow ever could! She felt a little heat in her cheeks upon recalling his self-assurance, even though she had behaved so very ill herself... But as he was shortly departing from Kent, and would probably never return to Hertfordshire, they were unlikely to ever meet again.

❦

Longbourn, Hertfordshire

'Lizzy returns tomorrow, I think,' said Lydia at breakfast. 'How long a time she has been in Kent! And would not it be very good fun if she was engaged upon her return?'

Mr Bennet shook his head. 'I have very little hope,' said he, 'of disposing of even one of my daughters much before luncheon.'

'I cannot *think*,' fretted Mrs Bennet, 'what has become of my pale pink ribbands. I have no notion where they might be!'

Mr Bennet shook his paper open and said knowingly, 'Perhaps Lydia might have seen them?'

'Oh, Lord!' cried that young lady.

And Kitty, rather nervously, coughed.

A Heliotrope Ribbon

'I am sure,' said she, 'I cried for two days together when Colonel Miller's regiment went away. I thought I should have broke my heart.'

'I am sure I shall break *mine*,' said Lydia.

'If one could but go to Brighton!' observed Mrs. Bennet.

'Oh yes!—if one could but go to Brighton! But papa is so disagreeable.'

'A little sea-bathing would set me up for ever.'

'And my aunt Philips is sure it would do *me* a great deal of good,' added Kitty.

(from *Pride and Prejudice*, Chapter 41)

'Oh heavens, it is Wickham again,' said Lydia to Mrs Forster, adding to that gentleman, 'And where have you been, this long age?'

'Are you sure you wish to know?' said he, with a little smile.

'I should *not* wish to know,' said Lydia impertinently, tapping his knee with her fan, 'for I am very sure that you have been up to no good… And so, does no one fancy attending me to the library?'

'A circulating library!' mocked Denny. 'What dog-eared volumes could it possess, worth the reading?'

'I shall not hear a word against the library,' said Mrs Forster. 'Thanks to it, Lydia and I have been enjoying quite the silliest book committed to print and laughing loud enough to be heard in Church Street!'

'What is the name of this masterpiece?'

'*The Castle of Otranto*!'

'Great heavens!' said Colonel Forster. 'Why, my own sister has read it.'

'She shares that honour,' said Wickham, 'with my poor self. And surely with you, Colonel?'

But Forster denied it. Upon which his wife pouted, 'He will never read any novel – which is why I insisted upon Lydia's being one of the party! For who would read plays and books with me, and be properly silly, else?'

'And I thought it was because I was your dearest friend!' cried Lydia.

'And so it was, I vow, but *that* is because you always make me laugh!'

'But,' said Colonel Forster, who felt most comfortably settled, 'What need have you of the circulating library, if you have already borrowed so edifying a tale as *The Castle of Otranto*? Unless you wish to be purchasing trinkets, either there or along the way, in which case I can comprehend its allure.'

'The library, I assure you, is merely an object,' said his wife.

'For who knows, lounging about here, what delicious curiosities we might observe on the Brighton promenade?' cried Lydia.

In the end, Lieutenants Denny and Wickham, Harriet Forster and Lydia Bennet set off. And as Colonel Forster watched his pretty wife retrieving her bonnet he thought, 'She is young, she is young indeed! And yet there is no harm in her. She is all agreeableness and amiability, instead.'

But when he recollected Lydia he did sigh a little, for she was not the intimate friend that he would have preferred his wife to have chosen. How unlike she was to her elder sisters! He had been quite smitten by Miss Bennet's softness while Miss Elizabeth's wit was almost as generally admired. Secretly, the Colonel believed Lydia more resembled her aunt, Mrs Philips – in her general boisterousness, particularly… He felt relieved when she was gone.

He felt concerned about Lieutenants Denny and Wickham, too. He had been reliably informed – for Brighton, despite its recent expansion, still boasted a village atmosphere – that they had been frequenting a few venues where serious gambling took place. He had promised himself to warn them about this at the first opportunity – though not before the ladies. Thus, the next time he chanced to be alone with Wickham, he said, 'I believe you made one of the party last Thursday at Mackay's?'

'I did,' said Wickham, 'though I never conceived my movements of any interest to anyone beyond myself.'

'Mackay's reputation, as you must know, is extremely bad.'

'Yet his events are so amusing!'

'Was Quigley there as well?'

'He was. Though one can generally contrive to avoid Quigley, however.'

The Colonel frowned. 'I would most strenuously advise that you do, my good fellow – for he has inveigled more officers into debt than most people can have any notion of.'

'You need not fret on my account, Colonel – I know enough to steer clear of the Quigleys of this world!'

'I hope you do, Wickham – I trust you do. And also, were I myself still unwed, I should be a bit less free with my attentions to the young ladies hereabouts, as well.'

'Really,' thought the amused Wickham, 'the colonel could be such a stick, at times!' But all he said was, 'You refer, I suppose, to Miss Johns? – for I have never been there above twice.'

'*She*, of course, is quite notorious – but, to say the truth, ever since the Prince has taken such a fancy to it, Brighton's character seems to have altered for the worse. The society ladies are greatly exercised about it.'

'Some people,' said Wickham drily, 'might attribute that to the militia itself!'

'It is true, amongst that better sort, there may be *some* believing that we are scarcely a force for good. But though some of the men may be a little uncouth, they could never rank with such fellows as Quigley or Mackay.'

After this conversation the Colonel allowed himself to feel reassured. Though he still fretted that Lieutenant Wickham was not perfectly reliable. He said as much to his wife that night as she prepared for bed.

'Heavens!' cried she, in mock indignation. 'I should hope that he is not reliable, for that would destroy his wicked charm at once, and he is *such* a favourite of mine and Lydia's! His compliments are so impish, and his dancing such perfection!'

'Yes, he seems to have a reputation with the ladies as being rather a dashing fellow.'

Harriet tossed her curls and said, 'Well, the others must do without him, for he is *our* particular pet!'

The Colonel could not help laughing. 'You cannot help being everyone's favourite, my dear, but take care that your friend Lydia does not compromise herself. For she is nearly as much the regimental pet as you are yourself!'

''Tis her sense of fun, I vow,' said his wife, brushing her pretty curls, 'for her complexion is not perfect.'

'Her complexion is well enough for the officers, for she seems half-besieged by them. But please recollect that – here, at least – we stand in place of her parents, and must be considered responsible.'

'Responsible!' she mocked, 'and for Lydia, besides! I should not take such a responsibility as *that* for a hundred guineas. And now, you must come and tickle my ankles.'

Once he saw that she was in no mood to be sensible, the Colonel dropped the subject. After all, he was concerned with military manoeuvres upon the Downs – as well as the tickling of ankles.

❦

'It is shocking,' said Lydia, 'how these society ladies arrive in such glorious gowns and clog up the balls so dreadfully!'

'It is not their fault that they are in society,' argued Harriet Forster. 'And some of their dresses are divine! That silvery silk of Mrs Turner's – and oh – Lady de Grey's roses!'

'I would give anything in the world for just one of Lady de Grey's confections,' said Lydia, 'though some of the others' gowns are very dull indeed. But how I wish that they would stay at home! For *they* have so many more opportunities of dancing in town than I am likely to enjoy, even in Brighton!'

'Nay, you must have sat down for all of two dances last Thursday!'

Lydia giggled. 'True, but at Longbourn I shall only have the silly Meryton assemblies to look forward to – and not a single officer to flirt with! How I wish Kitty was here, to see how many officers I dance with.'

'But with one officer, more than all the rest,' said Harriet Forster slyly.

'True, I did dance twice with Wickham on Tuesday. But *that* was a charity, for I saw that dreadful Mrs Johns making eyes at him. And so – and so I asked him to stand up with me!'

'You did not!' cried her scandalised friend.

'Well, I did *ask* him to ask me.'

'Lydia, you are impossible! Did your mama never teach you that it is only men who may request a dance?'

But Lydia did not laugh. Instead she said, very solemnly, 'I do believe, Harriet, that I may be falling in love. I have stoutly resisted – again and again – when I was fifteen, but now – truly, I think that I *might* be.'

Harriet hesitated. Lydia did not appear to be in jest. It might be true and – if it related to Wickham – Harriet did not want to believe it. This was partly because she did not wish to tell her husband, and partly due to certain, rather complicated, feelings about Wickham of her own. But before she could decide what to say, Lieutenant Denny was asking her to dance...

❖

My dear Kitty, How I wish you were here for everything is mighty <u>*delightful*</u>*! Because Brighton – not only the pavilion, but the sea-bathing, the company of the officers – but Brighton, itself – is so more pleasing than I ever imagined. The events, the atmosphere and the sea air are all so charming! And the balls are, in the main, so much better than our silly little dances at Meryton, for the quality of the people, the surroundings and the music, is so superior! Nor is that all, for I hardly have the chance to sit down and catch my breath, for Harriet and me are both so popular we need never sit down if we do not wish to!* <u>*There*</u> *is a change! To be sure, there is great disorder about the Prince's new mansion, the Marine Pavilion, which the Colonel thinks quite disgraceful. However, though the Prince himself has remained in London, there is a great deal going on and the dresses are beyond my describing – Lady de Grey's, especially. Not that it is all so superior, for a lady quite* *notorious, one Mrs Johns, dresses so shockingly that Mama would have ten thousand fits! And by the sea there are still dippers – horridly fat old ladies who immerse the infirm in the sea and hoist them out again – However, Harriet and me ignore them and enjoy the shallows on our own. Men and women swim apart, so it is all correct enough. Most of the ladies, especially those of the ton, dress with great discretion, and change properly... But now I must leave off, for Wickham and Denny have come to escort us to town...*

♭

The Forsters had not been married long before the Colonel's regiment was transferred, first to Meryton, and from there to Brighton.

The second-eldest daughter of a clergyman in a small Wiltshire town, Harriet had early rather chafed against her fate, having a vivid nature, an infinite gift for finding routine matters dull, and an immense frustration with the small town in which she had been born. The arrival of the regiment had quite entranced her, and – rather like Lydia – she had rapidly and delightedly fallen in love with officer after officer.

To her father's intense relief, however, she soon found herself courted by Colonel Forster, the kind of mature and logical fellow capable of giving young Harriet the guidance so young and skittish a bride required.

If Harriet's father was relieved, however, Colonel Forster occasionally wished that he had not been quite so precipitate. At eighteen, Harriet was beautiful, generous, and affectionate – but also rather flighty. He was acutely conscious, as she never seemed to be, of the glances, the rolled eyes, of the officers' wives, when she appeared in a ballroom, of the rather frigid courtesies of those regimental spouses whom they encountered on the street. Part of this, he supposed, must be jealousy... Harriet, with her light hair and hazel eyes, was so very pretty!

But the criticisms such ladies might scruple to make of the Colonel's wife her inseparable companion could never escape. In short, Lydia was every bit as unpopular with the regimental ladies as she was favoured by the officers, who unanimously considered her 'unstuffy, unaffected and quite excellent fun'.

As he entered the ball one evening with Harriet and Lydia, the Colonel observed Colonel Pearson's wife whispering spitefully to Mrs Carter. He was pleased to see the solid Captain Carter beg Harriet to dance, if rather less delighted to observe Wickham, with equal alacrity, securing Lydia Bennet. Truly, he might better have saved his breath as far as Wickham and ladies were concerned! But how well the fellow looked, smartly attired, the tallest man in the room, and the handsomest...

'How the old cats stare!' Lydia said, with a laugh. 'Have they have never seen any couple stand up to dance before?'

'Let them stare,' said Wickham lazily, 'for no one will likely ask to stand up with them, for Mrs Carter is about as scraggy as a fox, and Mrs Pearson very little better.'

'But not nearly as *thin*,' said Lydia.

'Neither can compare with any of the truly fine-looking young women in the room.'

'Have you any particular woman in mind?' she asked archly.

'I have the greatest respect and admiration,' said Wickham gravely, 'for the Colonel's wife, Mrs Forster –'

'Oh! You are quite impossible!' cried Lydia crossly.

'– and for her dearest friend–'

'Well, *that* is very much better!'

'– to my mind, the prettiest of all the famous Bennet sisters.'

'Oh, fie!' cried Lydia, very well-pleased. 'For as everyone knows, Jane is *much* the prettiest. 'Tis only after Jane that there are arguments!'

'Miss Bennet is exceedingly attractive,' said Wickham astutely, 'but lacks fire.'

'Well, *Lizzy* has fire, at least!'

At this, rather a shadow crossed his handsome face, for Wickham had – at one point – greatly admired Elizabeth Bennet and had even been in some danger of becoming besotted with her. She might still, depending upon his mood, be described as his secret ideal – if only she had money! But as she had not, he said, 'Miss Elizabeth is too satirical. A bit like our sour Mrs Pearson in years to come, I suspect!'

Lydia secretly felt this rather unfair. Her own feelings about Wickham varied with the weather. At times she felt that he was perfectly charming, as well as incontestably the handsomest fellow she had ever been in company with. But her sense of justice was strong. In truth, despite her reckless air, Lydia was quite an innocent creature... She had been shocked as well as titillated when Harriet had drawn her attention to a famous adulteress in a Brighton tea shop, and had turned round several times to get a fuller view...

My dear Kitty, I have just written to Mama, but of course I could tell them almost nothing! It is wretchedly dull today for there is no ball and the officers are all busy with silly manoeuvres on the Downs. We did watch for a bit, for Harriet had told the Colonel that we should, but, from a distance, one cannot tell one officer from another, though the townspeople and some of the ton, and what Harriet calls the quasi-ton, bring luncheon baskets and seem to find it diverting enough. Yesterday we saw a race at sea – that was far more amusing than the manoeuvres. Two of the craft collided and tipped over – how we laughed! Harriet and me spend a good deal of time exploring the walks and wandering about the shops, though of course we can afford almost nothing, for the Colonel gives Harriet very little more to spend than we get ourselves. How I dream of marrying high and being properly attended to in such shops as these! And – who knows? – it might yet happen, for Lieutenant Pratt's father owns land in the Indies – though you know whom I prefer, even to dear Pratt...

Lydia was walking with Mrs Forster's maid the next day when she encountered Wickham bidding adieu to companions outside a coffee house. Now women did not usually frequent such places – not that there was any harm in them, or so Harriet Forster believed. Wickham begged to know where she was going.

Lydia took his arm, and airily dismissed Sally. 'Mrs Forster is engaged,' said she, 'while I was just admiring the bonnets in that shop. If only we had such shops as these in Meryton!'

Wickham smiled in his saturnine fashion, for the shop in question was full of what he considered fripperies. But he said, and very handsomely, for he had just won at billiards, 'I have no objection to attending you inside.'

'What an angel you are! I must only *look*, however. But is not that a divine little purse, with embroidered roses?'

Wickham could see nothing divine about it, and instead asked the shopgirl whether they had not any finer ribbons. She blushed, moved to a drawer, and emerged with some very lovely ribbons. However, Lydia lingered so long before some shades of heliotrope that he grew bored enough to say, 'My dear Miss Bennet, if you admire them to such an extent as that why, I shall buy some for you!'

Lydia turned shining eyes upon him.

A HELIOTROPE RIBBON

('Really she was not at all an ill-looking girl,' thought he.)

'Oh heavens no, for *that* would not be proper,' said Lydia, vaguely remembering her mother's admonitions regarding gifts. But perhaps she had misremembered? And the heliotrope, close to, made her eyes seem so vivid a blue! And the cost was nothing, really, to any officer of the militia.

Wickham said gravely, 'Ribbons, I assure you, are perfectly proper, especially when one considers how well the colour suits you.'

'Oh! Well, in that case – if you *do* buy me a ribbon or two – why I shall never forget you. Every time I wear them, whether here or in Meryton, I shall think of you!'

Wickham smiled and paid for the ribbons, which the assistant bound up in a neat little parcel. As they left the shop Lydia said impudently, 'Well then, what have you done with my ribbons? I hope you are not going to give them to some other blue-eyed lady!'

'I have not the slightest intention of doing so,' said he, glancing round to ensure that no member of the regiment was about. 'But first you must pay me for them. Though not with money.'

'But how else could one pay for anything?'

'My currency differs from most people's,' said Wickham boldly. 'I wish to be paid… with a kiss.'

This was just the kind of flirting that Lydia liked. She was about to make some arch comment when she found herself – kissed. Colour flooded her face at the sensation – so often imagined, but never experienced before.

'Why, how dare you!' she demanded delightedly.

'What, did not you like it? At any rate, *here* is your reward!' And with that, he tucked the flat little parcel beneath her lace fichu about her neck, just stroking the skin beneath.

Lydia laughed. 'Oh, you are impossible! You do realise that you are impossible?'

'I have often enough been told so.'

'So, do you make a habit of kissing ladies, then?'

'Only if they are excessively pretty.'

'And do they never object?'

'That depends,' said Wickham judiciously.

'Upon the quality of the kiss?'

'Upon the quality' said he, 'of the lady.'

Then Captain Carter's judgemental wife came into view, with her emphatic, bustling stride. Instinctively, Lydia dropped Wickham's arm. It occurred to her that it might perhaps look a little odd for them to be observed together in the centre of Brighton. But how delightfully impertinent he was!

With the sea breeze blowing her about, she feared for her light little parcel. She put the ribbons in her pocket, and they were both excessively merry all the way home.

Later, she thought, 'It was true that he had taken advantage… but how charmingly he had taken it!' And the ribbons so perfectly suited her colouring and truly, he had been so very often at Longbourn as to be quite the friend of all the family. Had not she once heard her father recommend Wickham to Lizzy as a man agreeable enough to 'jilt her creditably?'

And then, the kiss had been so very nice! She wished he could have kissed her rather longer, despite rather uneasily recollecting a scene at Longbourn a fortnight before…

✦

'My dearest Lydia, now that you are going away, and without any of your sisters, I beg you to recollect that you must never let a man touch you disrespectfully.'

'But, my dear Mama, how am I to recognise disrespect, even if it should happen?'

Jane said, 'I believe she means what I experienced in London, when I was almost sixteen. I was at a box in the Little Theatre when some man just – just took my hand and kissed it.'

'The same fellow who wrote those verses on you?' asked Lydia eagerly.

'No, not he. But it did not feel quite – right – to me.'

'Nonsense! The kissing of *hands* is always acceptable,' said their mother. 'It is a kiss *elsewhere* which is not. A gentleman ought never to risk such behaviour of course but, as my sister Philips complains, a few of the militia *will* take a drop of liquor more than they ought. Which is why, Lydia, you must never allow yourself to be alone with one.'

'With a drop of liquor?' joked Lydia.

'Ha ha, very clever, my love!'

Lizzy sighed. 'What Mama *means* is that you must not allow yourself to be alone with any man, lest he might be tempted to take liberties.'

'Lizzy is quite in the right. And so I beg that you take care, Lydia, for men are deceivers ever. Also, you must never accept presents from a man, particularly not a jewel or an ornament, for *then* they are bound to try to take advantage. I remember, years ago – but never mind!'

'What about when a man chooses to take advantage in public?' asked Jane. 'Again in London, an acquaintance of our uncle's once offered me his arm, but then he pressed mine so very hard, and fondled my hand so – and even said something about my eyes – until I knew not where to look!'

'I am very sorry to hear it,' said her mother. 'An acquaintance of your uncle's ought to have been more genteel! But *you* were not to blame, my love. To take a man's arm is always proper, whether in town or in the country.'

'The comment about your eyes however,' said Mary, 'ought rather to have been censored. Had I been you, Jane, I should have said, "Such comments are most distasteful to me, Mr so-and-so. I bid you guard your tongue better."'

'Lord!' laughed Lydia, shaking her head. 'Were I to tell off dear Denny or Pratt in such a fashion, I should never be asked to dance again!'

'I believe,' said Lizzy, 'in tailoring the rebuke to the offense. At my very first Merton ball a man pulled me so hard towards the set that I said, "I must dance ill indeed, for you to think me in need of such support as this!"'

Jane laughed but added, 'Truly, a single look can sometimes suffice.'

'But a rebuke must be still more persuasive,' argued Mary, 'for looks can be misconstrued. *I* should suggest saying, if imposed upon, "Unhand me, sir!" – for that is brief, clear and to the point.'

Then Lydia barked, 'Unhand me, sir!' in such theatrical style that her mother and Kitty both burst out laughing...

Back in her room in Brighton, Lydia decided that, while the gifting of a heliotrope ribbon must be acceptable for, to be sure, it was no jewel, a kiss might still be considered 'taking advantage'. But she could not help wishing that Wickham might be emboldened by the experiment to take advantage again. It had been so very nice!

※

Wickham was promenading along the Steyne with Denny and Pratt. They were abusing the taste of the Prince in a fashion which that royal personage would have been less than pleased to hear when a rather ill-kempt man approached them.

'Mr Wickham!'

'Be off with you,' said Pratt, in disgust. 'You reek of snuff! And we have no coins to give you!'

'True enough,' said Wickham grimly, 'but walk on, I beg. I shall be with you in a moment.'

Denny and Pratt walked on while Wickham said to the man, in an undertone, 'Here is a guinea. The rest by Friday.'

'But 'tis *nine* guineas you are owing!' said the man, raising his voice. 'And you promised Mr Quigley the whole by last Friday!'

'Not so loud, man! – Until Friday, I swear it.'

The fellow's lips thinned unpleasantly. 'A debt of honour, Wickham –'

'Yes, yes, but what can a few days matter?'

'A few days! –'Tis a fortnight already! And just recollect what happened to Manson!'

'Do not dare to threaten me!' said Wickham coldly. 'You know that I will pay you. And do not dare to address me when I am with my friends, either!'

'I have my orders, same as you,' sneered the other. And then, with a curl of lip. 'Would be shocking, would it not, for you to have so sad an accident as poor Manson did?'

Wickham stalked off to rejoin his colleagues.

'Good Lord, Wickham! When did you start befriending every beggar in Brighton?'

'And so snuffy a b——, besides!'

But Wickham was in no mood for raillery. How confoundedly annoying it was to be so constantly in need of money – and how infuriating to recall that Darcy, who could so easily have amended his situation, was as rich as a lord! He had occasionally considered attempting a rapprochement but, after the overt contempt with which Darcy had treated him in Hertfordshire, he suspected that *that* would never answer. He had considered approaching Georgiana – she had the kindest heart – but Darcy had made it painfully clear that even a letter would never be tolerated. (He had twice encountered her accidentally in town – how violently she had paled!)

At least in London he still had a few contacts willing to loan him money. He might have to resort to these, in order to make Brighton endurable – for without the spice of the occasional gamble, it was confoundedly dull being buried in Sussex, instead of in town. Worse, there seemed to be no wealthy woman in Brighton whom he might hope to ensnare into marriage. Society here was too confoundedly small, the kind of place where everyone knew – or pretended to know – everyone else's business. His chance of captivating some rich woman would have been much fairer in London – and fairer still in Paris or Vienna…

'What d'you suppose is amiss with Wickham?' asked Pratt later, of Denny.

'Money. Or rather, the lack of it!'

'Well, *that* the same for us all.'

'But worse, I think, for those brought up with expectations,' said Denny thoughtfully. 'I mean, a proper school and living at Pemberley – which they say is as fine as a castle! And with Wickham treated almost as a relative by Darcy's father, besides! *We* might be hard-up and never feel it. It is not the same with Wickham.'

❖

'Colonel,' Mrs Carter told him, standing up very straight and speaking in the emphatic fashion he most detested, 'I *believe* it only right that you should know that I *myself* saw *Miss Bennet* walking with *Lieutenant Wickham*, just along Ship Street. And laughing and shrieking and generally making a *great deal* of noise.'

The Colonel's heart misgave him, but he said, 'I was already aware of their encounter, ma'am, for she mentioned it herself at supper that evening. However, so far as I am aware, there is no law against young men and young ladies walking along Ship Street – or even on North Street, itself!'

The feathers on Mrs Carter's bonnet bobbed in a displeased manner.

'My dear Colonel, I entirely *fail to comprehend* your attitude in this matter. Truly, I am doing you a *favour*, by observing that a *young lady* – a rather *empty-headed* young lady, by all accounts – and one entirely under *your protection* – was seen in public, unattended, with an officer of your own!'

Colonel Forster was a patient man, but he had just endured a dressing-down from his superior about several men of his regiment having been drunk and disorderly. While he so detested her style of speech that he could not help wondering how Captain Carter could bear it.

He said, 'First, ma'am, allow me to inform you that Miss Lydia is a very good kind of girl, and not the sort to get into trouble. Second, the Bennets are a most respectable family. I knew them well, myself, in Hertfordshire. And finally, Mr Wickham is well-known to all Miss Bennet's family. I cannot count the number of times we supped together at Longbourn!'

'You are entitled, Colonel, to your own opinion of *both* young people, I daresay. But, as I said to my husband, it is quite *shocking* the way some officers behave, and a *great many* of the enlisted men besides, and as for *Lydia* Bennet – I know nothing of the *rest* of the family – she is *quite* the loudest young lady in Brighton. I had to *cover my ears* by the seaside the other day! Whilst I overheard some *quite shocking* gossip, just last Wednesday – or perhaps it was Tuesday – about *Lieutenant Wickham*.'

The Colonel seized his chance.

'Yet Dame Gossip, as you must know, is wrong as often as she is right! In short, I greatly appreciate your kind concern but – I assure you – there is nothing to be concerned about.'

Later, the Colonel imitated the worthy Mrs Carter's emphatic style of delivery, until his wife rolled about on the bed, laughing. But then he grew serious again. 'I fear that there is some ill-feeling abroad against the militia. I remain mortified about their behaviour last Wednesday and fully intend to track down every man responsible. But Wickham is no one's idea of a fool.'

'And everyone's idea of a flirt,' added his wife, with a laugh. 'Did Mrs Carter truly cover her ears?'

'So she said.'

'How I wish I had been there! And now, do come to bed, my love, for my tiny toes are chilled and you must warm them!'

⁜

Lydia first wore the heliotrope ribbons at Thursday's ball though, upon glancing around she was disappointed not to see Wickham. He arrived while she was dancing with Denny.

'Ah! There he is, at last!'

'Who, Wickham? But he is always late!'

'That is very true, but still annoying, when we could have been flirting this long half-hour already!'

'Do you think of nothing but flirting, my dear Miss Bennet?'

'Why… oh! He has asked the new lady to stand up with him. Do you know her?'

'I know *of* her – a little. She is a Mrs Townsend, a widow with a very good jointure, a property at Hove and a house in town.'

Lydia pouted. 'But what is she like? Is she as charming as Harriet and me?'

'I have never been introduced to the lady, but surely *that* is not possible!'

Lydia sneaked another glance. 'Her face is too thin.'

'Quite, but she is not actually plain. And – to be blunt – perhaps our friend Wickham cannot afford to be so very particular.'

Lydia was silent. Finally she said, 'Do you truly think that Wickham would marry for money? For nothing in all the world could be more odious, I think!'

Denny laughed and said rather dryly, 'Do you perhaps recollect, when we were all back in Meryton, a girl called Miss King? A tall girl?'

'Indeed, really too tall – and too pale. And as dull as ditchwater!'

'Perhaps so, but her fortune – of £10,000 or thereabouts – proved so captivating to Wickham that he certainly wooed her and would have wedded her, if he could. But once her guardian got wind of the notion he whisked her away… I should suppose Mrs Townsend *twice* as well-off as Mary King – and not an ill-looking woman, either.'

Lydia was not so well-satisfied with this conversation as to continue it, though Denny noticed that she looked again, and rather more thoughtfully, at Mrs Townsend. Very demurely attired, she was a little woman and neatly made, but lacking in both complexion and countenance.

'She looks prudish,' Lydia said, at last.

'Ah yes! I recollect now. She is an evangelical.'

'And what is *that*?'

Denny laughed. '*You* would not care for them, Miss Lydia! Evangelicals believe that one should never stir of a Sunday – scarcely from one chair to the next – and that we are only put on earth to read the Bible. I have not the slightest doubt that the lady sponsors missionaries in foreign parts and thoroughly disapproves the Book of Common Prayer – I mean, for being unbiblical.'

Lydia began to feel a little better. Hard as she might, she could not imagine her friend Wickham liking so strict a lady, for he often travelled on Sundays, and sometimes made jokes about the Bible. However, he still deserved punishment for having asked Mrs Townsend to dance and so, when he, twinkling, begged her to stand up with him, she tossed her curls and recommended he 'ask Mrs Townsend, instead!'

'No,' said he very gravely, 'for she is sporting not a single heliotrope ribbon, and you must know that I only care for ladies wearing heliotrope – and with eyes to match!'

'Do you truly like the ribbons?'

'Why, did not I myself buy them, for a kiss?' Lydia tried to blush but was unable. The amused Wickham added, 'They suit you very well.'

'Better than Mrs Townsend's pearls suit Mrs Townsend?'

'Why, there can be no comparison, the ribbons are so irresistible! And she is elderly, besides.'

'Oh! yes – I should think her nearly thirty,' said Lydia, to whom this seemed a very great age indeed.

'Then, pray, stand up with me.'

'I suppose I must then, as no other officer has had the common politeness to ask me!'

Meanwhile, Mrs Townsend confided to her friend Mrs Edmondson, 'I find Mr Wickham personable, but I *have* heard that he is without a penny. Do you happen to know if this is true?'

Her friend lowered her voice. 'I believe it to be very true indeed. The late Mr Darcy loved him dearly, but the *present* Mr Darcy cannot abide him. Still, his manners are much admired – in Brighton, at least.'

Later that evening Wickham risked Lydia's displeasure by asking Mrs Townsend to dance again. The lady hesitated at first but then accepted, and after a few minutes of inconsequential discourse, inquired, 'I understand you are Derbyshire-born, Mr Wickham?'

'I am,' said he, a shadow crossing his handsome countenance. 'And years ago, I was promised a most excellent living in that county but – unluckily – the donor died before I was in a position to take it. His son disposed of the living – no doubt, for a tidy profit! But there – it is the way of the world!'

'You wished to be a clergyman, then?'

'It was my dearest wish,' said Wickham, without being struck by lightning on the spot. 'But alas – it was not to be.' And he made his expression as noble as possible.

'Yet the church must be reckoned difficult enough, without the security of a living!'

'So I understand. After that I attempted the law, but – between ourselves – I found the morals of those in the profession extraordinarily disheartening. I was forever being passed over. Ability and discipline seemed to count for nothing while, if born an idle young dandy with high connections, one's prosperity was guaranteed!'

'I do pity you, Mr Wickham, most sincerely.'

'I am grateful, ma'am. And thus, with my last pittance, I procured a commission, despite having been designed for higher things.'

'It seems a very well-ordered regiment.'

'My fellow officers are an excellent body of men – but some of the enlisted troops cause us no little concern. Why, just the other evening there was a distressing incident not a hundred yards from hence!'

'I believe I heard something about it,' said Mrs Townsend.

'Exceedingly disrespectful remarks were made – and to ladies, besides.' Wickham sighed. 'It is heavy work, ma'am, to teach manners to such fellows as these!'

'But surely, they are not bad at heart?' asked she anxiously.

'No, ma'am, they are not – though some, even many, are in desperate need of religious instruction. But far from all! Far from all! I have myself loaned one promising young fellow a book of John Donne's.'

'Oh, Mr Wickham! You could not have done better, you could not, indeed! – I hope it was the book of Holy Sonnets. Tell me that it was his Holy Sonnets!'

Wickham smiled – a very different smile from the one with which he had – and so recently – favoured Lydia.

'How did you guess, ma'am? – for *they* have ever been my favourite.'

As Mrs Townsend told Mrs Edmondson later, he seemed a perfectly well-behaved young man, and one 'not lacking in serious feeling'.

As they returned to the barracks, Lydia mercilessly mocked Wickham for his attentions to the widow, observing, 'And truly, she ought never to have been dancing at all, for they say her husband has only been dead these nine months!'

'No,' said he, 'it has been above two years. And she puts me so in mind of my dear mama!' – though she did not. But Lydia, squeezing his arm, assured him that he was entirely forgiven.

❖

Colonel Forster permitted himself a little wit at Wickham's expense, upon receiving a letter from Mrs Townsend the next afternoon, 'What, and so you told the good widow that the men required more piety, did you?'

'No, no, 'tis too much to recall in daylight the arrant nonsense of the night before! Besides, one is obliged to do the civil thing, while dancing.'

'I cannot conceive what made you ask the lady in the first place! Still, a few godly pamphlets can do the men no harm – I suppose they will make paper darts from them. You admire this Mrs – let me see – Townsend, do you?'

'Not in the least. She is perilously dull, as you can see from her note, but she puts me in mind of my dear mother.'

'And I had thought you could scarcely remember her!'

'I remember her,' said Wickham, shaking his head, 'quite well enough.'

❦

'I fear that I have promised to visit a fellow I was once at school with, near to Hove,' said Wickham, when refusing to accompany the ladies to an afternoon concert.

'Who is this tiresome fellow?' said Harriet, pouting.

'His name is Patchett,' said Wickham – the only schoolmate's name that he could immediately recall, beyond Darcy's.

'And he lives at Hove?'

'Near to Hove, I believe. He lost a leg in France.'

'Well,' said Lydia, 'the concert will be very poor fun without you! Should I send Sally to fetch Denny, Harriet?'

'Oh, yes! Pray do – and Pratt, as well.'

Wickham rode off, thinking affectionately, 'What a sweet, silly creature Miss Lydia is, though amusing, all the same!' But then he strove to remember all that he had heard or could surmise about Mrs Townsend, the person on whom he truly intended to call. He had taken a great deal of trouble to procure an invitation, for – 'I am scarcely out of mourning, Mr Wickham, and have very few visitors' – but she had relented upon his mentioning her volumes of poetry.

The house was modern, standing on gently sloping ground not far from the sea. He found the lady reading a well-thumbed copy of the Psalms, which she put down at once.

'Mr Wickham! I had not imagined that you would take so early an opportunity to call.'

'I do not wish to intrude, ma'am. But I have been visiting a poor fellow who lost his leg, not far from here. A regimental acquaintance.'

'How very good of you! However, I must admit to encouraging very few visitors,' said she, adding to the butler, 'Do bring the tea at once, if you please. I am excessively sensitive to atmosphere, Mr Wickham, and do not wish the serenity of the vibrations disturbed.'

'I understand.'

'But an admirer of Donne is rather different – I was most struck by what you said, about Donne's passion for awakening.'

'Indeed,' said Wickham, '"And we sleep all the way; from the womb to the grave/ we are never thoroughly awake."'

'I expect he was referring to our sad feebleness in faith.'

'I am quite convinced of it.'

'Although my beloved husband always maintained… Oh, thank you, Betty. I hope you will have a little tea, Mr Wickham, though it may be a trifle weak for you, just at present. Perhaps you might let it brew a little longer?'

Mr Wickham had a little tea.

He had never been more bored in the entire course of his existence.

✦

Wickham, I must trouble you for the thirteen guineas you promised last Friday. If you fail again, consider this a warning. Josiah Quigley, Esq.

Wickham failed to recognise the men who brought the note but had no difficulty guessing who had sent them, and why. The first was a navvy, roped with muscle, his companion wiry and piratical, a harsh scar across his hand.

'One moment,' said Wickham, perspiring. He was relieved to find that he still possessed some of his winnings from the previous night – these, amounting to four guineas, he handed to the fellow.

'What! Is this all?'

'Ah – yes, just at the moment. I should have the rest – shortly.'

'We was told 'tis your *last* warning!'

'Tomorrow,' said Wickham fervently. 'Tomorrow, I swear it, as I live and breathe!'

The heavier man stepped forward, shoved his thumb against Wickham's chin and pressed upwards. Pain shot dizzily up his jaw, then the man stepped back.

'Tomorrow,' said he, 'or –'

'Tomorrow!' promised Wickham, fervently massaging his jaw.

Once they had gone, Denny returned from Colonel Forster's lodgings.

'You were greatly mourned,' said he, 'by both Mrs Forster and Miss Bennet. Oh, and one of Quigley's fellows was seeking you in the mess, as smelly a creature as I ever struck. Were you at Mackay's?'

'I was not,' said Wickham, who had been enduring Mrs Townsend's views on Donne's 'Death be not proud' – of which his own opinion was that Donne must have had a skinful when he wrote it.

'Well, I should advise you to show your face at the ball tonight, or be cut ever after – by Miss Lydia Bennet, at least!'

Wickham thought feverishly, 'Dancing! What good is dancing? – It is money I want! And without it…' He stood up and pulled on his coat.

'What, are you off *again*?'

'Tell Miss Bennet I shall come to the ball,' he said, and flung himself out of the room. Denny stared but Pratt joked, 'He looked as if he had seen the ghost of Hamlet's father!'

'Money, d'you think?' asked Denny.

'Down to his last farthing. But Wickham's like a cat – he always lands on his feet!'

⁂

Mrs Townsend was both startled and displeased to be informed that Mr Wickham had returned. She was a lady exceedingly conscious of appearances, and – delightful as he was – two visits in the space of several hours had a strange appearance, particularly in a young officer calling upon a widowed lady. Before admitting him, she resolved to tell him so.

'Mr Wickham, again! Why, has something occurred since I last had the pleasure of your company?'

'No, ma'am, not at all. It is merely that I have come to a decision.'

'About the poor enlisted invalid of whom you spoke, the one who lost his leg?'

'No, not Patchett.'

'I had thought his name was Patchley?'

'Your pardon, I must have misspoke before. But my errand is not about Patchett, poor fellow!'

'He is dying?' she asked anxiously.

'No, it is I who is dying, ma'am!'

She almost jumped. 'What, have you weak lungs?' – for her husband had perished of this complaint.

'No, ma'am,' said Wickham intensely, 'I am perfectly well in myself, but I am dying of love, for you!'

'Why, Mr Wickham!'

He fell to one knee and captured her unresisting hand. 'Have pity on my state, I beg! I can neither eat, nor sleep, nor do my work, for thinking of your sweetness, your angelic expressions, your gentle goodness!'

'Mr Wickham, we have not known each other a fortnight!' she cried, as he thought how sheeplike her narrow face was.

'Ten minutes,' said Wickham fervently, 'might have been enough!'

'And, as well, I could never possibly agree! Why my beloved Jacob was only buried two years, three weeks and two –'

'I assure you, not a soul will know of our engagement, beyond ourselves,' said he, his warm hands cupping hers. 'Not a single soul!'

She rose, distressed, but also moved and obscurely gratified. 'Oh! 'Tis far too sudden – I had never once imagined... *My* ardent hope, Mr Wickham, was that you and I might – between us – contrive some reformation in the men about whom you care so deeply. I never once thought – oh, never!'

He thought disgustedly, 'All my delicate insinuations, then, were entirely lost!' But, recollecting Quigley, all he said was, 'So there is no hope at all then, that at some point in the future, you might – conceivably – consider –'

'Truly, I do not know, Mr Wickham,' said the lady faintly. 'However – it is, I daresay, an old-fashioned view – but my period of mourning feels but just begun!'

'I understand,' he murmured, secretly cursing her stupidity, for how could any woman breathing have failed to comprehend his gentle gallantries? However, as it was as well to keep every possibility open, he said, 'Mrs Townsend, such feeling does your heart the greatest credit, and only serves to inflame my admiration more! Forgive my importunity, I beg, and permit me to hope!'

She hesitated. 'Should it be God's will, Mr Wickham! But now, while thanking you for the honour of your kind esteem, I fear that I must bid you adieu.' And she extended her hand in quite a definite farewell.

As Wickham rode off, he thought bitterly, 'I would have done a good deal better to have tried to extract some sum for the legless Patchett! Still, if I can only extricate myself from this quagmire, she should be easily enough managed! But what the devil am I to do for money?'

And in the end, he rode directly to the only Brighton moneylender with whom he still had credit. Mr Sidney was doing accounts in his office – coatless, cravat awry, sleeves rolled up to his elbows. He glanced up as Wickham entered and shook his head. 'I hear you have annoyed our friend Quigley.'

Wickham swore.

'You are far from alone,' said Sidney, consolingly. 'Though he is not a fellow I would recommend anyone to fall foul of!'

'The truth is, I have no time to waste,' said Wickham. 'I need

152

the money by tomorrow.'

'How much?'

'Between nine and ten.'

Sidney whistled. 'Pounds or guineas?'

'Guineas.'

'It cannot be done! – not in the time.'

As Wickham turned to go, Sidney said, 'There might be some chance if Quigley –'

'I thank you, but no,' said Wickham, and flung himself out. He thought briefly of Mrs Johns – he had won a good deal at her house soon after the regiment's arrival – but not even *he* could win such a sum in a single evening, especially since the local gamblers had by now a wary respect for his skill.

At Castle Tavern the fiddles would be tuning up, the ball beginning... A curse on it! – he was in no mood for dancing. But then, just as swiftly, he changed his mind. Most of Brighton society would be there – some sportsman might still bail him out. It was either that – or flight! He provisionally booked a carriage, in case he continued unlucky, his handsome lips set in a thin line as he changed into a fresh uniform and combed his curling hair.

At Castle Tavern he was just giving Mrs Carter a rather sardonic bow – they detested each other – when pretty Lydia Bennet rushed up to him. 'How dare you be so late, you wicked thing? I had begun to think that you would never arrive, and that I should be obliged to stand up with every ugly creature in the room!'

'But how could I resist, knowing that you and Harriet would be here?'

'You have not been at Hove, again? You can never have wasted this long age with some silly schoolfriend!'

'I am one of the few people I know,' said Wickham, with heavy irony, 'who persists in doing the proper thing, regardless of self. So says my friend, at any rate! In fact, tonight I go to town, on his behalf. But that is a secret, my dear Miss Lydia. You must not breathe a syllable to a single soul!'

'To *town* – but why? And why is it to be so secret?'

'I dare not tell the Colonel, lest permission be denied, and I obliged to let down poor Patchley.'

'Patchley? I had thought you said Patchett?'

'Nay,' said Wickham hastily, 'his name is Patchley.'

'Well! I still think you are using me very ill,' said Lydia, with a coquettish toss of her head, and he escorted her to the set. And as they wended their way back, part of a merry throng of militiamen and young ladies – she asked tenderly, 'When will you be coming back? Tuesday or Wednesday, perhaps?'

'Can you keep a secret, my dear Miss Bennet?'

Lydia hesitated, for she had never kept a secret in all her life. However, there was no reason why she should not begin, for had she not already promised not to tell Harriet that he was leaving? She said, 'Why, of course!'

Wickham drew her into a little side-alley. She had a fleeting recollection of her mother's strictures – for they were entirely alone, with high brick walls on both sides, and the rest walking onward without them.

'I leave Brighton tonight,' said Wickham recklessly.

'So you said already, you silly creature! But when will you return?'

'I shall never return, Lydia.'

'What!' she cried, divided between pleasure at his use of her given name and a thrill of fear at the violence of his manner.

'I shall never live in this hellhole more! Instead, I go to town and thence to Paris.'

'You cannot mean,' said Lydia, very white, 'that you intend to leave the country?'

'I must!'

'Then – then – why then, you must take me with you!'

He laughed, astonished, amused and even a little moved. 'You are mad, for *that* must be impossible! And with your every connection chasing me, besides! I only thought, just now, that since we must part –'

'No, my dear, my dearest Wickham, you must listen! If we were to leave tonight for town, we should be ahead of any pursuit by hours!'

'Such is my ardent hope!'

'And a couple, you know, is much less noticeable on the road than any single officer would be!'

'I daresay that is true, and yet –'

'For *you* might be thought to be deserting. And we could easily get married in London! For who would know us there?'

'But it would only cause still more trouble and difficulties – and for us both! No, just one kiss – for luck – and I shall be off.'

'What is a kiss,' cried Lydia fiercely, 'compared to love? I love you, Wickham! I cannot live without you! And if you leave England – I know it – I should never see you more!'

Wickham was worked upon. He had often enough captured ladies' hearts, but the heart of so young, lively and innocent a creature! And it was not only her affection. He thought, 'To have a companion would make me less conspicuous, as well as less lonely, for what would any lieutenant be doing fleeing, else?' Her face so imploring – so soft and pretty in the shadows – and it was entirely her own suggestion – and her father so idle a fellow! It would take his mind from the business, at least for a moment! And her eyes shining!

'Well, come if you like, but you must be quick!'

'Oh Wickham!' cried Lydia, kissing him in ecstasy.

'A quarter of an hour,' warned he, 'and not a moment longer! You must be at the gate in a quarter of an hour.'

But it was half-an-hour before she arrived, her cloak pulled round her, breathless with excitement. He had just determined to order the coachman not to wait – but he relented when he saw her cheeks flushed with joy in the dim light and did not reproach her.

'Quickly,' said he, 'for we have no time to spare!' and he pulled her inside. He could not relax until they were beyond the city boundaries – well past North Street, with all its little shops fast shut – and cantering steadily up the London Road. Then, in sheer relief at his escape, he grasped her hand and squeezed it. It was a very warm hand. Exhilarated – even transported – with relief at having left Quigley's men behind him, he put his hand inside her gown and caressed her breast, fastening his lips onto her own.

Just as dawn was breaking, the Forsters were awoken by a wild rapping on their door.

'Colonel, Colonel!' shouted his corporal.

'Why, man! Whatever is the matter?'

''Tis Wickham, sir. The captain says as he is gone!'

'Gone? Gone where? – to London, do you mean?'

'Why sir, it must be so, for 'is trunk is gone and all else besides!'

'I am coming,' said the Colonel grimly, lighting his candle and reaching for his trousers.

'Why, whatever is happening?' asked Harriet sleepily, as her husband tightened his belt and glanced round for his coat.

'I do not know, but I *suspect* that Wickham has fled his creditors!'

'His creditors?'

'He owes a fair amount,' said Forster grimly, pulling on his boots. 'Denny may know something of the particulars. But whether he has gone to town or to France or even to the colonies –'

'The colonies! What – and without telling you?'

'Of course not, for *I* should have put a stop to it! It is the last thing we need, with matters as they are, for officers to desert, leaving debts of honour behind them!'

'Poor, poor Lydia!' cried his wife, curling down cosily again. 'She is so fond of him, that she will feel it a great deal – and he *is* an amusing fellow!'

But the Colonel had already departed.

He had been gone only a quarter of an hour, and his wife was drowsing again when she heard a hurried knock.

'Ma'am!' cried Sally, ''Tis a note for you, and from Miss Lydia!'

'What,' said Harriet crossly, 'has she gone out so early, then?'

'Oh, ma'am! I cannot tell you.'

'Whyever not?'

'You must read it, indeed you must!'

'Well then, I shall, if you only give it me!'

My dear Harriet, You will laugh when you know where I am gone, and I cannot help laughing myself at your surprise tomorrow morning, when I am missed. I am going to Gretna Green, and if you cannot guess with who, I shall think you a simpleton, for there is but one man in the world I love, and he is an angel! I should never be happy without him, so think it no harm to be off. You need not

*send them word at Longbourn of my going, if you do not like it, for
it will make the surprise the greater when I write to them and sign
my name Lydia Wickham. What a good joke it will be!*

'Good heavens!' cried Harriet, 'And so, she has truly eloped,
the silly creature?'

'Aye, ma'am. Just as quiet as quiet!'

'Goodness! Does anyone else know of this, Sally?'

'No ma'am, for I found it myself when I went to see about the
fire. But – oh ma'am – 'tis a terrible thing!'

'Well,' said Harriet philosophically, 'they always did like each
other. But' – to herself – 'they shall be quite pitifully poor! For
Wickham was treated very ill by the Darcys, and the Bennets are
not very well-off!'

Sally was emboldened enough to inquire, 'What think you,
ma'am – will he marry her?'

'Marry her? Why, of course he will marry her – he *must* marry
her! Whatever do you mean, Sally?'

'Oh, ma'am – I should not say.'

'Say what? Speak up, I beg! What can *you* know of Wickham
that *I* do not?'

Sally said unwillingly, 'He – He has not a good name, ma'am,
about the town.'

'But that will be jealousy, for he is well-favoured and
handsome.'

'Quite, ma'am – but he also owes a deal of money.'

'Oh Lord, Sally, almost every officer owes money! 'Tis the
gambling, as the Colonel always says, for *he* has no patience with
it. He would never gamble, not to save his life!'

'If only they were all like the Colonel, ma'am, but – truth to
tell – they are *not*. And Mr Wickham has been often seen at – at

Mrs Johns's, ma'am.'

'Gracious. Is that not a place of ill-repute?'

'Yes, ma'am and – and – what if he was to – to use poor Miss Lydia unkindly?'

Harriet jumped out of bed. 'No, no, for that *must* be impossible. I have known Wickham for months and months! I *know* him, Sally! He could never betray the Colonel so, nor treat a lady so very ill!'

'If you say so, ma'am, it must be right,' said the maid but so very faintly that Harriet said, and with resolution, 'I must go to the Colonel this instant – or better, send Peter to find him! He must wed her, he *must*. Else – oh, else we shall *all* be blamed for it!'

'I shall, ma'am!'

'And not a word, Sally, not to anyone. For all might still come right!'

'Yes, ma'am,' said Sally, and fled.

'I must own that I am surprised, sir,' said a tousled and sleepy Denny. 'Not that *she* would wed *him* – and that in a trice! – but *he* has had his eye on some rich widow down Hove way. He has been calling on her every other day, in hopes of persuading her to the business, while pretending to be assisting some fellow who lost his leg in France!'

Vaguely, the Colonel recalled having heard the ladies rallying Wickham about this unlucky schoolmate. But his sense of honour flatly rejected the notion that any man of his own company – of his own *acquaintance* even – could use a woman so.

'I see,' said he, keeping his voice steady with an effort. 'He has been courting the wealthy Mrs Townsend, has he? He always used to jest that he must marry money, in some way or other! But to seduce Miss Bennet and – you suspect – with not the slightest thought of wedding her! It is outrageous, appalling, indecent!'

Denny rubbed his chin and said, though without conviction, 'I might be wrong, sir. But though he likes her – for Miss Lydia is so saucy – the Bennets lack for money, and Wickham wants money more than anything! And it might have been – begging your pardon, that – that she threw herself at him. She *is* rather hasty, and but sixteen.'

Pacing, the Colonel found that he could not contest Denny's opinion. Though he had not been in company with the pair as often as Harriet, he had heard enough of their banter to imagine that *he* merely found Lydia amusing whilst *she* – oh, it was a wicked, wicked business, a shocking business! For the Bennets were gentry, and no end of Bennet sisters to be dragged into the mire. And it *was* mire. How the spiteful old cats of Brighton would revel in Lydia's downfall! – and how ironic it was that Mrs Townsend, of every woman in the area, had been the woman deceived! And it was not impossible that Lydia had thrown herself at Wickham – and he himself held responsible! And secretly he even thought, in the self-revulsion of that moment, 'Oh, why did I ever choose so young a wife as Harriet!'

He stopped pacing long enough to ask, 'Did Mrs Townsend truly like him, then?'

'Well sir,' said Denny, 'he had hopes that she was weakening, at least. And truly, he might be desperate enough to wed any rich lady as would have him! – but Miss Lydia has no money.'

'And yet to ruin her? No, never! I cannot think so ill of him as that!'

Denny said nothing because, mostly, what Wickham thought about was money – which women had money, which card-player he might skin for money, which moneylender could be relied upon to advance him money... And he as fussy as a woman about the finest boots, the finest cravats, besides!

Colonel Forster swivelled towards him, gripped his shoulders and said, with resolution, 'You do not truly think that he could – could take her, and *fail* to marry her? Tell me straight, Denny, for 'tis I who must confess the truth to Mr Bennet!'

But Denny had no words. He only nodded – thrice.

⁂

Mrs Carter to Capt. Carter: 'A *shocking* business, and how the Colonel will ever be able to hold his head up again I *cannot* imagine, for she was his own wife's dearest friend, and who is to say that *she* herself – running after the officers as she does – will not end up in *similar state*? And as for Miss Bennet's laugh – well! I had to *shield my ears*!'

⁂

And Quigley swore and smote the messenger furiously across the top of his head. 'Why did you not guess what the great blackguard had in mind? You are a blockhead indeed!'

⁂

Mrs Townsend said to Mrs Edmondson, in a tone of quiet indignation, 'Well, I cannot believe it, not for a single moment. *Such* a civil, thoughtful, respectful young man, one of such exceedingly good principles – so knowledgeable about Donne – so eager to bring the men in the regiment around to correct patterns of thought! Oh, it is quite shocking how good people can attract such spite and calumny! There is very much more to this tale than meets the eye, I am sure of *that*... The young lady shall be found, quite separate from Lieutenant Wickham, and some very good reason supplied for his disappearance!'

And Mrs Edmondson quite agreed with her.

◈

Sally, shaking her head, 'I always knew 'twould would be so. That time she begged me to return home, for *he* would bring her back. And the store she set by those heliotrope ribbons!'

◈

It was a soft, verdant evening in Hertfordshire, but Colonel Forster had, ever since leaving Brighton, been dreading the very view that met his gaze – the view of Longbourn from the road, grey-stoned, respectable, solid. Such a journey – such a business! While, as for Lydia's exuberant note to Harriet, he felt as if it was scorching a hole within his pocket.

As they broached the brow of the hill, he rapped on the glass. 'Please,' he told the coachman. 'I need to collect myself, just for a moment, before we arrive.'

He got out and paced a little upon the verge, hands clasped behind his back. For within that house was a family already alarmed and concerned, already shocked at the express he had sent informing them that Lydia had eloped with Wickham, and all this – God knew – quite bad enough. But now it would be his duty to tell them that, in all likelihood, it was no elopement but a seduction instead, and that Wickham had, almost certainly, no serious intention of wedding their youngest daughter. (Damn and blast the fellow – a scrounger, a wastrel and a cad!) And *he* in charge of Lydia all the while!

But the Colonel had never wanted for courage. After a few minutes, he sighed, squared his shoulders, and said to the coachman, 'Continue to the house, I beg, for I am ready.'

Lady Catherine Regrets

Lady Catherine was extremely indignant…

(from *Pride and Prejudice*, Chapter 61)

I had no sooner sat down – my nerves in no fit state, as you can imagine, to bear very much more – when Lady Linbury was announced.

'My dear,' she said, without preamble, 'you will never – no, *never* – believe what I just heard at the Dalrymples'!' And her manner so excited as to appear faintly ill-bred. But then, it is not everyone who has my sensibility on such points.

'I daresay,' said I, though the Dalrymples were never amongst my favourite members of the aristocracy, for Lady Dalrymple pretends to great good humour while stabbing her every acquaintance in the back, and the Honourable Clarissa is insipid to a degree.

'Well then! It transpires,' said Lady Linbury, 'that the rumour I mentioned – about Darcy – is quite true. He is indeed pursuing one of those dreadful Bennet girls!'

'I should be obliged,' I said coldly, 'if you would not be quite so absurd. For I have it on the highest possible authority that Miss Bennet – as featherheaded as most young girls but apparently *unusually* attractive – once entranced Charles Bingley, instead.'

Lady Linbury smiled with the most odious condescension and said, 'But, my dear Catherine, there is more than one Bennet girl –

there are six, at very least! I *did* hear that there were seven, but *that* was Madame St George, who is never to be depended upon.'

'There are certainly no more than five.'

'I daresay. Yet, whilst the eldest might perhaps be courted by Mr Bingley, the second-eldest, or perhaps the *third*, is pursued by Fitzwilliam Darcy, himself!'

I could not help smiling then, for *this* I could not believe. Not that Darcy might neglect my daughter Anne, for I have never been entirely easy on that point, but because he is so proud – and very properly – of his lineage. If any well-born fellow might be capable of pursuing a young lady who only scrapes into the-gentry by the skin of her teeth, it would not be Darcy!

In other words, had such a rumour involved an infatuation with Lady Diana or Miss Rowbotham, I should feel far more seriously concerned. Or had the *Colonel* been named – I could far more easily believe that Colonel Fitzwilliam might disgrace his house, for he has, while abroad, imbibed some rather curious notions about the equality of all men. As it was however, I was able to say, 'My dear Alexa, this could never be!'

'Wait, I beg. I heard the tale from Mr Bingley's own *sister*, Caroline. She believes Darcy entirely besotted, and you know how inseparable he and Charles Bingley have always been!'

'Fitzwilliam does, I must admit, rate Mr Bingley's abilities a great deal more highly than I can do. But it is far from uncommon for men of ability to relish the company of their intellectual inferiors. My own father, the Earl, maintained a few acquaintances of whom Mama could *never* approve. However, he would not have contemplated marrying their sisters!' I left her as soon as I could, in order to bathe my temples in eau de cologne and, despite my bravado, to consider all that I had heard.

I recollected first that I had once believed Miss Bingley herself a threat with regard to Darcy. There has been evidence, and for years, that she was trying for him. And Fitzwilliam has long been *most* deplorably attached to Mr Bingley, for all that young man's lack of intellect and even breeding – for who the Bingleys were, before Bingley's father made his fortune, I have never been able to ascertain. And does not their very attachment suggest that Darcy *might* have been corrupted by Colonel Fitzwilliam into believing birth and status less important than they truly are?

It is far from impossible.

Now this was not the first occasion that I had considered Darcy rather lax in his pursuit of my daughter. Oh, he *says* the correct things about her delicacy, charm and elegant accomplishments – it is all very proper – but when does he seek to sit by her, attempt to solicit her opinions, or regard her with actual devotion?

Of course, to do so might be considered ill-bred, yet how it would have eased my mind! Particularly when people ignorant of his destiny have said, 'Apparently, he greatly admires Miss Albright's Italian or Lady Imogen's singing' – or whatever it is. It is almost as if he conceives it more a matter of *duty* to court his cousin – instead of its being a tacit engagement, and one of two decades' duration, besides!

I felt exceedingly unsettled that evening. Dismissing my maid as soon as I could, I sat thinking, while staring out of the great curved window from which one enjoys so fine a view of Hyde Park. However, in the end, I resolved not to interfere. It seemed so unlikely that such a match could ever be, while even to *suggest* it might only serve to implant notions in a young man's head – for Darcy was still rather a young man. I also comforted myself with the notion that the badly bred have nothing to do beyond fomenting idle rumours about their betters. The following week would surely be soon enough to suggest to Darcy that it was time to make Anne's position and his own rather clearer – to the remainder of the family, at least.

However, the arrival of the first post the next day completely altered my thinking. I recognised Mr Collins's punctilious handwriting at once.

Your Ladyship, Please forgive this gratuitous intrusion into your precious time in town, which I hope and trust is providing you with a great many hours of pleasure and enjoyment. That I am so daring as to impose upon your great good nature, as I believe might be acceptable to your good self, is due to a rather disturbing letter from Lady Lucas which my wife received yesterday. This communication described a call her mother Lady Lucas made at Longbourn on Monday, during the course of which Lady Lucas was told that Mr Bingley had offered to Miss Bennet – and been accepted – despite the fact that she, though generally admired, has no fortune to speak of! But I am not trespassing upon your valuable time for the purpose of pointless gossip alone. Instead, my wife deems it my duty – and her judgement never fails her – to acquaint you with a matter of far higher import. For the surprising union of Mr Bingley with Miss Bennet is in danger of being eclipsed by an alliance of far greater moment. In short, Mr Fitzwilliam Darcy is rumoured to be courting Miss Elizabeth Bennet, the same young person of whom you took such exceedingly generous notice while she was visiting my dear wife at Easter!... At first, I must confess, I refused to credit even the possibility. Engaged as he is to his lovely cousin – herself possessed of such exemplary birth, elegance, and charm – how could your nephew even consider such another? It is likely no more than Dame Rumour. Yet were it ever proven to be true, you would have every right to feel betrayed by my never mentioning it. For, as I cannot stress too often or too fervently, my loyalty to Your Ladyship is second only to my allegiance to a Higher Power...

There was a good deal more, for Mr Collins' loyalty is second only to his prolixity, but by this point I was already ringing the bell for Elsa whom, as I had already determined, would be attending me into Hertfordshire.

Now the wealthy and the well-connected are inevitably targets for wicked gossip, and Darcy must rank as one of the most eligible young men in London. Still, I was shaken – more shaken that I wished to own, even to myself – and therefore proposed to represent the true nature of the case to the second-eldest Miss Bennet, and *that* without loss of time.

I also determined to write nothing to Anne, down at Rosings. Anne has so often been reminded of her destiny that I cannot conceive of her doubting it. Despite this, I cannot help blaming her for not having made rather more effort to attract her handsome cousin… For while I never precisely *advised* Anne to attach Darcy, I have always taken it for granted that she would recognise her duty to do so. Had she only been less languid, less complacent – had she, in short, bestirred herself – my own immediate exertions might have been rendered unnecessary.

Though I had little doubt of their answering, for my powers of persuasion, in common with all of my powers, are formidable.

I merely told my ladies' maid that I was attending to personal business. Elsa is as discreet a creature as I have ever employed – however, there is not a servant in the world who does not gossip, and my purpose is to halt rumour in its tracks, rather than to spur it onwards. Lady Alexa had been quite inquisitive enough.

'What, at once?' she exclaimed.

'I doubt that I shall be gone above a day – two, at the most.'

'I do hope,' said she, insinuatingly, 'that dear Anne is well?'

'I have no reason to suppose otherwise. But I am not going down to Rosings.'

'But surely there must be some quite shocking alarm?'

'You know my spirit of activity, my good friend. If something is worth doing, it must be worth doing as soon as may be!'

'Well, I daresay you know your own concerns best,' said she, rather discontentedly.

Once Elsa and I had set off, I found that I recalled Miss Bennet quite well – dark, slim and pert, not ill-looking but assuredly no beauty. I recalled too her saucy mien, which could veer perilously near impertinence. ('My age? With three younger sisters in society, you can hardly expect me to own it!')

Truly, I was shocked that Darcy could admire so superficial a creature, assuming that he had not been entirely mistaken by the Collinses and the Lucases, as was possible.

By the time we reached the depths of Hertfordshire I was feeling rather fretful. It seemed to me that Mr Collins would never have dared mention the business, were there not some cause for alarm. And men can behave so inexplicably! We were twice obliged to stop for directions, and Elsa doubtless heard me inquiring about the exact location of Longbourn. The countryside about was not unpretty, in its flat, spare Hertfordshire style, and Meryton itself seemed prosperous enough, with tidy shops and a cobbled high street. As we turned into the drive at Longbourn my first impression was that the house was tolerable – luckily for the Collinses, who will one day inherit it – though its hedges appeared rather ill-kempt, and its principal gate a little loose upon its hinges.

'Your Ladyship, would you perhaps wish me to –' asked Elsa delicately.

'No, no, I beg that you remain. The Longbourn servants will

assist, I am sure, should you require anything, and I shall not be long.'

Now that the moment had arrived, I found that I no longer felt the slightest apprehension – indeed, upon observing the faintly down-at-heel style of the Bennet property, I rather wondered that I had ever regarded the business as worth travelling for. I had also attempted, during the drive, to imagine Darcy smitten with *any* young woman and in this, I must say, I had failed. In short, I was more than ever convinced that Mr Collins had been misled by the normally sensible Charlotte into a quite ludicrous alarm.

After all, my nephew had visited at Longbourn. Surely any such property, observed by such a man as Darcy, must instantly dampen any serious regard for its owners? – It was redolent of such an insufficiency of means, of so crabbed and penny-pinching a style of existence! I even felt a little annoyed at the Lucases, for having inadvertently wasted so much of my time. But there it was!

Having gathered up my reticule and adjusted my bonnet, I accepted the Longbourn footman's assistance – there was grease on his cuff – and descended to the gravelled drive. The entrance hall was sadly dark, and there were precious few portraits to be seen as I followed the butler (who positively *stared* upon hearing my title – probably, I was their first titled visitor).

I entered the drawing room hard upon his rather scuffed heels. There I perceived a stout lady of forty or thereabouts by the window, an exceedingly young lady doing needlework, and Miss Elizabeth, reading a book. She rather started as I was announced, while her mother seemed equally struck. After refusing refreshment, I disposed myself upon a chair and waited – in vain – to be introduced. Finally, I deigned to inquire the identity of the young sister.

Mrs Bennet spoke with gratified alacrity. 'She is Kitty, Your

Ladyship. My youngest daughter is recently married, and my eldest is walking about with a young man whom, we hope, will soon become part of the family.' (I felt a little shocked at her even mentioning Miss Lydia, given all that Mr Collins had confided as to the circumstances of her marriage.)

I presumed that the young man alluded to was Mr Bingley, whom I had no desire to encounter. I was not best pleased with Bingley, for was it not Darcy's incomprehensible affection for that very ordinary young man which had caused all the trouble in the first place? – Had Darcy never attended him into Hertfordshire, he might never have encountered Elizabeth Bennet at all!

Determined to lose no time, I suggested that she show me about the garden. Once we were far enough from the house, and the *pourparlers* dispensed with, I presumed that she had surmised the purpose of my visit.

'Not at all! I have not been at all able to account for the honour of seeing you here,' said she, with a most affected air of astonishment. (As if *I* could be toyed with in such a fashion!) I instantly said that I had heard, 'not only that her sister was soon to be most advantageously wedded but that *she* was rumoured to be courted by my own nephew – though *that* must be a most scandalous falsehood.'

At this, she did colour a little but only retorted, 'If it is so impossible, I wonder at your coming so far. Whatever would Your Ladyship mean by it?'

'Why, to hear it instantly contradicted!'

'Your coming to Longbourn,' said she, with a lofty little smile, 'will be rather confirmation of it – if such a report truly is in existence.'

'If! Do you then pretend to be ignorant of it? Has it not been most industriously circulated by yourselves? Do you not know that such a report is spread abroad?' She denied it. I pressed on. 'And can you likewise declare that there is no *foundation* for it?'

A little hesitation and then, 'I do not pretend to possess equal frankness with Your Ladyship. *You* may ask questions, which *I* choose not to answer.'

I thought, 'This is not to be borne!' but only said, 'Miss Bennet, I insist upon being satisfied. Has my nephew made you an offer of marriage?'

'Your Ladyship has declared it to be impossible.'

'It ought to be so, while he retains the use of his reason. But *your* arts and allurements may, in a moment of infatuation, have drawn him in!'

'If I had,' said she, 'I should be the last person to confess it.'

I was astounded – and heated, too – by the mixture of archness and impudence in her tone. Could such assurance possibly spring from a secure confidence in Darcy's regard? – It was just conceivable... Collecting myself, I said, as best as I can recall, 'Miss Bennet, do you know who I am? I am almost the nearest relation Darcy has in the world and am entitled to know all his dearest concerns!'

'But you are not entitled to know *mine*, nor will such behaviour as this ever induce me to be explicit.'

'Let me be rightly understood. This match, to which you have the presumption to aspire, can never take place. Never! Mr Darcy is engaged to *my daughter*. Now what can you have to say?'

'Only this,' said she, 'that if he is, then you can have no reason to suppose he will make an offer to me.'

I sighed as, clearly, a great deal of tedious spadework would be called for. However, recollecting my dear Anne. I said, as patiently as I could contrive, 'The engagement between my nephew and my daughter is of a peculiar kind. From their infancy, they have been intended for each other – the favourite wish of *his* mother, as well as her own. While they were still in their cradles, we planned their union – and now, at the moment when the wishes of both sisters would be accomplished – is this to be prevented by a young woman of inferior birth, of no importance in the world, and wholly unallied to the family? Are you lost to every feeling of propriety? Have you not heard me say that from his earliest hour he was destined for his cousin?'

'Yes,' said she, with a little lift of her chin, 'and I had heard it before. But what is that to me? If there is no other objection to my marrying your nephew, I shall certainly not be kept from it, by knowing that his mother and his aunt wished him to marry Miss De Bourgh. You both did as much as you could, in planning the marriage – its *completion* depended upon others. If Mr Darcy is neither by honour nor inclination confined to his cousin, why is he not entitled to another choice? And if I am that choice, why may I not accept him?'

At this impudence, I must admit, I began to feel very angry. I have been celebrated, all my life, for my quickness and celerity – the unfortunate consequence of which is temper. If I have a weakness, it is surely *that*. Breathing rather quicker, I said, 'Because honour, decorum, prudence – nay, interest – forbid it. Yes, Miss Bennet, interest! – Do not expect to be noticed by his family or friends, if you wilfully act against the inclinations of all. You will be censured, slighted and despised by everyone connected with him. Your alliance will be a disgrace – your name will never be mentioned by any of us!'

'These are heavy misfortunes,' replied she, with a complacent little simper. 'But the wife of Mr Darcy must have such extraordinary sources of happiness attached to her situation that she must, on the whole, have no cause to repine.'

She was doubtless gloating over Pemberley, where the mischief must have occurred. For, had poor Darcy been smitten by her at *Rosings*, it could never have been lost upon myself. No, the mischief had surely occurred in Derbyshire. And to be fair, Pemberley, even leaving its glorious setting aside, might be enough to addle any country girl's brain. Its astonishing gold plate, its magnificent paintings, its splendid dining hall... Really, was it so surprising that the girl's head had been turned by what was, truly, one of the finest houses in all of England?

But it was her *manner* that so goaded me, a combination of impertinence and assurance. Had she herself – like timid little Georgiana – been born to Pemberley's magnificence, she could not have appeared more disdainful – she, whose uncle was in trade, whose family was undistinguished, and whose estate was entailed!

I cried, 'Obstinate, headstrong girl! I am ashamed of you! Is this your gratitude for my many attentions to you last spring? Is nothing due to me upon that score?... Let us sit down. You are to understand, Miss Bennet, that I came here with the determined resolution of carrying my purpose – nor will I be dissuaded from it. I am not in the habit of brooking disappointment.'

Here she murmured something sardonic about what a pity that was. Undeterred, I continued, 'Hear me in silence. My daughter and my nephew are formed for each other. They are descended on the maternal side from the same noble line and, on the father's, from honourable and ancient, though untitled, families. And what is to divide them? The upstart pretensions of a young woman without family, connections, or fortune! Is this to be endured? It must not be, it *shall* not be! Were you sensible of your own good, you would not wish to quit the sphere in which you have been brought up.'

'In marrying your nephew, I should not consider myself as quitting that sphere. He is a gentleman – I am a gentleman's daughter – so far, we are equal.'

'True. You *are* a gentleman's daughter. But who was your mother? Who are your uncles and aunts? Do not imagine me ignorant of *their* condition!'

'Whatever my connections may be,' she said, and I am not sure she did not add 'Madam' – 'if your *nephew* does not object to them, they can be nothing to *you*.'

'Tell me once and for all, are you engaged to him?' It was one of the longest silences of my life before she acknowledged that she was not. I thought, 'So, all is not yet lost!' and pressed home my advantage. 'And will you promise never to enter into such an engagement?'

'I will make no promise of the kind,' said she.

Really, one could hardly credit that she was the same young creature as I had known at Rosings! See what Darcy's mad infatuation had accomplished! A perfectly respectful and even conversable young lady had been transformed into arrogance, by a single viewing of Pemberley and the faintest hope of having roused my nephew's admiration!

However – my strength of character never fails me – I set my teeth and persevered. 'Miss Bennet, I am shocked and astonished. I expected to find a more reasonable young woman. But I shall not go away without the assurance I require.'

'And I certainly shall never give it. I am not to be intimidated into anything so unreasonable. Your Ladyship might wish Mr Darcy to marry your daughter, but would my promise make such an alliance any more probable? Allow me to say, Lady Catherine, that the arguments with which you have supported this extraordinary application have been as frivolous as the application was ill-judged. How far your nephew might approve of your interference in his affairs, I cannot tell – but you have no right to concern yourself in mine.'

Now I had previously promised myself never to mention Miss Lydia's elopement, to preserve the Collinses from reproach at having told me of the business. But I was so provoked – so thwarted, so disdained – that I cried, 'Not so hasty, if you please! You must know that I am no stranger to the particulars of your youngest sister's infamous elopement. I know that her marriage was a patched-up business, contrived at the expense of your father and uncle. Is *such* a girl to be my nephew's sister? Is her husband, son of his late father's *steward*, to be his brother? Heaven and earth! – Are the shades of Pemberley to be thus polluted?'

Again, her shamelessness astonished me. 'You can *now* have nothing farther to say,' she resentfully answered. 'You have insulted me, in every possible method. I must beg leave to return to the house.'

I had no choice but to turn as well. 'Unfeeling, selfish girl! Do you not consider that a connection with you must disgrace him in the eyes of everybody?'

'Lady Catherine, you know my sentiments.'

'You are then *resolved* to have him?'

'I have only resolved to act in that manner which will constitute my happiness, without reference to you or to any other person so wholly unconnected with me.'

'You are determined to ruin him before the family – to make him the contempt of all the world!'

How her eyes flashed! – 'As to the resentment of his family, or the indignation of the world, if the former *were* excited by his marrying me, it would not give me one moment's concern – and the world in general would have too much sense to join in the scorn.'

'So,' I said, lowering my voice, for we were then near to the house, and who knew what parent or which chit of a sister might be listening? – 'So this is your final resolve! Very well. I shall now know how to act. Do not imagine, Miss Bennet, that your ambition will ever be gratified. I hoped to find you reasonable but, depend upon it, I will carry my point.' And by the carriage, still lower for Elsa's sake, for I could see her reading – or perhaps pretending to read – within it. 'I take no leave of you, Miss Bennet. I send no compliments to your mother. You deserve no such attention. I am most seriously displeased.'

My maid must have overheard at least something of this, or – if she had *not* – she would have been a fool indeed not to have inferred, from the language of gesture alone, that Miss Bennet and I did not part as friends. However, she behaved very well, acknowledging, in answer to my rather hasty queries, that she had not required more refreshment than the tea the coachman had procured her. I then instructed the fellow to make haste to the inn we had passed, for I found myself quite parched after such an unfortunate scene. And, after a little refreshment at the inn – appalling tea and a quite inedible biscuit – we made our way back to Lady Alexa's.

There, a more promising repost was laid in the garden room. Once we were finally relieved of servants, she lifted an eyebrow and murmured, 'And so, you have actually been into Hertfordshire!'

'I must confess,' I told her, 'that there appears to be a grain of truth in the rumour you touched upon last evening –'

'I am sorry for it,' said she, with a sigh that did her heart great credit.

'– but the hussy's little schemes will never answer – *that* much I can promise you.'

'Why, whatever can you intend? Surely you cannot mean to apply to Darcy, himself!'

'I can, indeed.'

'My dear Catherine, I beg that you think again!' At this, I must own, I stared, for Alexa is generally the first to object to inequality of situation. She said, 'Darcy will never forgive such interference, as you must know – and besides, he is of age. You had best say nothing. You will only be getting ill-will.'

'I am astonished that you, of every person, should take such a view!'

'But when Lord Granville Leveson-Gower –'

'Darcy, for all his faults, is no Lord Granville Leveson-Gower!'

'Certainly not, for Darcy is of exemplary character, I believe.'

'He *is* of exemplary character, I assure you!' I countered rather huffily. Because – for all that I was still annoyed at Darcy – exceedingly so – he is still my nephew, and head of the family, besides. 'My only concern about Darcy, with regard to Miss Elizabeth, is that he may have imbibed some of Colonel Fitzwilliam's strange ideas with regard to all men being created equal.'

'There are a great many strange ideas about these days,' said Alexa disapprovingly – and I agreed with her – 'but I cannot imagine Mr Darcy subscribing to them. His air is rather proud and his manner rather stiff – which *was*, or so it was always said, why Lady Diana never tried for him. One could imagine him cutting you – yes, even you! – for presuming to tell him what he ought best to do. No, in your position, I should leave it to his common sense. With the family as impossible as you say – really scarcely *gentry* at all – he will likely think better of the business and desist. Though the family is reputable, is it not?'

'The family is respectable enough and the property not derisory, if rather down-at-heel. But the mother is untidy, blowsy, and uncouth – how she stared as I entered!'

'And yet, as even *you* must concede, you arrived with no warning at all. And what of Miss Elizabeth? – I assume she is pretty. Is she also clever, mannerly, well-spoken?'

I was forced to admit – recollecting our interview, bitter as it had been – not only that the flush upon her countenance had been only too becoming but that she had spoken well enough. I finished, 'But Alexa, all the world knows that her youngest sister eloped, and with that appalling Wickham fellow! How many young men of exceptional breeding would even *consider* an alliance, after so shocking a scandal?'

But at this, Alexa shook her head again. 'Sadly, an elopement is not considered such an infamy as it used to be. *That* shameful business is all mended – neatly scotched, indeed – and now these Wickhams, though never likely to rise, will be acceptable enough to many. How unlucky it is that the uncle had sufficient funds to salvage the situation!'

'But an elopement –' I persisted.

'It is true that, had the fellow *not* been bribed into the marriage, no man of any standing could ever have courted the Bennet sisters – but *that* is all gone by. And so, do you still intend to call at Grosvenor Street?'

'I do. I am grateful for your opinion, Alexa, but such influence as I have – which is not small – shall all go one way.'

'Very well. My own hope,' said she, 'is that the young lady is flattering herself, and that your nephew's pursuit – if pursuit it was – has since slackened. He can scarcely be besieging her in Hertfordshire, at any rate, if he is still in town. Even should the worst occur, and they wed, you must not despair of dear Georgiana– even of your own Anne. Should Darcy persist in marrying beneath him – really, almost a misalliance – *they* might still make brilliant matches, perhaps.'

I agreed, of course, though secretly thinking that Anne's delicate looks are not of that showy, blatant sort that young men these days appear to prefer, while Georgiana – though admittedly both lovely and accomplished – has always been painfully shy.

And shyness, it seems, is no longer the fashion.

✦

The following morning, I awoke early to sort out my thoughts, for I did not wish to be betrayed into such annoyance as I believed myself to have displayed – were the chit capable of understanding it – whilst in Hertfordshire.

I determined to be sensible but aloof, for Darcy and I have never been particularly close. Georgiana has often confided in me, and in her cousin Anne as well – but Darcy is self-sufficient to a fault – which may be why I cannot imagine him in love. There is always, somehow, a little barrier with Darcy – not only between him and myself, but between him and every other person... I am not, I daresay, as interested in other people as many – nor as addicted to novel reading as Alexa is – but I have the instinctive understanding of human nature that every woman is born with, as well as a mind my governess admiringly compared 'to that of a man'. These two advantages, I trusted, would see me through the interview with my nephew.

He seemed greatly surprised upon my being announced.

'Refresh the tea,' he ordered his butler in an undertone, and to me, 'Your Ladyship! I little thought to see you here.'

'I should rather think not,' said I. His exquisite appearance, as I had entered, roused my ire. He had been reading and as he rose, he looked taller, handsomer and more elegantly attired than I could ever recall seeing him. How broad his shoulders were, how distinguished his countenance! How outrageous it was to contemplate him – and Pemberley, besides – being wasted on that pert little miss at Longbourn! In that moment, I would have found it infinitely more bearable had he succumbed – as so many had before him – to Lady Diana's remarkable charms. Heavens! *They* would have been a couple worth looking at!

He said, 'I fear you find my staff unprepared for this honour – I am in town only a few days, on business. Is this chair to your taste?'

'I should prefer one somewhat higher if you please. I am a trifle weary.'

'But surely you have not travelled from Rosings today?' he asked, looking surprised.

'No, only from Lady Alexa's. But yesterday I travelled, with my ladies' maid, to Hertfordshire and back.'

'Truly, in one day? To see the Skinners, I suppose.'

'No.' I said, very levelly. 'I was visiting at a place I had never been before in the whole of my life. A place called Longbourn, near Meryton.'

At this, he frowned and was silent. Luckily, the servants then appeared, bearing a few prettily arranged biscuits and cakes. While Fredericks remained – how long he took! – nothing, of course, could be either said or done, beyond ascertaining whether I wished for more sugar in my tea. The moment we were alone I said, 'You can imagine my errand at Longbourn, I am sure.'

'I fear that I cannot,' said he, but I could not believe him. He was hardening himself – he was resolving upon something.

I said, 'Surely you cannot be the *last* to know that your name has been linked – and in the eyes of all the world – with that of the second Bennet girl?'

He took a deep breath.

'I promise you that I have never, in the entire course of my existence, heard one single syllable of this.'

'Yet so it is – for Mr Collins himself assured me of it! While Lady Alexa most certainly overheard, at the Earl of Weybridge's, that Charles Bingley was to wed *one* sister, and Darcy of Pemberley the other.'

'I greatly fear, ma'am,' said he seriously, 'your information is deficient. The rumour-mill is, in this case, but half-true. Bingley is indeed engaged to the eldest Miss Bennet. I had a note from him yesterday, and only this morning wrote to wish him joy. However – and strictly between ourselves – I made my own proposals, in due form, last spring at Hunsford –'

'What!'

'Permit me to finish, I beg – to Miss Elizabeth – and the lady would not have me.'

'She *refused* you?'

'She did.'

'Refused you? *Refused* you!' He acknowledged it again, and I cried, feeling almost affronted, 'Refused you! Upon what plea? For what reason?'

'I am not at liberty to say.'

'Utter arrogance! And from *such* a family!' Now I should, of course, have been delighted – and did assuredly feel greatly relieved as well as shocked – at this information. And yet there was such regret, such sorrow, in his face! And then, this deplorable marriage of Bingley's probably meant that he would soon be returning to Hertfordshire, where the hussy, of course, still remained. I simply *had* to know whether any farther application was in his thoughts.

'Yet surely, after so signal an insult, you can have no notion of offering to her again?'

'That, ma'am, is a question which I am not prepared to answer.'

Almost the same form of words as her own! I said then, as well as I can recollect, 'You must not, you *shall* not! Fitzwilliam, you must be aware that I am not one to throw my weight about. I would be, I daresay, the last, the *very* last, to lay down the law to any person. And you know how I pride myself upon weighing up the evidence before entering upon any judgement – why, our own lawyer has described my mind as acute and incisive! However, this much I *will* and *shall* say... I interviewed Miss Bennet at Longbourn – we walked about her garden – and I found her utterly obdurate. Not to mention unmannerly, obstructive, resolute and impossible!'

'If I might ask, in what respect was she unmannerly?' he asked, almost sharply.

'Why, in every respect! She absolutely disdained me! When I asked whether she was resolved never to engage herself to you, she refused to tell me. When I reminded her of my kindness to her last Easter, she omitted to thank me. And when I described the accord as to your destiny that your dear mama and I reached – that sacred accord which no doubt softened my sister's deathbed – she merely remarked, "You both did as much as you could in planning the marriage. Its completion must depend upon others." Have you ever heard anything likelier to offend, in the whole of your life?'

Darcy took a turn about the room, doubtless as struck by this level of ingratitude as I had been. Finally, he said, 'Aunt, first, I accept that the ownership and destiny of Pemberley must appear of prime importance to you.'

'Precisely as it does to Georgiana and to the Colonel and to our every other relation. It is of paramount importance to us all! It is, after all, the primary seat of –'

'And, as I said, I appreciate that such is the case. However –'

'And nor is that all, Fitzwilliam! For Anne is devoted to you. Devoted!' (I had intended to say this earlier but, in my agitation, it had slipped my mind.)

'And I am equally devoted to Anne,' said he, at once. 'She is a lovely girl and has grown into a most elegant and admirable young lady. But though I love my cousin, and always have, I could never become her husband. I know that such an idea has been mooted – my late father himself begged me to consider it. But Anne is like a second sister to me. I could no more wed Anne than I could wed my dear Georgiana!'

Now this was, indeed, a blow, and an irrecoverable blow at that... I felt, in that moment, as if ice had been poured about my heart. *A second sister*! There was, then, no chance for my own Anne. I had never actually *observed* any brotherliness of Darcy's towards Anne – beyond solicitude for her health, perhaps. But nor, I reminded myself, had I observed any evidence of a stronger affection.

And again, I recollected Miss Elizabeth's dark eyes, sparked with indignation, as they had been in the grounds of Longbourn. It was difficult to believe that her elder sister might be still *more* attractive! Perhaps there was some part of myself – never considered a beauty, though always 'handsome enough' – that distrusts beauty, on principle? Anne's looks might be the epitome of all that is delicate and highly-bred, but Miss Elizabeth – those eyes! – was as confident and careless as a society belle. She had the air of someone too sure of her attractions to be concerned about them. Impertinent and lively, she was perhaps the *last* woman I should have thought likely to entrance someone of Darcy's reserve – yet had he not already offered to her? – an infatuation, indeed!

I asked him for a glass of wine and water, which he procured himself rather than to summon his servants. Finally, I said, 'It is a blow, Fitzwilliam, I cannot deny it. It has long been the first wish of my heart – as it was the first wish of your mama's – that the two estates be united. But if such is not to be, Anne will still marry – as well or perhaps even better – while there is still time for you to see through the ambitious pretentions of the second-eldest Miss Bennet.'

'I cannot see how she pretended,' said he.

I thought, but did not say, 'Did not she pretend to be merely an agreeable friend of Mrs Collins's, while poaching on my own daughter's preserves?' And yet the chance was too fair not to make one last attempt. Therefore, I said, 'I would strongly advise that you think, Fitzwilliam, not merely about the personal attractions of your wife, but about her breeding, too. Surely you would never wish to imperil Georgiana's chances by allying yourself to a woman of inferior rank, pert manners and a lamentable level of accomplishment, whose mother is less than genteel and whose youngest sister is a disgrace!'

He stirred as if to speak, but I continued, 'Nay, hear me out, I beg!... You have decided – in defiance of your extended family and all sage advice – against Anne. So be it! But there are many well-born, well-bred, and thinking young women beyond Anne! Do not hasten, I beg, to disgrace yourself in the eyes of the world by pursuing the second-eldest Miss Bennet, whose ambition, upon viewing Pemberley, has apparently so worked on her dislike as to make it not inconceivable that she might someday accept you!'

His mouth was set in rather a thin line as he rang the bell. 'My dear aunt, you are tired, you are unwell. I recommend that you return to Lady Alexa's, where you can rest. Fredericks, I should be obliged if you might assist Lady Catherine to her carriage.'

Yes, it was – or very nearly – a dismissal! I left feeling spurned, angry and almost repenting what I had said at the last but, as the carriage swept through the street, I gradually grew more in charity with myself. I had not been supine and silent, at least. No doubt I had grown a trifle warm – but surely I could not have reasoned for so long *entirely* in vain? It would take a great deal of confidence in any young man to apply twice, and to someone so inferior, as well! And, after all, had Miss Bennet not said, with that little lift of chin, 'I am not engaged to him'?

To be sure, Anne's chance is gone by, but I cannot believe Darcy so entirely lost to common sense. Some clever noblewoman or society beauty might still intervene, ruining the ambitions of the second Miss Bennet. This, at least, must be the ardent hope of that majority of the family, the part unafflicted by the inanities of love!

March 25th

Dear Lady Linbury, With regard to the Dalrymples, there is an old saw about the broken clock being right twice a day, and I should put this rumour in much the same category. I daresay the marriage will be called off before the banns are read, for I have met the young lady, and more than once. She is tolerable, in terms of looks, but her <u>*manners*</u> *are quite impossible.*

April 2nd

My dear Georgiana, Nil desperandum, as I was taught at your age, or thereabouts. It is all most unpleasant, and most unfortunate too, but you must not let it disrupt your music, your reading and your Italian. Your new sister – assuming that the match is not called off – will never be able to improve you, but it is not impossible that your sweetness of manner might inspire her to rather more gentility. More, I fear, cannot be hoped for at this stage, but, whatever happens, you must bear it with your usual good grace...

April 11th

Dear Mr Collins, I thank you for your note, which was most thoughtful and which – I am aware – has never received proper acknowledgement. I have not been well – London at present does not agree with me. However, it was good of you and Mrs Collins to write. So unfortunate a turn of events! – but not one that could possibly have been anticipated. Who could have imagined, when we were all comfortably at Rosings last Easter, such an outcome as this! But human nature is unfathomable!

April 21st

Dear Alexa, Perhaps you were right, and my interference only served to impel Darcy onwards, but I cannot think so. I hear that they are to marry next week, very quietly, as is only appropriate, in Hertfordshire – Still, I suppose he has a week to return to his senses.

April 29th

Lady Catherine regrets that she is <u>not</u> at home this Thursday.

Of Tact and Tactics

(Author's note: This story is based on my Susan: A Jane Austen Prequel. *In this book I enjoyed imagining what Lady Susan, Austen's stunning and manipulative 35-year-old widow, might have been like when just sixteen. In fact, this story is a prequel to my prequel – as well as offering some explanation for the transformation of Lady Catherine's daughter, Miss Anne de Bourgh.)*

'And what sort of young lady is she? Is she handsome?'

Mr Collins said, 'She is a most charming young lady indeed. Lady Catherine herself says that, in point of true beauty, Miss de Bourgh is far superior to the handsomest of her sex, because there is that in her features which marks the young lady of distinguished birth.'

(from *Pride and Prejudice*, Chapter 14)

'How handsome Lord Cuthbert is!' thought Anne de Bourgh. Really, it was almost indecent to have such shapely legs, and at such a length besides, and though Amelia teased him for the streak of silver in his dark hair ('My brother, the badger!') it was really most attractive... His sardonic sense of the ridiculous also appealed to her and – though the Cuthbert family was not particularly well-off – all in all, she counted herself amongst those ladies who found

Lord Cuthbert's only disagreeable quality to be his perfect indifference to herself. While he teased his sister with such style that, at times, she felt quite envious of Amelia's having a brother...

These thoughts occurred to Anne as she settled in the carriage. She did not particularly wish to return to Kent – she felt better amused in town where, in addition to more diverting society, there were plays, balls and concerts. (Despite the fatigue of attending concerts whilst tone-deaf, she enjoyed watching others in the audience and had, for the purpose, perfected an expression of charmed expectancy.)

In addition, there was not a single marriageable male in or about Hunsford, and she was beginning to fear that she was – in terms of marrying – somewhat running out of time. Although as the heiress of Rosings she must always be sought, by someone or other, she found the cackhanded attempts at flattery by elderly members of the nobility often demeaning and occasionally infuriating. As if *she*, who – were there a spark of justice in the world – should by this point have been mistress of Pemberley, need settle for a man old enough to be her father!

However, she had heard that the Johnsons were still in the country, and Anne quite failed to share her mother's dissatisfaction with them. Despite their being new money, and Mr Johnson unashamedly in trade, he was so incurably sociable as to make her sojourn in Kent a far less tedious prospect than it would have been otherwise.

◈

Mrs Johnson died, very quietly, just after ten, while Mr Johnson was dozing over *The Times* racing reports. The maid, having briefly left the room, was shocked to find her mistress gone upon her return.

Though Phoebe could not help thinking that, where there was no hope of recovery, perhaps it was a blessing?

Hastily, she closed her mistress's eyes but found herself in two minds about awakening the master. She moved about the room, purposely making a little noise, first with the chamber pot and then with the bed-warmer, in hopes that he might stir, though 'twas never easy to see death in a face, and a wife's face, besides…

Finally despairing of these ploys, she trotted downstairs to ask the young master what she had best do. She found Mr Henry talking quietly with his sister Caroline. Curtseying, she said, 'I greatly fear, Mr Henry –'

'What, already!'

'The surgeon *did* say, sir, that it could be at any time, in this week or the next.'

'I shall send the apothecary word,' said Miss Johnson, rising. 'Where is my father?'

'Asleep, ma'am,' said Phoebe. 'And I could not decide whether to waken him or not.'

'Of course you must,' was Henry's opinion.

'But sir, it seems such a liberty!'

'Then I shall do it,' said he heavily, 'for it must be done.'

He ascended the stairs, two at a time, with Phoebe scuttling behind. Upon entering, Henry was struck by the almost marbled beauty of his mother's face in the candlelight, First, he leaned down to kiss her. Then, with a little sigh, he touched Mr Johnson on his shoulder.

'Save the women and children!' shouted that gentleman, still caught fast by some dream. 'Eh, eh! Who is that?'

'It is I, Henry. I am very sorry to be the one to tell you – but it has only just occurred. Our beloved mother is gone.'

Mr Johnson jumped to his feet. 'Gone, and without a word to me! The poor creature!'

'Indeed, she was a paragon,' said Henry and Phoebe murmured something both fervent and indistinguishable.

'Gone! Gone! And what, I ask you, am I to do without her? I was always afeard,' he said confidingly, 'that she would die before me, for there was always this or that amiss. Women's troubles! But then, women *will* have their little niggling pains and nothing to be done about it!'

'Indeed,' said Henry, though very well-aware that it was no little niggling pain that had carried away his mother at the last. Then he asked, 'Perhaps we might pray?'

'But how, man? The rector will have been abed long since!'

'*I* shall pray,' said Henry quietly. 'Lord, receive the soul of my dear mother, who suffered so much, so bravely, and so long. To your loving mercies we deliver her!'

'Aye, well done. You did that well,' said his father, smacking him on the shoulder. 'Did he not, young Phoebe? Better than I could have done, I am very sure. Ha!'

'Amen,' said Henry, but the maid, unsure which master to answer, said nothing at all.

❖

The date set for the funeral and the body removed, the condolence visits began. Lady Catherine de Bourgh, owner of Rosings and the ranking landowner of the parish, was an early visitor. Though, as she mentioned to her lady's maid, in whom she had grown rather into the habit of confiding ever since that dreadful Darcy business, 'as poor Mrs Johnson had been bound – and for life – to that appalling fellow, perhaps it might be considered a blessed release.'

OF TACT AND TACTICS

In Lady Catherine's opinion, the offences of the Johnsons were many and grievous. They were not only in trade, but quite shamelessly so, for Mr Johnson spoke with enthusiasm of his business and – however often his wife attempted to turn the subject – had never apologised for his mining concerns. He also relished his fortune to an almost indecent extent, not only tripling Warleigh's size but tacking 'Hall' onto its title, and *that* for no good reason, for not even Her Ladyship could deny that Warleigh had always been of sufficient size to rank as a hall. But 'Warleigh Hall' sounded cheap, to her mind, compared to the elegance of Rosings – or indeed of Warleigh, plain and simple. Still worse, Mr Johnson had recently determined on starting up a hunt – something which ought to have been organised by Colonel Fitzwilliam – if a hunt was required, which it was not.

As for Warleigh itself, its wall paperings were too garish, its plate too ornate and its principal carriages quite pitifully pretentious. While its only admirable inmate, in Lady Catherine's view, had been lost with the death of Mr Johnson's modest and thoughtful wife, who had, though with such signal lack of success, attempted to check her husband's exuberance these twenty years and better.

Still, they were near neighbours, and it would look exceedingly strange were she not to visit. She was rather shocked, upon being admitted, to find Mr Johnson's cravat tied very sketchily and his waistcoat positively flaunting a line of silver thread. His elder daughter, Caroline, rose to greet her with a becoming air of sorrow.

'So kind of you, Your Ladyship,' said she. 'My brother will be grieved to have missed you. He is consulting with Mr Collins at the rectory, about the funeral arrangements.'

'Ah,' said Lady Catherine, 'Mr Collins will do very well indeed.'

'Oh, certainly,' said Caroline, though she secretly held no very high opinion of Her Ladyship's rector.

Meanwhile Mr Johnson instructed a servant, in what he fondly believed to be an undertone, 'Fetch the muffins, my lad, and take care to bring the freshest ones.' And he rubbed his hands with a zeal as he added, 'There is not a cook in the country who can make muffins like ours. See if you do not agree, Your Ladyship. You will want precious little at luncheon after, I am sure!'

Lady Catherine said, with a rather steely smile, 'I was so grieved to hear about your poor mama, Miss Johnson. That lady had the patience of a saint.'

'And needed it – ha!' cried Mr Johnson, but then, as if struck, 'And yet – 'tis true enough – she was never one to complain. The only thing she *would* complain of was if I should come back from the Assizes a little loud and waken her, which I never intended to do!'

'Our loss is very great,' said Caroline.

'Aye, for she was loved across the parish!' boasted Mr Johnson. 'Not like some I could –'

'Mama,' said Caroline Johnson, fervently wishing to kick her father's boot, 'always did a very great deal for the poor.'

'True, true, for she was forever doing it,' said he. 'Why, she would never let those poor Pritchards be! There could scarcely have been a day, Your Ladyship, when Mrs Pritchard could say to herself, "Alone at last, to get on with my own business" – what with the soup and the herbal draughts and the bits of game and the inquirings after!'

'The Pritchards have been peculiarly unfortunate, I believe,' said Lady Catherine. 'You have made this room charming, Miss Johnson. *Such* a sweet collection of Tunbridge ware by the pianoforte.'

'Oh, but it cannot compare to Rosings! I trust Miss de Bourgh is well?'

'She is visiting with a friend in London,' said Lady Catherine. In fact, Anne had been ordered to visit Amelia Cuthbert, as Lord Cuthbert, Amelia's brother, was one of London's most eligible young men and – heaven knew! – she must wed, and the sooner the better. In fact, to Lady Catherine, Anne's fate was beginning to become rather concerning. Her accomplishments, whether through ill-health, impatience or possessing no ear at all for music, had always been restricted to embroidery and to the designing of attractive but useless little tables. Worse, after Darcy had been taken in by that appalling Bennet girl, Anne seemed to have altered from a passive, frail and slightly fretful young lady into a satirical one…Though Lady Catherine comforted herself by recalling that, as the striking Lord Cuthbert himself possessed rather a sardonic air, perhaps they might suit?

After Her Ladyship had departed, Mr Johnson said heartily, 'Well, there is one visit done, at least – I know no one who can look down her nose sideways better! But I think I spy the Richardson's carriage. I shall be very glad to see the Richardsons, for their daughter is as fine a creature as ever I set eyes on.'

'Oh Papa, you must not say such things, and Mama not yet buried!'

'Heyday!' cried he, stung. 'I was as fond of my wife as any man alive, but I hope I should always notice a pretty girl when I see one.'

'He will *not*,' said Caroline to Henry later, 'understand the first thing about tone. He *will* be hearty, when he ought to be stoical, and sportive when he ought to be sorrowful. I believe that he loved our mother as much as he could love anyone, but I fear that, the moment our period of mourning is over, he will make a great fool of himself over some young lady or other. Perhaps more than one!'

'Once the funeral is past, perhaps I shall have a word,' said Henry comfortingly. 'We can only do the best we can.'

❖

The day of the funeral dawned sunny and clear.

'So much the better for everyone at Warleigh Hall!' Mrs Collins thought, as she tended her hens behind the Rectory. ''Tis a miserable business for all the Johnsons, I am sure, but such a strain on William, as well!' For she had heard her husband practising his eulogy in the front room, whilst still keeping a diligent eye upon the road. No one knew better than Mr Collins the movements of the great people at Rosings, or was quicker to cross to the window, to assemble a most gratified bow.

He was still rehearsing his speech when Charlotte returned.

'Her sweet and gentle womanly nature or – perhaps better ?– her gentle and sweet womanly nature made her ever a friend to the poor… A *friend* to the poor… A friend to the *poor*… Oh heavens, it cannot be so very difficult!'

'It sounds very well, dear,' said Charlotte Collins. 'I am only sorry that I cannot hear you deliver it.'

'Oh heavens, never! Only recollect the scandal when Mrs Lefevre attended her husband's funeral! And *that* in town, besides! Will – ah – will the Richardsons come, do you suppose?'

'Oh, I should think so. And the Earl, I am certain, for Lady Catherine had a note from the Countess.'

'The Earl! You do not mean the Earl of Bittlesham?'

'Why, who should I mean, else? And why should he not?'

'The Earl of Bittlesham! – For *he*, you know, has a great deal of interest. A great deal of interest, indeed! Why, 'twas Bittlesham who got young Herbert a stall at Westminster!'

Charlotte turned away to hide a smile, for a stall at Westminster was reserved for the clerical elite – or at least, for the immensely well-connected. She could not imagine it befalling William – and besides, she was far happier in the country, with her books, her walks, her apple jam and her hens. But she hastened to soothe him. 'You will do perfectly, my dear, whether the Earl is listening or not! Why should you be concerned about an Earl, when you dine every week with Lady Catherine, herself?'

'Nay, 'tis not the same,' complained Mr Collins testily, 'for Her Ladyship and I comprehend each other perfectly.'

'Which is to say,' thought his wife, amused, 'you comprehend each another still worse than you both comprehend most other people!'

Mr Collins's nerves did not lessen. Once his wife had left he grew still more agitated – so much so that he went to his desk and extracted a little flask he kept in a bottom drawer, for the direst of emergencies. For surely an important eulogy, spoke before the cream of Kent (and even Sussex) society, was nothing less than the direst of emergencies? Just a few sips to clear his throat, and just such another dose before he left for the service, could do no harm at all...

'And how did you get on in town?' inquired her mama, the moment Anne had settled in her chair.

'Oh, it was all very agreeable,' said Anne, inspecting her fingernails.

'Lord Cuthbert keeps a famous cook, as all the world knows.'

'Certainly, their cook is well enough.'

'Did you attend any concerts?'

'Nothing beyond the usual. There was the most tremendous fuss about some new violinist called Janiewicz or Jancewicz, but *I* could see nothing so very wonderful about him. Violins always sounds so scrawny and thin – when they go high particularly! I would rather hear a pianoforte at any time.'

'What was Lord Cuthbert's opinion of his performance?' asked Lady Catherine – she believed, artfully.

'As to *that* I could not say, for at the concert he did nothing but hang about Lady Diana.'

'Lady Diana, did he? Did he, indeed!'

'While *she* was quite the disgrace, Mama, with Lord Cuthbert on one side and Mr Stoles on the other, and Sir Richard just behind, staring down her gown – if it could be termed a gown, for there was not enough of it to quite qualify – while tapping Mr Thornton and Sir Reginald in the first row with her fan! She quite set the place a-buzz – rather like the violinist. For his tone buzzed like a bee inside of a jug!'

Lady Catherine did not care for the sound of this (any more than her daughter had cared for the sound of the violinist). Despite the invitation from Lord Cuthbert's sister, there seemed very little chance of Lord Cuthbert's offering to Anne. She pressed a little harder. 'Did you ride out in the park very often?'

'Not with Lord Cuthbert, because he was forever fussing about his racehorse, Summer Sands or Shining Lights or whatever it is called... Amelia and I rode out when we could. But then, the weather has been so tedious! There were three days when we were absolutely confined, beyond one, very wet, visit to the Ellisons.'

'What,' inquired her mama, 'is the point of a racehorse?'

'I believe, to eat a great deal, and most of it money. So said Amelia, at any rate. And to run about at Newmarket or at other rather odd places. Some of them jump over fences, as well, but Lord

Cuthbert's horse does not. At least, I do not think so.'

Lady Catherine felt a renewed spurt of anger at her nephew Darcy – every bit as well-bred, well-off and well-looking as young Cuthbert – who she and her late sister had agreed would marry Anne. But *that* ship had sailed. Meanwhile, Darcy and his wife lacked even the common decency to appear unhappy, for they seemed quite sickeningly attached, at least as far as anyone could tell… Indeed, Mrs Darcy, for once properly dressed, had made a modest stir in town – why, there was even some rumour of Thomas Lawrence painting her portrait!

And all the while Anne, at nearly thirty, might almost be considered an old maid. Certainly no one of proper estate had yet sought her, unless one counted Lord Harvey, so greatly her senior, or that dreadful Mr Wright. Perhaps Anne might be obliged to consider a young man whose good fortune and excellent manners might compensate for his lack of breeding – a young man such as Mr Johnson's heir, Henry.

Henry Johnson! Was the idea really so impossible? Lady Catherine wondered. As Lady Alexa so often reminded her, times were changing – nothing was as sensible and well-organised as it had been in their day – while the younger Mr Johnson was not only wealthy but gentlemanly with it. Further, Warleigh Hall was situated in a very decent county and – once she herself was dead – Anne could live at Rosings, and Warleigh made over to Miss Johnson instead… She began to wonder how she might, with her usual tact, broach the possibility to her daughter.

✦

Mr Collins peeped dizzily into the sanctuary of St Mark's. The church was full for the funeral, although of course only men were allowed. The Earl of Bittlesham was there, looking more hawklike than ever, along with Mr Johnson and Henry, Mr Richardson and his sons and a great many others, some drawn by the memory of Mrs Johnson's many kindnesses and others by the still more urgent necessity of remaining in the good graces of the Earl, the Richardsons or the Johnsons themselves.

Mr Collins retreated to his tiny room behind the choir cubicle, feeling just a trifle giddy… A trifle giddy in the, ah, head, which made him feel even worse than he had during his little fit of nerves at the Rectory. Perhaps it had not been the wisest idea to drink from the flask, several times at home and then so very close to the beginning of the funeral? He rather wished, just then, that he had *not*, as he fumbled in his pocket for his well-thumbed, well-rehearsed eulogy.

It was not there. Appalled, Mr Collins fumbled again, in his other pocket, amidst his books, about the little desk and – in increasing panic – beneath his neatly ironed surplice, which he had yet to don… In his haste not to be late, he must have left the eulogy at the Rectory, for it was nowhere to be seen, and his curate Templeton already knocking at the door, saying rather urgently, 'Sir, Mr Collins sir, everyone is waiting. They are indeed!' Upon hearing the rector groan, he entered, asking, 'Mr Collins, are you quite well?'

In fact, Mr Collins had never felt less well in the entire course of his life, for he was entirely unused to stimulants, and had never drunk more than a thimbleful before. 'Goodness gracious!' said he, sitting down, rather hard, on the bench beneath the stained-glass window.

'What must I do?' asked his curate.

A wiser man might perhaps have said, 'I beg you, Templeton, tell them that I am unwell!' But Mr Collins was obstinate – and the

200

eulogy lost – and his hopes of a stall at Westminster, perhaps, lost along with it! And he had rather a poor opinion of his youthful curate, besides. (Templeton give a eulogy before an Earl? – never!) Thus, he rose, sighed, shook his head as if to set it to rights, and followed Templeton into the church sanctuary.

As he stood in the pulpit, swaying like a poplar in a breeze while doing his best to recollect the words of his eulogy, he noticed Henry Johnson's pallor. Poor fellow! Poor fellow! He cleared his throat, and blinked hard to stop his gaze from swimming, though why he felt quite so dizzy was beyond his understanding.

'Dear friends, friends and those who cared for the lady – I allude, naturally, to Mrs – to ah, Mrs – to the lady we are burying, that good, sweet, gentle soul – whose, ah – nature was one of sweetness and gentleness. And sweetness. Never forget *that*! Forget that, gentlemen, at your peril! – And, indeed, goodness. Which I had intended to mention before. In short, her sweet and gentle nature, or her gentle and sweet nature – either, really – led her to be a poor friend to the sweet, while her gentlemanliness was, unarguably, sweet indeed. And her gentleness, likewise! I venture to say that never were such gentility and manliness united – or indeed untied – as in the later lady – I should say, the late lady. Unless it might be in Lady Catherine, herself!'

At this, the curate Templeton – with whom Henry Johnson had been most urgently whispering – advanced towards the pulpit, nervously suggesting that they proceed to the churchyard.

'Just so,' said Mr Collins. 'Just so. I thank you, my good Sparkes, for reminding me. And for visiting from your stall at Westminster!' (For Sparkes had been his curate before Templeton, though he had never been to Westminster.) Then, with the comfortable sense of having been as impressive as possible, Mr Collins proceeded to lead the way to the graveside at a stately, if notably uneven, pace.

'Nay, sir, for I could not,' Templeton meanwhile whispered to Henry Johnson.

'But great heavens, man, the fellow is incapacitated!'

'I *am* sorry, sir! But – but I cannot!'

Briefly, Henry considered whether he himself… but surely one need be ordained? And in the end, Mr Collins managed the burial satisfactorily enough until, in a fresh wave of giddiness, he advised, 'Into your hands, O Lord, we commend your servant, Mr Johnson.' (Sensation, through which Mr Collins soared triumphant.) 'As our bodies come from the dust of the ground, we return the dust to the ground. Ground to ground! The Lord taketh away, but also giveth! Blessed be the name of the Lord!'

And with that, Mr Collins turned majestically, bowed, tripped over a sod of earth, and half-fell into the arms of the curate Templeton.

'I think,' said Henry to his father, 'we should lead the way to the carriages ourselves. And at once.' For the carriages, waiting in a queue down Church Lane, were to take the mourners to Warleigh for the funeral meats. But his father remained aggrieved.

'What the blazes did the great blockhead mean, by saying that *I* was dead?' he wished to know.

❦

The funeral concluded – though forming the basis of all manner of ribaldry, while the landlord of the Queen's Head made rather a speciality of imitating Collins's peroration – Lady Catherine lost no time in suggesting her latest scheme to her daughter.

'The truth is,' said she, 'that you must marry *someone*, for the sake of the line. And, from all that I can gather, Lord Cuthbert has not the slightest intention of settling down – for Lady Diana, I am quite sure, would never have him. For that reason, I believe that you should make more of an effort with Henry Johnson. He is a *most* respectable young man, though hampered by keeping his father in order.'

'At the funeral,' said Anne pertly, ''twas all he could do to keep your dear rector in order!'

'Mr Collins was most unwell,' said her mother icily. 'He is subject to bouts of giddiness, Charlotte tells me, when particularly overworked. The apothecary's own opinion –'

'Well, every soul at the funeral said that he was clearly in his cups.'

'What nonsense! Mr Collins is a *most* temperate young man! Why, he never takes more than a finger of wine at Rosings!'

'But how could he have claimed that *Mr* Johnson was dead, whilst burying *Mrs* Johnson, else?'

'He misspoke, he admitted as much to myself. A mere slip of the tongue, as might happen to anyone. He suffers from a nervous disorder, inherited from his own father, one which has occasionally afflicted him ever since his university days. But I do not intend to discuss Mr Collins but your duty instead – for *I* shall die at some point, just as poor Mrs Johnson did!'

'But do not fret, Mama, for when you *do*, I daresay that Mr Collins will claim that you were as gentlemanlike as she!'

'I beg,' said her mother sharply, 'that you give my opinion the consideration it deserves!'

'Well then, if we *must* be serious, the difficulty is that I cannot help rather liking Lord Cuthbert, while Henry Johnson is so tedious and prosy, so predictable and dull!'

'Lord Cuthbert might yet come to his senses. It is not impossible. But it is as well to have another young man in reserve, in case he should *not*. Henry Johnson is a steady young man, who has never had anything to do with his father's business – though being in trade is not the social impediment it once was, as Alexa is forever reminding me. It would be an immense honour for him, beyond a doubt, but you might go a great deal farther, and do a great deal worse!'

'I do not mind *every* young man connected to trade,' said Anne thoughtfully, 'only the tedious ones. And Caroline did say that they would call. But it is such a manoeuvring business, altogether!'

'Marriage,' said her mother heavily, 'is indeed a manoeuvring business, and always was. When I think of that encroaching Bennet girl –'

'Quite,' said her daughter.

❦

The call being paid, Henry felt rather taken aback to find Miss de Bourgh standing by him, rather closer than was usual.

'I hope you and your sister have recovered from all that has occurred,' said she.

'We are doing, I believe, as well as might be expected... I trust that you enjoyed your time with Miss Cuthbert in town?'

'Tolerably,' said Anne, 'but such a rush. So much to do, so many fittings, so many events and engagements! I prefer the quietness of the country, after all.' And this was clever, for she had heard that Henry Johnson was not especially fond of London.

'I am quite of your mind,' said he. 'I feel a rush of pleasure every time I arrive in town – yet, after a few days, I find I cannot breathe easily there.'

'Nor I.'

'I do not know his sister, but Lord Cuthbert is a most amusing fellow.'

OF TACT AND TACTICS

'A bit of a rattle, perhaps,' said she, while thinking – with regret – how very much more amusing he was than Henry Johnson.

'I *did* hear that Miss Amelia has all the sense that Cuthbert lacks, for his good luck has gone all to pieces, I understand. Excuse me, I beg, I must just have a word with my father.' For his father was wandering towards the collection of cakes, before anything had been said about them. Really, he was as much trouble as a child!

Anne was half-inclined to rush after Henry, to appeal for more information – though *that* would never do. But what in heaven's name did he mean by Lord Cuthbert's luck 'gone all to pieces?' And how could she possibly inquire without betraying how greatly it affected her? Although there might be a chance during the dinner, for she would certainly be seated by Henry Johnson, and Her Ladyship by his father...

And thus, between the first course and the second, she murmured, 'Forgive me, Mr Johnson, but when you said that my dear Amelia's brother might be – perhaps – in some slight difficulty – whatever did you mean? I have been fretting ever since, for my dear Amelia's sake!'

'Forgive me, I beg,' cried Henry, 'I never wished to alarm you! Cuthbert is certainly not in the kind of trouble you might be thinking of. Indeed, I expect it is all nothing. However, his horse, Shining Sands – you know he owns a racehorse, I suppose?' Anne murmured an assent. 'As fine a beast as was ever seen – Irish-bred, I believe, and fancied at Ascot and Doncaster. At any rate, the creature broke its leg in training and *that* after costing poor Cuthbert a pretty penny, what with the purchase, the trainer, and all the other expenses besides!'

'That is very ill luck, indeed!'

'But I daresay all will end well, unless he has borrowed a vast amount on the strength of its future winning which, to be sure,

Cuthbert is far too canny to have done.'

Anne felt almost faint with shock. The racehorse! – Did it alter anything that Cuthbert had gone from being the envied owner of a famous racehorse to – perhaps – suffering some level of serious debt?

She believed that it did. She found herself recollecting Cuthbert's sudden want of spirits when his trainer's bills arrived… his sister's chaffing him about the horse's prospects… and his friends' ribald jests about his riches to come. In short, while only last week – with Cuthbert's hopes for Ascot all alive – she herself would have been nothing more interesting than some friend of Amelia's, *this* week she might be perceived in quite a different light, as Lady Catherine's sole heir. Though she was far from being the only heiress in London, of course. There were a few who were very much richer… She thought of Lady Rosalind, rumoured to have £80,000, and of the still more extravagantly endowed Miss Williamson – though she was a literary recluse and said to be rather odd. Yet both had been extensively courted for years, and by men of far greater pretensions than Lord Cuthbert!

'When,' she asked in confusion, 'I mean, forgive me, but when did the poor horse fall?'

'Last Saturday, I believe,' said Henry vaguely. 'Unless *that* was only when my father heard about it. Have you ever ventured to Ascot yourself, Miss de Bourgh?' But Anne's mind was too engaged to respond.

'So recently!' she thought. 'Since I returned to Rosings!'

And she wondered if she might not contrive some excuse to return to town, though so swift a retreat might appear rather strange, especially as she had made such a point of longing for her native air… But she was wild to discover how Lord Cuthbert might be affected, and to offer lashings of sweet womanly sympathy with regards to his unexampled plight.

Oh, he would precisely suit her, with that saturnine quickness of his! She longed for escape from her mama – but, most of all, she longed for someone young, handsome and lively. It was not country air she truly hungered for as much as for freer, headier air... Lord Cuthbert was widely travelled, and his sister had often mentioned his fondness for Switzerland and Italy. What a release it would be, after Rosings! And then, that impudent way he had of lifting his eyebrow, that flash of silver in his hair!

The rest of the visit to Warleigh passed in a great blur, for Anne was passionately impatient to be back at Rosings, where she could write little notes on hot-pressed paper to each of her connections in hopes of an invitation to town – for which she must invent some plausible excuse. (Another scratching violinist – perhaps a pain in her tooth?) It was imperative to be on the spot, at such a moment!

Lady Cuthbert! – it did sound well – and would brilliantly erase the ignominy of being disdained by her cousin Darcy! There was nothing *amiss* with Henry Johnson – she believed him honest and trustworthy – but the stain of trade still occasioned in her an instinctive recoil, for Anne was, at heart, her mother's daughter. In Lord Cuthbert she recognised ambition and a daredevil spirit that matched her own... and then, his height, his delightful manners!

My dear Mary, she wrote, *<u>Such</u> a nuisance, but I find I am obliged to return to town after all... My dear Emily, Indeed, I have heard Janiewicz, and how I long to be transported again! I was wondering if you planned on attending next week's concert and, if so, if there might be the slightest chance that you could procure me a ticket? ... My beloved Martha, As I must return to town to consult my dentist, I was hoping that you might conceivably find space for me...*

But all these pretty notes, dispatched by the first post the next morning, were rendered utterly unnecessary when Anne received, by the second post, a note from Amelia Cuthbert – to whom she had not dared to write at all.

My dearest Anne, Should you possibly be allowed to return to town, sooner rather than later, it might be a very good thing. I have news of great importance – at least to us, and even, perhaps, of some slight significance to yourself. I cannot say much but, recent as was your visit, I quite yearn to see you again. Do let me know if your mama could spare you! Your devoted Amelia

Lady Catherine was unhappy, and even shocked, when her daughter admitted at dinner that she planned a return to London – and almost immediately. 'My tooth,' said she, 'is so exquisitely painful that I cannot bear it. And Amelia has not the slightest objection.'

'Dear me. And I had only just told Caroline Johnson that you might ride with them on Friday!'

'Oh! Mama, if you only knew what I am enduring! As if red-hot pincers were –'

'Oh, very well,' said Lady Catherine, in dissatisfied tones. 'What a pity that there is no dentist closer! However, you need not stay beyond next Tuesday, I am sure.'

❖

As soon as Anne de Bourgh arrived, Amelia pulled her into her dressing room. 'I did not dare to write more explicitly,' said she.

'About your brother?'

'Yes! I know that you do not dislike him – and I only hope that you will *not*, when you learn that he has, in truth, been rather hasty.'

'Why, in what respect?' asked Anne, her heart beating quicker.

'It is all the fault of that silly racehorse of his. On the strength of two wins, he has borrowed against all the grander winnings he *presumed* that it would achieve, throughout the entire season. And it has hurt its leg so badly that it can never race more!'

'The poor creature!'

'Indeed, and poor Sidney as well, for now he cannot pay his debts.'

'Heavens!' cried Anne. 'I would give you everything that I possess, in all the world, but I have little beyond what Mama gives me. I could never –'

'Oh heavens, I am not asking *you* for money! It is only that – that – oh, 'tis so embarrassing! But well – were Sidney to *marry* – marry sensibly, I mean –'

'Good gracious!'

'I have been thinking, my dearest Anne, of *you*.'

Anne looked shocked. (She had practised looking shocked before the glass while still at Rosings and been not displeased with the result.)

She said, 'But I never, in all my life, imagined –'

'But how I beg that you imagine it now! For then, not only would all our difficulties be over, but we would be sisters! And truly, Sidney is as good a fellow as exists, in all the world! He *can* say a rather superior, rather cutting, thing but he is so loving a creature at heart, and the best brother, and the most loyal friend, and the kindest son to our mama! My dearest Anne! *Do* say that you might be willing to think about it, at least!'

Anne thought, in amazement, 'Cannot she see that I am very nearly thirty, and that I am tone-deaf – not only to music, but to all those silly little airs and graces that can attach a man? It is as if

Amelia imagines that I, in common with Lady Diana, have half London at my feet, instead of resembling – bad poetry aside – the reclusive Miss Williamson instead!'

Anne was entirely silent, as if shocked. Finally, she said, 'My dear Amelia, you have quite taken my breath away! For I never, in all my life, thought of your brother and yet, and yet – it is not impossible. For I always liked Lord Cuthbert, for your sake!'

And, as the fair ladies fondly embraced, Amelia felt the first sense of relief since her brother had confessed his debts – for, as he had gloomily confided, 'Your Anne may be my only hope, for I believe, in all of London, there is none other with sufficient funds whom I could bear!'

On Sidney's advice, Amelia had secured the Crawfords for dinner. They were two of her brother's prime favourites, for Henry Crawford was clever and insinuating, his sister Mary dark and lively. *She* was full young for the company, but as adept at society as she was said to be at playing the harp.

'How fares the Admiral?' Amelia inquired of Mary.

'His moods are plaguing indeed!'

'In what respect?'

'Why, in every respect, for they test my patience and that of his housekeeper, and his cook as well. How his wife can bear him, I cannot conceive! But there! I must not complain, lest I appear as contrary as he.'

'Nay,' teased her brother, 'but *that* will never stop you!'

Mary vouchsafed him a look, but a look such as would have persuaded most brothers to turn the subject, which Mr Crawford instantly did, and smoothly too, 'I trust, Miss de Bourgh, that you have a little relief from your toothache?'

'Oh! It was quite like magic, the way he removed it – and all my discomfort – away!' cried Anne, who had not troubled her dentist, for fear of losing a tooth, and all for nothing.

Later, under cover of a gap in the courses, Lord Cuthbert leaned towards her and whispered, 'I suspect you did not attend the dentist at all, Miss de Bourgh!' And then, observing her little start, her little blush, 'I suspect we understand each other – for we always *have* understood each other, have we not?'

To which she could only smile.

It was the beginning, as Anne recognised – that single comment, in so intoxicatingly private a tone.

On Tuesday they were seen at a concert, Miss de Bourgh with that famously rapt look in her eyes, and a complete conversion to the artistry of the violinist Janiewicz. On Wednesday, they rode out with Amelia on Rotten Row, where they were seen by any number of people. On Thursday John Thorpe noticed them laughing immoderately at a play – *Hamlet*, as it happened – nor did the significance of three consecutive events go unacknowledged, for Thorpe mentioned his suspicions to Sullivan, and between Sullivan, Thorpe, the clubs and the coffee houses, it was common knowledge by Friday that the fall of Shining Sands had done the business, and that Miss de Bourgh – thin, pale, delicate and under-sized as she was – was to be wooed and won at last.

My dear Alexa, wrote Her Ladyship triumphantly, *Between ourselves, I never once thought Darcy quite clever enough to suit Anne, but I believe Lord Cuthbert will make her very happy. The house at Richmond is to be sold – for Anne has never much cared for Richmond – and they are looking for a property rather more extensive, perhaps in Grosvenor Street. They are to tour Italy following the wedding, but only once the weather might be depended on. I shall miss her a great deal, but it must count as quite a conquest, and she did well to bide her time, for there were any number of others* – (for zero was still a number) – *I may tell you, waiting in the wings but none as quick and lively, as charming or as well-looking as Lord Cuthbert is. How I look forward to seeing you, upon your return from Scotland! Yours ever, Catherine.*

Mary Rose

(Author's note: Some very genuine Austen enthusiasts can't bear any of Austen's heroes to be less than pure on their wedding nights. If you feel this way, I respectfully suggest that you skip this short story and scroll on to the next one.)

Mr. Knightley's answer was the most distinct.

'Is Miss Woodhouse sure that she would like to hear what we are all thinking of?'

'Oh! no, no' – cried Emma, laughing as carelessly as she could – 'Upon no account in the world. It is the very last thing I would stand the brunt of just now.'

(from *Emma,* Chapter 7)

The other day, as a newly wedded gentleman, I fell to remembering. And, as my Emma has preceded me to town, and as this is the time of year when there is least to do about Donwell Abbey, I have resolved to read through my old diaries before destroying them. I wish there to be no danger of their falling into my wife's hands upon my death for, as I am sixteen years Emma's senior, I will likely die before her.

These diaries could be of no possible interest to any other person, but Emma might, perhaps, be made unhappy by discovering that, many years ago, I loved another. They possess no literary merit – indeed, I will doubtless blush while rereading the volume

213

in question and wonder that I had not burned it long ago! For years I preserved it, assuming that I should never feel such passion more – but I find that, as I pick up the little book – leather-worked, rather fine, it might have been used for accounts instead – that I feel a little curiosity to recollect all that occurred, in the light of my new love.

My wife in town and the servants all abed... Come, courage to remember!

July 29th

'The new maid,' said Mama. 'Sullivan, could you ask the new maid to come? Oh! and do remind me whether she is a Sophie or a Jane or whatever her name might be.'

'Yes, ma'am. Her name is Mary Rose.'

'Then Mary will do... I wish to see her about my lace shawl, as she might perhaps be able to mend it. She is said to be very clever with her needle, and my eyes are so tired.'

As my brother and I were playing at backgammon, and as I was losing, I used the excuse of this interruption to say, 'Since the rain has stopped, John, do you not fancy a ride, instead?' But John, who was born with all the thorough meticulousness that I lack, merely reminded me that it was my turn. I was still considering my move when the new maid entered.

Though related to my mother's ladies' maid, she in no way resembled her. Mrs Hook was alert, solid, stodgy and beady-eyed. By contrast, Mary Rose was small, slight and excessively pretty, with high cheekbones, a pointed chin and a few, very fair, curls just escaping her cap. Her gown was neat and her feet tiny. She curtseyed to Mama and asked, 'What must I do?' in a voice as light as her figure.

Mama explained what she wished for, and Mary bore the shawl away. By then I had lost the game and John had agreed to ride out with me. As we walked to the stables he complained, 'You did not play nearly as well as usual.'

'I was distracted.'

'You are a good deal too easily distracted, as Mr Culbertson always complained.'

This was too true for argument, so I let it pass. We had been at the same school before I started at Oxford, and Culbertson had been housemaster to us both. John – still a pupil there – excelled in every respect, while I had succeeded only in cricket and in history. I much preferred being up at university, where I was not obliged to study every subject. Mama had once sighed, 'It is a good thing, George, that you are the elder, for while John has the application to succeed in whatever he has a mind for, *you* need only manage the estate.'

The older George Knightley thought, 'And she was correct for I have found, over the years, that managing the estate has grown to fascinate me as much as history, while John has certainly succeeded a great deal better at the law than I could have done... Though I certainly know families where birth order could well have been reversed, in our own, I believe, it was for the best!'

In truth, I had been distracted by the unusual beauty of the new parlourmaid, though to have said so would have scandalised the strait-laced John.

As we rode, he annoyed me by slowing at times to recommend again what crop might work – once I had eventually succeeded our father – in this field or that. Yet even John can surprise, for as we were heading back, he asked, 'Do you think Father is all right, George?'

'Father? In what respect?'

'I do not quite know.'

I grappled with this. Our father, then aged about forty, had scarcely had a day's illness in his life. He worked hard, engaged us in estate business and – as a rule – only fretted over those of his tenants who were failing or over legal issues at the Assizes. But John was intuitive as well as clever and that evening, after Mama and he had gone upstairs, I decided to inquire.

'I am well enough, but, as you are now nineteen, you ought to know that I am worried about your mother,' said Father brusquely.

'She has always been delicate.'

'Quite – her lungs, particularly… Also, I am having difficulties with the accounts.'

'But your steward sees to the accounts, does he not? And how often have I heard you say how greatly you rely on Hook!'

'I expect you have. However, as you will learn, George, no one is absolutely to be depended upon. Tenants regularly as reliable as clockwork dodge their rents, neighbours generally agreeable decide to encroach. Even Hook himself – but enough said, I think!'

❖

How well I would have understood him now – and how ill I understood him then! This was perhaps the first time he vouchsafed anything serious to me – and I mistook his meaning.

I was perhaps a little afraid of Hook, steward of Donwell and husband to Mama's ladies' maid, for I had once seen him violently cuff a stableboy and he was ferocious in collecting money from the tenants. John once said that Hook had two tones, a gentlemanly one with Papa and quite a growl at other times…

❖

MARY ROSE

Today, Mama told John and me the story of Mary Rose. She is 22, though she looks no older than sixteen, and had been briefly married to a butcher called Hartley or Hartman. But the butcher had died, and suddenly too, so Mary found herself returned to Donwell. Until she can get another place, Mama has taken her on as a parlourmaid, though we have two parlourmaids already. As she said, 'It is always good to be kind and, as everyone knows, parlourmaids rarely last long, for they are forever getting wedded and moving away. I suspect that Mary will wed again herself, for she is unusually well-looking and, after all, she has no child. A babe is what will deter most men, after all!'

'So, she has been married,' I thought, almost in wonderment. All that beauty had belonged to some butcher, who had collapsed in his shop and never come home again… I wondered if Mary had been very attached to him, and if she had been very unhappy at his death. I can guess nothing at all from her manner, for it seems always the same, whether she is neatly gathering up the tea things, or asking Mama what she wished done about a bit of lace. She has a soft, pretty voice, and deft, swift movements. Elaine, the principal parlourmaid, seems to dislike her, for I heard her say to one of the footmen, 'Such airs and graces! One would have thought her married into the gentry itself, instead of some butcher, baker or candlestick-maker!'

On Tuesday, while I was crossing from the stables, I met Mary struggling with a great deal of laundry. 'Here,' said I, 'I shall take that. Where are you going?'

'Oh no, sir. 'Tis not fit!'

She was correct, in that it might not look well, so I proposed calling Charles or Harry to help. But even that distressed her.

'Oh no, sir, you must not trouble Charles, for he is with the master!' cried she and, in one breath, 'I *shall* be teased, if you do. I can manage well enough – though I thank you kindly all the same!' Thus I was forced to let her continue, as unsteadily as she might, and to oblige myself to turn away in case she wished to set it down without fear of my interference.

Ever since, I cannot help noticing that, when she comes into the room for some service, or to inquire of Mama, she will sometimes look at me and, should she happen to catch my glance, colour a little.

'I hope,' said John this afternoon, 'that your new parlourmaid is healthy, Mama.'

'Why, I hope so too, for a cleverer hand with a needle I have never encountered! But why should she be poorly?'

'Her colour varies so! She enters the room, as pale as paper, and then turns pink, and then returns to pallor again… I daresay it is nothing, but I did read that it might be symptomatic of a blood disorder.'

'Did you? Well then, I shall mention it to Mrs Hook.'

It was something I had noticed myself, but would never have dared to mention, the fluctuations of colour on that lovely face.

August 13th

On Thursday, recollecting an invitation I had left in the coach, I went down to the stable yard, where I stumbled across Mary Rose, in tears.

'Are you all right Miss – ah –' (I had almost said Hook, for I could never recollect her wedded name.)

'Oh yes, sir! You need not – you need not think –'

'But something must have occurred to distress you! Unless you are still grieving, perhaps?'

'No,' she said swiftly, 'I am not grieving, sir, not at all. I am extremely grateful and happy to be here at Donwell.'

I hated myself for asking but could not help it. 'And yet you were much affected at the time, I am sure?' She looked downwards but said nothing. 'I mean,' said I, 'It cannot be easy, to lose a husband!'

'No, sir,' said she, but her tone did not convince. I took a step closer and said impulsively, 'Surely you cared for him?'

'No, sir,' said she, and this time she did glance up, her eyes swimming with tears.

I felt shocked, exhilarated, speechless. I knew that I should leave, that it was most improper to speak so personally to a servant. And yet I asked, in a low voice, 'He was unkind to you?' She could not answer my guess – it was nothing more – but her gaze entreated me not to press her. Longing to comfort her, I strove for a more normal tone, one like my father's, saying, 'I am glad, at least, that you are happy here. My mother would be exceedingly sorry if such was not the case, Mary.'

She looked at me, as if wishing – even yearning – to trust me, but merely curtseyed and left. Later that day, my mother chanced to ask the butler why Mary had not brought in the tea.

'Begging your pardon, ma'am, I gave her leave to go into Highbury,' said Sullivan.

'But why? It is not her usual half-day off!'

Sullivan said, 'She requested it, ma'am, most particularly.'

'Oh very well,' said Mama. 'But do let Mr Hook know, once she returns.'

He lowered his voice. 'I fear, ma'am, that was why she so urgently wished to visit a friend at Highbury. I did wonder if Mr Hook might be displeased with her, for some reason.'

'Did you, indeed? Do you have any notion why?'

But then he spoke too softly for me to hear. I trusted that Mama would do anything needful for, once she interests herself in anyone, she is generally fearless in their defence. Still, Hook was what my father called 'invaluable' – and there could surely be no contest between an invaluable steward and a superfluous parlourmaid. But why should she wish to avoid her own father, who had taken her in after she was widowed? Did he frighten her? Was that what she had almost told me in the stables – before shame or embarrassment had stopped her?

The next day – yesterday – I asked Mama, as casually as I could, 'Has Mary Rose returned?'

'You mean Mary? Oh yes! It was only a little misunderstanding, I believe, between herself and Hook.'

But I remained unconvinced, and upon spotting her making a fuss of the new litter of puppies in the stables, I boldly asked, 'Why did you wish to avoid Mr Hook the other day, Mary Rose?' (I was the only person in the house to use the 'Rose', which I secretly preferred.)

'Oh sir, 'tis not fit for *you* to know!'

'It is fit for me to know, if you might be ill-treated in my father's house!'

'I think not, sir,' said she, very quietly.

Unsure whether or not to feel offended, I asked, 'Am I to understand that you refuse to tell me?'

She nodded, but with tears in her eyes.

'You refuse?'

'I *am* sorry, sir.'

I said impulsively, 'I believe he beats you!'

She almost whispered, 'Yes, sir. Sometimes.'

'This cannot be permitted!'

But she had turned, as if to run away. I stopped her. 'Can you show me?'

'Oh, sir! Never.'

I felt myself go hot and cold all over. 'Then tell me – where did he – ?'

She said, with the greatest possible reluctance. 'My shoulder.'

Her shoulder. I reminded myself that she was under my family's protection – the estate's protection – even from her own father, if required. I said, very formally, 'If you would not mind – if it be compatible with modesty, of course.'

After hesitating, she pushed her collar an inch downward, revealing a vile raw stripe, near the base of that white neck, as if from a tiger's claw. I could not help crying out, 'Not a whip?'

'Oh never, sir! Only his belt!'

There was precious little difference, in my opinion. I recalled – very inconsequentially – Mr Ladner, a master at our school, who had used to relish whipping the younger lads with his belt whenever they misbehaved. I said, 'Replace your collar, I beg. My father shall know of this the instant he returns!'

'Oh no, Master George… for if he does, then *my* father might lose his place!'

And really, this might be true, for my father's notions of chivalry are far in advance of most people's. He would surely scorn to employ a steward who could lift a belt to a child, even to an adult child… Again, I knew not what to say.

She said urgently, 'Also, it may be that I have found – a place – and even a means – of running away.'

'You have friends elsewhere?'

'There was a woman – so very kind! – where I lived when I was married.'

221

'A relative of your husband's, perhaps?' I asked, doubtful whether this knowledge was a relief or not.

'No sir, the wife of the rector. *She* would take me in, or else find me a place, I am sure. But oh! – you must not tell the master!'

I bit my lip. I felt then – as I feel *now* – that I could not remain quiet about so serious a matter – for if Hook could beat his own daughter, might not he bully others of the servants? But perhaps it would be safest to wait till she had run away? And yet, if that happened, I would never see her more! That thought, her trembling, the wound to that sweet neck, undid me.

And so, fool that I was, I kissed her.

✦

'Fool that I was, indeed!' thought Knightley, almost twenty years later, pushing the little book away in disgust. How dared I compromise her so? For not only might we have been seen, but I had already put her in as impossible a position as my own! Caught between ruining her father and ruining herself, she chose to give in to me.

Not at once, for she fought her inclination bravely. But in the end, that was what it amounted to – and entirely my own fault, besides.

I kept fretting meanwhile that she might secretly resolve to flee – and, at least partly, from myself! And – as I later learned – such was the case. However, her mother discovered her plan, begged her to remain, and promised to speak to Hook. (Which Mrs Hook assumed was her sole concern. I do not believe that Mary Rose confessed anything about me to her mother.)

✦

MARY ROSE

August 14th

I had never kissed anyone before – though I knew many at university who had, and a great deal more besides – and the sensation was so astonishing and unexpected that I could not get it out of my mind. I could think of nothing else, dream of no one else. I used to long for her to come into the dining room, but it was almost never she. I had not, you see, been able to interpret Mary Rose's expression, before she fled. Had she been terrified, mortified, flattered, embarrassed? Had I comforted her, increased her worries – or merely made it still likelier that she would flee? I fretted about this constantly.

Most often, I believed her to have been shocked – but, as I reminded myself, I was not only several years her junior, but infinitely her junior in terms of experience of life, for I had never been beaten – nor married, either. I was so distracted that I failed to concentrate on my work, and Father had to remind me twice to call at Hartfield and, even then, I suspect that my answers made very little sense.

During Thursday and Friday I saw her not, but everything seemed exactly as usual, and I began to feel a little calmer. For, thinking it over, how could she be conveyed to the house of the rector's wife, so far from hence, without her father's approval? And, even if she *could* contrive to get so far, how could she be assured of this woman's assistance? – while it would be madness to go without! It was only today when John said, 'I hear that Hook's daughter is to leave us.'

My heart stopped.

'Leave us! But why?'

'I do not know, and Mama would not say, but what *I* think – what I guess, I should say – is that Hook, whose temper seems

223

increasingly uncertain – that business with the Martins, for example – is quite likely unkind. Were I our father, I might even consider dismissing him.'

'*Consider* it!' I cried hotly, for *I* would have dismissed him long since.

'Indeed. For, excellent at figures and clever at business as he may be, I suspect him to be getting ill-will where the tenants are concerned and, in addition –'

'He is wicked!' I said, so fervently that John seemed rather alarmed.

'Wicked is a strong term, George. Though I cannot think that it reflects well upon the estate that –'

'Hang the estate!' I cried and ran down to the stables. There I found clueless stable lads and bewildered stable hands, but an entire shortage of information. I ordered the youngest to the kitchen, to discover where the maids might be.

'Elaine and Sarah are upstairs sir, and Mary seems to have disappeared. Would not Harry do?'

But Harry would most assuredly *not* do. What if Mary Rose had fled Donwell, altogether? I spent so long hovering about the stables – for the servants had to pass through the stables to move between their own quarters and the Abbey – that the head of the stables, old Hutchings, risked a little jest at my expense, 'Why, since when were you so keen on horseflesh, Mr. George? 'Twas not three years since you told me ye'd no mind even to hunt, for not liking the foxes to be killed!'

Suddenly I spotted Mary Rose, who was rushing past with some folded linen. Heedless of Hutchings, I caught her up at once.

'I heard that you were leaving,' I said, as casually as I could contrive.

'I may be, sir,' said she, not looking at me, but straight before her instead.

'Your father?'

'In – in part, sir.'

'Or me?'

She turned aside to hide her countenance, murmuring, 'Again, sir – in part.'

I said, in my straightforward way, 'Come, we must talk this through.'

'Nay, sir – *we* must never talk at all!'

'Because you have been told off for it?'

'Because,' she said, turning to face me, ''tis not safe. Not for either of us.'

'At last I comprehend you. You do not trust me!'

And her look as she spoke, I believe, will never leave me as she said, 'No, sir. Instead, I cannot trust – myself!'

Suddenly I noticed Hutchings staring at us across the courtyard. He could never have overheard her – or could he? – for nothing was sharper than Hutchings's hearing! Inwardly cursing the fellow, I said brusquely, 'We cannot speak in public. I shall return at eleven.' And without waiting for her response – for I feared that she would refuse – I left. And by the time I dared glance behind me, neither she nor Hutchings was to be seen.

Briefly, the elder Knightley wondered if the occasional rumour that had surfaced about his past might have been old Hutchings's doing. Not that it mattered, for there was no proof, beyond that securely locked in his brother's law office...

How hard this had been on his impulsive youthful self, Knightley recollected perfectly. But looking back, how confoundedly hard it must have been on Mary Rose! What an arrogant, selfish, casual, obnoxious and entitled young fool he had been, thinking only of himself and his own passion! And he flung the leather book from him, with half a mind to burn it at once.

But then he forced himself to retrieve it. It was of use – of use, at very least, in humbling him. And some unacknowledged part of himself still wished to remember.

Almost two decades ago – it was a period! Two decades was a period!

❖

She was not there when I arrived, but I heard a hesitant step soon after. I pulled her into a vacant horse bay – it was very dark by then, of course, but there was a little light from the sconces. She let out a startled gasp, so I said at once, 'Forgive my impetuosity, but we cannot risk becoming a subject of gossip. Has he beaten you again?'

'No, sir,' said she.

'Thank God! Now I have given the matter a great deal of thought, Miss – Mrs – Mary Rose – and I am not the correct person to address Mr Hook. Would that I were! But I am not quite of age, while my father –'

'Oh sir, but no one must! – You have been most kind, and I am grateful, but I ought never to have –'

'Permit me to finish, I beg. But *someone* must speak to Hook, and – given my father's own hastiness – I believe that the someone must be a woman. Your own mother now –'

'She has promised to, sir, but she fears him too!'

'What of the housekeeper, then?' For our housekeeper was famously formidable.

'I believe,' she said, 'that there is none who lacks fear of him, except young Harry.'

'Harry, the footman?'

226

'And I only wish *he* feared him more!'

Longing to see her countenance clearer, I said, 'It is no more the place of a footman to report a steward's wickedness than it is my own – for Hook must be the footman's superior and I, of course, ought not to know the first thing about it. But this is unendurable! Does he beat your mother, as well?'

'Almost never, sir, and yet he uses her ill.'

'And does she bear it?'

'She does, sir.'

'I wish,' I said impatiently, 'that you would not be forever calling me sir!'

'I must – sir.'

'Oh, very well! In that case, would you permit me to speak to my own father? For what have we done that was wrong, beyond the once?' (When I could not help myself, I did not say.)

'Oh no, sir, for my father would think that I had told of him! Then everything would be worse than ever!'

Then she burst into tears, as people say. I put an arm about her – but she removed it. 'Nay sir, you must not – for that will also make matters worse!'

I am not proud of what happened next for – I believe – I lost all reason. No sooner had I touched her than she half-stumbled into my arms. I held her fast, hoping to comfort, her heart – to my inflamed fancy – beating like an injured bird's. I believe I kissed her cap first, and then her temple and then… and then, with a little cry, she broke away – and ran away, too. In the stable yard she turned, and the expression on her face, just lit by the sconce, truly startled me. How many times did I attempt, later, to read her expression! Terror, exhilaration, misery… I could not begin to disentangle it all! Then she fled.

❖

The older Knightley recalled that he did not see her again for several months, for he left as early as he could for university the next day, and saw none beyond Harry, the footman, at breakfast.

✦

October 2nd

Oxford, I swear, will be my cure. Work will be my cure. I swear it, here, in these pages. Never again shall I add to poor Mary Rose's woes with my childish selfishness!

October 12th

I have, for these past weeks, attempted all that I promised, pushing that illicit embrace to the back of my consciousness, astonishing my tutors with my industry, and performing better than I ever did before.

I *did*, last night, confess my feelings to my closest friend, who said with a laugh, 'Love? You are not in love, my poor Knightley – not a bit of it! Instead you are most certainly quite deeply in lust and the cure for that – ha! – lies all round Oxford! Come with me tomorrow night and I shall prove it!'

But I believed that I was indeed in love, and refused so steadily that I finally shook his confidence in the diagnosis.

'What, you had three conversations with the girl – and those mostly about this rabid father – and a single kiss – and you have since lost interest in any other living creature?'

I acknowledged, almost humiliated, that this appeared to be the case but added, 'I believe, Johnson, that I am fool enough to fall in love with almost anyone. I have the disposition for it. So much so that the first woman I engage with at one of these houses you mention would probably entrance me similarly! In short, I am convinced that I am one of those rare and unlucky fellows who had best wait till safely wedded!'

'So much the better – or so much the worse! – There are risks in both directions, perhaps. You have heard of poor Latimer's pox, I suppose, and small wonder. It is said that there was not a virgin left in Basle, after he left the place!'

December 11th

Johnson kept my secret, but once the time came to return to Donwell for Christmas, I found myself in a turmoil of apprehension – for I had heard nothing of the Hooks, not even from John, and must presume that nothing had altered.

Nor had it, or so it seemed. I arrived midday yesterday, the 10th. Mary Rose coloured deeply when I met her in a corridor, and answered me hurriedly, 'Oh, everything is so much better, sir! I am only grieved to have caused you the slightest concern!'

'Truly?'

'Yes, sir.'

'I am very happy to hear it!' I returned, but this afternoon I met her in daylight, when she seemed still more anxious to pass by.

'Wait, what is amiss?'

'With what, sir?'

'Why, with your eye! Have you a stye in it?'

She touched it almost guiltily, and said, 'Truly, sir, I do not know – there is no pain.'

I spun her round and said grimly, 'So all is well, is it?'

'I know not what you mean, sir,' said she. But she would not lift her head but averted it, too late – too late altogether. For I had already seen the bright bruise – and I had played enough cricket to know what a single hard blow could do!

'I cannot believe you,' I said at last, releasing her, 'but I am obliged to respect your wishes, I suppose!'

And moved on, greatly disturbed. I loathed the thought of thwarting her – but the alternative must be almost as bad. After a wakeful night, I ordered her mother, Mrs Hook, to my – study, I call it but, truly, parted from the Bodleian at Oxford, little enough study occurred there. Mrs Hook came at once, her thimble still on her finger. She looked fearful, for I had never summoned her before.

I said, 'Forgive me for troubling you, Mrs Hook, but I happened to notice that your daughter has a bruised eye. She refused to tell me how she came by it. However, I *have* heard that Mr Hook can be, perhaps, a little hasty – with the tenants and so forth – and I wished to be reassured that *he* was not responsible.'

The lady clasped and unclasped her hands but said nothing.

I then added, in a softer tone, 'If I have guessed right, have no fear that Mr Hook shall ever learn of it. And if I am wrong, I should be very glad to be set right.'

Her silence told me all – there was no need for her to burst forth with, 'Oh, Mr George!'

'Speak without fear,' said I, as steadily as I was able.

'I durstn't!

'Because of Hook? Or for fear of what my father might say?'

'Oh, sir, I durstn't! You see, Mr Hook has long since taken against Mary Rose. He cannot credit that she is a true child of his. Although she *is* his child, sir, I swear it!'

I took this in. 'And *this* is why he so dislikes her?'

'Yes, sir.'

'And beats her?'

'Oh! Most rarely, sir – mostly, he only sneers.'

'Mostly! – and she no child but a woman grown! And beats *you*, as well?'

'Heavens, sir, almost never!'

'Almost?'

'Hardly ever, sir,' she said and given her strength of stature, I found that I could believe her. The silvery, slight Mary Rose must be far more easily imposed upon. But could any man beat a woman for what he imagined her own mother's sin?

'Why does he suspect… what you said… of Mary Rose?'

'Why, because she looks so different from her brothers, is all,' said she, rather flustered, 'for *they* are so dark and strong and tall!'

'She has brothers?' – for I had never interested myself enough to find out.

'Yes, sir. Three fine young fellows – the youngest two 'prenticed out, and Sam with his own shop down Croydon way.'

I could not help thinking, 'What a pity that none of them is nearer!' A brother might be just the ally I required! But I only said, 'I wish you and all of your family very well, Mrs Hook.'

'I thank you most kindly, sir. Will that be all?'

'Indeed – but I beg that you would be so good as not to mention our discussion to anyone.'

'Oh no, sir, never!'

Writing this now – and doing my best to recollect all that passed – I feel still less satisfied than I had pretended to be at the time. I remain a little astonished at Hook's suspicions – Mrs Hook is so very plain and heavy – but perhaps he possesses a suspicious temperament, a temper to look for the worst in people? And truly, Mary Rose resembles neither of her burly parents. It also made me wonder whether the Donwell servants might not all be caught up in turmoils of their own…

MARY ROSE

December 22nd

The Abbey is full of visitors for Christmas festivities, and Highbury altogether – the Crown, Hartfield, Coney Hall – exceptionally lively, with balls, dinners and concerts, some of the concerts not too bad. But I am in no fit state for enjoyment. Mama upbraids me for not dancing with the correct young ladies – the richest, of course – but they all seem either dull or coy, for this one smiles too much, and that one seems too desperate and they all make the same comments, and so affectedly too, about the weather and the dinner and the music. As do their mamas. ('Gracious, Mr George, you put me so in mind of your handsome father, when he was young!' And: ''Tis rare for a young man to dance with such grace as you, I must say!')

Though I think the only difference is that some of the young men – my brother John among them – do not feel the music as I do.

And all the while I cannot get Mary Rose from my mind. At our own ball, in honour of my uncle, and in hopes that he will leave my brother his estate, I kept noticing her – waiting at table, running errands, fetching wraps – always with that variable colour. It is if her looks remain imprinted upon my consciousness, till superseded by the next glimpse. There was not a lady in all the crowd who could compete with her delicacy of feature and lightness of tread! I obliged myself to engage with them all, and with Lady Kneller and Miss Peters in particular, but I felt bored, dissatisfied and out of spirits.

And perhaps I was not alone in this because, just after dinner and before the musicians began again, who should I stumble upon but Mary Rose, being imposed upon? It was in the room farthest from the dancing, and the importune fellow the younger son of some baronet – I cannot recall which for, though he had been mentioned by one of my partners, we had not been introduced. She seemed to be objecting, her lips compressed, her cheeks afire. She looked up imploringly at me and I said, more sharply than I intended, 'Mary Rose, go downstairs' – and to him, 'I must insist, sir, that you leave my father's servants alone!'

The fellow muttered something about there being 'no harm meant,' and I stalked on, in no condition to amuse Miss Peters, Lady Kneller or any other guest. I was utterly mortified. For what had he done, or tried to do, that I had not? If *he* was badly-behaved why, how badly-behaved was I?

Which is why – writing this – what I wish most of all is simply to beg her pardon. For though I must believe myself to be better-looking and better-spoken than Mr S---- I am no less contemptible.

PS Just as I was putting my journal aside, I thought of a method to compensate her for my appalling behaviour. From now on, I shall have on my person the book which most reminds me of Mary Rose. I am sure she would love such a book.

December 23rd

The Abbey rambles over a good deal of ground – over the centuries there have been sections appended, while other parts have been allowed to fall into disrepair. It lacks the assured compactness of Hartfield, though I prefer it. At any rate today, as Mary Rose rushed down the back staircase of the deserted west wing, she almost collided with me.

'Oh, sir! How you startled me – but I quite forgot to feed the hens!'

'I am sorry for the hens then,' said I, 'but I have been carrying this about, in hopes of seeing you.' And I handed her the book.

She looked longingly at it, but put both hands behind her back, saying, 'I must not, sir. But I thank you for – for thinking of me.'

'What, are you never allowed to borrow a book?'

'Oh no, sir – I often do. But *such* a fine one!'

'It is one of my favourites, by Wordsworth.'

Again, the look of longing – again the refusal. ''Tis not my place, sir.'

'It is but a loan,' said I hastily, 'and I insist.' And pressing it into her unresisting palm, I forced myself to turn away.

December 26th

I saw her occasionally over the next two days, but only in the course of her duties, and did not permit myself so much as a single word. But today, Boxing Day, when I observed her again by the hens, I pulled up my horse and hastily dismounted. She started upon seeing me.

I said, 'I did not mean to alarm you. I only wished to know what you thought of the book.'

'Oh, I loved it!'

'Truly? Did you? Which poem did you like best?'

She faltered, '"She – dwelt among the untrodden ways", I think.'

'"A violet by a mossy stone/Half hidden from the eye – "'

'"Fair as a star, when only one/Is shining in the sky,"' she finished, almost reverently. 'But they are all so beautiful!'

'How strange it is, however, that you have chosen the very poem that reminds me of you.'

She ducked her head down, saying, 'Oh, sir, this is too much foolishness!'

'But who could possibly be fairer than you, Mary Rose?'

'A great many people, sir.'

'Nonsense! Who can you be thinking of?'

'The mistress of Hartfield,' said she, at once.

'Mrs Woodhouse is certainly very lovely, even after having two young children,' I admitted, 'but she does not put me in mind of –'

'And Miss Peters – Such elegance, and so perfect a complexion!'

'Miss Peters's complexion is admirable. But she is far too – real, somehow – to feature in lines such as these. There is no elfin delicacy in Miss Peters!'

'I must beg you, sir, not to say such things to me,' said she in a very low voice, 'or to give me such books, either. Why, the lines run through my head by day and by night – when I should be about my work, I mean.'

'But surely it lightens your work, Mary Rose?'

She hesitated then, 'I cannot say, sir, that it does *not*. But I cannot concentrate for thinking of them. They tempt me to – to daydream, about the Lakes and – other things. And there is such – such feeling – such regret, even – in a few that –'

'Perhaps,' I said boldly, 'the regret was that the poet did not take his chances, with the "Lucy" of the text?'

'Perhaps so,' said she, turning that glowing face to mine. '"But oh the difference to me!" And to think, Mr George, that he is still writing, perhaps at this very moment, and by Lake Windermere, too!'

'We can only hope so,' I cried. 'But you do not ask which is my favourite.'

'Well, sir,' said she, with a smile that seemed to go through my entire body, 'which is your favourite, then?'

'My own favourite,' I said – impetuously – 'is, "Three years she grew in sun and shower/Then Nature said, 'A lovelier flower/On earth was never sown/She shall be mine, and I will make/A Lady of my own."'

But she had already turned away from me. 'Nay, sir, this is too much of foolishness!'

'But foolishness, if it lightens the work of every day, must be no foolishness at all!'

She laughed – her laugh was charming, if a little embarrassed – and said, 'Well, I must thank you for the book, sir, and I promise to replace it in your study the moment I have copied the poems I loved best.'

'When might that be?'

'Why tomorrow, sir, if I am not needed in the evening. Will that be too long?'

I denied it but could detain her no longer, she would go.

December 27th

Two days later I was in my study, having remained on purpose, when she appeared with the book. She started upon observing me.

'Oh, sir! Forgive me, I had thought that all the family long since gone out!'

'And so they have, beyond myself – my parents and brother are gone to Hartfield. I see you have brought the book.'

'And I thank you for it!'

'But I would like you to keep it, Mary Rose. I can always buy another upon returning to Oxford tomorrow.'

'Oh never, sir! For everyone would wish to know how I came by it!'

I was forced to recognise the truth of this, though I had never thought of it before. She handed it to me with a curtsey, saying, 'Bless you sir, for your kindness!'

'Wait!'

She did look a little distressed then, and said tremulously, 'I cannot, sir.'

'Just one kiss, Miss Mary. To save my sanity!'

'No, sir. I cannot – not even for your – sanity.'

'Why ever not? No one will ever know!'

She took a deep breath then and said, 'Why then, sir, for the sake of my own.'

She half-ran to the door. I caught her there.

How long we kissed, I cannot tell. Only the softness, the scent of her, and the torrent of curls which *would* escape, descending halfway down her back. That softness, that scent, and the sense that I was not only lost but – simultaneously – had found my way home at last.

Knightley then recollected that it was not Mary Rose who had told him. Instead, he had learned from John, who, after gravely mentioning in the body of his letter that Hook's temper had finally become sufficiently 'erratic' for him to be threatened with dismissal, added in a postscript, 'It seems that Hook's daughter, the parlourmaid, is certain to be dismissed, and for the usual reason. Though I cannot think but that the culprit will confess, and make an honest woman of her, for the sake of the child.'

March 4th

I told my tutor I would return as soon as I could. 'But the seminar, Knightley!' he objected.

'It is important, sir.'

'I should hope it is! What of the defence of your essay?' And after I made such a point of the Senior Dean's coming!'

'I shall be back by then, I swear it!'

'Is someone dying, Knightley?' he asked, rather more mildly.

'No, sir. But I must go, and at once.'

I spent half of one sleepless night in a hostelry, to rest my horse, but was back on the road at daybreak, having determined to reach Donwell before even the servants had breakfasted. And with the rain's easing it was very little later when I first clattered into the stables.

Old Hutchings lifted one eyebrow as I tossed him the reins, and the butler exclaimed, upon finding me in the breakfast room.

'Why, Mr George!'

'It is I. Where is my father?'

'No one is down yet, sir, that I know of.'

'I should like breakfast all the same. Perhaps – perhaps – Miss Mary could bring it.'

She came into the room with the tray – more exquisite than ever.

'You are sure?' I asked, but I was already convinced. She looked a little fuller in the figure, and then, her face!

'Yes, sir. I can do nothing – it is too late, indeed!'

'You must trust me,' I said, almost reverently.

'No, sir. Instead, I must go away.'

'No, no, I beg! Just give me one chance, to see what might be done.'

'*You* must pretend to have nothing to do with it! I can – contrive. Your mother has been so kind!'

'I will not have you – dispatched – to some godforsaken place, as if *you* had done wrong!' I cried fiercely.

'I *have* done wrong, sir.'

'It was entirely my fault.'

'No, sir,' she said, with quiet definition, and her expression, I believe, will stay with me forever.

'In any case, I shall not desert you!'

Her eyes filled with tears. 'But you *must*, sir! You must trust me to look after – after my child!'

And, for once, I did not mind the 'sir' but kissed her forehead, her temple – and then, her hand. How I wish, now, that I had dared kiss that trembling lip, as well!

'*Our* child,' I said. 'And you must trust me, likewise!'

Then John entered. He took in the situation – my presence, our near-embrace – in utter consternation. 'Oh, God!' he cried. 'It was never *you*!' And as I bowed my head, and as Mary Rose fled, 'How is it possible, in heaven's name? – and have you admitted it to Father?'

'I am here to do so.'

John crossed to the window and back, frowning. 'Oh George! This is desperately ill news!'

'It is certainly unlucky.'

'It is very much more than unlucky. The fact is – but how could you know? – our father accused poor Harry, last evening, of being responsible!'

'Harry, the footman?'

'Yes. It was Hook who blamed young Harry. Harry has been – fond of Miss Mary for some time, apparently.'

'Wait! Hook accused *Harry* of seducing his daughter and our father then –'

'But not in public, George! Only Mama and myself were by!'

'*That* makes precious little difference!'

'But Harry denied it. Then Papa rated him which now, I must say, does seem *most* unfair – but George! Of what were you thinking? – This was badly done, indeed!'

This reproach, and from John especially, I felt through all my body and soul. How could I have done such a thing, and to so rare and lovely a creature? I deserved to lose my brother's respect!

I cried, 'But I love her!'

'Why then, you should have resisted! I cannot imagine such a girl seducing *you*. No, you took her, and now – *now*, I greatly fear – you must take the consequences, as well.'

'Can you imagine that my heart has not been telling me this, ever since your letter?'

Mother came in then, alarmed at our raised voices – and more than alarmed at my unexpected appearance.

'George! What do you here? And why are you arguing?'

John gave me one last serious look and departed.

I took a deep breath and said, 'I have come, Mama, because *I* am the father of Miss Mary's child.'

For a moment I thought she might faint. Instead, she swayed a little, braced herself against the table, and was silent for a long moment. 'It is not true,' she said at last. 'It *cannot* be true!'

'It is, Mama. And the fault was entirely mine.'

'Oh George! What have you done? And your father attacking poor Harry, as well!'

'*That* I cannot understand! How dared anyone accuse Harry, whatever Hook might have said?'

'Wait! Harry – though guiltless – might still wed Mary. Something of the sort might be arranged, for he has admitted being fond of –'

'*He* shall never wed her,' I said.

'Why not? – for I think he likes her very well.'

'Because, Mama, *I* must wed Mary Rose myself.'

At this she screamed and one of the footmen – not Harry – rushed in.

She whispered, 'Oh, George! Have you lost all reason?' How pale she was! But then she dropped my gaze and said to Frederick – it was as if she could not bear to look at me – 'Frederick, fetch Harry, and at once.'

She said nothing at all as we waited, but poured herself a little tea, with unsteady hand.

Harry looked thinner than ever, all his usual mischief set by. Mama said directly, 'Harry, I wish you to know, and at once, that we have been exceedingly unfair to you, as it turns out, and that we are sorry – very sorry, indeed! My husband will wish to apologise himself, I am sure, but now you may go. We will speak later.'

Harry did go, with just a single darting glance at me – a complicated glance, comprising envy, relief, respect, detestation, and a thousand other things, besides. His mind must have been in turmoil for, only moments before, he must have been both fearing for his place and – perhaps – hopeful of his marriage…

'Now George, you must not remain. *I* shall tell your father about this business.'

'No! It is my responsibility –'

'It is. But I fear for your hasty temper – and for *his*, as well.'

'But Mama, I have ridden through dark and rain to tell him! As I must!'

'Good heavens, George, have we not enough trouble without you and your father fighting each other? Have you not already done your best to set the whole household about by the ears? Go to your room, I beg! I shall send for you once the worst of his wrath has passed.'

I turned on my heel and went up to my rooms, probably with very ill-grace. How humiliating it felt, to be ordered upstairs, like a child!

❖

241

Though I was very little more than a child, reflected Knightley, twenty years later. I never learned, either from my mother or from John, who was summoned to calm our father's temper – exactly what transpired. Though I suspected it was fiery enough, for by the time he was prepared to see me, he was still exceedingly angry.

✦

'And so, George, you have let me down appallingly – let down the entire family, indeed – and caused me to be appallingly unjust to young Harry.'

'I am very sorry, Father. However, I must just say –'

'So you should be! Because you wanted the girl, you took her – and now you have ruined her!' I dared not speak. 'The worst of the business is the position in which you placed her, for – as the young master – she surely feared to say you nay! How could any son of mine treat any woman so? The arrogance, the thoughtlessness, the – the utter selfishness! I cannot believe it of you!'

'I am shamed indeed, for *she* was not in the least to blame.'

'And now she is the lifelong responsibility of this house! – as, of course, is her child.' Then, as if an afterthought, he added, 'She must leave, and at once.'

I steeled myself to resolution.

'If she must, sir,' I said, 'why then, I must leave with her.'

He wheeled round. 'What!'

'I agree with every word you say – I deserve your every rebuke! However, I greatly fear, Papa, that I am in love with Mary Rose.'

'In love? In *love*? Utter nonsense! At your age, *you* can have no notion of what love is about!'

'I believe that I do, however.'

'Then you are not only arrogant, but a young blockhead,

242

besides! Love is not the same as wishing to – to couple with some pretty young creature! You might admire her character – but that is not love! You are warm-hearted – no bad thing, if not carried to excess – but again, that is not *love*. You are too inexperienced to know the first thing about it!'

'It is true, Father, that I have never been in love before, but I believe it is love which makes me long to protect Mary Rose from her father. It is love which makes me long to shield her from society – and love, too, which makes me long to gift her the respectability she now lacks! Were I to marry her –'

'Marry her? *Marry* her? Why – why – you could never, conceivably, marry her! How could a parlourmaid called Mary Hook be wife to the heir of Donwell? What education, what knowledge, what attainments could *she* possess that – oh heavens, man, she would bore you within a fortnight – and be an embarrassment for the whole of your life!'

'You do not *know* her! She has read a good deal – and thought a good deal besides.'

'What, enough to acquit herself in society? What could she have learned, beyond such maths and reasoning as some village school might have supplied? Can she sing, paint, embroider? Has she Latin, Italian, French? How on earth could a parlourmaid possibly comport herself properly in society?'

'She cannot be the only woman to –'

'Our every acquaintance would sneer in disgust. Donwell – the maid as mistress, indeed! – would become a laughingstock. Whilst in town – should you ever dare to *brave* town in her company – she would be cut, or disdained at very least, by all our acquaintance!'

'She would be my wife. This must be enough.'

'It was not enough in Mrs Ratcliffe's case and *she* had at least been sufficiently educated to work as a governess. Though she was apparently so distressed by society's scorn that she never returned to town again! Ratcliffe did *her* no favours, believe me. Think, man! What might all your high-minded stupidity bring to such a girl, beyond confusion upon confusion, misery on misery? This is not decency – it is idiocy, instead! And not love, but mad infatuation!'

I denied it as stoutly as possible – yet secretly, my heart misgave me. Would Mary Rose *truly* be capable of being the wife my position demanded? Could her allurements, intellectual curiosity and sweetness compensate for her lack of education? Could I possibly be infatuated?

'And even if it *were* love, it would make no difference. In your position, you cannot *expect* to marry for love. Love is a bonus few can afford! No, no, you must marry for alliance, instead. Though you unluckily have no suitable cousin, and the infant girls now at Hartfield will always be rather too young, any number of society ladies would gratefully accept of your proposals. For people of our position –'

'But 'tis not fair, Father, for her to suffer so, and all alone besides!'

He softened a little and said, 'It is, but such is the way of the world. She has been unlucky – unlucky in becoming attached to a man of your standing, and unlucky in the expectation of a – but you cannot alter the rules every man must live by! You might buy her comfort, but never respectability – not with a child. And were she *not* carrying your child, surely you would never contemplate such a marriage at all!'

'I might,' I said stubbornly.

But at this my father entirely lost his temper. 'Not in England! I cannot prevent you, from eloping to Scotland – with Cook or the scullery maid, if you like, let alone with Hook's daughter! But I tell you straight that, if you do, then I shall disinherit you! – I swear it, by this hand! John can take your place. *That* is what is at stake – not merely the ridicule and contempt of our every connection – but your entire inheritance! Should you elope with Miss Hook you shall give way to your younger brother, who at least has *some* measure of common sense... Now go away, for the sight of you sickens me! Go! Go now! – and send me word tomorrow what you decide.'

I went straight to the stables, not from any hope of seeing her – for at that hour on a Thursday she was always engaged – but to take out a horse, for I find that riding always calms my spirit.

The sun was setting. Indeed, I doubt that I have ever seen Donwell look lovelier than it did that evening, every line of grass illuminated, an orange soft as clementines suffusing the fishponds, and splinters of dark gold spangling the bend in the river where the Martins' pretty cottage lay. Donwell Abbey glowed creamily, half its windows candlelit, its great oaks, elms and cedars scattered round.

'To give up all this!' I thought. And yes, I also thought – 'For all this to be, instead of mine, my brother's!'... I am as fond of John as I had ever been of any fellow, but what man could consider, with perfect equanimity, everything of his own made over to his brother?

Yet, what price honour? I had not defiled her virginity – but I had still put Mary Rose into an impossible position. Before my intervention, there must have been some hope of the respectable remarriage of which my madness had deprived her. I would not escape all calumny, of course, but there were always excuses made for the guilty man... Oh! Whatever had possessed me, to take her at all?

She had possessed me. The pursuit was mine, but she had half-seduced me, in the end, despite resisting so firmly before. But how

I had longed for her to! – I had loved her – I still loved her – and she had confessed, in the moment of culmination, that she loved me. And yet, how well did I truly *know* Mary Rose? I had always imagined courtship as a process of gradual enchantment and growing certainty (she is the one, she is not – nay, she *is*!) By contrast, Mary Rose had come as a tumult, a madness! And in the end, I returned the horse to the stables, doubting her, doubting myself, doubting everything.

March 5th

This morning, my brother's influence was tried – and how one must feel for poor John – still a lad of seventeen and a lad possessing the strictest possible notions of decorum, besides. He disapproved of my sin passionately – as passionately as he has ever disapproved of anything. And yet my time at university and my misdemeanour – rather, my crime – have put me as far beyond him as an entire decade, despite my being his senior by only two years.

We were walking about the rose garden and on his side it was all, 'The honour of the family… the scandal that must be scotched… widely mistaken in your feelings… really rather impulsive behaviour…'

It was lawyer-talk, and I scarcely listened until the moment true feeling crept in. For he finished thus, as well as I can recall, 'However, and having said all this, my dear George, I have no wish to take what is rightfully yours! How could I ever feel remotely comfortable, knowing that I had usurped an estate not my own! And so, and for that reason, should you choose to marry Hook's daughter, I have determined to refuse it.'

'What!'

'I have told our father that I cannot take it. Though *he* only bade me to think again.'

'But John, whether you wish it or not, if he wills it, it must be!'

'Oh, do not say so! Do not force me into such misery!'

'Misery, do you call it?' I cried, shocked, almost winded. For I had already thought that, were I in John's place, nothing could be more agreeable than to usurp my elder brother's position, thus escaping all the inconveniences of a profession! But John – as so often – felt differently.

'It would be utter misery to *me*,' said he, 'and not only because our father's unfairness would lie so heavily upon my heart. I have the greatest distaste of being looked up to, supplicated to, and bound to such an enormity as Donwell Abbey is! I love to think of what might be grown in such-and-such a field – I love to imagine what great bull to buy – but not with serious considerations riding upon my every decision! I beg you therefore, if you love me, to reconsider not only all that you stand to lose, but all that *I* stand to lose, as well!'

I embraced him strongly.

'My dear John,' I cried, 'you are too good!'

'A man,' said John fervently, 'can never be too good.'

'By God,' said I, 'if ever a man *could* be, then – but I shall attempt to mend matters – if I can – without causing her to suffer more!'

⁂

In other words, thought the older George Knightley, the promise of Donwell – to me, the very breath of life! – seemed to John a most onerous imposition. What he most wished for was what he has since accomplished – the pretty wife, the numerous children, the London property, the thriving firm. Though he loves to visit Donwell, he is always grateful to depart from it to his own home again. In some ways, he and Isabella are the luckiest of all, for there is nothing they wish for not already within their compass.

✦

Circumstances being so strained, I could not be surprised to be summoned to Mama's dressing-room this evening.

For the first time in my life I had to summon resolution to encounter her, though I knew – as the child concerned always does know – that I was her favourite. My father's regard was more evenly divided, but I was my mother's son.

Her sternness of the morning was quite put-by. Instead, she embraced me, crying, 'Oh my poor George! She seduced you!'

'It was the other way about, I fear,' I said, remembering how I had caught her by the door.

'A young widow – *she* would know what she was about!'

'But one most unhappily wed, Mama, and abused by her father besides.'

'And you so young and so impulsive!' Now I felt unconvinced about my impulsiveness. Compared to John, I am impulsive, indeed! – but has not John been teased for excessive caution throughout his life? She added, 'And so affectionate! – You were always so loving, George. Do you recall your dog, Arrow? How deeply his death affected you!'

'Of course I remember,' I said impatiently. 'But Mary Rose –'

'Your very first nurse told me, "He has the winningest character, ma'am, I ever –"'

'But Mama, the fault is mine! *She* must not be allowed to suffer for it!'

At this she sighed. 'That the blame for misbehaviour is unequal,

248

I concede – but truly, what man would marry an unwed woman with a child?'

'The man before you.'

'What, would you ruin yourself? – for your father will not have it!'

I strode about the room wishing – fruitlessly – that there might be a third way, as if I were a King in the Old Testament and could keep a concubine, whom I would treat as well as my wife! But this was truly mad. No, my choice was between comparative poverty, living – perhaps at some resort, perhaps under an assumed name, with Mary Rose – or else to leave her and never see her more.

'I cannot abandon her.'

'But she shall not be abandoned!' cried Mama. 'Instead, she shall be comfortable forever! She shall want for nothing – and have a nice little pension – and be attended by a responsible lady. *Where* she might be so attended though, I cannot say, for it cannot be here. The family reputation –'

'You mean to send her far away with my child?'

'With – with what I expect is indeed your child. Though even *that*, George, must not be –'

'The child is mine!'

'In any case, we must ensure that the child – he or she – has every possible chance. A school, a governess, whatever you wish for – but, oh George, do not break your mother's heart!'

I stopped and thought. It was far beyond what most families would do. It would be considered exceedingly generous by many. But to my mind, it was still a kind of death. Never to see Mary Rose again!

I said, unsteadily, 'I must think on it.'

And left her there.

MARY ROSE

January 3rd

Thanks to Mama, I was allowed to see Mary Rose before returning to university.

I write this now from my room at Jesus College, looking down on the quad. A different world, a different world! I should be working at my thesis, but the words will not come. Instead, I keep reliving the scene in my mind.

She came, for the first time, straight to me, curtseyed and said, 'Oh sir, you have been so good!'

'I have not, Mary Rose,' said I, embracing her. How tightly she held me! 'I wished to marry you but was not allowed.'

'I never thought of it,' said she, very simply. ''Tis not for the likes of myself, with neither birth nor education, to be lifted above so many fine young ladies! Only you could have thought it possible!'

It was what I had told myself, again and again, but the prettiness of her voice made it sound almost intolerable! I gripped her slim shoulders.

'You must wait for me, Mary Rose!'

She smiled faintly. 'What, you think so many young Essex men will wish to offer to a penniless girl with a baby?'

'My father cannot live forever. Then I shall be free to marry as I choose!'

'Even if that is so, sir, you must not think of me! You have given me all I need. Thanks to you I shall never be subject to a man of bad disposition – or to any man at all! I am the luckiest unmarried woman in England, thanks to your goodness!'

'All the same, I beg you to promise me. Promise me that you will wait.'

'Oh sir, if you truly wish it, I shall promise – but *you* need fear no rival for,' with a little breath, 'there is no one on earth with your warmth of heart!'

I felt a little comforted. But still – to have to go so far away as Essex, and with no one she knew, and to have a child – assuming it lived, for many did not – though she seemed quite fearless about it. Then she added, 'But I wish to be clear, you must never feel bound to *me*!'

'But I am bound to you!'

She smiled but shook her head. 'It – it may not always be so, sir.'

'And yet it may!' said I, capturing her hand.

'What I mean, is that it need not be.'

'I have something for you,' said I. It was the book, of course. Her eyes widened upon seeing it again.

'Oh, sir, you ought not –'

'No one,' said I, almost savagely, 'will ever dare to ask whether you came by it honestly, for I have inscribed "to Mary Rose" inside the cover.'

'Oh, sir! So beautiful a book!'

'And to think,' I said, 'that he might, and at this moment, be by Lake Windermere, writing lines as beautiful as "Three years she grew in sun and shower"!'

She did not refuse it then but looked up at me with tears brightening her soft eyes.

'I thank you, sir, with all my heart!'

September 10th

Last Wednesday, while I was at the Bodleian, my serving man found me, in order to tell me that my father was come.

Perturbed, and fearing for Mama, I rushed back to my rooms.

Father, however, was not in mourning – and I breathed a momentary sigh of relief.

'Why, what do you here, Father?'

'I fear, George, I come with heavy news.'

'Not my mother?'

'The news comes from – from Essex.'

'The baby is dead,' I cried, thinking, "Poor little creature!' – but so common a grief!

'The baby thrives, but at the cost of its mother,' said Father, very steadily.

'Mary Rose is poorly?' I asked, but already an icy chill had closed its fingers about my heart. His silence told me – everything.

'Oh, God!' I cried – and began to weep.

My father's hand, strongly, uselessly, gripped my own – but I could think of nothing but Mary Rose.

Heedless of the protestations of my tutor, I determined to go at once to Essex. It was my first visit to that county, and I half-blinded by tears for most of the journey. Being in no state to ride, I hired a chaise, and travelled two nights upon the road. Far, far too late to see her, but the baby was expected to live. It seemed somehow crucial, to see my child.

I had not expected to like Essex so well – too flat in comparison to Surrey, I had been told, and of no particular distinction or beauty. But the village where Mary Rose had dwelled was close to the coast – the air pleasing, the inhabitants clean and well-spoken.

Mrs Smith admitted me rather hurriedly, and apologised – unnecessarily, and several times over – for the disorder within.

The wet-nurse was in the back room of the cottage and engaged in rocking the sleeping child. Sublimely unconscious of all the anguish its short life had occasioned, she lay, tiny fingers curled into fists, wearing a cap that – presumably – Mary Rose had herself embroidered.

It was unexpectedly moving simply to look at her, sleeping. Though as I did she stirred and stretched, arching her tiny back and opening those minute fists. Then the eyes opened.

'A beautiful baby,' said Mrs Smith, and the wet-nurse said, 'Such eyes! And such fair hair!'

Mary Rose's shade, with perhaps of touch of darker gold, the eyes an ocean blue.

'The lady said she was to be called Harriet.'

I said, 'Harriet. May I hold her?' and, instead of answering, the wet-nurse picked her up, supporting the delicate neck, and handed her to me. She weighed less than a puppy, but I was enchanted by her quietness, her satiny skin. And as I carried her to the window – the two women conversing in low tones behind me – I whispered to my tiny, glowing child, 'My daughter. My only child. Grow, tiny Harriet! – grow wiser and surer and even fairer and still more beautiful. You will probably never learn who your father was, but he shall always care for you, even after his death, for my brother has promised. But know – always know – know in the deepest part of your soul – how much your father loves you!'

Then, struck by a thought, I turned back to the women, who fell instantly silent.

I said, 'Did her mother choose a second name?'

'No,' said one and the other shook her head. I handed the baby back as if it had been made of china instead of my flesh and another's.

'Then,' said I, 'I should like her to be christened Harriet Rose.'

And they promised me it would be so.

Afterwards, I asked the coachman to take me down to the coast, where I walked for an hour, until the salty winds had lock-dried the tears to my face.

And thought, 'Three years she grew in sun and shower/Then nature said, "A lovelier flower/On earth was never sown./This Child I to myself will take/She shall be mine/And I shall make/A lady of my own."'

Knightley closed the diary, eyes blurring, thinking, 'It is now my duty to burn it, my duty towards Emma. For, should she find it after I am gone, how hurt she might be – there is still such strength of feeling here!… It must be burned, indeed!'

Though, in the end, he found that he could not.

In that moment – shadows falling, candles failing – with what a wave of relief did he recollect his brother.

John – acquainted, as he had always been, with the whole! His own hand could not set his past afire, but John's – always the steadier – might be relied upon. After which, there would be nothing of proof in all the world. And if, in his weakness, he kissed it before surrendering it, no one would ever know…

❖❖❖❖❖

A Highbury Christmas

From the diaries of Mr Perry

(Author's note: In Jane Austen's Emma, *Mr Perry is the local apothecary, a minor character, who receives no lines at all. However, Austen just hints that he has a sense of humour he cannot quite trust himself to display. It was the passage below that first inspired my idea of the good apothecary as a humourist – and even as a mimic.)*

Mr. Perry was an intelligent, gentlemanlike man, whose frequent visits were one of the comforts of Mr. Woodhouse's life; and upon being applied to, he could not but acknowledge (though it seemed rather against the bias of inclination) that wedding-cake might certainly disagree with many—perhaps with most people, unless taken moderately. With such an opinion, in confirmation of his own, Mr. Woodhouse hoped to influence every visitor of the newly married pair; but still the cake was eaten; and there was no rest for his benevolent nerves till it was all gone.

There was a strange rumour in Highbury of all the little Perrys being seen with a slice of Mrs. Weston's wedding-cake in their hands: but Mr. Woodhouse would never believe it.

(from *Emma*, Chapter 2)

I was immersed in *The Times* and my good wife sweeping when she observed, 'You have not been to Hartfield these two days. I fear Mr Woodhouse will pine away, drift into a decline and perish altogether.'

'But Mr Woodhouse has believed himself to have been in a decline ever since I first encountered him, when he was as hale and hearty a fellow as ever I clapped eyes on.'

'Yet still, I wish you would attend him.'

'Are you trying to rid yourself of me, Mrs Perry?' I inquired humorously.

'Well, I have a great deal to do about the house, and your legs are in the way.'

(Did I mention that I have very long legs? – so long that I can look rather comical – or so I have been advised – when on horseback.) I kindly shifted mine to assist my wife as she added, 'Also, were you to go to Hartfield, you might learn something about all these rumours.'

'Which rumours do you mean?'

'Why, that Miss Woodhouse might wed Elton, after all.'

I sat up so sharply that I almost banged my head upon the sconce. 'Wed Elton! Who, I beg, could believe so nonsensical a tale?'

You see, I had the advantage of knowing Elton well. The rector of Highbury is a sprightly, well-set-up young man, reasonably well-born and considered unusually well-looking. He greatly relishes society, though I believe him to be better value at the whist club, for in mixed company he can stress the gallant to excess. However, these tactics have answered so well – so many ladies pine for him, so sought-after is he for dinner engagements – that many men in such a position might be in danger of conceiving even Emma Woodhouse within their compass.

But Elton is not such a fool. Elton knows – to the shilling – how much his cook spends on meat each week, and how much his every parishioner pays in tithes. He can estimate as well as anyone how much Miss Cox might be worth and how immensely rich Miss Woodhouse must be. Therefore, he must know that he might as well offer to a duchess and have done as to offer to Emma – for Emma *does* have moments of duchess-like disdain, as well as great kindness, to her father particularly.

We all have faults, and if Miss Woodhouse's is to have rather too high an opinion of herself, my dear Clara's fault is to gossip. There is no reasoning with her, in this department. No, she *will* imagine herself to have spotted some intrigue, illness or injustice, and will have informed her every acquaintance before it can be contradicted. In this respect, she is rather a difficult wife for an apothecary to have. There have been patients of mine Highbury supposed dead and buried less than an hour after I mentioned to Clara that they were poorly – which can prove most embarrassing, particularly when they recover. However, the first rule of marriage is to hold one's tongue – though it is a rule very difficult to keep.

Clara said, 'I cannot see anything so nonsensical about it. Does not Elton spend hours every day at Hartfield, mooning over Miss Woodhouse while *she* sketches young Harriet Smith? And reading till he is hoarse, all the while!'

I took a little tea and said, 'I have, I concede, observed Hartfield in just the state that you describe – I have even seen the celebrated artwork upon its easel. And I have – assuredly – seen little Miss Smith being spoilt by injudicious praise and heard Elton reading to the ladies. But such a rumour is nonsensical, all the same.'

'Why, I beg?'

'My dear, if you will listen, I believe that I can satisfy you. The truth is, that there is a vast gulf fixed between Miss Woodhouse, heiress of Hartfield, and the eldest Miss Cox – and I suspect that the Coxes' is where Elton will take himself a-wooing at some point – though Miss Cox would, I daresay, have him tomorrow.' And here I attempted to mimic Miss Cox's breathy tones. 'Why, Mr Elton! Dear me! Good heavens! I had no more idea – you do me too much honour! I am not worthy, not in the least, while my surprise is beyond anything – but I can certainly fit in some time to marry you, perhaps Tuesday week or the following Thursday. Indeed, but for the state of my shoes, I could even contrive to wed you this afternoon –'

'Oh, hush! – You will be overheard at your play-acting someday, Mr Perry, and not a soul in Highbury will ever trust you more! And you should recollect, too, that the "vast gulf fixed" which appears so obvious to you might not appear quite so obvious to Mr Elton.'

'It will appear obvious enough to Miss Woodhouse, I assure you. If Elton imagines – because the lady finds her father a trifle tedious, that she would accept the local rector, he is a fool indeed!'

'I should not call him a fool,' said my wife, pausing in her sweeping. 'An opportunist, perhaps. He might be trying for it, for why should he not? – *he* has nothing to risk by venturing, beyond a little dignity, for young ladies love to be courted. As for the eldest Miss Cox, if Miss Woodhouse *does* send him packing with a flea about his ear, she might still get her chance, shoes or no shoes!'

'My dear, Elton will never offer to Emma Woodhouse. He cannot think so well of himself as to offer to Emma Woodhouse!'

But Clara was having none of it. 'You suggest that Miss Smith is being spoilt – but I consider Mr Elton every bit as spoilt as Harriet Smith. He is of very good family – the finest young man in Highbury – and every girl at Mrs Goddard's sighs with yearning whenever he deigns to ride past. Why, even their teachers –'

'Aye, and on club evenings he can be witty at their expense!'

'Perhaps so, but Miss Woodhouse most certainly encourages him. To invite him to Hartfield, every morning and most afternoons, must suggest the most rampant encouragement! And nor has it gone unnoticed, for when Miss Bates said on Thursday, "I declare, Mr Elton has ridden to Hartfield every day this fortnight!" everyone laughed most knowingly.'

Rather struck, I asked, 'They laughed, did they? Did they, indeed!'

'They did. And so, were I in your place, and forever visiting at Hartfield, I should put a little word in Miss Woodhouse's ear. For she would detest the notion of being gossiped about.'

'Nay, I could have no right! Now it may be true – I certainly cannot dispute it – that Elton is very often at Hartfield. But what jurisdiction have *I* over the lady of the house, and how she might choose to waste her afternoons? Nor have I the slightest wish to offend Elton, else our whist evenings might be forfeit… Should he have imbibed a wrongful notion of Emma Woodhouse's intentions, she will bring him to his senses soon enough.'

'But would he not come to his senses rather sooner, were you to quiz him on the subject on whist night?'

'Never – for Knightley might take it amiss, with the family connection. And 'twould be a devilish dull standard of play, were Elton and Knightley both missing at the Crown.'

Clara thought for a moment and then, 'Knightley! Surely, had he the slightest inkling about the gossip, he would dare to give some advice to Miss Woodhouse, himself? By all accounts, he treats her with precious little ceremony, upbraiding her for ignoring her music, teasing her for preferring romances to –'

'True enough, and rather he than I! Miss Woodhouse has had a temper since she was a child, when she determined that she "would" do this, or "would not" do that… How well I recollect the pains her poor mama took – and all for nothing! For Miss Emma *would* go her own way, as her father always doted on her, and her elder sister married far too soon.'

'And so, you will say nothing?'

'If Knightley himself says nothing, then who am *I* to speak?' And I took up my paper while my dear wife, tossing her head in discontent, moved to attack the kitchen instead.

Now, between ourselves, I have for years cultivated a habit – a habit priceless for any medical man – of managing, in almost every circumstance, to appear calm, confident and urbane. It is a habit worth many guineas a year to me. But I did not feel quite as easy as I pretended because, the more I considered the matter, the likelier it seemed that my good wife might be in the right. I found myself recalling Elton's joyful alacrity at being asked to carve at the Hartfield dining table… I remembered Emma's giving him a playful little push at some gallantry or other… and I recollected how, when addressing the Woodhouses' butler, he sometimes possessed a near-proprietorial air. ('My good Serle' indeed!)

Of course, should Elton dare to offer, Miss Woodhouse would likeliest send him packing. But what if she was secretly smitten – that flirtatious little push – and executed some appalling error of judgement? She was a strange creature by way of an heiress, for she had never once tasted the delights of Bath – or even those of Tunbridge – and had only rarely been to town. In short, whom had Emma Woodhouse ever encountered of a rank sufficient to address her? And was it truly so impossible – that obduracy of hers – that she might insist upon degrading herself?

But it was scarcely my place – it was Knightley's place, for 'twas his brother who had married her sister – to instruct Miss Woodhouse in her duty. And thus I began to wonder if it might not be politic to have a word with Knightley at whist – should the moment seem propitious.

＊

It *was* propitious. The very next evening Elton was missing from our little company at the Crown – he had been dispatched to London, on purpose to get Miss Woodhouse's famous portrait framed. At the very end of the evening, Mr Knightley and I were the last remaining, engaged in counting the cards at the final table. The candles were guttering low and the proprietor nowhere to be seen when I cleared my throat and said, 'I do not wish to say anything out of turn.'

Knightley said, with great good humour, 'If you did, no one would be more astonished than I. I should back you there, against any fellow breathing!'

'It is merely that I have heard a strange rumour, and I was wondering whether it had reached you likewise.'

'I am unaware of any rumour, I assure you, whether strange or not strange. It has nothing to do with me, I hope?' He spoke lightly but I hastened to reassure him, for the only rumour I ever heard of George Knightley was that half of his tenants trespassed against his great good nature – and once – years ago – a hint about some woman he had loved and lost.

'It has nothing to do with you, at all. It is merely that idle report supposes Elton to be courting at Hartfield.'

He smiled rather oddly and said, 'Elton! I think not.'

'Just what I said. But I did wonder, were Miss Woodhouse to be informed that ignorant gossips believed him to be, that she might cease to –'

'– encourage him unfairly?' he asked. Which silenced me, for I should not have put it quite so strongly – though it was what I had meant, all the same.

Knightley finished counting the cards. Then he said, 'That she has some little scheme in mind is certain – Miss Woodhouse always has some little scheme in mind! But I cannot think that she would permit herself to be imposed upon. She would be affronted, I believe, at the very suggestion.'

I was glad to hear my own view endorsed, and said as much, but he continued, 'As for Elton, I doubt if he could nerve himself to the business. He is thin-skinned and easily mortified – far more easily mortified than one might think. So put out was he, upon failing to receive an invitation to the Assembly, that he left the last Assizes in rather a temper! I also think he relishes the adulation of Highbury in general too much to care for any young lady in particular… But I am obliged to you for your confidence, all the same.'

And with this he shook my hand – something I felt at my heart. I admire no man more than Knightley – for directness, equability and intellect he has not his equal. His one fault is that he is a character impossible to burlesque, for the subtlety of his own self-mockery is much beyond my skill to reproduce.

Clara stirred as I slipped into the bedroom with my candle but grew livelier when I confided what I had done, as 'Knightley listened and was not offended. And I believe he will recollect it.'

'I am quite certain of it. Are you hungry, after your long evening? Would you care for a boiled egg?'

And so lightened did I feel that I answered in the style of my favourite victim, the immortal Miss Bates.

'Nay, I do not wish for an egg – though never were there such eggs as our hens lay, and how wonderfully dear Patty does them justice! How I wish, my good Mr Perry, that you had been passing yesterday at half-two – or perhaps it was a quarter past – when she made her tiny cakes, the ones with just a touch of nutmeg, brown sugar and – I believe – cinnamon. I am not quite certain about the cinnamon – but heavens! how we did indulge! For that reason, we have no little cakes with which to tempt you – though I must own to just a touch of colic today for which the cinnamon – if 'twas cinnamon – might be to blame. But I can be colicky, you know, when the winds are excessive – and they have been unusually strong, for poor Patty was wakened by the wind and recollected dreaming that hundreds of tiny mice were crawling about her coverlet. To be fair, mice have long given Patty the shivers, because when she was four – no, I believe she was five – 'twas her sister who was four, and there was but a year between them –'

'Enough!' cried my wife. 'Would you try my poor patience to death?'

'Oh my dear, I hope to try your patience for many more years before *that* happens.'

But there was a little dimple in her cheek which made me fancy myself forgiven, as I snuffed out the candle and eased my long legs into bed.

⁂

'Twas not a week later, and nigh on Christmas eve, when I next saw good Miss Bates in person. Pulling up my horse in consternation, I cried, 'Miss Bates! Whatever can you be thinking of, to come out in such weather? I have never seen a clearer promise of snow!'

'I have not been out long,' argued that lady stoutly, 'not more than ten minutes, or perhaps twelve although, I must confess, I wish that I had brought my other gloves, though I believe Patty is washing them. Not that they will come to the slightest harm in that case, for there is no soul on earth more careful than Patty. She is so exceptionally careful with all our things! – and rightly so in this instance, for my grey leather gloves are particularly pleasing, a gift from our dear, good Colonel Campbell – and, considering I was not by when he chose them, it is astonishing how wonderfully they are fitted! I must admit that the gloves I am wearing are just a trifle loose in comparison, though they have *this* advantage –'

I dislike interrupting Miss Bates but, as I had not yet had my supper, I did interrupt her, and without compunction. 'Gloves or no gloves, my good madam, it is exceedingly likely to snow. Of course, snow is delightfully seasonal – my children will be leaping for joy in pure anticipation at this very moment – but *you* would be far better advised to be sitting at home and toasting those tiny feet of yours by the fire.'

'Well! I thank you, with all my heart, for such kind consideration – though I must just say that there is nothing actually *amiss* with these gloves, 'tis only that the leather has worn a little on the cuff, and just *here* on the right seam – no, the worn seam is on the left – how very odd! I was persuaded 'twas on the right...' And, by the time she had finished assuring me, several times over, that she would toast her feet by the fire, I was late for supper, and Clara a trifle testy in consequence.

'I am sorry, my dear, but I encountered Miss Bates, as she was returning from the butcher's.'

'What, in this bitter wind?'

'Exactly what I said, but –'

'– but *then* there was no extricating yourself. Well, let us see what you think of the pie, then, for *I* think that Mrs Attings has contrived it to admiration. So much so that she dispatched a portion to Mr Elton's cook for her opinion, quite in triumph. You recollect their rivalry, of course.'

I *did* however tease my lady as we went upstairs by observing that no amount of ice and snow would keep Mr Elton from his intended that evening, as he and the Hartfield party were all to dine at Randalls. But she only said, 'Well, I am as convinced as ever I was that he will ask her.'

'No, no, for should he do anything half so mad, he will never be welcome at Hartfield anymore.'

＊

All evening long the snow fell, and well into the morning.

Christmas Day was too snowy for most to attend church – and Boxing Day about the same. The trees looked weighted with their powdery burdens and the graveyard very pretty while, within St Peter's, the holly was extremely festive, with trails of ivy about the altar. Our children had the Christmas of their lives, making 'angels' and snowmen not only in our own gardens but in everyone else's. Afterwards they, along with every other child at Highbury, went sledding down Church Hill as long as the light endured.

Of course, it could not last. The winds having departed, and the snowmen almost melted, I yesterday made the rounds of my most delicate patients. In this select band I included Mr Woodhouse, as he considers himself likely to expire at any moment – despite a system reasonably robust for a man of his years. As I expected, I found him as much disconcerted by the snow as if he had never witnessed such an event before. After accepting some tea I gave him a tonic – whimsically wondering whether I dared smuggle some portion of the tonic into the teacup of his lovely daughter.

Emma seemed extraordinarily out of sorts. After greeting me rather absently, she answered her father sharply indeed – 'Really, Papa, it is not to be supposed that Mr Perry can remember your every symptom with exactitude!' – and quite snapped the head from her butler's shoulders, 'I have told you before, Serle, that I cannot bear this kind of tea, tasting, as it does, principally of dust.'

This was not the Miss Woodhouse I knew so well! – and really, one might almost call such sharpness ill-natured. Perhaps you will say that girls will be girls, particularly those girls blessed with both fortune and figure, but Miss Woodhouse as a rule is both genial and generous – as she can well afford to be.

Not long afterwards, a note was delivered to Mr Woodhouse.

'Nay,' said he to Serle, 'this must be for my daughter. 'Tis Elton's hand.' The butler politely reminded him that the envelope was addressed to himself. Mr Woodhouse, though easier after his tonic – though there is nothing in it but a little valerian – still insisted on the note being given to Emma instead. 'You may read it to me, my dear, if you would be so good. I do not wish to complain – Mr Elton is always so attentive! – but I do find his writing inconveniently small.'

Emma caught at the envelope with an eagerness which brought Clara's theory to mind, murmuring, 'Addressed to you – how very odd! – for it *is* his hand.' As she read it she flushed a little and pursed her mouth – never a good sign in a woman. Then she said, 'It is merely a note, Papa, to say that Mr Elton is gone down to Bath.'

'To Bath!' he ejaculated in horror, 'So far from hence!' Because, as Mr Woodhouse never stirs himself, he can never endure the notion of anyone else's stirring anywhere.

'Yes, Papa,' said Emma impatiently, 'but Mr Elton has his own carriage and horses.'

'But why should he wish to go to Bath?'

'But why should he not? – for Bath is always cheerful, and all the world knows how Mr Elton relishes society! Who could be more of a general favourite than Mr Elton?'

Was there a touch of derisiveness in this, some little barb? – I could not quite determine.

In either case, Elton's note proved the ruination of Mr Woodhouse's comfort. He was utterly miserable. To him, there was something terrifying in the ordeal of travelling – his mind *would* assault him with broken wheels and horrible accidents, of misbehaving horseflesh and innocent passengers dispatched to the ground, of snapped necks and broken pelvises. In fact, his imagination was *too* good – just as his every headache seemed to presage some terminal illness, so every journey contained the threat of disaster. It was rumoured about the town that his parents had always shielded him. Would they had resisted!

Emma was obliged to work, and with a zeal. 'For Papa, Mr Elton is young and the journey, which would be so very trying to you, will be as nothing to him… Overnight? I am very sure that he will rest overnight, probably twice… I do not think *many* inns as bad as the one that you recollect, Papa, else they should not remain in business… *You* might well detest such a trip, but fresh scenes, fresh verdure and fresh company delight many… As for Bath, I have never seen it myself, but it is said to be remarkably fine, and the countryside nearby – What say you, Mr Perry? Should not every young man, providing he has sufficient means, experience Bath?'

Upon this appeal, of course, I said all that I could think of in support of Elton's scheme – though secretly surprised and even annoyed that he never mentioned it to me. 'Twas so *unlike* Elton not to have done so, in fact, that it made me wonder if the trip to Bath might have been a rather impulsive, last-minute decision.

There was also *this* evidence in favour of Clara's imaginings when Mr Woodhouse mourned, 'And how you shall miss him, my dear Emma, for he visits here more than anyone!'

For a moment she looked a little confused, before saying, 'But Papa, he shall not be gone above a fortnight! Really, one would think that Mr Elton had proposed to explore the Hebrides, or to get up some expedition to foreign parts!'

Her father only shook his head, 'But – dear, dear – such traveling in-between!'

In truth, to Mr Woodhouse no news could possibly be good, for news – by its very nature – implies change and as he so often remarks, 'Change! It is always for the worse, is it not, my good Perry?'

But that there was a little confusion in the lady, at the mention of Elton's attentions, I was sure, and of his trip I remained suspicious. I passed Knightley on my way out and shared the news of Elton's journey, for which he thanked me, with a little smile. Then I rode off to assure myself that my other invalids had weathered all the ice and snow.

That night at supper, I found my wife exceedingly self-satisfied. She said, 'I have something to tell you that will astonish you not a little.'

'I cannot doubt it,' I said, very cordially, 'for such has been the case ever since we met. I venture to say that you have astonished me, with regularity, throughout the whole of our acquaintance. Indeed –'

'Do you wish to hear what I have to say, Mr Perry, or do you intend to drivel on indefinitely?'

'I do not *intend* to drivel on at all.'

'Good! – for much has transpired. Mrs Attings has heard the whole, and from Fergus!'

'Our Mrs Attings? And who, in heaven's name, is Fergus?'

'Fergus, as all the world knows, is the second coachman at Hartfield. And 'twas he who heard Mr Elton propose to Miss Woodhouse! There's for you!'

'Did he propose to her in the stables then?' I jested, for I did not believe a word of it. Highbury servants, one and all, are addicted to gossip. Come to think of it, in that respect if in no other, my wife would have made a most excellent servant.

'In the stables, indeed! 'Twas in the snow-bound second carriage, as they returned so hastily to Hartfield from Randalls, just before Christmas.'

'Impossible, for someone else must have been by. Mr Woodhouse would never permit his Emma to be alone in a carriage with any man, not even the Archbishop of Canterbury!'

'Yet so it was, for the rest were all bundled in the first carriage, though Fergus was as astonished as you that it *should* be so. And Mr Woodhouse confined the first coach to such a snail's pace that he overheard almost every word, while thinking how immensely tedious it was, to trundle along so torturously in less than an inch of snow.'

'He should have blessed himself, to have been so royally entertained! – And so, Miss Woodhouse was in the second coach with Elton alone? And he really dared to pop the question?'

'He did! Precisely as I predicted. While you laughed in your sleeve at the thought! – and he popped it in some style as well, for 'tis not every woman who is told that her lover would die should she disdain him! Instead, as I recall when a certain gentleman offered to me –'

'No, no, 'tis too much to recall the inanities of youth, in middle-age!'

'But there were none to recall! Instead, you stood in the East room, as straight as a judge and said, "My dear Miss Clara, I have thought it over a great deal, and I truly believe that you and I might contrive to be a most happily wedded couple."'

'And truer words were never spoken!'

'But where was the *romance* in it? You never threatened to die had I refused!'

'I did not, for a man must be a blockhead to say any such thing – and, besides, I was sure of Miss Banks, had you disdained me – but go on about Elton.'

'Well! And so he says his piece – about his trembling with fear and his readiness to die if she disdained him – but *she* pretends not to believe him! "No more of this to me, Mr Elton," says she. "Any message for *another,* I should be most happy to forward but no more of this to *me*, if you please." And then he grew warm and swore that his attentions had been too marked to have been mistaken. And then *she* says that any attentions *she* had observed she had set down to Miss Smith's account.'

'Miss Smith!' I repeated.

'And he said just the same. "Miss Smith! I am astonished! I am not in such despair as to sink to the level of Miss Smith!" – Though perhaps those words were not exact, for Mrs Attings was not quite certain, but that was the sense of it.'

'So, Elton had entirely mistaken the business,' I said.

'*He* had believed himself, and for some time, to have been courting Miss Woodhouse, while *she* had no more notion of it than a Dutchman!... And then she grew cool and said that "had she believed herself to have been his object, she would have thought him ill-advised in making his visits so frequent" – and a final slap – "I have no thoughts of matrimony at present." What a set-down for poor Elton! And so, my dear Mr Perry, you must admit that I was right.'

I said, 'I believe that we were both in the right, for *you* foretold his proposal, and *I* foretold her refusal!… But what a scene – and what could he have been thinking of? A spoiled, petted young lady like Miss Woodhouse, with such an inheritance! She would have been as likely to accept the hand of the eavesdropping coachman!…

And yet, they had been celebrating Christmas at Randalls, with good food and good wines. Mr Elton was in his cups, I suppose, and under the influence of her fine looks – all alone with the lady – and unexpectedly, too! Aye, that will have been the way of it. You will find, in the end, that poor Elton was not himself, and that he apologised most ingratiatingly the next morning.'

'Not so! I forgot to tell you. For Miss Woodhouse herself accused him – of unsteadiness, I mean – in the middle of it all, and he denied it. And with such eloquence that Fergus, at least, quite took his part.'

I recollected then, 'And neither could he have abased himself, for I chanced to be at Hartfield when Elton's note about Bath was delivered. And when Miss Woodhouse read it, she was most displeased... There can have been no abasement, no apology, but a breach, instead –'

'– which Elton has attempted to brush over, with his hasty removal to Bath,' said Clara, 'which, by-the-bye was not much to the taste of his cook, for *she* got no notice at all.'

'But truly, a man cannot be blamed in such a case. How mortified he must have been! He had either to arrange for his own decease or else some more temporary disappearance. Nothing less would have sufficed, after swearing to end it all should his suit be spurned.'

'Well, *I* still believe that she encouraged him, whether she intended it or not.'

I shook my head. 'I have yet to observe Miss Woodhouse encourage any man, and I have seen her with Elton a thousand times... No, no, there is no excuse for him, beyond ambition. 'Twould have been as if I, instead of choosing you to be my wife – '

'– or Dora Banks –'

'Nay,' I said hastily. 'I never had a thought of Miss Banks – it was as if I had petitioned Miss Woodhouse's own sister, instead!'

'About Miss Banks –' began my wife.

'She had a jaw like a boatswain,' said I, and took another puff upon my pipe.

Now, I have already shared my first rule of marriage. Perhaps the *second* is that a man must learn to abuse the looks of any woman to whom he does not happen to be wedded. I held my tongue – along with my breath – and my lady moved on. 'Of course, Miss Woodhouse is very pretty.'

'But spoiled and rather arrogant.'

'Perhaps, but might not she have encouraged Mr Elton's visits with little Miss Harriet Smith in mind? Are they not very intimate? And did not she make up a marriage for her own governess, before? You have seen them all together, time and again – did you never imagine it might be so?'

'I confess that I did not. Perhaps *you* might have.'

'I dare say I would.'

''Twill be diverting for you to watch them together once Elton returns – to see if *she* remains offended, or if *he* unbends so far as to apologise.'

'It will indeed,' said she and then, at last, I was left to the contentment of my wife's most excellent pork, and to the conviction of a job well done.

❧

When Elton returned, I dared to tease him a little about Christmas Eve.

'Utter nonsense. Truly, Miss Woodhouse must be the most conceited woman in existence! It is quite true that we were confined in the same carriage – John Knightley's manners are not perfect –

and that she was a little flirtatious, but nothing out of the common way. As for making the lady an offer, I should as soon offer to my cook! – Miss Woodhouse is not at all the sort of woman I like… But I will share with you, my good Perry, that I am an engaged man.'

'What! So did Miss Cox –' I cried.

'Miss Cox! I should think not! Chilly as she is, I would take even Miss Woodhouse over Miss Cox! No – in confidence, Perry – I am engaged to a Miss Hawkins. A Miss Augusta Hawkins, of Bath.'

I gathered my scattered wits. 'Well, this is news indeed! I wish you joy!'

'And permit me to tell you, that no Highbury lady could compare. She is piquant – charming, in fact – witty, clever, musical – and the nimblest dancer in all the world!'

'Well, I wish you both very happy,' said I. 'But what a sly dog you are! To rush to Bath, almost overnight! I suppose you heard that Miss Hawkins was to be there – and you were off!'

He looked conscious, which made me guess that he had instead first met the young lady at Bath. Then he said, 'I am sure you will like her, for who could not?'

'Who, indeed?'

It was difficult not to tell Clara that evening – I quite longed to tell her – but I recollected that time when all Highbury believed Miss Bates, who had caught a chill, dead and buried – and forbore.

She would discover it, soon enough – and then, what pleasure she would have in telling *me*!

Pride and Perjury

'Oh! for myself, I protest I must be excused,' said Mrs. Elton; 'I really cannot attempt – I am not at all fond of that sort of thing. I had an acrostic once sent to me upon my own name, which I was not at all pleased with. I knew who it came from. An abominable puppy! – You know who I mean...' (nodding to her husband).

(from *Emma*, Chapter 7)

'Permit me, Miss Hawkins,' said the master of ceremonies, 'to introduce Mr Elton. Mr Elton, Miss Hawkins.'

'Enchanted,' said Mr Elton, and – at least partly – he meant it.

Miss Augusta Hawkins seemed a vast improvement on his previous partner, whose teeth had been quite fascinatingly terrible. He had scarcely been able to take his eyes from them as they had danced down the set, while the lady concerned appeared so unaware of the offence that he had felt quite unreasonably cross with her. In addition, she danced only tolerably. In short, to have been bound for two dances to Miss Lovett had put Mr Elton in rather a temper.

Miss Hawkins, by contrast, had a piquant countenance, a light foot, and was extremely conversable – most conversable indeed! By the end of their first dance in the Lower Rooms, Mr Elton's head was reeling, though rather enjoyably.

'Quite. Just so,' said she. 'What I always say is, if my dear Selina is wrong once, she is right ten thousand times! My sister was perfectly correct about Mr Jackson, but by *that* point I could do nothing to discourage him. He dogged my footsteps – he visited every other day – he brought me flowers… But there it is! It should be a lesson to me, never to take a young man at his own estimation, but to judge for myself, instead!'

'I hope you do not intend to judge too harshly in the present case,' said Mr Elton daringly.

'Oh, I should not so presume! But there are *some* young men who are nothing more or less than puppies!'

'Your brother-in-law's seat is near to Bristol, I believe?'

'It is. Though boasting the most complete retirement, Maple Grove is not above five miles from Bristol. Its situation suits my dear sister perfectly. Why, this very evening we had to *prise* Selina from the house – she would as happily have spent the entire evening closeted with her music and her embroidery although – to own the truth – I find that I cannot observe her, just at present. Perhaps she has escaped our vigilance and trotted back to Laura Place, in spite of all!'

Mr Elton inquired further of Maple Grove, and there was clearly no dislike of the subject.

'There is nowhere, Mr Elton, where I feel more *myself* than at Maple Grove. The elegant restraint of its design! Its topiary – the view from the valley to the east – the line of oaks to the west! Oh, everyone who beholds it must admire it – but to me it has been quite a home.'

'I suppose there are maples there, as well as oaks?'

'I believe so. Truly, there must be. But my brother-in-law's grounds are so extensive, Mr Elton, that I cannot say where they might be found.'

'I assume that your sister was first introduced to Mr Suckling in town?'

Miss Hawkins laughed. 'Nay – 'twas here – just here, in the

Lower Rooms! It was indeed! I was not present, else I should have been the first to suspect the attachment... For no one is quicker at a hint than I – though I say it myself, as ought not!'

Mr Elton declared himself convinced, and their dances continued to their mutual satisfaction, at the end of which he begged permission to call at Laura Place, a permission very readily granted.

Upon hearing of it, however, Augusta's sister lost no time in locating her husband. ('For Augusta is so impulsive! Do, I beg, contrive to discover who and what this Mr Elton might be.')

Mr Suckling, swift to oblige, then learned that Philip Elton was a rector, of good family and possessed of an excellent living in Surrey. And that night his wife said thoughtfully, 'Mr Elton has rather too high a colour for my taste, but his *manners* seem unobjectionable. He might do very well for Augusta.'

'Quite,' said Mr Suckling, who owed his reputation for suavity to his never quite saying what he was thinking. In this case, he was thinking that any man with the requisite number of legs and a few working teeth would 'do' for Augusta, provided that the gentleman's situation was such that she would be obliged to remove from Maple Grove. Mr Suckling could never decide whether it was the shrillness of Augusta's voice, her provoking titter, or her air of knowing a great deal more than anyone else that most grated upon his nerves, but his sister-in-law could not be settled too soon. And Surrey was at a most admirable distance. They might not encounter Augusta above twice a year, were she to remove to Surrey...

Back in his lodgings, Mr Elton felt equally encouraged. What an excellent idea it had been, to come to Bath after Christmas! The splendour of the Assembly Rooms, their scalloped alcoves and glorious chandeliers, were all to his taste, as was the creamy stone of Bath's buildings – not to mention the society. At Bath he felt still more appreciated than he had felt at Highbury.

And he winced as he recollected, for the hundredth time, the crisp contempt with which Miss Woodhouse had dismissed his suit on Christmas Eve. ('As it is, the disappointment is single and, I trust, will not be lasting. I have no plans for matrimony at present.') The loftiness of her countenance, her sneering tone! While her conviction that he had, all along, been wooing her empty-headed little friend was perhaps most insulting of all.

Miss Smith, indeed! Miss Smith, forsooth! Miss Smith – not an ill-looking girl, to be fair, but with no money, no family, no known *parentage*, even! Did he really appear the kind of fool to throw away his every advantage on a parlour boarder at a village school? He, whom almost every female in Highbury made eyes at, sometimes within the precincts of St Mark's church itself?

It was usual, so Elton believed, for even the strongest anger to soften over time, for the sting of every insult to gradually ease away – but the fire of his own, stoked by a resentment so just, had yet to abate… Only a woman of astonishing stupidity could have imagined that such a man as he – good-looking, well-mannered, well-born – but then, he had often considered Miss Woodhouse's judgement suspect. Though given that she possessed, wrapped round her finger, so fond and feeble a father, perhaps humility was not to be expected? Yet when – as rarely happened – Elton mused on suitable topics for sermons, how often modesty, meekness and feminine submission sprang to mind!

He could fancy penning such a sermon – aye, and delivering it too, upon his return to Highbury!

❦

On his first visit to the Sucklings, he was greatly struck by his host's civility. He cried, 'Mr Elton – How exceedingly good of you to call!

278

Maxwell will show you into the drawing-room, where I hope to attend you ere long.'

In the drawing-room Elton found Mrs Suckling leaning against her tambour frame, an accessory she fancied – like her harp – peculiarly becoming, though she detested music and needlework about equally. Miss Hawkins, her sister, brightened a good deal upon his entrance, set down her book and made a parade of ringing for fresh coffee as, 'I am very sure you are in need of it. I can never look out the front window without observing hundreds of young men rushing about their business!'

In fact, Mr Elton had no business at all at Bath, beyond soothing his ruffled feelings after the sting of Miss Woodhouse's dismissal. He assented, however, and took care to admire the house and the furniture.

Mrs Suckling received these compliments graciously, though the property was rented and its style not to her taste. Upon inquiring about his own abode, she learned that the rectory was well-maintained, capacious and excessively pretty, boasting a cottage garden, a shrubbery and a respectable number of servants. It all sounded most promising for, after all, no member of the family had ever imagined that Augusta could marry quite as splendidly as Selina had herself.

'It is not far from the road,' he finished – and truthfully, for the vicarage walls were hard by its edge, 'but the garden extends for over an acre, with a little grove of apple trees at its conclusion, while my nearest neighbour is a hundred yards down Vicarage Lane.'

'I assume there is a great house at such a place as Highbury?' asked Mrs Suckling.

'There are two, ma'am, perhaps even three, which might be so described. Perhaps the name of Mr Knightley, of Donwell Abbey, might be known to you?'

'Perhaps it might.'

'A most worthy fellow, and my dearest friend. As is Mr Weston, who is likewise often in town. But I cannot imagine you will have heard of old Mr Woodhouse, for *he* would never stir from Hartfield unless forced, at gunpoint, by some highwayman.'

Miss Hawkins laughed – her teeth as neat as they had appeared by candlelight. Her gown was charming too, as were the tiny pearls clasped about her throat. She cried, 'But surely there are some well-born ladies at Highbury? There would be little enough music, were there none at all!'

'None to compare with present company, I am sure,' said Mr Elton, in secret – if vicious – retaliation against Miss Woodhouse. 'Miss Fairfax, Miss Cox and Miss Woodhouse are the principal performers, of which Miss Fairfax is incomparably the most gifted. Are you fond of music, Mrs Suckling?'

'Devotedly,' lied his hostess, 'while Augusta plays and sings delightfully, when she finds the time. But who has the energy to burnish their accomplishments in Bath, with the shops and the Rooms, the shows and the concerts, and so many acquaintances arriving every day?'

Mr Elton owned that he quite longed to hear Miss Hawkins sing, whereupon Selina said, 'Perhaps, if not engaged, you might care to attend us on Thursday? Augusta and several of her friends can generally be persuaded to perform on Thursdays. And last week the Earl of Evesham honoured us, though he rarely ventures anywhere!'

Just as the gentleman accepted the invitation, the coffee arrived and the butler simultaneously announced, 'Miss Bingley.'

'My dear!' cried Mrs Suckling, though secretly rather put-out, 'how charming of you to find the time! Permit me to present Mr

Elton, of Surrey. Mr Elton, Miss Bingley and I were friends at school.'

'I am sure,' said the ever-gallant Mr Elton, 'that you can have hardly left it!' – though he found little enough to admire in the newcomer. Nearer to thirty than to twenty, she was sharp of feature and sardonic of tone, with none of her schoolmate's soft graces.

'Do you intend to remain long in Bath, Mr Elton?' inquired Miss Bingley.

'Three weeks, alas, is all that I can spare from my duties.'

'What a pity! For Bath must boast pleasures even Surrey cannot equal.'

'Oh, you need not tell him that! He is *quite* the convert!' cried Augusta Hawkins. 'Did not you tell me, and only last night, that you were smitten with Bath?'

Of course, the gentleman agreed and, once their visitors had gone, Selina ventured, 'Mr Elton is well enough, is he not, Augusta? At least, one meets a great many worse.'

'Oh indeed,' said Augusta. She picked up her book and read a little before pensively crossing to the pianoforte. 'Mrs Elton,' she thought, as she dispatched some finger exercises. 'It does not sound ill.'

And that night she dreamt of pretty shrubberies and hawthorn hedges, and of the chiming of distant church bells.

❧

Elton called at two other houses before luncheon, at one of which he was startled to discover that Miss Bingley was twice as well-endowed as Miss Hawkins, with close on £20,000. (Miss Woodhouse's fortune, of course, was finer still, but *she* had, 'no thoughts of matrimony at present'!)

Yet £20,000 – or thereabouts, for such rumours rarely proved exact – still provided rich food for thought. For had he not come to Bath secretly vowing to return to Highbury an engaged man? *That* would show Miss Woodhouse how he might be valued by better-judging members of society, while £20,000 was a handsome fortune! And if Miss Hawkins might be considered as reaching an age of some concern, might not Miss Bingley be supposed to have already reached it? Both sister and brother were settled – though neither to extraordinary advantage – but even *that* fact was rather encouraging than otherwise. Clearly, the Bingleys were not fortune-hunters. And whenever Mr Elton considered Miss Bingley's £20,000, she never seemed quite so particularly plain…

Mr Elton was delighted, once Thursday arrived, to find Miss Hawkins and Miss Bingley disposed together upon one of the Sucklings' settees. (Indeed, he was rather taken with the company altogether, being mostly comprised of young ladies and sleepy married men.)

'Why, Mr Elton!' tittered Miss Augusta. 'Had I recollected that *you* might attend, I would have practised rather harder!'

'I am sure,' said Miss Bingley loftily, 'as occupied as we have been, that *I* am the one most in want of practice. Besides, I never feel perfectly comfortable when separated from my own instrument. Sentimental of me, I daresay, but there it is.'

'Truly?' laughed Augusta. 'It is all one to me what pianoforte I play!'

'And yet to a true *artist*, there can be quite a considerable difference… Are you from the West Country, Mr Elton?'

'No, I was born in town and reside in Surrey.'

'The garden of England!' cried Miss Hawkins.

Miss Bingley's rather superior smile suggested that *she*, at least, had visited many counties rather more deserving of that accolade.

'Are you by any chance related to the Eltons of Berkshire?'

Mr Elton denied it, whereupon Miss Hawkins said viciously, 'I am very glad, for I never heard a good word said of them.'

'What a pity it is, in that case,' said Miss Bingley, 'that they are *such* friends of my brother's.'

Mr Elton hastened to soothe both parties by remarking that, where such varying reports prevailed, interested parties were oftenest to blame.

Meanwhile, as Mrs Suckling wished the music to commence, there ensued an anxious parlay over which young lady should lead, and five young ladies performed, though not one in any danger of throwing their audience into ecstasies.

Charles Bingley arrived during his sister's Italian air and enthusiastically applauded during a pause in the middle. For this he was roundly teased which, to Elton's secret astonishment, he did not appear to mind in the least...

Mr Elton left the Suckling's convinced of having acquitted himself well. Miss Hawkins had twice reminded him of the ball on Monday, and the elegant Miss Bingley had deigned to recommend a poetry reading that she expected to patronise ('Some very gifted young men, I assure you, though I cannot answer for them all...')

Miss Hawkins, and Monday's ball, also proved an item of conversation at the Bingley's.

'I find Miss Hawkins's superior airs,' said Miss Bingley, 'utterly insufferable. It was all "my beloved Maple Grove" and "my brother's charming new barouche landau." While her singing was so appalling that I noticed her brother-in-law, the master of Maple Grove himself, discreetly slipping into the garden.'

'Must we attend the ball, Caroline?' asked Mr Bingley wistfully.

'Jane must not think of it, given her condition. But I should be most grateful, Charles, if you attend me.'

283

'Oh indeed!' cried Mrs Bingley, 'you must not feel obliged to stay home, my dearest, and be dull.'

'But I am never happy unless with you!' objected her husband.

'Yet Caroline *must* be attended, while I shall be perfectly content with my book, by the fire.'

For the first time in his life, Bingley sympathised with his friend Darcy's distaste for balls. How dull such an event would be, without his wife, Jane! But his sister also had a claim, and it ended in his agreeing to accompany her.

➣

At the ball, Mr Elton found himself in a position of most enviable discomfort, as he was positively besieged by young ladies anxious to dance. (As he later bragged to his mama, 'Everywhere I turned, another pair of eager eyes sought my own. I almost wished I could have danced with two or three at once and got it over!')

It was not only that Mr Elton was considered eligible. There was rather a dearth of unmarried men in Bath that week, a situation recently exacerbated by the arrival of a gentleman with six daughters. Even the good-natured Bingley felt obliged to dance far oftener than he wished to.

'Really,' said Mr Elton to Miss Hawkins, 'do young ladies never lose their appetite for dancing?'

'As for myself,' said she, 'I am never happier than when sitting at home in Maple Grove, quite quietly, with a book. But it is not everyone who has such resources as I!'

'You are fond of novels, I suppose?' inquired Elton, who had no patience with them.

'*Some*, perhaps, yet I love to feel that I am expanding my mind – if that does not sound just the tiniest bit pretentious!'

'Not in the least – I honour you!' returned Elton, but rather absently – for Miss Bingley had just danced past and, to his mind, it was as if her £20,000 had danced with her.

Miss Hawkins said, 'To my way of thinking, 'tis a young lady's *duty* to improve her mind. Compared with gentlemen' – that tinkling laugh again – 'we have little enough to think of, else!'

'Not at all! It was always my father's opinion, Miss Hawkins, that women are philosophers by nature.'

'Was it, indeed? Well, *I* cannot aspire to philosophy. I cannot pretend to be anything beyond what I am – unusually thoughtful and well-educated, but assuredly no conjurer… Though I *have* been put in the way of absorbing more information than most, at Maple Grove.'

'I do not doubt it!' cried the gentleman.

'In addition, as well as bringing us up to appreciate the finer things of life, our dear Mama never disdained more domestic matters. Selina, of course, is everywhere lauded for her embroidery, but half my acquaintance vies to seek my advice on dress, and I have also completed designs for several sweet little tables.'

'How I long to see them!' cried Elton – and on that note they parted.

Elton's next partner was a most serious young lady, from whom he felt obliged to wrest opinions on the Rooms, on various walks about the countryside and on the agreeableness of Bath in comparison to London. He turned from her with such relief that he almost backed into Miss Bingley.

'Forgive me, I beg,' said he with a bow. 'I hope I have not tumbled your beautiful gown?' (It was possibly the finest in the room, gilt-coloured silk, with gold ribbons.)

'Not at all, Mr Elton! It was my fault entirely!'

And there she stood, waiting to be petitioned. 'I do not suppose,' he offered, 'that you would care to dance?'

'I should have no objection,' said Miss Bingley archly, 'as the Earl of Evesham is unlikely to apply!'

Now Elton did not mind a well-bred archness, of which he saw so little in Highbury. Here, archness seemed the fashion, like oysters at dinner. But how he wished that Miss Woodhouse had been there to observe his social triumphs! He noticed Miss Hawkins opposite, dancing with rather a foppish-looking young man wearing a crimson waistcoat.

'It is rumoured,' murmured Miss Bingley, 'that the fellow's waistcoat cost quite a frightening amount, yet *I* cannot admire it.'

'Your brother is the only well-looking fellow in the room,' said Mr Elton, steering her neatly down the set.

'Oh, I think *not*,' said she, to his secret delight. 'Though one cannot, of course, expect the same class of young man here as in London and – Oh, heavens! Is that not Lord Castlereagh at the door? You must recollect – the cabinet member obliged to resign after dueling with the Foreign Secretary?'

Perhaps Elton was distracted by Castlereagh – or perhaps the fop had led the usually nimble Miss Hawkins astray? All that Elton could swear to, either then or afterwards, was that the incident happened too swiftly for his comprehension. One moment he was observing Lord Castlereagh – and the next, Miss Bingley's pretty gown had a rent of some inches near its base, where Miss Hawkins' equally pretty shoe had trodden on it.

'Oh heavens!' cried Miss Hawkins. 'I am *mortified*! Your lovely gown!'

'It is nothing,' said Miss Bingley, smiling through her teeth. 'Just nothing at all!'

'I am very sure,' cried the fop with a laugh, 'it can be mended in a trice!' just as Mr Elton began to commiserate with his partner.

Miss Bingley said, 'I greatly fear, Mr Elton, that I must excuse myself, before the damage is compounded.'

Elton submitted – yet, as she left to adjust her dress, found himself perplexed as to the etiquette of the situation. There remained any number of unpartnered women – mostly fanning themselves – one of whom he was probably obliged to petition, in Miss Bingley's place. (Or was he instead obliged to mourn the bereavement – the bereavement, at least, of an intact gold-ribboned gown?)

'What a pity,' said a stout young fellow by his side, shaking his head.

'Quite,' said Mr Elton.

'The ladies set such store by their gowns! To own the truth, my good fellow, I cannot comprehend it. One gown looks just like any other, to my way of thinking.'

'And to mine,' said Elton cordially.

'My name is Thorpe. Would you care to play at three-card brag?'

Mr Elton was very persuadable. He fancied himself as useful as the next man at cards. After all, had not Knightley of Donwell described him as the best whist player in Highbury? – Three-card brag was never his favourite – there was rather too much luck in it – but it was good-natured of this Thorpe fellow to rescue him.

In fact, it was far, very far, from good-natured – for it was not twenty minutes before a perspiring Mr Elton discovered that the best whist player in Highbury was no match for John Thorpe, who regularly defeated some of the most famous players in London. In the beginning, Elton believed himself in the ascendent, but as the ante rose, he found himself in deep water – even sinking. How fervently he wished that he had remained in the ballroom!

A little crowd, hearing that a serious sum had been reached,

gathered to observe the battle. ('A clergyman, did you say?'…
'Nay, they all gamble nowadays!'… 'Smart as a whip, and does not
lack for nerve'… '*That* will never do, against a player such as
Thorpe'…)

Elton began to feel almost dizzy – the fetid air, the stench of
tobacco, the nearness of the onlookers. But Thorpe's face had
briefly clouded upon the last drawing of the cards. Though he had
been swift to crack a joke, his opponent felt a tiny spurt of hope.

'And so,' inquired Thorpe, 'what have you to offer, my good
fellow?'

Elton turned over his cards and hope surged again. His was
assuredly no triumph, but it need not be a rout… He displayed the
cards: an eight, a nine and a ten. But then Thorpe, with masterly
deliberation, unveiled an ace, a two and a three – and in matched
spades, besides!

Elton's face drained of colour, as Thorpe was feted and
congratulated.

His opponent cried, 'Well met, sir!' but Elton's mouth was too
dry to respond, and Elton's head was reeling. Indeed, he felt almost
sick with fear and mortification. Why, he had lost, in less than an
hour, almost half the money he had brought to Bath! Having made
over his note of hand, his only wish was to escape.

He found Charles Bingley by his side, who had procured him
some wine and water. A few moments later both men were
gratefully breathing in the chill night air. Elton thanked Bingley,
who said somberly, 'It was nothing! I am only sorry that I did not
see you leave the ball with Thorpe.'

'What, is the fellow so notorious that you would have warned
me off going?'

'No, no, Thorpe is well enough – we have quite a few friends in
common. But he has a reputation for sharpness, beyond a doubt.'

'The fellow is an actor!'

'So I understand. I did not observe the whole.'

'But what am I to *do*?'

'Why, in what respect?'

Elton hesitated. He did not know Bingley well – he had only called upon him twice – yet he had so open, so trustworthy, a countenance! And then, what other friend could he boast, here in Bath? Two cousins – one aloof, the other intolerable!

'Might I confide in you, Bingley?'

'Of course, my good fellow!'

'Then my difficulty is simply that, in order to fulfill my note of hand, I shall have to –'

'You mean, you have not funds enough?'

'It is not as bad as that – but, well, should I pay the fellow in full, I should have to return home before my visit has expired.'

'Which you would prefer not to do?'

'Indeed,' said Elton thinking, with a shudder, of the embarrassment of returning early, chastened and humbled, to Highbury. He imagined Emma Woodhouse's barely veiled contempt, the whist club's open ribaldry, even Knightley's and Weston's quips at his expense. No – he had no wish to leave Bath before he could do so in triumph, flaunting an engagement to – to some young lady or other!

'Then suppose I advance you some part of it?' asked Bingley.

'What! You would do so much for me, unrelated as I am?'

'I would indeed. I feel for you sincerely – and some little guilt besides, that I did not warn you about Thorpe – why, these days he can hardly get a game, in town! And you will honour your word, I feel sure.'

Elton grasped his hand. 'I am moved sir – moved and grateful!'

'It is no more than any man, in easy circumstances, might do.

You have not been in Bath long enough to be wary... Mind, I do not say the fellow cheats, for I never would while lacking proof of it – but a better-judging fellow than Thorpe, I am persuaded, would have stopped long before the sum you reached!'

Elton thanked him with a secret sigh of relief and made over his note of hand. Then they returned together to the ballroom, where Elton made a point of requesting both Miss Hawkins and Miss Bingley – in her mended gown – to stand up with him.

❧

Mr Bingley had never had any doubt of his wife's approving what he had done. Jane Bingley's sympathy was instantly aroused. 'What, and so Mr Thorpe simply kept raising the ante?'

'Quite.'

'And this against no gamester, but some gentleman rector up from the country? Heavens! Why did Mr Elton not quit the game?'

'No doubt, my love, he should have quit it, but so many were watching – it would have taken a strong nerve to do so. But I am glad that you approve.'

'Oh, *you* did well, indeed! He will repay you and – even if he did *not* – you will have done something good and kind and like yourself.' Though Bingley could not help reflecting that loaning money to Mr Elton was rather safer than loaning money to Lydia Wickham, which he was always being asked to do, and all without the slightest hope of being repaid.

Bingley also admitted to himself that his sister Caroline's flagging prospects might well have influenced him. A fellow like Elton – of established family, sound position and good looks, settled in a pleasing part of the country... Caroline might go farther and do worse!

PRIDE AND PERJURY

Meanwhile, in the Pump Room the next morning, Elton was heartened to learn that his embarrassment was far from unheard-of. ('Oh heavens, 'tis as common as common! These rattles think nothing of cheating at any game upon the cards!') He was reassured too by the warmth of his reception at Laura Place, where Mr Suckling took care to engage him in conversation, Mrs Suckling smiled sweetly upon him, and Miss Hawkins played and sang, in his own opinion, at least as well as Highbury's much-vaunted Jane Fairfax... He had never rated Miss Fairfax, a rather ethereal creature whom George Knightley considered a beauty – Miss Hawkins's liveliness was much more to his taste.

'Would you care to accompany us in the park later?' inquired Mrs Suckling, as he rose to leave.

'I should like nothing better!'

'First, I must call upon the Bragges, but we should certainly be about by noon. Shall we say, the west entrance, by the great oak?'

Mr Elton declared himself entranced, for he remained convinced that gallantry was the path to every lady's heart, despite its having so signally failed to answer with Miss Woodhouse. Though he thought of the Highbury heiress with rather less ire than he had before, being mollified by his triumphs at Bath. It was her loss, was his commonest opinion, for who else would consider offering to so conceited a creature? No, Miss Woodhouse would grow lonely, old and haggard and learn to regret that she had not accepted Mr Elton's hand, when still young and well-looking!

And during the rest of the morning, while Miss Hawkins fretted over which of her pretty spencers best became her new gown, he attempted to write a poem. Now Elton considered himself not ungifted in the rhyming arts, despite his riddle in Highbury having been so lamentably misconstrued. Half an hour's crossings out later...

Augusta, thou art a beacon bright,
Rare jewel amidst bleak star-shorn night,
Thine eyes, twin stars of heav'n's pure blue
In them, my heart finds solace, 'tis true.

Like lilies, thy visage does perfect impart
A grace to lift the world-weariest heart.
Thy smile a soft sunbeam in a world of gloom,
Its warmth dispelling all clouds of doom.

Each note that falls from thy melodious tongue
Resembles songs of angels, sweetly sung,
Thy laughter, brook's pure babbling stream,
Soothes sorrow with love's enchanting dream.

Augusta, be mine – I beg you – forever!
In love's embrace, we shall ne'er part, not ever!
Together treading life's wondrous way
Through joys and through sorrows, come evils that may.

He was unsure about the 'clouds of doom' – (gloom? bloom?) – but otherwise felt not dissatisfied... And really, given that both Augusta and Caroline contained three syllables, his pretty effusion might 'do' as well for Miss Bingley, should he alter his allegiance... In an attempt to clarify his thinking on this point, he called upon the Bingleys, interrupting the lady's singing practice.

'How grieved I am to part you from your muse!' cried Elton.

'Oh, as to that, my muse – as you call it – can wait. I adore all music and most books, but conversation has charms that neither can equal!'

'Indeed,' said Mr Elton fervently. 'Especially converse combined with so charming a view – you at your instrument, the sweet verdure of the garden beyond!'

'Oh, do you like our tiny patch of green? 'Tis nothing in comparison to what we are accustomed to, I assure you! I suppose you have an excessively pretty garden down in Surrey?'

Elton reflected gloomily that his vicarage encroached so nearly on Vicarage Lane that it could scarcely be said to possess any front garden at all. But he merely said, 'I cannot pretend to know half of what my garden contains – but my cook is as prodigiously proud of her vegetables as any cook in England.'

Miss Bingley rather liked the sound of the cook for, having been raised by her mama with an emphasis on the fashionable arts, she was sadly lacking in the more domestic variety. But then, recollecting that the dashing Mr Elton was also a rector, she said, 'Mrs Bingley and I have been amusing ourselves making pinafores for the poor children down the road. What think you of my smocking?'

'It is most beautifully worked!'

'Jane and I generally contrive to find employment, even at Bath... though we *had* thought of venturing to the park this afternoon, as the weather is so fine.'

'Which section of the park is your favourite?'

'Oh! 'Tis hard to say, it is all so delightful!' said Miss Bingley, repressing a sneeze. 'Why do you ask?'

'I had hoped, if possible, to increase the chances of my encountering you twice in one day.'

'Well!' – most graciously – 'Well, in that case I daresay we might contrive to be near the pavilion by three.'

This could scarcely have been more satisfactory. Thus the canny Elton secured the pleasure of walking in the park, first with the chatty Miss Hawkins and later with the elegant Miss Bingley – and in both instances with the happiest connivance of their guardians, for Mr and Mrs Suckling were sufficiently mannerly to *appear* as absorbed in each other as Mr and Mrs Bingley truly were... Yet that evening found Elton's clarity of mind none the forwarder, for while Miss Bingley was unquestionably both plainer and older than Miss Hawkins, her dowry remained stubbornly in the region of £20,000, while Miss Hawkins's thousands could hardly be greater than *ten*.

Later, Mr Suckling complained to his wife, 'Just as I begin to think your sister secure, I learned from the Priors that Elton was also accompanying Miss *Bingley* about the park today.'

'Was he, indeed? – and yet, as he is not actually engaged to Augusta, surely he is at liberty to walk in the park with every young lady in Bath!'

'Well, *I* believe that he is trying to decide between the two. At least, such is my impression.'

'If he is, though, there is nothing in the world that we can do about it,' said she – but Mr Suckling never answered her.

♦

Miss Bingley's sneezes worsened that night, and so prevailed the following day that she decided against attending the ball for, as she complained to Jane, 'my nose is red beyond possibility of disguise, and I have such an aching in my throat!'

As Elton entered the Lower Rooms, he overheard Miss Hawkins confiding to a dark-haired young lady, '*Such* impertinence!'

'Good evening, Miss Hawkins,' said he.

'Oh! Are you here again, Mr Elton? How very delightful!... Isabella, I do not believe you know Mr Elton, of Surrey. Mr Elton, my friend Miss Thorpe, who is here with her mama, and her brother

John… Well! As I was just telling Isabella, I received, this very morning, an acrostic on my own name – and unsigned, besides!'

'How romantic!' cried Miss Thorpe, clasping her hands together.

'Say rather, how shocking. Here, you may read it, and judge for yourself!'

Miss Thorpe, nothing loth, took up the paper and read aloud:

> *'Augusta, Augusta, my true heart's delight*
> *Unmatched in sweet charms, a radiant sight,*
> *Graced by thy smile, my soul takes flight,*
> *Unfathomable esteem, pure as starriest night.*
> *Soft whisper of hope may my heart's soul ignite*
> *That you my adoration might perchance requite,*
> *Augusta, Augusta, my true heart's delight.'*

'Such sweet lines,' cried the lovely Miss Thorpe. 'And the rhyming is perfection!'

'But so entirely improper! Surely you would never permit anything of the same sort to be sent to yourself?'

'Oh, heavens, *I* could never resist! But then, I have so much heart – *too* much heart, I sometimes think, for my own comfort…'

'And recollect – *unsigned*!' Miss Hawkins reminded her, fanning herself violently.

'But are not such tributes generally unsigned? And "graced by thy smile, my soul takes flight" – oh! – 'tis quite divine!'

Miss Hawkins appealed to the gentleman. 'Surely you agree, Mr Elton? Surely *you* would never send so impertinent a missive to any lady, however much you happened to admire her?'

Mr Elton trusted that he would not, for the composition was quite appalling – but he understood Miss Hawkins to be appealing to his sense of propriety rather than to his critical judgement. (How fortunate it was that he had not risked his own poem!) He said, 'Certainly not,' just as she added, 'And, my dear Isabella, I am almost certain that it is Mr *Jackson's* hand.'

'No, no – for he would never dare!' cried her dear Isabella.

'But as he trod on my feet last Monday he told me that I danced with grace and fire.'

'And so you do,' said Mr Elton, in gallant parenthesis.

'Oh fie, Mr Elton! Spare my blushes, I beg!'

Far from sparing her blushes, Elton was sufficiently emboldened to add, 'Forgive us, Miss Thorpe, but might you perhaps be willing to show your grace and fire on this occasion, Miss Hawkins, and stand up with me?'

'Why, of course! Only too pleased – but I shall find you later, Isabella, for we must together devise a proper punishment for Mr Jackson's impertinence.'

The ball being crowded, Mr Elton could not discern quite every syllable of Miss Hawkins's vivacity, though its thrust was clear enough. ('Abominable puppies... Maple Grove... the *idea* that I should ever... *some* young men... not the slightest notion of how to behave... Mind, I am not saying that the *family* is to blame – I daresay not... very good sort of people, considering... My dear Selina... Maple Grove...')

Despite this pretty exhibition of ruffled feathers, Elton believed the lady less offended than flattered by the 'puppy's' presumption – or, at least, that she *would* have been flattered, had Mr Jackson only had sufficient sense to have been rather better-born. But he liked to hear her – she was no trouble to entertain, he had only to agree – and then, she danced so prettily, and smiled so well. And what an affable, unpretending fellow her brother-in-law Suckling was – actually seeking him out to canvass his opinion on the situation in

America and the flavour of the punch!

'I suspect that all our worries about Miss Bingley are at an end,' said Mr Suckling to his wife that night. 'She would have attended the ball, else.'

'I am glad you think dear Augusta secure,' said his wife vaguely. 'But – though nothing is quite perfect in all the world – Mr Elton *does* live at such a distance from Maple Grove. It could scarcely be less convenient, unless it was in Northumberland or the Scottish borders!'

'It is a drawback, without a doubt,' said Mr Suckling, with a shake of his handsome head. 'Yet as you say, nothing is quite perfect in all the world!'

The next morning in the Pump Room, while admiring the view from the long windows, Elton was disconcerted to find himself again accosted by John Thorpe. (Surely the fellow was not petitioning for his winnings at three-card brag quite so soon?)

'Here you are, at last! I say, Elton, I am sure that there are no hard feelings between us –'

'Why, none at all,' said Elton. It was no part of his policy to make enemies – not even of Thorpe – and surely Bingley would have the money for him by Friday.

'– but there seems to be some wild idea making the rounds that I took advantage of your good nature the other evening. Utterly ludicrous, of course – ludicrous, indeed! – but 'tis the worst of Bath. 'Tis blighted by cantankerous old cats with nothing to do but gossip and by young girls who do not know their own minds from one day to the next! Believe me, Elton, I had no more thought of driving my own *sisters* about –'

'Quite,' said Elton.

'– but *that* is all by-the-bye. At any rate, I should be most grateful if you would do me a favour.'

With the mental reservation that the favour had nothing to do with cards, Elton assured him of his kindest assistance.

'Well then – to own the truth, I am in love.'

Elton inquired if congratulations were in order.

'Not quite,' said Thorpe, 'but very nearly. Catherine Moreland is her name. The most delightful creature! Sweet, gentle, pretty, unaffected – a little absent-minded, I grant you, but otherwise without a drawback – and monstrous rich. The Allens are as rich as Croesus, and *she* is the heir – and famously close to my sister Isabella, besides.'

'I have met Miss Thorpe, but not Miss Moreland,' said Elton.

'Well, well, it does not signify. What *does* signify, and most confoundedly, is that little Miss Moreland was head-over-heels in favour of my suit – had never seen my equal and so on. But since then she has heard from some malicious old crone or other that I supposedly took advantage of you last week – and it seems to have rather shaken her good opinion.'

'And so,' said Elton, growing impatient, 'you wish me to cadge an introduction to this Miss Moreland and to reassure her that you did not take advantage?'

Thorpe clapped Elton so powerfully on the shoulder that he began to cough. 'You are quick, by the heavens! And as for cadging – never fear – I shall introduce you to Miss Moreland, myself!'

The cough had perhaps stimulated Elton's brain, into which darted an idea.

He said, 'I should be only too delighted, my good Thorpe. And all I should ask in return is that return of that note of hand I gave you when we played at three-card brag.'

At this, the light of enthusiasm faded from Thorpe's countenance, for there was a curricle-hung gig he rather fancied buying with his winnings. Then he rallied. Catherine Moreland had a neat ankle, a soft manner and a prodigious amount of money. Were he to wed Miss Moreland, he could afford any number of curricle-hung gigs. And if he did *not*, surely there were any number of other fellows he could defeat, whether in three-card brag or in any other game upon the cards?

'Of course, absolutely, just what I was about to suggest! But you *will* reassure Miss Moreland, will you not?'

'I will, indeed.'

It gave Elton a great deal of satisfaction to inform the good-natured Charles Bingley the next day that he was no longer in need of a loan.

'I am not at all surprised,' said Bingley, at once. 'Thorpe is not a bad fellow at heart. Such a tale renews one's faith in human nature!'

Elton could not help reflecting that it was his own guile, rather than any qualms of conscience on Thorpe's part, which had wrought this transformation – though he decided not to mention it. At the same time, he could not feel at ease till he had fulfilled his own side of the bargain. As it happened, Thorpe was so late at the Upper Rooms that Elton had almost given him up when he appeared, rather dusty from inspecting some gig or other, and with temerity enough to suggest that *he* had been the one kept waiting.

'Ah, Elton! Found you at last, by the kingdom! Where have you been this long age? At any rate, let us get on... As you have doubtless conjured, Miss Moreland is the fair girl in cream, on the left. The girl with my sister Bella.'

'There!' Isabella was telling Miss Moreland, with a toss of her black curls, 'I knew that you would tease me quite unmercifully, but he was so determined – he made such a point of wishing to dance with me – he kept claiming that there was none in the room to compare and no end of similar untruths – and so, in the end, I could not say him nay.'

'Oh, *I* should never tease you!' cried her companion anxiously. 'I am sure you did very right by dancing with him.'

'Miss Moreland,' interrupted Thorpe. 'I should like you to know my good friend Elton. Mr Elton has traded the vile boredom of some foul hole in the country for a few weeks at Bath.'

Miss Moreland welcomed the new acquaintance warmly, saying, 'I am so glad to find you gentlemen such friends!'

'We are indeed,' said Mr Elton firmly, 'and always were.'

'Even with regard to cards?' asked the earnest Miss Moreland.

'Particularly with regard to cards,' said Elton.

'And *this*, you see, is why you must pay no attention to tittle-tattle, my dear Miss Moreland!' cried Thorpe, exceedingly well-pleased. 'My sister's, especially!'

'For shame!' cried Isabella, tossing her ringlets until it occurred to Elton that she must have been advised how well their tossing became her.

But Miss Moreland urged, 'You must not listen to him, Mr Elton – he will give you quite the wrong idea of his sister. *She* is no gossip, I vow!'

'Aye, do not listen to me,' said Thorpe cheerfully. 'A very good rule to live by! And so, Miss Moreland, why do we not show everyone in the room how this dancing business is supposed to be done?'

Miss Moreland yielded, though not, Elton believed, without a regretful glance in the direction of another young man across the room. His own notion was that Miss Moreland, had she ever favoured Thorpe's suit, favoured it no longer.

He thought, 'If so, I cannot blame her, for Thorpe is a rattle as well as a rake – but perhaps she only bears his company to oblige his sister... How odd it all is! I daresay that, after next week, I shall never see these Thorpes or Morelands more – they will be less to me even than Miss Woodhouse herself, for I shall never escape *her* company. But how Bath seems to consume one, all the same!'

❧

The next morning was chilly and, after admiring the soft cream of the local stone, Elton decided to warm himself in a coffee shop. There he found Thorpe complaining to an older gentleman, 'He must have the sorriest equipage in all the kingdom, yet the Moreland family itself is exceeding well-off, while *Miss* Moreland – And here is Elton! Fancy a turn at three-card brag, eh? Eh?'

As this quip had been deployed more than once since their battle in the cardroom, Elton forced a smile and declined.

'In that case, Elton, my good fellow, is it true that you are courting Bingley's sister Caroline?'

'I like the Bingleys very well, but I am in no hurry to settle – I prefer to take a little time to look about me.'

'She is well enough, Miss Bingley,' said Thorpe tolerantly, 'and she is nobody's fool.'

'And has £20,000 besides,' said his older companion, pulling deeply on his pipe.

'Nothing like!' scoffed Thorpe. 'For, as all the world knows, her father lost half his fortune in Antigua when that hurricane felled his crop!'

'*Half* his fortune? Who told you so tall a tale? You forget what vast amounts he had set aside before,' said his friend, laughing.

'And hurricanes do not come every year! 'Tis said, and probably truly, that Bingley's father made up his lost ground ten times over! Why, Miss Bingley might have as much as £30,000! – But then, was not her heart quite broke – or so I heard – when Fitzwilliam Darcy preferred some impoverished gentleman's daughter?'

'Perhaps so,' said Thorpe thoughtfully.

'What!' cried Elton. 'Not Darcy of Pemberley? Are he and Bingley, then, so very well-acquainted?'

'Aye, and always were,' said the older man. 'Long before Bingley wedded one sister and Darcy the other.'

Elton felt an unexpected pang of sympathy for Miss Bingley. To have had hopes of, only to be disdained by, Darcy of Pemberley – one of the most distinguished men in all the kingdom!... At the same time, this information made her seem still older, almost as if she had been married already. Augusta Hawkins benefited by the comparison, for few could 'do' youthful sprightliness with quite Miss Hawkins's *esprit*…

◆

'Elton is certainly taking a great deal of time in coming to the point,' objected Mr Suckling to his wife a few days later, 'considering that he has only a week and a bit left in Bath.'

'Has he, indeed? – Heavens! How the weeks fly by! But caution is no bad thing, in a young gentleman particularly. One would never wish to marry one's only sister to a John Thorpe, a Thurgood Jackson or – heaven forbid – a George Wickham… Though, should Mr Elton venture, I suspect that Augusta would have him, for she likes him very well.'

Mr Suckling said, 'I shall not be long, my dear. I promised to see Prior before he returns to town.' But instead of calling on his friend Prior, Mr Suckling wandered into the nearest coffee house where, as he had anticipated, he found Thorpe.

'Suckling! *You* do not often honour us at this hour! Coffee? Or a touch at billiards?'

'I thank you, no. Instead, there is something you could do for me,' said Mr Suckling. 'That is, if you were thinking of attending the Lower Rooms this evening.'

'Something of what nature?' asked Thorpe, rather warily.

Mr Suckling glanced round and observed some naval officers at a nearby table.

'Let us take a little walk,' said he, 'and I shall tell you.'

The dancing had almost begun – the couples forming, the fiddles tuning, and Miss Hawkins greatly displeased in consequence – when Mr Thorpe asked her to dance.

'Oh, Mr Thorpe, I fear that I cannot oblige you. As I just told Mr Jackson – I seem in *such* demand this evening, I vow! – I have already promised these very dances to our good Mr Elton.'

'But Elton is not about,' said Thorpe impatiently, 'and a thousand things might have arisen since he secured you. In fact – by the heavens! – he said as much to me, this very morning.'

'He told you *this very morning* that he might not attend, did he?'

'He did – upon my word – in the Pump Room. I recollect it perfectly now.'

Miss Hawkins hesitated, but only for a moment. After all, it was no bad thing to appear sought-after – and rather embarrassing to appear *not* to be, though a great many young ladies were sitting down. As Thorpe bore her off to the set, he said, 'I believe you live with the Sucklings at Ash Grove. A famous place for shooting, is it not?'

Miss Hawkins laughed rather shrilly. 'Not *Ash* Grove, Mr Thorpe, but *Maple* Grove. The elegant restraint of its design! Its noble topiary – the view from the valley to the east – the line of oaks to the west. 'Tis a delightful place – everyone who beholds it must admire it – but to *me* it has been quite a home!'

Upon his arrival, Elton was most discomfited to observe Miss Hawkins's arrangements, particularly as his lateness was the result of his landlady's having ruined his best cravat... The two dances that followed put him back in charity with Miss Hawkins, if not with his landlady, but Thorpe then requested the next two, to the lady's affected consternation.

'Heavens, am I not to have a single disengaged moment? Well, if you *insist*, Mr Thorpe. For there is Mr Jackson, like the troops of Midian, prowling round! Do not desert me in *his* vicinity, I beg.' And in a lower tone, 'He composed an acrostic upon my name – at least, I am *almost* certain it was he.'

Elton felt a spurt of jealousy. Whatever was Thorpe thinking of, to be paying such attentions – and such marked attentions too – to anyone beyond Miss Moreland? Why, the man must have confided his pursuit of Miss Moreland to all of Bath! (For that matter, where *was* Miss Moreland?)

It was quite Miss Hawkins's night of triumph – she was constantly being petitioned to dance, for others seemed to queue up in Thorpe's wake. Mr Suckling looked on with his rather catlike smile – while Elton consoled himself by vowing to call at Laura Place as early as he could the next morning.

❖

'Ah, Elton,' said Mr Suckling silkily, 'A trifle chilly out, is it not? But so good of you to call. You will find the ladies warming themselves by the drawing-room fire. I shall join you once I have finished my letters.'

However, he did not. Instead, he interrupted the party in the drawing room some ten minutes later, saying to his good lady, 'Forgive me, my dear, but I would be most grateful for your advice.'

Mrs Suckling rose at once, saying, 'I shall be quick, Augusta, but I beg that you pay the greatest attention to Mrs Bragge once she arrives, for I expect her at any moment.'

For fear of Bragges, Mr Elton wasted no time. The moment Mrs Suckling's footsteps faded down the hall, he said in a fervent undertone, 'What a delightful opportunity to speak to you alone! Permit me to seize it, for I have something most particular to say to you.'

'Why, Mr Elton! Whatever can you mean?'

'Surely you can guess?'

'Oh, Mr Elton!' she whispered, lifting one pretty palm.

'Nay, from the moment we were first introduced, my ardent admiration must have been evident, especially to one of your quickness! Nor can I imagine that our striking congruence of feeling could have escaped you. Why, when we dance together, our two hearts seem to beat as one!'

'It is true,' said she, attempting a pretty confusion, 'that we seem curiously in tune with each other's feelings. And that we do appear to think alike on every important point. But still, I never –'

'Your beauty and your dancing first kindled my admiration. Your vivacity and wit then charmed me. But it was only last night – you were dancing with Mr Thorpe – when I recognised that we might have been made for one another! And this being evident, what impediment could there be to our marriage? Why should we not be united, in the eyes of God and man?'

'True – true, indeed! And yet'– remembering a line from a

novel – ''tis all so sudden, that I hardly know whether I sleep or wake!'

'Your lovely eyes are open,' said Elton, recollecting his poem in his turn, 'like twin stars of heaven's pure blue! Therefore, you cannot be dreaming!'

'But truly, it has the feel of some delightful dream!'

'Miss Hawkins, I can promise to make you comfortable as well as happy for though my family is a little sunk from its days of glory, I am assured of being remembered by my uncles and cousin, while I command a delightful situation already.'

'Oh, I have no doubt of it!'

'In that case, might you assure me that I boast some measure of your gentle and maidenly regard?'

The lady sighed, but it was quite a sigh of pleasure as she said, 'Mr Elton, though replete with every possible advantage at Maple Grove, I am happy to accept of your proposals.'

'Dear Augusta!'

'Dearest Philip!'

And by the time Selina returned all was settled – beyond the date which was to make Mr Suckling the happiest of men.

❖

The wondrous news spread through Bath as swiftly as Augusta's prettily worded notes could contrive... Miss Bingley, still sneezing, looked sour indeed when she heard of it. But there was consolation in that, at the next Assembly, Mr Thorpe, recollecting his mistake regarding her fortune and thoroughly annoyed at every creature by the name of Moreland, greeted her with unusual warmth.

'Ah, the divine Miss Bingley has returned amongst us! Like a tender goddess!'

Miss Bingley looked up, rather startled.

And smiled.

✦

My dear Knightley, wrote Elton exultantly, *I wish you to be among the first to know that I have been fortunate enough to have persuaded Miss Hawkins of Bath to accept of my proposals...*

✦

'Well, *I* heard as you were courting that Miss Moreland,' said Mr Jackson, rather slyly, over the chess table.

'Me? Never!' said Thorpe, with a little shudder. 'Miss Moreland's fortune was nothing like as fine as she pretended. And *she* was the kind of empty-headed creature who never knew her own mind from one moment to the next. She quite longed to go for a drive, but then she could not come... Or she *could* have come, had she not forgotten her parasol or recollected some other engagement –'

'And then at the last ball you danced twice with that Miss Hawkins.'

'Now Miss Hawkins,' said Thorpe meditatively, 'is, I believe, greatly attached to me. Strictly between ourselves, I could wed Miss Hawkins with the lifting of my smallest finger. But then, her little airs, her affected laugh, her interminable praise of Maple Grove! No, no – Instead, you will soon find out, my good Jackson, the kind of creature who can command my heart. Someone entirely superior to Miss Moreland or Miss Hawkins – in fortune, in birth, in everything! Your turn, I think? I moved my rook before.'

✦

'I understand,' said Mrs Bragge, 'that congratulations are in order, with regard to your sweet Augusta.'

'We shall miss her a great deal,' said Mr Suckling, without being struck by lightning on the spot.

'I wish her very happy, I am sure. What kind of young man is Mr Elton?'

'He is a remarkably steady, respectable, pleasing young man, and exceedingly popular at Bath,' said Mr Suckling. 'Indeed, our one regret about the business is that Surrey – he resides in Surrey – is at *quite* such a distance from Maple Grove.'

If you enjoyed *Pride and Perjury*, please consider buying and reviewing Alice McVeigh's previous novels. (An excerpt from *Darcy: A Pride and Prejudice Variation* is given below.)

Susan: A Jane Austen Prequel
Harriet: A Jane Austen Variation
Darcy: A Pride and Prejudice Variation

Alice's website can be found here: https://www.alicemcveigh.com. She can also be followed on social media/BookBub at this link: https://linktr.ee/ASTMcVeigh.

Darcy: A Pride and Prejudice Variation

by Alice McVeigh

Chapter 1

London

'May we waken Mr Hurst, Louisa?'

As Mrs Hurst had not the smallest objection, Miss Bingley sat down at the pianoforte, pushed back her sleeves, and began to pound upon the instrument.

Mr Hurst started. 'Save the women and children! What is happening?'

'Nothing at all,' said Louisa, 'except that Caroline is practising.'

Mr Hurst rubbed his brow, yawned, and said, 'Well, I cannot see the point.'

The point, thought his wife, was that Caroline was not yet wed, that music was her most persuasive claim to accomplishment, and that there was precious little point in her having tuition if she was never to practise – but she said not a syllable of this, for her husband was quite as well aware of it as she.

'Where are Charles and Darcy gone to?' was his next plaint.

Louisa sighed. 'Charles has gone into Hertfordshire – as even *you* must remember – to look at some place or other. As for Mr Darcy, he is visiting the Admiral at Eaton Place.'

She did not mention that Darcy's absence was the reason for her sister's practising – but so it was, because it was her admirable policy not to attempt any work in Darcy's hearing until it was fit to be listened to. And then, the sonata she was practising – really, she seemed resolved to attempt one bar a thousand times! – could not be said to have attained any level of fitness at all. Somewhat to Louisa's relief, Mr Darcy then entered, and the semiquavers jangled to a halt.

'What, back so soon!' cried Caroline. 'Was the Admiral so desperately dull?'

'The Admiral,' said Darcy, 'was not within.' And he crossed to the table on which he had left his book.

Caroline, fluttered, thought how very good-looking he was, and how well his new coat fitted his strong shoulders, and how she rather liked his frown, as it increased the distinction of his profile. Closing her music, she said, 'What a nuisance for you! Would you care to walk, Louisa?'

'If you wish,' said her sister, perfectly aware – first – that it was cold and gloomy, and second, that *she* had only been asked in hopes that Darcy might be persuadable. However, as he continued to frown at the fire and as Caroline had no real desire for exercise, the notion was dropped. Not long afterwards, there was a bustle in the hall, through which Bingley's fresh voice could be distinguished.

Louisa cried, ''Tis Charles, I vow – I was not expecting him this long age!'

'I suspect he took one glance at the mouldering great ruin, and turned about without stopping,' said her husband, curling himself more comfortably upon the settee. 'He cannot have been gone long enough to inspect a Pembroke table, let alone a country house.'

But when Bingley appeared, he had a very different tale to tell. 'Friends, I am returned, to tell you that Netherfield, near Meryton, Hertfordshire, is the prettiest place I have been privileged to see, in the entire course of my life!'

'So much, my dear Mr Hurst, for your ruin,' observed Caroline, but Mr Hurst's eyes were most peaceably closed.

Charles removed his gloves. 'I cannot pretend that it has, of course, the maturity of timber, or indeed of architecture, of places such as Pemberley – it is in an altogether lighter, more modern, style. But the entrance is delightful, with gravel all new-laid, an open aspect, and a curved frontage – I was rather taken with the frontage – while the servants' quarters alone are twice the size of the place in Buckinghamshire!'

'But what of the society?' inquired his sister Louisa.

'Do not fret – I recollected your advice and it seems entirely unexceptionable. A Sir William Lucas and family are settled within a mile – there is a well-maintained hunt – the market town of Meryton is within a *very* easy distance – and there seem no end of excellent properties nearby. I passed at least five very decent-looking houses. The shooting –'

Caroline wrinkled her nose. 'But who would *live* in such a market town as Meryton?'

'At the moment, a great many soldiers, for the — regiment is quartered there. As I passed through, I observed any number of redcoats – as well as some pleasing shops and a few barouches. In addition, there are balls – though the housekeeper was too discreet to vouch for these. She is a Mrs Emmerson, a solid, sensible soul. I have asked her to stay on, as she received a famous recommendation from the Ibbotts and must know every tradesman in the country.'

'And you have truly taken it!' marvelled Caroline, while Louisa teased, 'Why, for someone as hasty as Charles, to have inspected it for ten minutes must count as the most devout consideration!'

But their brother defended himself. 'I was not hasty to no purpose, I assure you, for there was another family wishing to inspect the property had I not secured it. Besides, if one deliberates too tediously, one never gets anything!'

'My concern,' said Caroline, 'is merely that the society might prove unendurable.'

'Then *you* may stay in town, and allow Louisa to organise my dinners at Netherfield, instead.'

'My dear,' came from Mr Hurst, in the depths of the settee, 'my advice is that you not touch that idea with the far end of a bargepole. It will only involve you in a great deal of trouble and exertion.' And, in proof of his distaste for either, he began almost immediately to snore.

Darcy inquired sardonically, 'And so, you have taken it on a 24-month lease, with the option of continuing thereafter?'

'Nothing like it, and I can quit it at any time, so the solicitor said. Should we find that it does not answer, we can be off in a moment!'

'What, you had enough time to call upon a solicitor, as well?'

'Nay, for he was good enough to ride over from Meryton, for the purpose. There is a splendid drawing-room, with French windows and a charming view of open country.'

'I suspect that not a soul has asked to view the place since Michaelmas,' said Louisa.

But in the end, they agreed that it would be amusing to inspect 'Charles's folly' at the weekend. Once Darcy had assented, Caroline could entertain no possible objection – and so, to Netherfield they were to go.

Chapter 2

Longbourn

'So, what think you of Mr Bingley, Jane?'

'Why, what should I think of him? – except that he is inspecting our neighbours' house, with a view to renting it.'

Eliza laughed. 'No, for it is already decided that *he* is to take it and *you* are to marry him! Mama is entirely convinced and – of course – her instinct can never err!'

'What, has she said so?'

'She has not – but she is having her embossed gown altered for you, the one with the green ribbands. And as she declared her intent, the gleam of maternal calculation was glittering in her eye!'

'My dear Eliza, your imagination –'

'No, not at all, and – judging from the pursing of her lips on the subject of Mrs Long's nieces – she will push you at this Bingley as hard as she can… And it is not so hare-brained a scheme, at that. A spoilt young bachelor rarely looks farther than the nearest beauty, and your equal in *that* regard is hard to find.'

Jane cried, 'Oh heavens! For the last person Mama wished me to marry –'

'You mean Colonel Watson, I suppose?'

'I have never been more embarrassed!'

Lizzy, imitating her mother's tones: '"And here is Jane – the beauty of the family – and no creature could be better-natured, besides! What a delightful wife she would be, for the right young man!" The poor Colonel could scarcely keep his countenance!'

'But Lizzy, how can Mama be so certain that Mr Bingley will take Netherfield? Or, should he take it, that I should like him?'

'Why, as to that, you are obliged to like him! We are obliged to

314

like any man of good fortune, you know – be they bat-witted, beetle-browed or bow-legged. But *you* need not fret, for you like almost everyone. Indeed, you are celebrated for it, almost as much as for your divine complexion and your annoyingly obedient hair.'

'Do not tease me, Lizzy! – There is a very great difference between liking a man and – and *marrying* him!'

'I am afraid you will find that, to Mama, there is almost no difference at all.'

'And you say she is depending on it? Even though we have no means of knowing whether Mr Bingley might not be already attached – or might not *choose* to be attached – or might prefer someone slender and clever, like you!'

Lizzy laughed. 'No, *that* could never happen, for I should certainly – within the course of a single morning – offend so rich a man's entire acquaintance! Instead, I shall die an old maid – residing with Mary, or perhaps with Charlotte Lucas – condemned to good works and morning visits, along with a quite frightening amount of embroidery. But perhaps you might occasionally invite me to Netherfield, when no one more exalted might be expected!'

'Such a fate,' said Jane warmly, 'might happen to Charlotte – though I hope it shall not – but never to *you*.'

Elizabeth smiled. Secretly, she did not believe her prospects quite as bleak as she pretended. Somewhere, there must exist a gentleman willing to overlook her lack of fortune in consideration of her quicksilver wit... For the moment, she was perfectly content as she was.